BY THE
MOONBEAM
AND THE
MIST

THE ESHOLIAN INSTITUTE

BOOK 2

MARIAH MONTOYA

Cover Art by Lea Androić

Editing by Shannon Pring

Island map by Freelance Cartography

Campus map by Shepengul

For anyone who's ever wondered

if you're the hero or the villain.

Maybe we're all a little

bit of both.

Author's Note

As Rayna and her friends get older, the themes of each book will mature along with them. That being said, *By the Moonbeam and the Mist* is a bit darker than the first book in the series. Please be aware of the following potential triggers: forced drug use (the magic suppressants), attempted SA (not between main characters), branding, creepy crawlies, sexually explicit scenes, vulgar language, violence, and death.

EELER

THE
UNINHABITABLE
ZONE

BASCITE
MOUNTAIN

SICKIMORE

ALDERWICK

WYNDRIP

MERKWEI

GRAYCOTT

VARCHMOUTH

THE ISLAND OF
ESHOL

GILDENLEAF
HALLOW'S
PERCH
YELLOWSEEK
WASTEON
LLIVIEW
CARDINA
THE
ESHOLIAN INSTITUTE

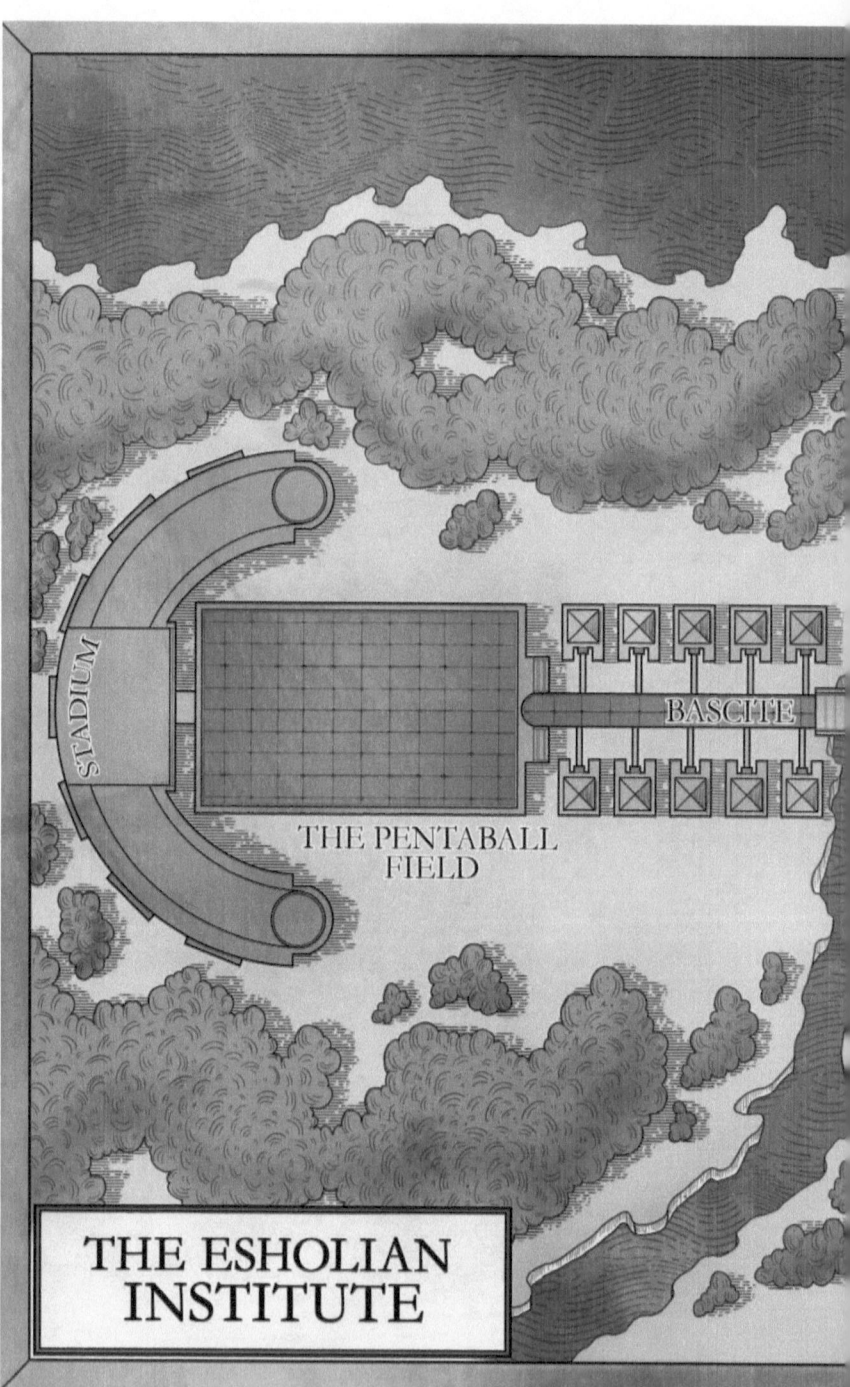

STADIUM

THE PENTABALL
FIELD

BASCITE

THE ESHOLIAN
INSTITUTE

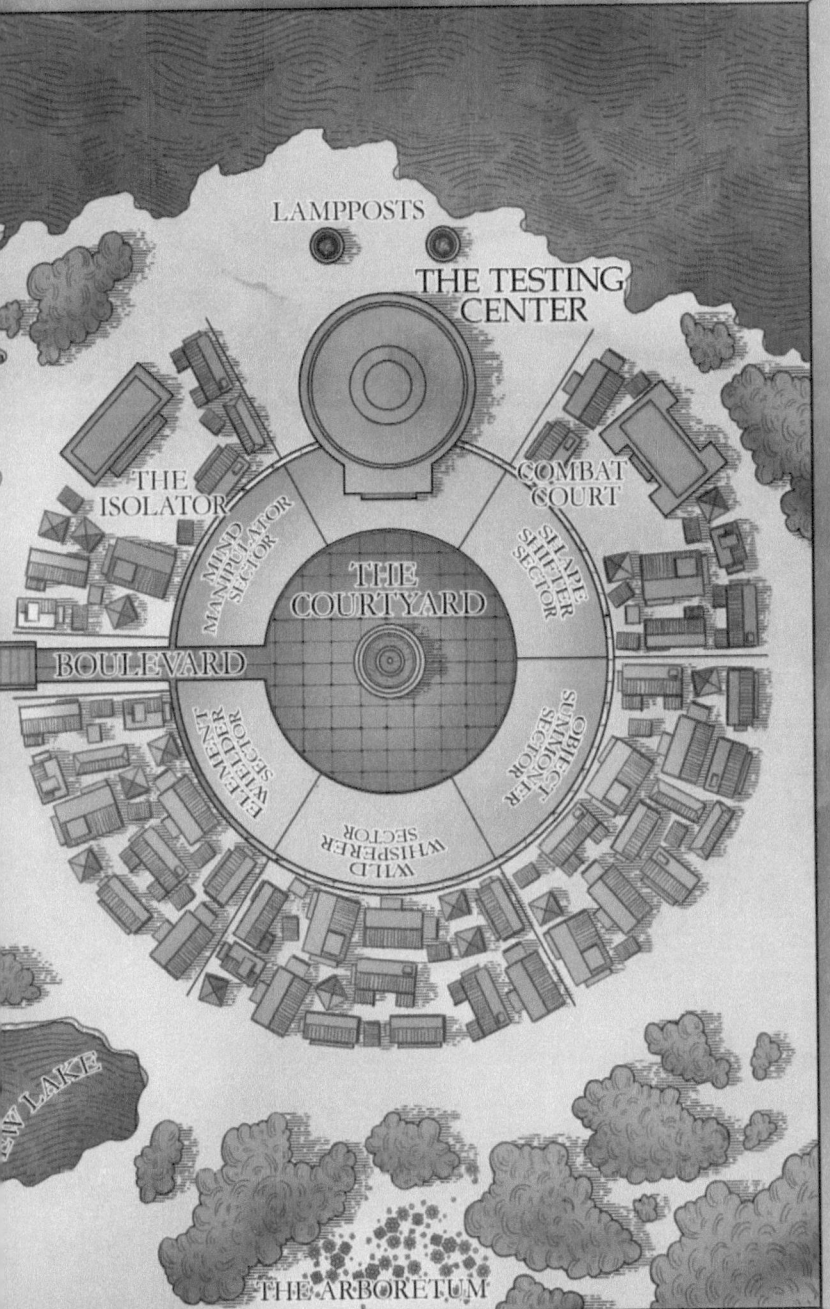

PROLOGUE

COEN

Even as a Mind Manipulator, I couldn't wipe the image of her from my brain.

That wild cascade of curls, those jade-green eyes, even the freckles strewn across her nose and cheeks, as if the God of the Cosmos had sprinkled a little extra stardust over her Making—I saw them all in the spaces of every blink as I stared across the vast expanse of ocean.

But even the memory of her face didn't absolutely suffocate me the way the memory of her voice did.

Please, Coen. Take whatever you want, but don't take away us.

My innate magic jolted, like a fishhook trying to tug me away, and I had to clench my fists and say her name in my head to keep myself tethered in place. To not let that endless darkness gobble me up and spit me back out somewhere I didn't want to be.

A small, furry shadow loped to my side, but I didn't glance down to where I knew the creature would be gazing up at me in concern. I didn't need concern right now. I needed to keep Rayna from exploding with *her* innate magic again... without her knowledge of my presence. Which meant I needed to focus.

But the creature's mental images oozed toward me anyhow—a little, nonhuman mind demanding I pay it attention.

So I made a quick dive toward it with my Mind Manipulating power and found a fuzzy picture of me on my knees, digging for clams, plucking something small and round from the bed of meat.

"Yes, I have one." I held up the black pearl pinched between my forefinger and thumb. It wasn't just a gift for Rayna, but a reminder, a declaration. A piece of me that I could leave behind without the Good Council's detection.

She had all my pieces anyway. This was just a talisman of that. A way to tell her subconscious that I would come back for her again.

And again.

And again.

"I'm ready," I told the creature through a deep breath. "I'll be back before you can even have time to trash the kitchen again."

That earned me a jab in the shin, and I *almost* smiled... but couldn't hold it as the memory of Rayna's voice permeated my mind *again*, wafting down every twist and turn of neurons, swirling with the mist of my memories.

Please, Coen. Take whatever you want, but don't take away us.

My little hurricane, I wished so badly I could have said. *I would never do anything to cause that light to leave your eyes.*

But I hadn't said that. And I couldn't regret it, even if she hated me now. Even if it scooped out every piece of me worth fighting for and left me a hollow monster with aching teeth.

So I wrenched my eyes from the sea's horizon where Garvis, Terrin, Sasha, and Sylvie would be bobbing on one of those ships past my newly sharpened line of faerie sight and turned on the pebbly shore.

2

Back to the jungle. Back to the Esholian Institute on the other side of the island.

Back to my reason for every beautiful thing I'd done and every wicked thing I still had to do.

CHAPTER

1

The sweet, earthy scent of black bamboo washed over me as I lay in the grove, closing my eyes and listening to the song of the jungle.

Wildflowers crooned around me. Shrubs and ferns sang in rougher, more bristly tones, while the bamboos themselves hummed excitedly, the pace of their synchronized voices matching the quick fluttering of their thousands of leaves.

This. This was the only place I could go to that seemed to calm the constant ache in my head where my memories had been wrenched from me against my will three months ago. Everywhere else just left me feeling cold and empty, but this grove of gracefully swooping plants...

Something tickled my senses, like the string of a spiderweb brushing over my closed eyes.

I grabbed the knife nestled in the grass beside my head and popped up to my feet in a single swift movement—

Just as a striped mass of muscle and fur pounced from the grove's deepest shadows.

Two giant paws slammed me to the ground, knocking the knife from my hand and the air from my chest. The white tiger licked his maw above me now, two strings of saliva dripping from his canines as he kept me pinned.

As soon as I caught my next inhale, however, I exhaled a whistle meant for the jungle and stuck out my empty hand.

The nearest bamboo bowed over to scoop my knife from the ferns. With a violent flick, it hurled the weapon back in my direction. I caught it by the handle and lifted it to the white tiger's throat before he could lower his head.

Jagaros chuffed and removed himself, padding backward with a flick of his tail.

"*You're getting better.*"

The words should have come out as a growl, but the magic the Good Council had branded into my skin, into my very blood, made me hear them as if he'd spoken in my own human language. As if the faerie-derived bascite swimming in my veins acted as a magic translator.

"And you're getting to be a pain in my ass." I hoisted myself up off my back. "You could have at least said hello before attacking me."

The thin strips of Jagaros's pupils surveyed me. "*You are the only human I would let talk to me like that without eating them alive.*"

I laughed, although the sound was instantly swallowed in the thickness of the jungle's hums and cheeps.

"I'd like to see you *try* to eat me alive after spending so much time training me how to avoid that."

Indeed, I'd been meeting Jagaros in this exact same patch of black bamboo every day for the last few months, forcing both my hands to get familiar with the craft of the blade. As soon as I'd let it slip to him that I had a weapon stowed beneath my bed, Jagaros had insisted I learn how to use it. He made me twirl it, throw it, and wield it as if he'd actually turn feral one day and try to chomp my head off.

But I knew what the knife practice was *really* for, although Jagaros had refused to utter a single word about the pirate breach and what he knew about it since that day on the beach: as a Mind Manipulator himself, Coen Steeler would know all about my Wild Whisperer abilities and could simply command me not to use them. If I came face to face with him, I wouldn't stand a chance without the knife.

With the knife, I might be able to catch Steeler off guard—hopefully by the throat.

"*Why don't you try actually hitting a mark before you get too cocky?*" Jagaros said now, sitting on his haunches beside me.

"Watch me," I replied, and shifted myself into a throwing position, already pinching the tip of the ridged antler handle.

Elbow up. Wrist back. Eyes on the widest ebony stalk, which was still only about the diameter of a large fist.

With a snap of my wrist, the knife spiraled through the air—heavy handle over curved blade—and rooted itself into the stalk half a head lower than I had intended.

I hissed a curse under my breath, but while Jagaros tutted through his canines, the bamboo laughed.

That was another reason I'd chosen these practice sessions here. As a type of grass, black bamboo grew so rapidly that a blade in their wood merely tickled them, scratched an itch they couldn't scratch themselves. A tree, on the other hand, would have been highly offended.

"Hey, you know what," I said as I stomped forward to retrieve the knife. "At least I've been getting it to stick every time. Remember our first practice, when the blade just bounced right off?"

"*Unfortunately*," Jagaros replied with a swish of his tail. "*Now do it ten more times.*"

"Can't," I replied, letting a bit of my smugness shine through the words. While I appreciated Jagaros's attempts to teach me how to cut through flesh and stop a heart, I wasn't particularly fond of anything that involved ten tries in a row. I knew he'd just sit and judge me with that tail flicking distastefully the whole time, then snarl at me about how disappointing I was. "I told my friends I'd meet them at the Element Wielder lake to see if the giant octopus is real."

"*You told your friends you'd meet them at the lake,*" Jagaros repeated, staring at me as if he couldn't believe such ludicrous words had come out of my mouth. "*To see if the giant octopus is real.*"

"Yeah." I slipped my knife back into its leather sheath. "Wren and Rodhi have been debating about its existence for the last few weeks, so Emelle suggested we put it to the test and see if any of us can actually spot it."

I knew it sounded stupid, knew it was ridiculous to try to have fun when murderous pirates were breaching the dome around our island and attacking seaside villages. But I also knew I couldn't skip out on too many things. I'd built a wall of ice around myself since Dyonisia Reeve had given me orders to capture Steeler, but I couldn't let Emelle or any of the others know about it. If they suspected that anything was off with me, they'd try to get involved.

And as much as I hated Steeler for what he'd done to me, I feared what Dyonisia Reeve and her Good Council elites could do to my friends even more.

No, I wouldn't drag them into this. Wouldn't let them know that I could now wield a knife, or that I'd been tasked to catch a pirate, or that most smiles on my face were part of a well-cultivated mask.

Jagaros inclined his head ever so slightly.

"If it's your wish to act like a half-brained monkey who just discovered a puddle, then go. I'll see you tomorrow."

"Don't let the monkeys hear you saying that," I muttered, and gave Jagaros a swift pat on the neck before trudging away from the bamboo grove, toward the Esholian Institute campus, my knife in hand.

The lake sat directly behind the Element Wielder sector, several jutting columns of rock rising from the water like fingers. Miniature waterfalls plunged down between the crevices in an endless cycle, spawned by elemental spells. Thankfully, the Element Wielders weren't picky about who liked to hang out on their turf, so there was almost always a group of Esholians lounging on its shore or island.

My friends were already there. I could hear their voices echoing from one of those crevices, but before I emerged from the tangle of jungle surrounding the lake, I sent a hum out to the trees.

Vines unraveled over my head and gently wrapped around the handle of the knife that I offered with outstretched hands. I watched them tug the weapon up into the thickness of the canopies, where I knew the jungle would keep it safe for me until I could stuff it back into the drawer of my bedside table in my new room.

"Thanks," I whispered to the trees, and touched the nearest trunk.

I could have sworn the limbs of the tree bowed in response.

Then I made my way toward the bridge of permanent ice that never melted, even with the current streaks of sunlight streaming down onto its path to the rocky island in the center of the lake.

They must not have heard my clacking footsteps over their own voices, because Wren and Rodhi's argument didn't falter as I drew near.

"I *know* that octopus exists, darling. I was at the Mind Manipulator house last night, and Penny Ickers said it groped her when she—"

"Penny Ickers," Wren interrupted with what sounded like a scowl, "likes to blow stories out of her asshole. She was probably just pissed no one else wants to grope her and made it all up to feel better about herself." I rounded the column of rock, and Wren's gaze jerked toward me. "Oh, hey, Rayna! Where've you been?"

"Meditating," I answered as truthfully as I could. During this three-month break at the peak of the dry season, it wasn't uncommon for a Wild Whisperer to go out into the jungle on their own and practice. And I *had* been meditating—until Jagaros had so rudely interrupted me.

I felt that wall of ice forming around me again, though, that familiar pain beating a dull melody at the base of my skull now that I'd left the grove of black bamboo. But my smiling mask was airtight as I turned to Emelle, Gileon, and Lander, and said, "Please tell me they haven't been bickering the whole time. I think my ears are already bleeding."

Oh yes, my mask was *good*.

Emelle rolled her eyes, a smile crinkling the edges of her face. "Trust me, I can't wait to get this over with once and for all." She turned to Lander, tucking a strand of loose brown hair behind one of her ears. "You ready, babe? Or do you need more time?"

Lander was flexing his fingers and bouncing on the balls of his feet nervously. When I cocked an eyebrow at him, he explained, "I think I can change all your clothes to wetsuits for as long as we're in the lake, if I can just concentrate hard enough."

"Really?"

As a Shape Shifter, Lander would eventually learn how to morph other people's forms for longer periods of time, but right now he wasn't too confident about changing any other corporeal thing besides himself. I was surprised he was willing to try Shifting all our clothes at once.

"Yeah," Lander said, giving a shy smile. "I've been practicing on my own. Turns out the trick to Shifting multiple objects at the same time is to imagine juggling them. So." He clapped his hands. "You all in?"

Actually, I couldn't think of anything I'd rather do *less* than, as Jagaros had so kindly put it, act like a half-brained monkey who'd just discovered a puddle. But old Rayna would have been all in just for the hell of it—for the sake of belonging—and besides, I wasn't a bad swimmer. Back in my home village, my once-best friend Quinn and I had splashed through enough ponds and lakes around Alderwick for me to know the basics.

The thought of Quinn made something deep inside my chest wring itself into a tighter coil. She'd been the only other one besides me to face interrogation in the Testing Center after the pirate breach. From what I'd heard, they'd found her deep in the jungle, surrounded by walls of her own magic-made ice, after she'd lost her memory as thoroughly as I had.

Yet the few times I'd tried to knock on the Element Wielder house door to ask for her, the girls who answered always told me Quinn wasn't available to talk. And that thing in my chest would just wring tighter.

Because despite our falling out, Quinn and I were both surrounded by our own ice, it seemed. Even though I doubted we'd ever be able to melt each other's walls...

Well, it would have been nice to be walled in together.

"I'm in," I said before I could overthink it.

Everyone else echoed the sentiment except for Gileon, who rubbed his arms and said, "I think I'll sit this one out. I don't like water." He pressed a mournful look onto the surface of the lake. "It's really wet."

Rodhi choked on nothing but air, while Wren reached up to pat Gileon's shoulder. "Okay, Gil. You stay here and guard us against any wandering Element Wielders who might want to come stir up the lake. I'm sure we won't be long, considering there's nothing to find."

Rodhi recovered from his almost-burst of laughter and blew Wren a sloppy kiss. "Hope you like tentacles, darling."

Lander rolled up his sleeves and fixed a look of utmost concentration onto his face. Like he was constipated.

Emelle giggled at me between her fingers.

A moment later, our clothes tightened in some places and melted away in others. The remaining fabric molted into a stretchy, waterproof material that reminded me of one of my silk dresses hanging in my new second-year closet back at the Wild Whisperer mansion.

I looked down and found a suit clinging to my body, its two-inch straps haltered around my neck and its bottom cutting off around my thighs.

The brand on my left shoulder shone in startling contrast. The opposite of silky, it was a rough red design of singed skin that formed a circle and a bulbed, five-pointed star. The same as everyone else's on the island of Eshol, although the Good Council themselves sported a bright red dot in the center to distinguish themselves as superior.

Everyone else besides Gileon wore similar suits, but Lander himself began to change from the head down, his ebony-colored skin slickening while his form became more tapered. In the span of time it took for me to blink water from my eyes, he'd become an upright shark-like creature that dove headfirst into the water.

"Damn," I said, watching the ripples where Lander had plunged through expand and shrink again when he didn't resurface. "I think that might be the creepiest form he's ever donned."

"Oh, you haven't seen him as a piranha," Emelle said, then turned to Wren and Rodhi with a teasing glimmer dancing in her wide brown eyes. "May the best Wild Whisperer win."

She jumped in after Lander.

And despite the pain unfurling in the back of my head, despite the sense that another cavity in my memory had just opened up, I followed.

CHAPTER

2

Wren and Rodhi plunged in after us. When all four of us were paddling in the water, Gileon waving us goodbye and Lander still somewhere beneath us in his shark form, I hauled in a sharp breath.

Then sunk beneath the surface.

Murky gloom filmed my vision, but I kept my eyes peeled open and propelled myself deeper, until I came face to face with a few angelfish.

"*Don't make eye contact,*" one of them glubbed to the other.

"*Wouldn't dream of it,*" the other glubbed back.

Fine, then. I didn't want to talk to them either.

I came up for a quick gulp of air, then barreled deeper than before, my cupped hands brushing past seaweed that swayed peacefully and sang heavenly melodies that made me want to close my eyes.

And suddenly my eyelids *were* fluttering shut at the thought of just... floating here. Forever. By the orchid and the owl, floating felt *nice* after three months of constant weight pressing in on my bones.

But no. I had a job to do. Catch Coen Steeler. Make him give my sanity back. Hand him over to the Good Council and watch him burn.

I opened my eyes against the sting of water.

And found myself facing a giant, flaming orange eye.

The octopus was bobbing along the lake floor, but when it saw my attention move from one eye to the other, its tentacles began to sway in fluid, lazy motions, and its skin... its skin went from warty brown to bright blue quicker than I could try to propel myself backward.

"*I remember you.*"

I almost made the mistake of gasping in a lungful of water. Not because the octopus was talking to me, but because its gently swaying body was utterly silent on this underwater floor—yet I still heard the words as if they were floating in the water. My Wild Whispering magic was translating the sign language of the octopus's tentacles into something I could understand.

"*You took a midnight swim with that lover of yours,*" the octopus continued, drifting closer, and my heart stuttered.

A midnight swim with a lover? I couldn't remember doing such a thing—which meant the octopus could only be referring to one person.

"*Oh, yes.*" It nodded. "*You were clinging to each other like coral and algae, your limbs so beautifully intertwined. I saw—*"

"*Pervert,*" I hissed at the eight-limbed creature.

A mistake. With the last of my breath leaving me in a torrent of bubbles, I kicked upward for the surface.

But a tentacle wrapped around my torso, reeling me closer to those massive orange eyes as large as the palms of my hands. My chest screamed with white-hot flames, and it took everything I had not to

15

inhale a lungful of lake water as the octopus brought me even closer to its body, the whole of it flickering into a mellow orange color.

"*Where is your lover now, hmmm?*" its free tentacles said.

I didn't have enough air left to answer, and there wasn't a single sign of Emelle or Lander in his hybrid shark form to save me. I didn't have Element Wielder abilities, couldn't conjure a pocket of air or make the water disentangle the tentacle from around my body.

The frantic thought scrabbled at the edges of my brain as my vision went cloudy: my Wild Whispering magic wasn't enough to save me if I didn't have the breath left to use it. Why had I parted with my mother's knife, even for just a silly little swim?

"*I do hope you find him,*" the octopus said dreamily. "*True love is such a rare thing to observe from these depths.*"

A rush of water around my ears, and I was suddenly slamming back down onto the slick edge of rock, gasping and retching as a sucker-lined tentacle wiggled goodbye and slipped itself back under the surface.

"You found him?" Gileon rushed over to me, thumping me on the back. "Oh, Wren is going to be so mad."

Before I could respond, Wren herself broke the surface of the water, spluttering and treading over to the slab of rock where I still knelt. She swept aside wet strands of feather-black hair as she climbed up next to us, a scowl scrunching her face.

"I passed him on my way up. I guess Penny Ickers was telling the truth for the first time in her life. Maybe Rodhi won't—"

But Rodhi popped up next second, already cackling with victory.

"Did you *see* the eyes on that thing? I swear, each of them was bigger than my face. *Someone* owes me thirty coppers, ten jokes I can claim as my own, and an apology in the form of a foot massage."

16

Wren crossed her arms. "I'll give you thirty coppers, fine, and the God of the Cosmos knows you need help with your jokes. But I'll convince a rhino to eat my hands off before I ever touch your feet."

Rodhi pressed a hand against his chest, pretending to pull an offended expression over his face as he clambered up next to us.

Gileon, however, furrowed his eyebrows at the lake. "Do you think Melle and Lander are okay? They've been under for a while."

"Lander's literally a shark right now," Wren replied with half an eye roll. I suspected her tone had taken an even sharper edge than usual in the face of her loss against Rodhi. "They're probably just making out among the angelfish."

No sooner had she said it than both Emelle and Lander popped up, spluttering out laughs as Lander melted back into his human self. My own wetsuit sprung back into normal clothing, and I wrapped my arms around myself, trying to calm the rattling race of my heart.

You took a midnight swim with that lover of yours.

Where is your lover now, hmmm?

True love is such a rare thing to observe from these depths.

No, no, no. I could *not* have been in love with a monster like Coen Steeler. I'd *seen* the memories the top Mind Manipulator on the Good Council, Kitterfol Lexington, had transferred to my own brain. Steeler had used me and abused me and then ripped himself from my head, leaving this throbbing pain behind. Even now, I could hardly concentrate on what Emelle was saying to me as that pain reached a new pulsing crescendo.

"What?" I asked, trying to refocus my vision.

Emelle squinted at me, the smallest of a concerned expression tightening the smile on her face. "I asked if you'd seen the octopus, too. Lander and I must have missed him, but Rodhi and Wren—"

She didn't get to finish her thought. The next second, a piercing scream ripped through the air in the distance.

"By the feather and the fang," Lander breathed, using his own sector's motto on instinct as we all swiveled toward that sound. It was coming from the direction of campus in echoing waves.

"That is *not* a scream of pleasure," Rodhi said, squinting.

Emelle glanced at me, and in that moment, it didn't matter that I had a wall of ice surrounding me. She saw right through it, saw the fear that must have been in my eyes, that dread reflected in hers.

The next moment, we were both running.

Back across the bridge, through the Element Wielder sector, toward the courtyard that connected all of campus, where that scream was still spearing the humid air. The others followed, our combined footsteps slapping cobblestone until the five of us nearly slammed into a crowd forming around the fountain at the center of it all.

It was Wren who dragged Gileon through the condensed barrier of bodies to carve a way for the rest of us. And when I saw where that screaming was coming from, my heart flipped over backward.

A young woman was on her hands and knees on the cobblestone by that fountain, which was tinkling merrily as if nothing was happening. As if the young woman *wasn't* blaring her throat out, bile dripping from her open lips. Her hair had grown back in rough patches, and her eyes were no longer bandaged, but open and unseeing.

Jenia Leake. A fellow Wild Whisperer.

Nobody knew what had happened to her at the end of our first year, but rumor had it that she'd gotten into an altercation with her boyfriend, Fergus, out in the jungle where no one could hear them. While Jenia had come out of it with her head and face mutilated,

Fergus himself hadn't come out of it at all. He'd simply disappeared, despite the Good Council's attempts to find him.

I'd never liked Jenia—not after that first introduction with Quinn, when she had surveyed me like I was a rotten piece of meat—but I couldn't remember talking to her much after that. And Jenia had been living in the sick bay ever since Fergus had disappeared. I'd rarely seen her out in public, even in the dining hall of our own house.

Until now.

Now, not only was she out in public on her hands and knees, but a whirlwind of butterflies spun in tight circles over her head, faster and more frenzied than any I'd ever seen. Two Good Council elites stood on either side of her like bodyguards, watching her scream without even twitching a muscle.

I didn't recognize them, but I would have known they were from the Good Council even without their attire: long, flowing cloaks clipped together with silver buttons, the left shoulders sporting a circle of sheer fabric to let us all to see those little red dots in the center of their brands. Beyond that, they had that aura of elitism dripping from their slightly tilted expressions, the ease and smugness I had begun to associate with anyone who came from Bascite Mountain.

"What is this?" Emelle whispered beside me.

I hated that I knew. Hated that the whispered words slid so easily from my lips.

"It's an early exile."

Because why else would the Good Council come for Jenia, who'd been accused of murdering her own boyfriend and disposing of his body deep in the jungle?

"Please don't," Jenia choked out now between screams, her fingernails scratching at the stone. "My sister... she's on the Good Council now. She won't let you."

"Your sister is one of our youngest, newest, and lowest-ranking members," one of the elites said. "She cannot defy Dyonisia Reeve's orders. And Dyonisia Reeve's orders state that anyone who kills a neighbor, tampers with the shield, or tries to run away from the Esholian Institute during their training years shall be exiled permanently without—"

"I *didn't* kill him!" Jenia spit, trying to crawl away now.

Something itched in the corner of my mind at that. Like a memory, tugging against the confines of my subconscious. Like I knew she was right. As horrible as Jenia was, as nasty as I remembered Fergus being, they'd been nothing but drooling, fondling lovers when it came to each other.

I strained to listen to Jenia's next words while the crowd around the fountain swelled even more, the quiet gasps of onlookers rising to excited whispers instead.

Excited whispers that sickened me. Because nobody was stopping this. Nobody was plunging forward to help her up or tell the Good Council elites to back the hell off.

"I don't know where Fergus went." Jenia was sobbing now, still crawling. "But I didn't *touch* him. Please."

"On behalf of the Good Council," the elite continued as if he hadn't heard her, "we hereby sentence you to eternal banishment, to preserve the safety of the worthy citizens of Eshol."

I expected Jenia to renew her screaming at that, but she froze instead, even as that halo of butterflies spun faster and faster.

I took a single step forward.

Don't you dare.

The voice echoed in my head, right where the throbbing was.

I jumped. Whirled. And found nobody looking at me, all eyes still pinned to Jenia in the middle of the courtyard.

Who are you? I thought furiously, wondering if a Mind Manipulator was messing with me from within the crowd. But that would have gone against the sector's etiquette, which usually discouraged Manipulators from entering a stranger's mind without permission. And I didn't know a single Mind Manipulator on a personal level. Unless...

The voice grazed my mind again, dark and fathomless, before I could solidify that terrifying thought.

Don't intervene.

My heartbeat flew into a frenzy as the image of a wickedly handsome young man formed in my mind, with dark brown locks of hair and eyes as cold and unyielding as smoky quartz.

It had to be him. Nobody else would have felt so horribly *familiar...* which meant he was on the island, on this side of the shield, perhaps watching me right now. A Mind Manipulator's power could only stretch so far.

Where are you? I asked now, my hands curling into fists, as if I could conjure my mother's knife just by pretending to hold it. My gaze scampered over the crowd around me, the buildings behind us, but I saw nothing, nothing besides onlookers craning their necks and my friends holding their breaths and various birds watching from the rooftops. *Why don't you come out and talk to me face to face?*

As if I could take Steeler on without my knife. My goddamned knife, which I *still* didn't have on me, for God's sake.

I could have sworn a low chuckle scraped through me.

Soon, he said.

No. Now.

A tongue clucked inside my head. *So impatient, as always.*

Clenching my jaw so fiercely it popped, I swung my attention back to the courtyard, where the two Good Council elites were already bending in unison to scoop Jenia up from where she still knelt.

Steeler had... had distracted me. And now it was too late.

As soon as they touched her, Jenia twisted and thrashed, shrieking viciously again—and almost managed to loosen herself from their grips. One of the Good council elites caught her by the sleeve. Fabric ripped, and for a split second I saw—

No. I almost fell into Emelle, who caught me with warm hands as I blinked at what I could not have possibly seen: a circle of seared flesh right beneath her armpit where that fabric had ripped.

Like Jenia Leake donned a second, hidden brand.

"You bitch," the Good Council elite cursed right after she managed to elbow him in the jaw with that same arm.

Except, her body didn't hit the ground.

It jerked right before impact, levitating, floating up to rest between the two men in a bubble of what I assumed was Summoning magic. I didn't have to see Jenia's fluttering lashes to know they'd made her pass out, probably by sending the blood from her head to her toes.

The butterflies that had been spinning above her head fell to the ground in heaps of membranous wings. Dead.

The elites didn't even glance down at them. They merely walked briskly through the path the onlookers had made for them, toward the Testing Center and the sea beyond it.

"Well, shit," Rodhi said, not a single spark of humor lighting up his voice for perhaps the first time in his life. His eyes were glued to the heap of dead butterflies where Jenia had been. "I've always wanted that to happen to her just to get her to shut up, but now that it actually did... well, that was fucked. Like, really, truly fucked."

Everyone else was hissing whispers to each other, and I knew that Dyonisia Reeve had ordered it to be so public to serve as a warning to everyone else. *Don't mess with the shield. Don't run away. And don't kill your fellow Esholians.*

But despite the fact that *she*, Dyonisia, was the one who had done this to one of her own citizens, I couldn't help the fury from spilling in a different direction. Toward that dark, invasive voice.

You monster, I seethed inside my own head, which had resumed throbbing. *Of course you wanted to stop me from intervening. You'll get all Jenia's magical scraps when they toss her overboard, won't you?*

Nothing answered within my own mind.

As if Steeler had never been in there at all.

CHAPTER

3

"I'll meet you guys in the dining hall," I said ten minutes later, when we'd all made our way back down Bascite Boulevard toward our houses. "I've got to go grab something for my head."

Indeed, my headache had only increased its tempo on the walk over, probably due to the burst of conversation as everyone who'd witnessed Jenia's exile ran off to tell the rest of the Institute what had happened. The birds, too, flew overhead, chirping and squawking about the gossip to every Wild Whisperer they could find. Only my own group remained somber, as if even Rodhi couldn't think of anything else to say.

"Okay." Emelle tried to smile at me, but her lips wobbled. "But don't be late. I heard Cook convinced some lemurs to bring her morel mushrooms for the potato pie tonight."

It was the best bit of normalcy she could offer after what had just happened. I squeezed her hand in thanks and nodded at the others before racing into my house's foyer ahead of them, up the stairs and to the second-year's floor. Here, chipped wooden doors lined the hallway, interspersed with windows where potted plants waved from their windowsills as I passed.

After our fourth quarterly test last year, my class of Wild Whisperers had switched from the communal bunkroom to this hall of four-person dorm rooms, so I now shared a space with Emelle and two others: a girl named Cilia, who hung with Mitzi Hodges, and Dazmine Temperton, who—

Walked out of our room right as I was opening it.

Well, shit. In the chaos of the last half an hour, I'd forgotten... forgotten that Dazmine had been Jenia's best friend. She rarely talked to any of us, always slipping out of bed first thing in the morning and returning late at night, her face always impassive, unreadable.

Now, though, Dazmine's usually perfect, bronze-toned cheeks were streaked with tears, and her chin was quivering.

"I'm sorry," I whispered before I could think twice about it. "I know Jenia and I didn't really get along, but I'm still sorry that it happened to her. That there was nothing anyone could do."

That there was nothing you could do, I meant to say beneath the layers, because from the puffiness of her face, I knew my frustration was *nothing* compared to her agony at losing her friend forever.

Dazmine took a step back. Her gaze squeezed into something hateful and cold.

"It should have been you," she said.

Now it was me who stumbled back. "What?"

"It should have been you," Dazmine repeated without flinching, crossing her arms. "I don't know what happened when those pirates everyone is talking about breached the shield, but I *do* know that Fergus and Jenia were trying to get me in on a plan to..." Her eyes darted behind my shoulder for a moment, as if to make sure the hallway behind me was clear, "to pull some kind of prank on *you*. I refused, and then—then suddenly Jenia comes back completely deranged and mutilated, Fergus doesn't come back at all, and you're just... completely fine?"

I took another step back. Not because this was the most Dazmine had ever talked to me, even as a suitemate... not even because she'd just admitted something horrible—that Jenia and Fergus had been planning to... to embarrass or hurt me in some way. No, I took that step back because I suddenly remembered what Quinn herself had told Dyonisia in the Testing Center three months ago: *There was a prank. I was just going into the jungle to play a little prank with my friends.*

Did that mean Quinn had been in on it, too—whatever it was that Dazmine herself had denied joining? Was *that* why Quinn had been interrogated right before me, because she'd been involved in an altercation with *me*?

"I know Jenia had her quirks, and sometimes she took things too far." Dazmine's throat bobbed. A single tear broke through the corner of her eye and marked a lazy path down her cheek. "But you did something to her, Rayna. You did something to both her and Fergus."

She took three steps forward then, until she was hovering right in front of my face and I could see that single tear wobbling on her jawline up close.

"And I'm going to find out what."

She brushed past me, not quite jostling my shoulder but whipping me with the flared edges of her braids.

"*Well, that was awkward.*"

I jumped at the voice, but it was just Willa, my dearest mouse friend, sniffling on her hind legs from my nest of pillows. Ever since I'd moved into this four-person room, she'd taken to sleeping in my bed with me at night.

"You heard all that?"

"*Well, duh. I hear everything. Except my cousin Barty when he snores. I put earplugs in for that.*"

I didn't even *want* to know what Willa's earplugs were made of.

Closing the door behind me, I strode to the arched glass window by Emelle's bed, where she kept her bedside table topped with a chiseled stone birdfeeder—every weekend, she foraged for seeds and nuts all by herself so that she could keep that feeder filled to the brim, a treat for any kind of winged visitor.

No matter how many times she opened that window to let a bird in, though, a tangle of ivy always cloaked the outside of it as soon as she closed it again. Like a curtain made of foliage.

Now, I grunted slightly as I nudged open the window as much as the ivy would let me, then hummed at the vines.

As much as I did need a pain reliever for my head, I also needed to bring my knife in for the night. The jungle could only keep it safe for so long before a monkey or sloth tried to steal it.

The process took a good two or three minutes, since all the vines had to pass my weapon along their endless, fibrous chain. During that time, my head spun and spun and spun with everything that had happened in the last half hour.

The octopus's claim. Jenia's exile and the second brand I'd spied beneath her arm. Coen Steeler *in my head.* Dazmine's accusation.

I could feel Willa watching me, her whiskers twitching in my periphery, but I didn't dare turn fully in her direction for fear she'd read it all on my face: absolute and utter chaos. A wrecked version of the mask I'd gotten so good at donning. I had half a mind to run back to that grove of black bamboo and bask in its scent all night, to forget...

The ivy outside the window twitched, and a single tendril of plant snaked inside the cracked opening, slithering in midair to place my knife in the palm of my hand.

I hummed my thanks, shut the window, and shoved the knife in my nightstand drawer, ignoring the sound of all the rolling, clinking objects in the back, before taking out a capsule of cat's claw extract for my headache.

Willa watched me swallow it, her whiskers twitching.

"*You don't have to pretend around me, Rayna.*" She scrambled closer to me, her little glass-black eyes shining with concern. "*This isn't the first rough day you've had since... since it all happened. This is just the first day you've let your hands shake a bit.*"

My hands were definitely shaking as I sat at the edge of my bed and clasped my fingers in my lap, trying to steady them. If nothing else, that rolling and clinking in the back of my drawer—that sound of the twelve little things I'd stuffed away—had sent me right over the edge.

Out of everything that had happened today, Steeler's voice in my head surprised me the least. *Predators can't stay away from their prey, dear one,* Dyonisia had told me three months ago. And despite the fact that Kitterfol Lexington showed up every week to ask me about my progress, despite the fact that I *should* have told him everything I knew, I'd managed to keep one thing from the Good Council's head Mind Manipulator: I was almost positive Steeler had been sneaking into this house, this very room, and watching me sleep every week since he'd left.

Who else would leave a little black pearl on my nightstand every Monday morning? Why else would I have twelve of those pearls rolling and clinking together in the back of my knife drawer right now?

It didn't matter how hard I tried to stay awake to catch him. I always ended up falling asleep and waking up to a new pearl staring me in the face until I hastily stuffed it away. As if I could deny the fact that Steeler had somehow cleaved through the shield again and again without alerting the Good Council's spies to his presence.

But I couldn't deny it anymore. He'd spoken to me. Alerted me to his upper hand. And now—rather than simply wanting to catch him and turn him in—my blood was singing to spill some of his.

Willa clawed her way onto my lap. I tried to soften my expression for her but... it just wouldn't budge. I could feel my face hardening again, and my fingers had already steadied themselves in my lap.

"*This isn't the right version of you, Rayna,*" she said. "*I know that. You know that. And I think your friends know it, too.*"

I didn't answer right away. I just gave her head a gentle, single-finger pet, then set her back down on the bed and started toward the door. Dinner. Emelle and the others would be expecting me for dinner, where I'd steal a slice of cheese for Willa herself.

When I reached the doorframe, however, I looked back.

And my words felt like I'd swallowed all those pearls one by one.

"I'll find the right version of myself again when Steeler is dead."

CHAPTER

4

The carriages came the next day at midmorning.

Emelle, Wren, and I watched from a balcony, lounging on wicker-woven chairs and sipping on coffee. Cook had made mine with all the spices I liked—cinnamon, clove, and nutmeg—so I let the heat prick my throat with all the warmth the sun couldn't give me.

"Oh, I bet you anything that one's from my village," Wren said, pointing at a wooden carriage that swept over the nearby jungle cano-pies on a supernatural wind, aiming for the courtyard beyond the estuary. "You can tell because it's the shittiest-looking one. Wyndrip always gets the shit end of the stick."

We were all carefully avoiding the topic of Jenia's exile as much as the rest of campus was talking about it. In part because she was a fel-low Wild Whisperer in our year no matter *what* she'd been like, but also because... well, I prided myself in having a group of friends that didn't pick out joy from other people's pain like vultures feasting on a fresh carcass.

Beside me, Emelle sucked in a breath, probably to tell Wren that the new carriage flying in wasn't as shitty as she claimed—then snapped her mouth shut again when one of the wheels popped off in midair.

There came a resounding shout from beyond our line of vision, but I knew the Element Wielding coachmen would have landed the carriage safely with or without all of the wheels intact.

"See?" Wren said, sipping her coffee undisturbed. "Told you. Shit end of the stick. Hey, buzz off. I already told the monkeys to scat."

She swatted at a parakeet that had fluttered to the balcony's edge, tilting its head at us and letting its beady black eyes rove over each of our figures. It wasn't until those eyes tacked onto mine that I recognized it and sat up a little straighter in my chair.

"You're Kimber Leake's... friend," I told it. Kimber as in Jenia's older sister. Last year's princess of our house who'd been assigned a seat on the Good Council after she'd passed her Final Test months ago. I'd probably never forget the patched yellow bill fluffing up her bird's neck, or the way it had looked at last year's inductees from its perch on her shoulder as if we were dirt between its talons.

Was Kimber *here*? Did she know what had befallen her sister? Had she come to oversee tomorrow's Branding or investigate Jenia's exile?

The parakeet, however, only coughed out a single word. "*Slut.*"

Then it flapped away, sweeping up and over the Wild Whisperer rooftop, before I could respond.

"What was that about?" Emelle asked, her eyebrows pinched.

"I don't—"

Again, my response was cut short by the flood of voices surging toward us from the courtyard. The last carriage must have arrived during the parakeet's little one-word speech, which meant the newest inductees were heading this way, led by our new princes and princesses who had been chosen during last night's elections.

A flash of yellow wings caught my attention just as the first of them flowed over the bridge onto Bascite Boulevard.

Kimber's parakeet flew against the tide, heading for campus.

"Rayna, where are you—?"

"I'll be right back!"

I was already up, my coffee mug almost cracking from how hard I slammed it down onto the chiseled balcony floor. I barged through the doors behind it—into Wren's four-person dormitory—and back downstairs until I was out on the street, sprinting in the parakeet's direction.

Slut. The bird had spoken with such an air of judgment that I knew *it* knew something—probably the vision Kitterfol Lexington had shown me at the end of last year. The way I'd been chained up and spread wide open for Coen to feast on. The way I'd had bruises lining my arms and neck. Whatever the pirate in disguise had done to me, it didn't qualify me as a slut, I knew... but that bird wouldn't have called me such a thing if it didn't know *something*.

I was almost at the bridge when the hundreds of new, sweating bodies converged on me.

Elbows and hips and hair lashed at me. The scent of anxiety and giddiness and desperation stung in my nose like acid, but I kept plunging against the flow of it all until—

"Rayna?"

My head jerked sideways at the familiar image of golden-brown hair and a pair of thick, knitted eyebrows.

"Wilder."

For a half second, my gaze tugged between the boy from my home village and the last flashes of the parakeet's wings.

Then Kimber's bird became nothing but a bobbing speck, and I knew it was a lost cause. But Wilder... he'd rooted himself to a standstill amongst the sea of his peers, watching me with those swirled hazel eyes I'd completely forgotten about until now.

"You've grown," I said, moving to the side of Bascite Boulevard to avoid that push of bodies. Wilder trailed after me without a second glance at the class royal he was supposed to be following, his hands slipping into his trouser pockets.

Indeed, I was squinting against the glare of sunlight as I peered ever so slightly up at him. Back in Alderwick, where we'd both grown up, he'd always been on the shorter, stouter side—I remembered *that* regarding the times we'd snuck into his uncle's shed to explore each other's mouths and tongues—but now he was just stout.

Wilder smiled slightly and toed the cobblestone. "Yeah, I guess I have. Meanwhile, you look the same." His eyes lifted to mine. Searching and assessing. "Except I heard you can talk to animals now."

"What? How did you—?"

Nobody at the Esholian Institute—save for the Good Council elites themselves—were supposed to have contact with the outside world. I'd certainly never written home about my new gift... or—had I? A too-familiar pounding behind my eyes told me there was yet *another* forgotten memory that might answer that question, but I ignored it, pushed the pain down and down.

"A crow told my uncle that he'd talked to you, apparently," Wilder said now, his half-smile freezing over his teeth. "My whole family's got the Whispering magic, remember?"

Yes, I had known that, but it was another tidbit of Wilder's life that hadn't crossed my throbbing mind until this moment. He'd even been named after the magic, for God's sake. After his eldest cousin, twenty-five years his senior, had come home from the Institute as an

Object Summoner, his mother and father had named him Wilder in the hopes that it would spur the magic to take their desired shape in his blood.

Purely superstition. The Branding activation had no rhyme or reason. The fact that most of his family had the Wild Whispering power was just a testament to how the sectors stuck together, maintained friendships, and married each other long after the Final Test.

I couldn't help the frown from creeping onto my face, though.

"A crow?" I couldn't remember ever meeting a specific crow. Owls and kingfishers and toucans, yes, but never crows. They liked to keep to themselves.

Wilder inhaled to respond. Inhaled—and then stopped.

A shadow fell over the space between us, and an oily, slithering quiet filled the buzzing in my head. As if the shadow had muted the world both inside and outside of me.

I turned to find Kitterfol Lexington's grin in my face.

"Catching up with old friends, are we now, Ms. Drey?"

Lexington's voice was as slimy and invasive as I knew his mind was, from the times I'd felt it probing my own. My stomach swooped in response, as if he'd placed me on the edge of that cliff behind the Testing Center and forced me to look down.

I pulled what I hoped was a neutral look over my face.

"He's not a friend."

I saw a moment of hurt flash across Wilder's face from my periphery, but I didn't let that neutral mask budge. No way in hell was I going to let Kitterfol Lexington, the most lethal Mind Manipulator on the Good Council and my personal tormenter, get his claws into Wilder. It was why I'd downplayed my friendship with Emelle, Lander, and the others around him, too, why I'd avoided thinking about my own *fathers*. To keep his attention away from the people I loved.

But as Lexington's eyes inched from me to Wilder, I knew *he* knew the truth. Knew he was penetrating the memories Wilder and I had shared in that shed so long ago, from both of our perspectives. He always pursued the most private, intimate ones that held his interest.

Which was why he'd never dug further into my mental images of those pearls. What use did he have in thoughts about jewelry pieces?

Now, Lexington's grin cracked wide open.

"Well, I trust your *not*-friend can make his way to the arena by himself." Lexington faced me fully with that cruel mirth swimming in his eyes. "Your presence is requested in the Testing Center."

"In the Testing Center?" I repeated, momentarily taken aback.

Of all the times Lexington had flown in to get me to report on my progress, he'd only ever cornered me in random places on campus, never taken me to the Testing Center for another official interrogation.

Lexington was already turning on his heels, his stringy braids flying.

"Dyonisia Reeve has arrived for the Branding," he said over his shoulder. "She would like a word with her... favorite student."

Every one of my muscles tightened at the mention of her name. Normal. I had to act normal, for the sake of Wilder and my friends and my two fathers, who were still back in Alderwick, unaware of the threats dangling over their heads from both the pirates and Dyonisia herself.

I would not want you to have to witness your fathers' bodies, broken and mangled and wrecked like this spider's, knowing their death was stretched out by the man who had you chained.

35

I'd managed to avoid thinking about that so far, but now, with Dyonisia Reeve returned, I'd have to face it again: the fact that my actions here could have consequences for Fabian and Don across the island. I'd have to spin Steeler's presence in my mind as something that made me look like *I* had things under control. Because I did. I *did.*

"Coming, sir," I intoned, and made my way after Lexington without glancing at Wilder again.

CHAPTER

5

It was just like it had been three months ago, only now Dyonisia sat in that glittering, throne-like chair without an audience behind her.

"Ahh, Rayna. Come here, child."

She motioned for me with one long, angular fingernail. Behind me, Lexington bowed his way out, and I found myself completely alone with the founder of this island and the head of the Good Council in this arched space beneath the Testing Center's dome.

I shuffled forward, barely daring to breathe. Her eyes—frosty blue and filled with nothing but a depthless void—tracked the path of my movement toward her, like a serpent eyeing a wandering mouse.

A glass of acai wine sat beside her on a limestone side table, along with a neat burgundy package wrapped in ribbons and bows.

Dyonisia smiled when I came to a halt in front of her.

"Sit."

I glanced down, trying not to let shock flare in my eyes. Sit? There was nothing to sit on, besides the arm of her makeshift throne or...

My body seemed to melt to the floor at her feet—sickeningly obedient under that watchful gaze—until she was towering over me.

Apparently satisfied, Dyonisia said, "Kitterfol has informed me that you have not caught any sign of our enemy since our last talk?"

Her voice sounded like the wall of ice I'd built around myself, except shattered: jagged and sharp enough to slice.

"I have recently succeeded in making initial contact," I said, choosing each word from the tangle of my thoughts ever so carefully.

"Oh? Is that so?"

Something flickered across Dyonisia's regal face. Shock? Pleasure? Pride? I didn't know. Only knew that I was glad Lexington had left the room, glad I couldn't feel his slimy presence in my mind to pick up on the little half-lies I was about to weave through the truth.

"Yes, ma'am. I—I opened up my mind and lured him in with..." I dipped my head, as if embarrassed. "—promiscuous mental images."

False. I'd just tried to help a fellow Esholian. But I obviously couldn't tell Dyonisia how much I abhorred her practice of tossing her own people away like literal pieces of garbage.

Dyonisia's tone became crisper. "When?"

"He wouldn't agree to a specific time or place, but he said soon."

Soon as in tomorrow night, when he'd leave a black pearl on my nightstand. But I couldn't tell Dyonisia that either, couldn't admit I'd been close enough to throttle him twelve separate times and slept through them all.

Dyonisia took a single sip of wine, smacked her lips delicately, and replaced the glass on that side table. Her sheet of midnight hair fell forward as she leaned even further over me.

"My sources tell me that you have been practicing some peculiar skills with your little tiger friend, child."

Little tiger friend. Jagaros would have sunk his claws deep into her throat if he'd heard that insult. I didn't dare correct her, though—not when I sensed danger hovering over each of her words. *She knew.* She knew I'd been meeting with Jagaros to practice with my mother's knife.

I waited for a blow, either a sharp reprimand or possibly the sting of her hand on my cheek. But only lethal quiet bore down upon me.

"Where is your weapon now?" Dyonisia finished, tilting her head.

I blinked up at her. Cleared my throat and tried to keep the mask over my face. "I thought it might not be... appropriate to carry a knife around everywhere I go." Especially considering the no-killing rules that Jenia had been accused of breaking—and banished for.

Dyonisia smiled, baring her wine-tinted teeth.

"Well, then, it's a good thing I have just the gift for you, isn't it?"

She turned and picked up the burgundy package beside her glass of wine. I hadn't given it much thought upon first glance, but now I watched her slide off all those ribbons and bows and unfold the box beneath, then hand me the complicated strip of leather inside.

"It's a thigh sheath," Dyonisia said. "I had the best of my black-smiths in Belliview tailor it especially for that knife of yours. So that when you *do* meet up with Coen Steeler—soon, as you said—your weapon of choice will already be on you. You will have to stop wearing those wretched pants, of course, and start wearing dresses like a proper Esholian lady. I will have some delivered to your room."

So many alarms blared through me at those words. The fact that Dyonisia had been spying on me, watching me so thoroughly that she somehow knew the exact shape and curve of my *knife* was one thing. The idea that I wasn't just her bait, that she truly expected me to fight a dangerous Mind Manipulator and potentially win—that was another.

I took the sheath and turned it over in my hands, feeling the cold nip of the buckles and the flexible pocket where my knife would go. There were also several other smaller pockets on either side of the main one, as if to host an array of shorter blades, too.

"I thought you wanted me to catch Steeler so that you could…" For some reason, the words lodged in my throat. "I didn't think you'd want me to…"

"Oh, I don't think you'd be able to kill a pirate, my dear." Dyonisia's laugh sounded like teeth splintering in her throat. "As I told you all those months ago, those pirates are becoming more and more powerful, breaking through the shield, planning more attacks on our seaside villages, murdering our innocents. But a well-aimed blow— perhaps to his undeserving brand—" And here, her fingers reached out and traced the brand etched into my own shoulder. "…it might hinder his magic as well as his strength."

I couldn't help but jerk away from her touch. Had she really said…?

"You mean to tell me that our magic can be destroyed if our brands are maimed?" I asked, horror clamping down in my gut.

Dyonisia whisked up her wine glass and brought it slowly to her lips. After she'd had a long sip, she said, "The brand itself is like the doorway to your magic, child. Shut the door, and there's no way for that magic to interact with the outside world."

It took every ounce of restraint within me to not trace my own fingers over my brand, to feel the scarred ridges of that so-called doorway. In my entire year of Wild Whispering, I'd never felt so much as a *tingle* from that circled star when I was talking to a plant or animal, but I supposed… supposed that it made sense, even so.

If I could catch Coen and stab him right on that spot…

"Can I ask you a question?"

Those words were tumbling out of my mouth before I could re-think them. Dyonisia raised a slender eyebrow briefly, but nodded.

"Is there ever a reason someone would have... two brands?"

Now her nostrils flared, as if scenting my fear. I didn't know which of the five types of magic she had, but I thought not Mind Ma-nipulating, or else she wouldn't drag Lexington around everywhere she went. Still, though, I tried to keep images of Jenia Leake out of my head just in case. Tried and failed.

Dyonisia had gone very, very still.

"Why would you ask such a preposterous thing, child? The Branding is a sacred process between humans and the magic those fa-eries discarded here centuries ago. What reason would someone have to get a second one?"

Again, the words just tumbled out.

"Maybe to strengthen their magic," I said, and for the briefest mo-ment, met the ice in her gaze. My own wall of ice seemed to quiver.

Dyonisia leaned back, smiling with her teeth.

"And why would anyone want to do that?"

I could have sworn she purposefully shifted her hair, then, her curtain of midnight black that always covered her chest and shoulders. A sliver of me thought I knew what I'd see: multiple brands, a display of strengthened power, a warning to me to quit asking questions.

Yet her bare shoulder flashed, and I saw... nothing.

Not a single brand, not a single scar, not a single burn.

As if she didn't have any of the five powers at all.

CHAPTER

6

"Where'd you get that dress?"

All the girls in my dorm room were getting ready for the Branding the next morning, Emelle and Cilia helping each other with their makeup while Dazmine braided her hair in silence. Willa usually liked to perch on my shoulder during these kinds of things, but today she'd had to help her family with some kind of altercation with royal spiders (whatever that meant) so I was readjusting my new dress without her high-pitched commentary in my ear.

Of course, I had prepared for Emelle to notice my new change of attire. I'd come home from the Testing Center yesterday to find a spread of sleek dresses already on my bed, all tight on the top and flowy on the bottom to properly hide the new sheath now buckled to my thigh. There'd also been four straighter, more slender knives that I'd stuffed in those other smaller pockets immediately.

I hated how much I loved it. Hated that Dyonisia had somehow known, not only my knife's size, but *my* size. The handle of my crescent blade pressed firmly against my leg, but the sheath itself fit around me like butter melting into my skin. After my daily session with Jagaros, I'd worn it to bed beneath my nightgown and woken up to trade that nightgown with one of the dresses before the others had even stirred.

Now, confident that the dress was tied back in all the right places, that it truly hid the knives buckled to my thigh, I said as nonchalantly as I could, "Oh, an older Whisperer who had outgrown this kind of style gave me some of her old clothes."

It *could've* been true. Here at the Esholian Institute, the peddlers from the nearest village only came once a year to sell their goods, so it wasn't abnormal for people to trade clothing amongst themselves.

Still, though, I cringed inwardly at the lie as Emelle's gaze narrowed with suspicion.

"Well, I think it looks sexy on you," Cilia said from where she sat powdering Emelle's cheeks. We hadn't known her too well last year, but ever since our new house princess had grouped the four of us together, she'd taken to Emelle and me nicely, and even tried to make conversation with Dazmine sometimes. "Maybe you'll meet someone new at the Branding ceremony tonight." She fluttered her eyelashes at me.

Dazmine seemed to pause her braiding. *I'm going to find out what,* she'd told me—which meant she was listening in on any clues about my current situation.

I threw what I hoped was a coy smile Cilia's way. "Maybe."

Meeting someone new was the *last* thing on my mind, but with Emelle and Dazmine listening so closely... I had to play the part.

Besides, I already had a meeting with someone tonight. Steeler would leave a pearl, but this time I'd catch him when he did. Because I wasn't planning on falling asleep or even climbing into bed, in case he'd been using his Mind Manipulating power to force me to pass out before he hovered over me like a goddamned creeper.

No, I was going to lead him far away from the house and my friends and confront him in the jungle, where the trees and vines would be at my beck and call and my knife would be strapped to my body.

For the first time since I'd been tasked with catching him, I truly felt like I had a chance. Ignoring the ache that was slowly but surely spreading in my head, I patted some tinted beeswax on my lips and puckered them, feeling a genuine smile forming there.

Because now I knew where to stab Steeler to make it count.

Five hours later, the whole of the Esholian Institute flooded the arena, all of us breaking off into our different sectors. Lander went off to sit with his fellow Shape Shifters, so Emelle and I waved goodbye to him and found Wren and Gileon smashed together in the Wild Whisperer section of the stands. Cilia and Mitzi Hodges were chatting behind them, but Dazmine, I noticed, was nowhere to be found. She'd left our room after finishing braiding her hair, and I hadn't seen her since.

"Where's Rodhi?" Emelle asked now, gently swiping away a moth fluttering near her face. The onslaught of dusk had beckoned all kinds of flying insects, it seemed—more than usual.

Wren shrugged. "I'll bet you five coppers he's off trying to woo Ms. Pincette for the hundredth time."

Ms. Pincette was the youngest instructor at the Institute—and the strictest. Rodhi had been obsessed at first sight.

Emelle snorted. "You just need more coppers after losing that bet to him. No way am I betting on that when you're probably right."

Wren chose to ignore this and swatted at another insect, this time a whizzing rhinoceros beetle with two tiny horns. "Can you get out of my *face* for like, one second?"

The rhino beetle whizzed over to Gileon instead, whose gaze went cross-eyed trying to keep track of it. To my surprise, he reached out a single finger until the beetle settled on it before saying in his slow, deep voice, "Don't worry about her. She's only mean on the outside."

The beetle cheeped something I couldn't hear from the other side of Wren. Gileon smiled, said something back, then gave a gasp.

"What? You don't have a name? Well, that's okay! I can name you. How about... uh... let me think. Uh..."

"Nuisance?" Wren supplied.

"Yes!" Gileon's whole face lit up. "Nuisance. Good idea, Wren."

"God help me," Wren muttered.

At that moment, Rodhi seemed to materialize from beneath us, squirming his way between bodies and squeezing himself between Emelle and me. "I'm here! It hasn't started yet, right? What'd I miss?"

"Gil is best friends with a bug now," Wren answered on cue, "and Rayna's being suspiciously quiet." I whirled to gape at her, my head pounding in response, but she just continued with, "How was trying to woo Ms. Pincette again?"

Rodhi didn't even question her assumption. He just pressed his forehead into his hands and sighed.

"Dismal, actually. I thought I'd win this round, but... maybe it's time for another strategy."

I cleared my throat, determined to contradict Wren's assessment that I was being *suspiciously quiet*—especially as that knife handle dug into my hip from the position I was sitting in. Suspicious, indeed.

"You make it sound like you're in a war, Rodhi."

Rodhi threw his arm around me and squeezed. "Sometimes, un-requited love requires one to enter the battlefield, darling."

"Oh, spare us." Wren glanced at Gileon, who was still conversing amiably with the rhino beetle on his outstretched finger.

Perhaps she would have said more, but Emelle pointed at the pen-taball field and said, "Look, I think it's starting."

Sure enough, the hundreds of conversations around us trickled to a quiet as the class royals led the newest inductees to their rows of seats. I watched, my blood curdling within me, as Dyonisia herself led Lex-ington and three other Good Council elites to the five chairs lined up right in front of the stage beneath strings of Element Wielder lights.

But it was the small-boned elite *behind* Lexington who caught my attention. I squinted at her as she sat on the other side of him.

"It's Kimber," I whispered to Emelle and Rodhi, tracking the yel-low parakeet on her shoulder. I couldn't decipher her expression from this distance, but the fact that she really *was* here, right after her sister had been exiled... I wondered what she thought of it all. If she still wanted to be part of the Good Council after they'd done that to a member of her own family.

But more than that, I wondered why Dyonisia had even brought Kimber rather than a more experienced Wild Whisperer. Those two elites who'd exiled Jenia had admitted that her older sister was as low-ranking as it got.

I was missing something, I was sure. Some vital piece of infor-mation about Dyonisia's motive. But I didn't have time to dwell on it as our president, Mr. Gleekle, clambered onstage and began his speech.

"Welcome, young ladies and gentlemen, to the annual Branding!" He stretched his arms wide, his voice amplified on the streams of wind that he sent out with his Element Wielder magic. "I want to personally congratulate you all on reaching this crucial stage in your cultivation as worthy citizens of Eshol."

It was much the same as last year, except now I didn't have nerves weighing down in my belly. In fact, I was pretty sure I must have blacked out from those nerves last year, because the more I thought about it, the more I couldn't remember the details of my own Branding at all. Just waiting and waiting for my name to be called, and then finding Jagaros beside me.

I wondered where he was at now, whether or not he was watching from the mountainside, as the elderly Mrs. Wildenberg dipped her hand into a giant upside-down sunflower hat and pulled out the first name for Mr. Gleekle to read.

"Manhi Wood!"

A terrified, shaking eighteen-year-old boy walked to the stage, attempting to keep his head high. We all waited with bated breath after Mr. Gleekle pressed the brand-headed poker onto his shoulder, imprinting him with the Esholian star.

Scales erupted all over the boy's body. The Shape Shifters to the left of us screamed with approval, morphing their own bodies into an identical reptilian humanoid, and the boy sauntered over to them.

On and on it went. I found myself watching the Good Council instead: Dyonisia's pristine posture and sheet of shimmering black hair, Kimber's parakeet jutting from her shoulder, Lexington's lifted chin.

It wasn't until Wilder's name was called that I jerked my throbbing head back to the stage.

I'd forgotten about him. Again. Guilt made itself a knot in my stomach as I watched him march up to Mr. Gleekle and roll up his sleeve, exposing his left shoulder to the new brand pulled out especially for him.

He's not my friend. I didn't regret those words, not when they might have kept Lexington from getting too interested in him... but I still absolutely sucked for not seeking him out and apologizing afterward.

I winced when Mr. Gleekle pressed the brand against Wilder's skin, but Wilder himself didn't. He just stared straight ahead, his fists clenched at his sides.

"C'mon, Wild Whispering," I muttered, and Emelle gave me a strange sideways glance. I'd explain it to her later. Right now, I was just hoping Wilder's random burst of magic would align with his family's wishes, for his sake.

The next second, however, Widler's fists flew to his head, and he clutched either side of his ears. As if he'd burst with the same kind of pain tormenting my own head right now.

"Shit." I leaned back. It was the classic sign of Mind Manipulating—to suddenly hear a thousand different thoughts would drive anyone crazy at first. Mr. Gleekle confirmed it a moment later, and Wilder stumbled toward the Manipulating section, looking dazed.

"Do you know him?" Emelle whispered to me.

"He's from Alderwick. I—he's always wanted to be a Wild Whisperer."

But as soon as I said that, I wasn't sure that was actually true. Had Wilder ever *said* he wanted to be a Wild Whisperer, or just that his family wanted him to be? What if he had actually been rooting for a different sector? What if he was happy to learn the art of Mind Manipulating?

And at *that* thought, it occurred to me: I knew next to nothing about the Manipulating art itself. Not that I was supposed to seek out information about other sectors, necessarily... but if I was going to trap and stab Steeler tonight, shouldn't I find out everything I could about the way his magic worked?

The next inductee's branding caused a storm to surge overhead, splattering the entire arena with a torrent of water until the other Element Wielders calmed it with upraised hands.

"By the orchid and the owl," Wren cursed, wiping water from her eyes with the back of her arm.

We protect and care, this we swear, by the orchid and the owl. I knew my sector's motto by heart, but it was time to learn Steeler's motto, too.

After the last person was branded, everyone began running toward their houses just like last year. It was easy to slip away from Emelle and the others in the chaos. Easy to follow the Mind Manipulators to their mansions of daunting marble pillars, where I snuck into the alleyway between the boys' houses and pressed my back against the wall next to one of the many windows.

My house would be all chatter and screeching and excitement right now, but through that nearby windowpane, all I heard was...

Moaning. And groaning. And... yep—that was the sound of someone throwing up.

Oh, gross.

I prayed Wilder was holding himself together, at least for the sake of his own dignity. Waving away a few lacewings, I willed my mind to calm, to not give away its location to any of the older Mind Manipulators on the other side of the wall, who would be busy gathering the newly-inducted and welcoming them to their new sector.

Voices rumbled from inside, soothing and so unlike the crisp, matter-of-fact way Kimber Leake had spoken to my house a year ago. I definitely wouldn't be able to make out what they were saying, unless...

"Hey," I whispered out into the muggy darkness. The sound of a thousand different chirping insect conversations stopped abruptly. "Any spiders around here?"

Nothing answered except a mosquito who whined in my ear, "*No spiders! Just me! And my sisters! And brothers! And you!*"

No spiders around? Weird. I massaged my temples for a moment, and was just pushing myself off the Mind Manipulator wall, ready to slip back into my own house, when a low, dark chuckle bloomed in the shadows of the alleyway.

"Trying to eavesdrop on other sectors, are we?"

I whirled to face it.

And there he was, in the flesh and blood. Not standing over me while I slept, but leaning against the wall of his old house, merely ten paces away, as if he'd been there all along.

Dark brown hair. Rich, tan skin. A smile that curved his mouth into something wickedly beautiful.

"Hello again, little hurricane," Coen Steeler said.

CHAPTER

7

In the space of half a heartbeat, I plunged my hand through the slit of my dress, yanked out the crescent knife, and threw it.

I might not have been the best at hitting a specific spot yet, but I could have sworn the blade was going to stick *somewhere*—in his neck, in his stomach, in the broad planes of his chest. If I could nick him now, I'd have a chance at getting close enough to that brand on his shoulder.

But my knife just clattered to the alleyway's weed-cracked ground. Right where Steeler had been standing a breath ago.

"What the—?"

I spun around to find him on the other end of the alley, where he was crossing his muscled arms. Somehow, he'd moved around me during that span of time it had taken me to blink.

A Mind Manipulating trick. It had to be some kind of advanced Mind Manipulating trick. My heart a raging tempest in my throat, I reached for one of the smaller, slimmer knives...

To find that Steeler had moved again. Closer.

He eyed my knife with interest.

"*That's* new."

"What the hell's that supposed to mean?"

I raised the knife again, but didn't throw yet, letting my eyes mark the spot where his brand would rest beneath his tunic to gauge the distance between us. The entire alleyway had gone mute, as if Steeler had blasted a bubble around us. I couldn't even hear the constant whining of the insects anymore.

"You mean in all your sick fantasies you used to subject me to," I went on, shifting my stance ever so slightly, just as Jagaros had taught me, "I never got to play with you like you got to play with me?"

Something shuttered in Steeler's eyes at that. Like the smoky quartz had sunk into the deep, dark cavern that was his wretched soul.

"All I need you to do," he said, his voice as dark and fathomless as it had been in my head two days ago, "is take this for me."

He raised his hand, and in the ribbon of moonlight shining down into the alleyway, I saw a single, pearl-sized capsule between his fingers.

What the hell was it? Some kind of Manipulating drug? A sedative, perhaps, or something to make my head hurt?

Of course, the pain in my head had gone curiously quiet, but perhaps that was just my adrenaline overriding it.

"I'll bite your hand off if you bring that thing anywhere near my mouth," I said, and threw the new knife.

It spiraled in midair, but it was so much lighter than my crescent one that my aim was off. I watched it draw close to him and slice past his jaw.

Then Steeler moved so fast, my scream didn't have time to leave my throat before two strong hands were pushing me against the Manipulator house wall, anchoring my wrists above my head.

The knife clattered to the ground a half second later.

"Get off me."

It was all I could say, even though I knew he wouldn't. God of the Cosmos, I'd never seen anything move as fast as him—unless he was jumbling up my brain's sense of speed and time.

I couldn't help what I did next. Couldn't help thrashing and yanking and kicking and squirming, trying to break that hold of his on me like the snared mouse I was. Every point of contact between us seemed to shock me, like little zaps of lightning trying to strike me down.

Steeler just surveyed me, unmoving and unrelenting.

I went still, panting, and cranked my head up to look at him. This close, I could smell his breath and sweat and—was that black bamboo? Had he been spying on my sessions with Jagaros, hanging out among the plants? Or was this another trick, another way to sedate me?

"Get off me," I said again, this time through gritted teeth.

"Are you going to reach for another knife and deliver another nick to my jaw if I do?" Steeler asked, cocking his head. Satisfaction squirmed through me as I saw the small trail of blood oozing from the cut I had inflicted. Just a nick, but enough to sting.

I'd *absolutely* reach for another knife to do that again if given the chance.

"No," I said.

Another one of those wicked smiles flew to his face, and now I could've sworn his teeth were as sharp and pointed as the rumors claimed about those pirates beyond the dome. He knew I was lying. He didn't even have to enter my mind to hear those loud and proud thoughts that were probably wafting right to him.

I tried not to let my eyes flick to the vines crawling up the wall of the opposite Wild Whisperer house. One hum, and I could have them

53

lasso his neck like a noose. But—shit. From the way his grin sharpened, those teeth flashing like goddamned fangs, I knew he was
hearing that plan unfurl as surely as if I'd said it out loud.

I'd have to wait, then, until he was thoroughly distracted. There
could be no forethought, no warning, or else he'd be able to move out
of the way in time with that strange lightning speed of his.

"Tell me where you learned to play like that," Steeler said carefully,
nodding down at the slit in my dress where I'd pulled the knife from.
"Is Dyonisia Reeve teaching you? I've never seen that sheath before."
His eyes skimmed up and down my body. "Or that dress."

I've never seen that sheath before. And what had he said earlier?
Hello *again*? I'd thought he was referencing our first meeting since
he'd erased all my memories three months ago, but what if...?

My breath left me in a single, livid gush.

"You haven't just been watching me while I sleep," I hissed as the
realization poured into me. I didn't care that his eyebrows shot up.
Didn't care that he almost seemed to loosen his grip on me before
pressing in harder. "You've been meeting me, *talking* to me, forcing
me to take whatever the hell *that* is—"

I nodded upward at his hands around my wrists, where he'd kept
that single pill safely and firmly pinched between thumb and finger.
Our altercation hadn't made him fumble it an inch.

"You're doing this every week," I breathed out, hating him, hating
him, hating him, "then erasing my memory of it every time."

Steeler spared a half-glance sideways, as if checking to make sure
his little Mind Manipulating bubble around us was still intact. It was.

"Not erasing anything of yours, actually. Burying them. Along
with all your other wonderful, winning memories of me."

I'd kill him. *Kill* him. I wondered if Dyonisia would fault me for
bringing back a beaten, bloodied carcass instead of a living hostage.

"I see you're a monster through and through," I managed to say. "No wonder my head's been getting worse and worse with you constantly meddling with it. Screwing with me once wasn't enough, huh?"

When his eyes flared open—in shock, it looked like—I hummed.

The ivy on the opposite wall sprung toward us like vipers.

Steeler moved again. There wasn't even a blur of motion, just him pinning me to the wall one second, slashing the vines with my crescent knife miraculously in his hand the next, and returning to pin me again before I could so much as twitch.

The remaining halves of the chopped vines slunk back to their climbing position on the wall, looking wilted. Defeated.

"How did you do that so fast?" I didn't dare look up at my knife, now clutched in his pill-free hand above my head.

Steeler didn't answer. He was panting, at least. Good. That *should* have winded him, however he'd done it. He returned his focus to my face, and all hints of that smug humor was gone.

"What do you mean your head is getting worse and worse?"

If he didn't want to answer my question, I *definitely* wasn't going to answer his.

But I felt him sink into my mind anyway, a deadly, murderous presence, to taste the answer for himself. To taste the way my head had been pulsing with pain more and more over the past few months.

He actually closed his eyes then. Just for a moment, but long enough for me to chance a glance upward at my knife poised above me.

When he reopened his eyes, I snapped my own away from the knife, to his moving mouth. "I'll make you a deal, little hurricane."

There it was again, that nickname. I hadn't thought much of it the first time he'd said it, too focused on his sudden appearance in the alleyway to care. Now, though, I tucked away the information for later. Assuming there *would* be a later.

"Take this pill," Steeler continued, "and I won't bury this memory of us. You can show it to the Good Council—how you nicked me."

He angled his face to bare his jaw for me again, and I almost bristled at the crusted blood. A scratch. That's all I'd given him. Just a stupid little scratch.

"How thoughtful," I crooned, and the venom dripping from my voice wasn't a lie. There was no mask in this bubble with Steeler and me. Just him and my unfiltered hatred. "But I'd rather you kill me than make a deal with you. You have the knife. Go on."

Maybe if he moved to slice my throat, he'd hesitate long enough for me to grab the handle and turn it against him. *That lover of yours*, the octopus had said. Surely, even if Steeler had mistreated me during our twisted relationship, he'd hesitate before spilling my guts out, right?

Steeler sighed through his nose.

"Please don't make me force you, Rayna."

Rayna. How dare he call me by my first name, the name my *friends* used. Hurricane was better. It matched the raging of my blood.

"Why?" I asked, giving my arms a yank. His hold didn't budge. "I thought you love forcing yourself upon me? Or do you deny that?"

For a shuddering moment, I almost hoped he *would* deny it. I couldn't get that memory Kitterfol had shown me out of my head, but perhaps the chains had been... consensual. The thought felt wrong, but what if...?

Steeler didn't answer, though—and that was answer enough.

Now my very bones seemed to quiver from the restraint, begging me to move, to get my arms around his strong column of a throat and squeeze. But there was no way out of this... not with his abnormal strength and speed.

"Did you make me do things other than have sex with you?" I asked now. The back of my nose stung as I felt the words form in my mouth, the fear I'd been holding back from even myself after Dazmine had confronted me in our doorway. "Did you make me... kill Fergus Bilderas? Or hurt Jenia Leake in some way?"

Pain. For a moment, all I saw was pain rippling in Steeler's eyes, a perfect mirror of my own. Maybe we were both monsters, if I'd murdered a fellow classmate—even as a Manipulated puppet.

But Steeler yanked a smirk onto his face the next moment, as if the pain truly had been just my reflection, and not his own.

"Oh, no. I didn't make you do anything back then. Killing that kid was all me. Now, open up."

This time, his words echoed in my mind, too, and I felt the Mind Manipulation work on me as I'd thought it would from the beginning: he dropped my wrists, but I couldn't run, couldn't move, couldn't do anything besides part my lips and open my treacherous mouth for him.

Steeler held my mother's knife with one hand and placed the pill on my tongue with those two large, steady fingers.

Okay, close your mouth now.

I did, loathing myself, loathing him. The pill was smooth and vaguely sweet and surely filled with some kind of pirate poison.

Swallow it.

I lifted my eyes to his, throwing every ounce of hatred I had into that gaze, and swallowed the pill.

He brushed a finger along my cheek. "Good girl."

Even though my legs still wouldn't move, locked in place against my will, I found my mouth.

57

"Fuck you."

Steeler laughed humorlessly. "You already have, little hurricane. Now..." He held my knife back out to me, and my fingers closed around the handle. At the same moment, he placed something small and round in my other hand, and my fingers closed around that, too. But my arm still *wouldn't move* as he began back-pedaling away from me at a leisurely pace. "See you next week, same time? I'm good with wherever—I'll find you no matter where you are."

With a distinct *snap*, I felt his mind bubble pop.

All the insect voices rushed back to me in one droning buzz, the hoots and howls and distant thunder of night sweeping in like a tide.

My legs unlocked. I swung my knife hand back.

But Steeler was already gone.

And when I opened my other hand, it was to find a single black pearl nestled in my palm.

CHAPTER

8

"*There* you are, Rayna!" It was Cilia, hiccupping and waving me over from where she stood with Mitzi Hodges and a group of nervous-looking inductees. "I was just telling the new girls about you and your famous Branding last year. You know, the tiger thing and all."

Our induction chant had come and gone, then, and nobody had noticed my absence in the pandemonium of it all.

Except—no, I realized as I wended my way toward Cilia. Emelle was glancing at me from within a knot of new Whisperers over by the cuckoo clock between split staircases, a hint of concern crossing over her features. And Dazmine wasn't even *trying* to suppress the suspicion written all over gaze as she crossed her arms on the other end of the foyer, tracking my movement deeper into the room.

Pretending I hadn't seen Dazmine and throwing my best attempt at a cheerful smile toward Emelle, I approached the group of young women all ogling me.

"Hi! Welcome to the Wild Whisperer house. How is everyone feeling?"

It didn't even sound like my own voice coming out of my mouth. It was much too high-pitched, too bright and bubbly compared to the deep, dark pit eating my stomach whole.

I'd slid my knives back beneath my dress, and the pearl—well, since I didn't have pockets, *it* had gone down the crack of my cleavage. I didn't know why I'd even kept it... except that I felt like I had to add it to my collection upstairs as a tally of sorts. For how many times Steeler had cornered me and forced me to take one of those pills and wiped away any recollection of the assault afterward.

A tally for revenge.

Cilia and Mitzi started introducing me to the new girls. Leyla. Randy. Kira. Idora. Shantelle. I tried to commit each of their names and faces to memory, but that was proving rather difficult when my memory itself was waiting for a certain Mind Manipulator to smear away the night's events at any second.

Only, that never happened, and as the mingling swelled into partying, drinking, and new cliques wafting to separate armchairs or sofas, I began to wonder if Steeler was really going to keep his end of the bargain even though I hadn't swallowed the capsule voluntarily.

Take this pill and I won't bury this memory of us. You can show it to the Good Council—how you nicked me.

I didn't want to show the Good Council, though. Didn't want Lexington or Dyonisia finding out that a wanted fugitive had been within my grasp—literally—and even with the knife and training and sheath, I'd managed nothing more than to mar his perfect jaw.

"Nice of you to finally join us."

I turned to find Dazmine striding past, a drink in her hand. I opened my mouth to make up an excuse, but her eyes lifted to something over my shoulder, and I turned to find Emelle, Wren in tow, pushing toward me.

By the time I glanced back, Dazmine had melted back into the crowd.

"Here." Emelle offered me a glass, but I shook my head—even though the whole memory removal thing had probably caused my sense of fogginess and haze last year, I still didn't want alcohol to cloud up my mind more than it already was.

Wren snatched the drink right out of her hand instead, but Emelle studied me with those big, brown, too-wary eyes. "Is everything okay, Rayna? I lost you right after the ceremony ended."

"Oh yeah, I... I had to step away for a bit." I thumbed my temples. "Headache."

It wasn't the whole truth, and God of the Cosmos knew guilt flooded through me when I said it, but it wasn't a complete lie, either. Now that my adrenaline had faded, the pain *was* creeping back into my skull, winding its tight band around my head.

"You should ask Gil what his mom does to treat chronic head pain," Wren supplied. "She's a medic, remember?"

"Or Rayna could just go to *our* house's medic," Emelle said, that look in her eyes only growing as I avoided her gaze. "You know, like I've been suggesting for the past three months."

"Yeah, well," I muttered, "for the past three months, our house's medic has been busy taking care of Jenia Leake." It felt wrong to utter her name, as if the memory of her was supposed to be banished, too. But I didn't think I'd be forgetting Jenia anytime soon. Not with Dazmine stomping around and Kimber as the representative Wild Whisperer on the Good Council and the truth about Fergus's death suddenly swirling around in my head, round and round and round.

Killing that kid was all me.

If I'd had any doubts that Steeler and his group of pirates were part of the breaches and massacres happening to coastal villages around Eshol before, I had absolutely zero now. He, Coen Steeler, had murdered one of my fellow Wild Whisperers.

Which meant he could murder my friends, too.

I cranked another smile onto my face and gripped Emelle's shoulder. Wren, I knew from experience, would probably swat me away like a mosquito if I tried to touch her, but I directed my words to her as well.

"I think I'm going to head to bed." *To add the newest pearl to my twisted little collection.* "We've got a long day tomorrow."

Indeed, tomorrow was when our second year at the Esholian Institute would officially begin. We'd have all the same classes, but we'd be expected to plunge deeper into our magic than ever before.

Wren drained her glass and held it up like a toast.

"As soon as you get your head to start feeling better," she said wryly, "we're going to work on getting you hammered."

"Goodnight to you, too, Wren," I said with a feeble half-laugh.

Emelle only pursed her lips, and I felt her watch me all the way to the staircase, where I begged myself not to stumble—or do anything else that might reveal what a mess I was—on the way up.

The silence of my cold, dark room hit me with relief. I was too drained to do anything besides collapse into bed, still in my dress, and pull the pearl from between my breasts.

As soon as I did so, a voice squeaked out, "*Do you still remember?*"

It was Willa, scampering across my pillow and sniffling against my hair.

"Yes," I breathed. "I remember."

As soon as Steeler had left me, I'd immediately run to the girls' Whisperer house—but rather than barge inside, I'd found some of Willa's cousins hanging out in the cracks of the foundations, taking advantage of the surplus of insects out and about. I'd told them to go find Willa herself, and when she'd scurried out to me five minutes later, breathless and asking what was wrong, I had poured it all out to her as fast as I could: Steeler, his speed and strength, the cut on his jaw, the pearl and the pill. I'd told her to relay it back to me in case I lost my memory of it.

Now, she nestled into the crook of my neck and said, " *Weird. At least he's a man of his word?*"

I snorted. "I don't care if he's the most honest man alive." *Or the most beautiful, with all that tan skin and those stupid muscles.* I swallowed against the dryness in my mouth. "He killed Fergus. And he force-fed me a drug against my will."

A drug I still didn't know anything about—whether it would make me act a certain way or think a certain way or simply kill me in my sleep.

"His people murdered innocent civilians a few months ago," I went on to Willa, "and are trying to get in to do so again. I... I've got to tell the Good Council that I need help—that he'll be here next week, in this very room, at dusk, and that I need help catching him."

The realization that I couldn't do it alone was almost a tougher pill to swallow than the one I just had. But even with Dyonisia's cold-cut gaze, hidden intentions, and toxic politics, she and I agreed on one thing, at least: Steeler's head belonged on a pike.

Before he finally grew bored of me and came for the people I loved.

After a hearty breakfast of cocona and scrambled eggs the next morning, we all headed out for our first classes.

Now that we were second-years, we'd be starting our week off with Ms. Pincette rather than A History of the Esholian Biome, much to Rodhi's delight—he was practically skipping down Bascite Boulevard as we joined the flow toward campus.

Still, it was strange not to head directly to that musty classroom Mr. Fenway had once haunted, where we'd first learned that bascite came from faerie blood. Stranger still was the idea that somebody else would be teaching in his stead, since Mr. Fenway had fallen ill and passed away last year. Try as I might, I couldn't remember much about his death beyond that he'd had some sort of fungal infection... which made me wonder if Steeler had been involved in that memory too, somehow. If he'd killed Mr. Fenway just as he had Fergus.

"How long till you think Rodhi jizzes in his pants?" Wren muttered, wrenching me from these thoughts as we crossed the estuary bridge and came to the courtyard where all the different sectors branched off. The angle of the sun made the Testing Center cast a long shadow over half of it, as if trying to cloak that spot where Jenia had been hauled away.

"Uh." I swapped glances with Emelle, who was biting her lip. "I'm going to pass on trying to imagine anything related to Rodhi's jizz."

"Hey." Rodhi whirled and pointed an accusing finger at us. "I can *hear* you guys tittering. Be warned—say one bad thing about my manly cream and I'll set an army of spiders on you."

Wren stopped and clutched her throat, gagging.

"Oh, *ew*. My breakfast just came back up." She resumed walking, her hand still clasped around her throat. "By the orchid and the god-damned owl, Rodhi, never say *manly cream* again or I'll have Gileon beat you up."

Gileon, of course, heard none of this; he was too busy lagging be-hind, discussing weightlifting with the rhinoceros beetle that had apparently stuck with him after the Branding. The beetle sat on his shoulder much like how Willa would sit on mine, occasionally flutter-ing its shelled wings when it got to a passionate part of the conversation.

"Alright, I'll see you weirdos later." Wren waved to us at the en-trance to the Wild Whisperer section, looking relieved at the prospect of parting ways. "I've got Predators & Prey with Mr. Conine, so hope-fully I'll encounter something dangerous enough to take my mind off the taste of vomit in my mouth. Have fun with your new lover, Gil!" And she whisked away down a side passageway.

"Nuisance is not a lover," Gileon called after Wren halfheartedly, then looked down at the small, horned creature on his shoulder. "He's a very special friend. Aren't you, Nuisance?"

The beetle cheeped a *yes*, and Gileon followed Emelle, Rodhi, and me down the familiar twists and turns to Ms. Pincette's classroom with a grin widening his face again.

The Wild Whisperer sector vibrated with life, as always. Monkeys chatted to each other on rooftops, tossing cringy jokes back and forth and pulling each other's tails. Birds—kingfishers and honeycreepers and herons—traded gossip as they swooped and zoomed over our heads. I could even hear high-pitched, breathy voices every time we passed a cloud of butterflies, although we didn't pause long enough to listen in.

Before long, we were back in Ms. Pincette's classroom, and it almost felt the same as last year. Except now I wore a slitted dress instead of pants, a knife handle pressed against my thigh beneath it, and I was all too aware of an unknown drug circulating through my body. I didn't feel any different, but perhaps it had yet to take hold.

"I won't tell you to settle down," came a punctual voice I hadn't heard in months. The last time I'd seen Ms. Pincette, she'd looked much too pale in the face of Dyonisia Reeve, but could I blame her? I was practically pissing myself at the thought of seeing Dyonisia again, especially to tell her I couldn't manage the task she'd given me.

But when Ms. Pincette snapped the classroom door shut and turned to face us, I saw that she looked much better than before. Her chestnut hair was tucked neatly behind her ears, her eyes glistened with their usual sharp intensity, and her chin was once more held high. Only the vaguest hint of undereye circles told me she might still be haunted by... something.

"I won't tell you to settle down," Ms. Pincette repeated, walking back to the head of the classroom, where a single, cloaked tank stood on a pedestal, "because you are adults, and it's your own lives at stake if you don't take this class seriously."

That shut everyone up. I'd never seen Rodhi go so still in his seat beside me, every hair on the back of his neck on high, predatory alert.

"Now." Ms. Pincette swung to face us once more, her hands clasped behind her back. "I'm sure you've all noticed the surplus of insects around campus lately. It's just our luck that we have a plethora of fire ants willing to help us learn about..."

She unveiled the tank before her with a graceful flourish.

"... the hive mind."

CHAPTER

9

Hundreds of flaming orange ants scurried around the tank, which Ms. Pincette had filled with waxy leaves and twigs. This far away, I couldn't hear more than their endless, raspy droning, but a small part of me shivered at the way their voices seemed to echo each other's.

Because they were all chanting the same thing, I realized with a jolt. Connected by more than just their formations and lines.

At that thought, the dull ache in the back of my head gave a jolt of its own, like it was trying to jump out. Fire ants. *Fire ants.* I'd known a fire ant once. Had talked to one. I was sure of it.

But I couldn't remember how, or why Steeler might have taken that knowledge from me. What did fire ants have to do with *him*?

"Ants," Ms. Pincette said, and my eyes jumped back to the front of the classroom, "have a special connection with each other that we as humans will never achieve. Their memories are collective, not individual, and they are able to transmit pieces of information to each other via the very air. Which..." She gave a rare smile down into the tank. "Comes in handy if you need to talk to someone over a great distance, for our ant friends can then relay those messages for us."

It took a few blinks from all of us before Ms. Pincette seemed to refrain from rolling her eyes and repeated herself.

"Wild Whisperers can talk to each other from across the very island, if they wish. As long as they utilize the hive mind."

Rodhi whistled. Mitzi and Cilia gave an *ooooh* from the back of the class. Gileon squinted at his rhino beetle he'd placed on his desk, perhaps wondering if the giant insect could do the same thing.

Ms. Pincette seemed to follow his eyes and train of thought.

"I'm afraid very few species of insects have the ability to pass messages down the chain of their kind. But while we have these ones here." She looked up from the fire ants, her eyes analyzing each of us in microseconds. I felt her gaze pause ever so briefly on me, then swiftly shift to Rodhi. "Mr. Lockett, would you be so kind as to—"

Rodhi's chair was already scraping against the floor from how fast he got up.

"—help me demonstrate," Ms. Pincette finished, her mouth twitching.

She dipped a hand in the tank, waited for one of the ants to scurry up her outstretched finger, and nodded at Rodhi. "Your turn."

"Yes, ma'am." Rodhi mimed a salute and dipped his own hand inside until an ant scurried up his finger, too.

"Now." Ms. Pincette didn't even blink when her ant trailed up her arm, to her elbow, and turned around to hurry back down. One bite, and her arm would form an itchy, swollen welt. "The trick to connecting with the correct counterpart is to describe your partner to your ant. And in an ant's case, smell is more important than any other type of description. So, Mr. Lockett..." She turned to Rodhi and spread her arms wide. "Let's get this over with. Sniff me."

Emelle shot me a wide-eyed look that I flung back at her. *Sniff me?* In what version of reality would Ms. Pincette ever ask Rodhi to *sniff* her in front of the whole class?

All around us, gapes and smirks filled the room. Even Gileon had looked up from his rhino beetle with his mouth hanging open.

Lost for words for perhaps the first time in his life, Rodhi didn't hesitate. He leaned forward, closed his eyes, and inhaled, looking as if he'd taken his Final Test and passed it early.

After a much-too-uncomfortable few seconds, in which I couldn't help but squirm in my seat, he pulled back with a sloppy grin. "Got it."

Ms. Pincette nodded. "And I have your scent down as well, I think. Okay, Mr. Lockett, describe me to your ant."

Rodhi brought his ant up to his mouth and said in a raw, raspy voice that mimicked the insect's accent, "I am looking to connect with a beautiful woman who smells like passionflowers in full bloom and the bark of a cinnamon tree when the sun's hitting it just right."

God of the Cosmos, that made *me* want to blush.

But Ms. Pincette's cheeks didn't warm a single shade as she brought her own ant to her mouth and said, in that same accent, "I am looking to connect with a young man who smells like coconut, obnoxious energy, and a hint of clove."

The ants wiggled their antennas.

"Alright, Mr. Lockett, now we'll see if we have described each other properly. If you'll go to that end of the classroom..." Rodhi was already jogging around all the desks. "I'll stay here, and we'll swap all the words we cannot tell each other face-to-face. Hypothetically, of course," Ms. Pincette added with a twist of her mouth.

This had to be the most intimate, awkward lesson I'd ever encountered, and it was only day one of our second year. But I supposed I shouldn't have been surprised. We were called Wild Whisperers, after all—and the wild animals of Eshol, much like the faeries who had gone extinct on this very island, relied on a sense of smell more than anything else.

I just never thought I'd hear Ms. Pincette relate Rodhi to a coconut. Wren was going to *die* when we told her.

Everyone had turned in their seats to watch Rodhi bring his ant to his mouth again, this time whispering something that nobody else could hear.

A moment later, Ms. Pincette brought her ant up to her ear, listened as it rasped something, and sighed.

"Yes, that would be something only Rodhi Lockett would say. Well done." She jerked her head at him, those sharp eyes alight with something I might have dared call humor. "The rest of you…" She faced the class again without whispering her own message to her ant, letting it spiral around her finger. "Please find a partner, grab two ants of your own, and practice across the room from each other."

Immediately, everyone began scrambling up, and Emelle and I clasped onto each other in a flash. I'd rather *not* sniff anyone's armpits today, but if it had to be someone, I'd definitely pick her.

"Go ahead," Emelle said once we'd retrieved our ants from the tank. Around us, everyone had burst into conversation—Rodhi now with Gileon, Mitzi with Norman Pollard, and Cilia tentatively facing Dazmine. Emelle spread her arms like Ms. Pincette had. "Take a whiff."

I did, my knife handle digging into my hip as I leaned forward, my ant tickling my palm where it scuttled back and forth.

"Hmm. Vanilla, I think? And… maybe roasted cocoa beans?"

A flush surged up Emelle's neck.

"What?" I asked.

"Oh." She shifted on her desk. "I just... I've always thought Lander smells like cocoa beans."

I shot her a smile that almost felt genuine on my lips. "Aww. Your scents have merged. How very primitive."

Emelle huffed and leaned forward to smell me now, her eyes scanning my new dress with a hint of yesterday's suspicion returning.

"Okay, I'm getting... climbing orchids. Like the kind that covers the back of the Wild Whisperer houses. And... is that bamboo?"

My skin prickled, as if a dozen fire ants were nipping at the back of my neck. Black bamboo—from Steeler's body pressed against mine in that alleyway, holding my arms above my head? Or simply from the grove I practiced in? Or both?

Emelle seemed to watch each of my heavy blinks.

"Ready to swap all the words we can't tell each other face-to-face?" she asked, a certain prickly note to her usually gentle tone.

I nodded, suddenly nervous, and we drifted to opposite ends of the classroom, where others had lined up to practice as well.

Bringing my fire ant to my mouth, I whispered Emelle's description to it. Emelle mirrored me from across the room.

Just as I was wondering what to say, all too aware of Ms. Pincette's attention scanning each of us, my fire ant rasped, "*Where were you really last night after the Branding, during the induction chant?*"

Shit. That was definitely Emelle's message, passed through the hive mind and straight into my ear. Thankfully, nobody around me would have been able to hear, considering how loud the room had gotten, but...

I caught Emelle's stare across the distance between us.

Another lie rose up my throat, another excuse.

But then I was whispering to my fire ant, "I can't tell you. I'm sorry. Please don't be mad at me."

Please don't leave me like Quinn did.

Emelle got the message. I could tell by the way her face fell.

"*I'm not mad,*" she relayed through my ant, "*Just worried. And so is Lander. We've both noticed you've been...off lately.*"

A ball formed in the base of my throat. I had tried so hard these last few months to throw on a smile, to keep Emelle and the rest of my friends far away from any part of this mission Dyonisia had shoved me into. I couldn't handle the thought of any of them getting exiled like Jenia had just because I couldn't keep my mouth shut about it.

But Emelle had seen through my mask. Lander, too. And now, even though I couldn't give them the truth, I couldn't lie to her either.

"I don't think you'll need to worry for much longer, Melle," I said, my throat thick. "I'll be back to normal soon, I promise."

When the Good Council caught Steeler this Sunday, to be exact. Then I'd lock away my knives and fold up these dresses for good.

Emelle didn't answer for a long, long time. That thickness in my throat swelling, I watched my ant trace each of my fingers before she had it say, "*Okay. Just promise me one thing, Rayna.*"

"Anything," I relayed back before I could think better of it.

Emelle's shoulders seemed to deflate from across the room. "*Remember that we have your back. There's nothing you could tell us that would make us turn away from you.*" My ant stopped scurrying on my palm, its mandibles flexing as it continued. "*So whenever—if ever— you're ready to share what's going on... Lander and I will be here. And I'm willing to bet a thousand coppers the others will, too.*"

The others as in Wren, Rodhi, and Gileon.

That tightness in my throat stung with tears. I would never deserve Emelle or her graciousness, that was for sure. Even if I knew I couldn't ever take her up on her offer. Couldn't ever involve her in the dangerous things she didn't have to be a part of.

Still, I whispered two words into the hive mind, into the vast invisible network I'd never given much thought about until now.

"Thank you."

Wren did almost die when Rodhi gushed about Ms. Pincette's scent over our quick lunch break between classes.

She covered her mouth, gagged, and choked out, "I remember that lesson from last year. Ms. Pincette paired herself with Lynthia Prescott to demonstrate back then, which made a lot more sense considering Lynthia slathers herself in lavender oil like, fifteen times a day." She shook her head, surveying Rodhi with something like awe. "Why would Ms. Pincette want to smell *you*?"

"Oh, I don't know," Rodhi said sarcastically, shoveling a bite of his quiche into his mouth. "Maybe because she's secretly in love with me too and has to hide it behind more professional interactions?"

Wren was still shaking her head by the time we all split ways for a second time that day. While she headed off to History, the rest of us flowed toward the arboretum, where Mrs. Wildenberg was waiting for us between perfectly pruned elderberry bushes.

"Hello class," she said in that warbling voice of hers. "Welcome to your second year as Wild Whisperers... and your first class with me where we will do more than lie on our backs and listen to the music of the flora around us."

Norman Pollard groaned. A few others echoed his sentiment. Last year, the Language of Plants 101 had been our reprieve from more laborious tasks. A time to just meditate and relax.

The Language of Plants 102, it seemed, would be a bit more rigorous.

"If you'll follow me, we're going deeper into the jungle today."

Mrs. Wildenberg turned. It was a painstakingly slow trek upward as she led us all at a hobbling pace away from the arboretum, away from campus itself, and into the lush density of foliage and trees and vines.

Thanks to my dress, my bare arms and ankles had taken about a hundred different bug bites by the time we all came to a thicket of strange, towering plants I'd never seen before.

Pale green stalks rose high above our heads, swaying slightly although there was no wind. Bristles covered each of them, red and bulbed, with diamond-like dew drops glistening at the end.

"Do you hear that?" Emelle whispered to me. I was thankful that she hadn't acted strange or angry after our talk in Ms. Pincette's class.

I strained to listen, but... no. I didn't hear anything. Not even the usual hum of the trees, the croon of wildflowers, or even the hundreds of whining conversations of the same insects that had bitten the shit out of me on the way up. It was as if the entire jungle had sucked in a breath and held it.

A second later, something snapped around my arm and pulled.

CHAPTER

10

I wasn't the only one who screamed.

All around me, my classmates kicked and shrieked as dozens of those stalks whipped out and curled around their limbs, too.

Mine was pulling me toward it, those bristles latching onto my skin like leeches. I tried to reach out for Emelle, but she was yanked backward into hers, and on her other side, Rodhi let loose a stream of curses as he was snared, too. Even Gileon's brute thrashing couldn't tear through the plant's hold, his rhino beetle fluttering around his head frantically.

Mrs. Wildenberg, however, remained untouched.

She calmly surveyed us in the middle of the thicket, and for a heart-stopping moment I wondered if she'd brought us here to die.

"Giant sundew," she crowed finally.

We all quieted down despite the slight stinging I was sure everyone else was feeling where those bristles had latched onto our skin.

Mrs. Wildenberg gave a wrinkled smile. "They feed on insects, rodents, and sometimes even larger creatures—such as humans."

Strangely enough, I caught Dazmine's eye from across the thicket.

She looked away, but not before I caught the slightly raised eyebrow that seemed to say: *yep, Mrs. Wildenberg is definitely insane.*

"Sundews take several hours to digest their prey," the elderly instructor continued, turning in a slow circle, "and that's when their prey are the size of our palms. So rest assured *you* all would take days." A dry laugh crackled out of her. "But we aren't here to dissolve into puddles of protein. We're here to learn a new language."

And then she began to make her hobbled rounds, clicking her tongue in eerie, rapid intervals. *Tk tk tk tk. Tk tk tk tk.*

One by one, the bristled stalks relaxed their grips on us and unraveled, lifting skyward to resume their gentle swaying. I rubbed my arms, where tiny, oozing dots had joined all the bug bites. Great.

"Now, what use do we have for our carnivorous friends?"

In the silence that followed, I couldn't help but think that if Fergus and Jenia were still here, they'd be throwing a hissy fit together about what had just occurred. Now, though, the class stood unnervingly still, listening with rapt attention. As Ms. Pincette had said, our own lives were at stake if we didn't take these classes seriously—because taming a sundew might be a part of our first quarterly practice test. Or even our Final Test.

"Anyone?" Mrs. Wildenberg asked.

Norman Pollard flashed two fingers in the air.

"Yes...uh...Nelson, isn't it?"

"They're good for infestations of invasive bugs?"

"Yes, but what else?" When no one answered, Mrs. Wildenberg said, "Security guards, of course! Historic Wild Whisperers have found that sundews are happy to act like guard dogs, so they've bred and magically altered these ones to heighten that characteristic. In fact, in Belliview, many of these plants are potted and placed on either side of high-security doors to ward off intruders."

"Shit, I knew that," Rodhi hissed on the other side of Gileon. "I've seen them guarding the entrance to the local bank."

"But don't they get... mad?" Cilia spoke up. "When they're uprooted and potted?"

"Oh no, no, no." Mrs. Wildenberg beamed. "In fact, sundews enjoy the superior status of transportability. But I warn you, it takes a special temperament to train them. None of the carnivorous plants take as kindly to the gentle type, as some of you found out when you were feeding the butterworts last year. But these beauties are a lot fiercer than butterworts."

She cast a dewy-eyed smile to the nearest sundew as if she'd never seen anything as cute, then started teaching us how to click our tongues in a way the sundews could understand. After we'd all spent a few rounds practicing, she began partnering us up to practice—not by name, but by pointing at each of us with a gnarled finger.

"You with you. And you with you. And you with *you.*"

By the time she'd paired me with Dazmine, I was one hundred percent sure our instructor still hadn't picked up on a single name or social relationship in the class. The glares Dazmine sent me as I trudged over to her could have come close to shattering my wall of ice.

"Hi," I said.

"Hi," Dazmine said flatly.

You did something to Jenia and Fergus, and I'm going to find out what seemed to hover between us. Trying to ignore it, I nodded at the nearest swaying stalk. "Do you want me to go first, or do you want to?"

Dazmine sighed and pinched the bridge of her nose. "I'll go."

She stalked over to the plant and touched its bristled edges.

Instantly, it snapped around her hand and spiraled up her arm, the bulbed bristles digging in. Dazmine didn't even wince. She just threw me a look over her shoulder and said, "Go on. Free me."

It wasn't really a command, I sensed. It was a dare. To see if I was the kind of person who relished watching others get hurt. To see if I'd hesitate to help someone trapped and in need of rescue.

I didn't hesitate. Immediately, I began clicking my tongue the way Mrs. Wildenberg had demonstrated. *Tk tk tk tk. Tk tk tk tk.*

The sundew twitched, but didn't relent.

"Dammit," I spat, and tried again. Dazmine watched me intently from within her confines of flesh-eating bristles.

"Wow, you really suck at this," she said after my fifth try. "It's supposed to be a click, not a *cluck*. What are you, a peahen?"

"Gee, thanks, Dazmine," I gritted out. "I'm literally trying to save your life right now, so how about some helpful pointers instead of insults?"

She scoffed, as if the prospect of acid spreading in her bloodstream right now didn't faze her in the slightest. "I talked to some of those fire ants over lunch break, and you know what they told me?"

I didn't answer her, sure that it was a trick question. I just tried clicking my tongue again... to no avail. The damn sundew only twitched.

"They told me," Dazmine plunged on, "that *you* asked a bunch of them to attack me, Fergus, and Jenia last year. And apparently, the ants obliged." She threw back her head and gave a bark of a laugh. "Now I know why I felt like I was on the verge of a panic attack when Ms. Pincette unveiled that tank. Why I could barely *breathe* during that class. But what I can't figure out—" She squinted at me. "—is why I don't remember the attack. Because when I think *really* hard about blistering, raging welts all over my body, I do remember it... but the memory is muddled. Like someone tampered with my head."

I gawked at her. The sound of the rest of the class clicking their tongues might as well have been miles away.

Had I set a horde of ants on Dazmine last year? And Jenia and Fergus, too? Back in Ms. Pincette's classroom, the pain in my head had certainly jolted, like a memory trying to unleash itself. But again, what did Steeler have to do with *ants*? And why would he have erased that memory from me—from all of us—if *I* had been the culprit?

Dazmine clicked her tongue in rapid succession.

The bristled stalks released her with an unspooling flick.

"Seems like you're better with trees and vines than you are with meat-eating death traps, Rayna," she said, a hint of triumph in her tone. Like she'd caught me bloody-handed. Which... maybe she had. "Kind of weird for someone who carries a knife everywhere she goes, don't you think?"

When the usual thumping sounds of partying began to ripple down Bascite Boulevard that night, I snuck to the grove of black bamboo and practiced throwing my new knives again and again, imagining that the stalks of dark bark were hundreds of murderous pirates with fangs.

As soon as I got the hang of them, they became easier to throw than my crescent blade. Swifter and deadlier, these ones hit more accurately, and I relished the feeling of finally hitting my mark perfectly.

"*You saw him, didn't you?*" Jagaros asked from behind me.

I didn't flinch. I'd known he would be watching.

"How can you tell?" I threw another knife.

"*Your smell,*" Jagaros said simply.

"Let me guess. Black bamboo."

I didn't know where the edge in my voice was coming from. But with the pain in my head gone for the time being, with my mask dissolved, I was just tired of... of trying to be *nice*. Of pretending that I might be a perfectly fine, completely whole person, rather than someone with this mess of ice shards swirling within me.

Jagaros didn't answer. I went to retrieve my knives and slowly turned to face him.

"That day you found me on the beach..." I began, tossing the knife from hand to hand. "You advised me to tell the Good Council I was... roughhousing with you." I'd had a cascade of bruises down my body back then—bruises I couldn't remember getting. Lexington had claimed they'd come from Steeler's own hands, but if Jagaros had wanted me to pretend otherwise... "What do you know?"

I'd asked him this question before, of course, but never so firmly. And he'd never done more than flick his tail and change the subject.

Now, though, the white tiger studied me with his head cocked.

"*A great deal more than you, Rayna Drey,*" he answered finally.

I caught my knife with one hand and pointed it at him instinctively. "Don't be a smartass. What do you know?"

There was more to Jagaros beneath that silky black and white coat, I knew—so much more than he was willing to let on. I just didn't know whether that something would end up hurting me or helping me.

"Why are you *really* training me?" I continued. "Is it just so that I can defend myself against Steeler, or is there another reason?" Tears blazed in the back of my throat, but I forced them back down. "If you knew he hurt me in the past, why would you try to cover that up?"

Jagaros eyed the tip of my blade with something like interest—and perhaps a flicker of surprise. Usually, he would threaten to eat me if I dared talk to him like that, but now he just rumbled, "*Everything will come to light soon enough, Rayna Drey.*" His eyes pinned me with a greenish glow. "*And this time, that light will be permanent.*"

Then he turned and padded into the darkness gathering beyond the grove, the jut of his shoulders alternating with each step. I stood there, frozen, my knife extended, watching him go in disbelief.

What he was doing to me was even worse than what I'd been doing to Emelle: not just keeping his own secrets, but keeping *my* secrets from *me. Everything will come to light soon enough*—that meant he knew about my past with Steeler and was hiding it from me, I was sure.

"Yeah, well, don't bother coming back until I see the light!" I called out, the words bursting past my lips before I could stop them. "I wouldn't want to be alone in the jungle with someone who might be working against me!"

Jagaros paused right on the threshold of the distant shadows, his spine stiffening as if he might say something back.

Only to slink forward again a moment later until his feline silhouette melted into nothing but night.

CHAPTER

11

Emelle side-eyed my dress the next morning on our way to History. Today, I'd chosen a longer one that would hide the various scrapes, bites, and pin-like puncture wounds from the sundew yesterday, so it swished around my calves with each step.

But I still felt self-conscious as I tried to brush off the weight of her glances. If Dazmine had noticed my knives, maybe I wasn't being as subtle as I thought I was. Maybe Emelle had noticed, too, and was just waiting for me to broach the subject myself.

"How was the party last night?" I asked before she could change her mind and start asking questions—not just about the dresses, but about why I hadn't come to bed until well past midnight. My hand still stung with blisters from all the knife-throwing I'd inflicted upon myself after Jagaros had left.

"Oh, let's see."

Emelle sighed as we weaved through the Wild Whisperer sector. Wren had been running late and told us to go on without her, and none of us had any idea where Rodhi was, so only Gileon trailed behind us, once again deep in conversation with his rhinoceros beetle.

"I actually managed to teach Lander how to grind," Emelle said. "Pierson Kadder got so drunk that he invited a gang of howler monkeys inside to play mini pentaball—trashed the boys' house completely," she added. "And then a few Element Wielder girls had a fight and ended up electrocuting the crap out of each other's hair."

"Wow." I bit my lip. "That sounds... fun."

Emelle smiled sadly at me as stray drops of rain peppered the stone pathways. She took a deep breath and said in a lower tone, "Look, I know you're not ready to tell me what's going on, but Lander's house is having a party on Friday. And I really think it would be nice if you joined us for real this time." She paused. "Not just to go through the motions, but to let loose. Like you said, have fun—even if it's the dumbest, most senseless fun you could ever imagine."

Fun. Could I have fun with the thought of Lexington arriving on Saturday for an update? Of the memory I had to show him—how I'd only nicked Steeler's jaw and needed help catching him when he came back to force-feed me another pill this Sunday?

Emelle was just inhaling a breath to say something else when we descended the stairs to the old History classroom. And both stopped dead in the doorway.

Gone was the musty, moldy scent that had accompanied Mr. Fenway. Gone were the cobwebs and swirling dust motes.

Now, the desks and chairs glistened with new polish, and—

"What the *hell*?" I yelped.

On every wall where old chalkboards and posters had once been, displays of dried insects faced us instead, their various wings spread wide and pinned in place. Stuffed animal heads glowered down from massive plaques nailed to the wall: red brocket deer and hippos and even a leopard. There were pairs of tusks and canines and rattlers and...

I closed my eyes against the onslaught of all the images, just as fresh gasps bloomed from behind me. The rest of the class had filed in, their cries of shock echoing the shriek of my magic within me.

"Don't look, Nuisance," Gileon whimpered.

"Settle down now, settle down," came a rasping hiss of a voice.

An instructor plunged through the jam of bodies near the doorway and stepped to the front of the classroom, her hair like inky quills sticking out of her head. I blinked. Then blinked again.

Because I *knew* her. She was the same hunchbacked woman who'd passed out our fourth quarterly History test last year...

Except she wasn't hunchbacked anymore. Her spine was straight as a spike now—almost too straight—and her nose looked less hooked.

The instructor surveyed us with undersized eyes rimmed in too many layers of kohl.

"I have assigned each of you a desk for the year, so please find your nametag and take a seat," she said in that same hissing tone.

We all glanced at each other. Assigned seats? We were all nineteen, for God's sake. I couldn't remember sitting in an assigned seat since I was five years old at the Alderwick schoolhouse.

"*Now*," the instructor said.

Glancing at Emelle, whose face had drained of all color, I edged toward the nearest row of desks to peer at the nametags placed neatly on each one. Norman. Mitzi. Dazmine. Pierson. Cilia. Gileon...

A minute later, everyone had found their seats and settled in, muttering under their breaths. Emelle was on the other side of the classroom from me, but thankfully I'd been placed next to Rodhi...

Who barreled in a few seconds later.

"I'm not late!"

He skidded to a halt before the desks, his mouth popping open at all the taxidermy. I tried to catch his eye and urge him to that empty desk beside me, but his eyes stayed glued to the nearest plaque of otter tails.

"No, you are not late," the instructor said, "but..." Her under-sized eyes strayed to a clock between stuffed heads. "Now you are. Please sit in your assigned spot before you become even more so."

Rodhi mouthed the words "assigned spot" with a dazed expression, but stumbled toward me and lowered himself into his chair.

I nudged his foot in an attempt to break him from his stupor. Rodhi did a double take, leaned in close to me, and whispered, "Looks like *someone* got some Shape Shifting work done over the dry season, huh?"

Thankfully, Mr. Fenway's replacement hadn't heard. She was too busy staring down her no-longer-hooked nose at Gileon in the front row.

"As you all may know, this is *History*, not Spiders, Worms, & Insects. There shall be no flying or buzzing things in here." She smiled at Gileon. "Please take your little pet back outside where it belongs." *Before I nail it to the wall, too*, she didn't have to say.

I'd never loathed an instructor before, but now my fingers actually twitched on my desk, begging me to grab my knife in case she got too close to my friend and the beetle he cared for.

Throat bobbing, Gileon hefted himself up with Nuisance perched on his outstretched finger. Every eye followed the trek of his heavy footfalls to the door and back.

Maybe it was for the best that Nuisance wasn't in a room with all his murdered and pinned-up peers, but I still hated the way Gileon slumped back into his assigned seat, empty-handed and looking as if he'd like to curl into something so much smaller.

"Very nice." The instructor returned her attention to the entire class. "Now, I'm sure you all remember me from last year. I am Mrs. Smetlar, and I am here to teach you about the Esholian biome—the flora and fauna of our island over the last few hundred years."

She didn't pace, but her eyes did—swinging this way and that as if to keep track of everyone all at once, a smile still stamped on her face.

"However, I would like to start off the year with a different piece of history that is crucial to our understanding of our jobs as Wild Whisperers of Eshol. And that is the topic of the Final Test... And the fraction of you who will be exiled in four years' time."

Rodhi's jittering knee fell still. On the other side of Emelle, Dazmine jerked her head up, and nobody else dared breathe.

Mrs. Smetlar pretended not to notice the reaction, but I saw the way her eyes had stilled. The way her lips had pulled up even more.

"You see, when Dyonisia Reeve first founded the island and learned how to recycle the discarded faerie metal at the top of Bascite Mountain, there were no tests or exiles at all. There was simply the domed shield of protection, the monsters beyond it, and the Esholian pilgrims safe and sound within."

Monsters beyond it—monsters as in Steeler. I pressed my fingernails into my palms to keep my hands from shaking as pain unspooled in my head. Rodhi glanced over at me, his forehead creasing with questioning concern, and reached out with his leg to tap my foot with his. The message was obvious.

Calm down.

Easy for him to say. This was only the second or third time *he'd* been calm in his life. But I dragged in a deep breath and willed my hands to uncurl.

Rodhi gave me a short nod and returned his attention to Mrs. Smetlar up front. Hesitantly, I followed his lead.

"—that kind of protection was vital," Mrs. Smetlar was saying, "But then the first unworthy citizen was gifted with Wild Whispering."

She waited for someone to make a sound, maybe a gasp of shock.

When nobody did, she said with a bit more impatience, "The new Wild Whisperer was given the simplest of jobs after her Branding: to protect the children of the settlement from predators while they played outside during the times their parents were busy."

I could see where this was going, and I didn't like it. Not one bit. Especially since it seemed like all those dead animal eyes were zeroing in on us. Watching our reactions to what came next.

"A leopard," Mrs. Smetlar said, nodding up at the stuffed feline head above her, "stalked a few of those kids and waited until all the other villagers were gone. Until only the Wild Whisperer remained to guard them. And then it pounced. And the pathetic waste of life who was *supposed* to be protecting them had no idea what to say or do to get the cat to stop its attack."

I tried not to look at the leopard head, so similar to Jagaros's.

"Afterward," Mrs. Smetlar continued, "the parents were so angry that their own powers began to malfunction. Magic-made storms and plagues and infestations threatened to destroy the entire island... until Dyonisia Reeve came up with a brilliant solution to ensure that nobody would fail their magic or their fellow villagers again."

The Esholian Institute. The Final Tests. Banishment.

For the first time in months, I let myself wish for my fathers. For the calm, calculating gaze Fabian would give Mrs. Smetlar at this news, and the exasperated, distrustful glare Don would throw her way. Although... perhaps they already knew. Perhaps Mr. Fenway would have told us the same thing if he were still alive—albeit without four walls of dead animals pressing in on us while he said it.

Mrs. Smetlar herself straightened her rod of a back even more.

"If it means maintaining the strength and prosperity Dyonisia Reeve has given this precious island, I shall be glad to watch the Good Council throw many more of you to sea after you fail your Final Tests."

And finally, her smile gave way to a leer.

Mr. Conine's double block of Predators & Prey came as a relief two hours later, when our whole class trudged to Building 3C.

Gileon had found Nuisance waiting for him outside on a low stone wall—thank the God of the Cosmos for that—so now he filled the beetle in on everything Mrs. Smetlar had said while we walked.

"Wren always used to complain about Mr. Fenway's digestive issues," Rodhi said mournfully, "but I bet she's gonna wish for his stink back when she meets *that* vulture of a woman this afternoon. If only I had the right kind of pan, I'd bake her into a pie and feed her to the—"

"I just hope Dazmine's okay," I interrupted before he could finish that horrible sentence. The last we needed was for a spider to report it back to Mrs. Smetlar... although I doubted a single living thing wanted to get within half a mile of that room surrounded by their own nightmares.

Rodhi, Emelle, and I glanced up toward Dazmine, who was walking ahead with her eyes glued to the stone walkway. I might not have cared for Jenia, but if it had been *Emelle* who'd been exiled...

I *might* have thrown my knife at Mrs. Smetlar for what she'd said.

None of us said another word until we got to Mr. Conine, who was waiting for us right outside the classroom door, his sideburns and circle beard as bushy as ever. When the entire class had gathered around him, he clapped his leathery hands and rubbed his palms together.

"Welcome back, Wild Whisperers. I had a whole lesson planned on gibbons, but it turns out our friends in the Object Summoning sector need our help. Lots of bugs out this year. Which means lots of food for the mice. Which means... lots of snakes. Specifically black mambas."

Murmurs broke the silence. We'd talked to snakes last year—and broken up a fight between a boa constrictor and a mongoose during a quarterly test—but only ever interacted with non-venomous ones.

Black mambas... I remembered Fabian and Don warning me to avoid them altogether in Alderwick. This should be fun.

"If you'll follow me," Mr. Conine said, "I'll explain as we walk."

He began to wind through the smallest passageways of our sector, and we followed in single file. His voice echoed back as he said, "The Summoners have used their magic to expel the snakes, of course, but..." A gruff laugh. "Mambas are prideful and can hold a mean grudge. No amount of physically removing them will keep them away for long, not when they know where all the food is now. So it'll be *our* job to make the mambas leave for good—by tricking them."

Interesting. Usually, Mr. Conine warned us *against* being deceptive toward animals. The fact that he was encouraging deception now...

Mr. Conine laughed again, probably hearing all our murmurs as we ducked under a painted arch and came to a row of quaint wooden classrooms clogged with objects hanging from strings over our heads: shoes and empty bottles, pocket watches and even some underwear.

"The boa constrictors we dealt with last year are downright docile compared to black mambas. Whereas boa constrictors value companionship in small doses, black mambas value trickery."

Mr. Conine turned to face us again, his expression tightening into something serious.

"They will try to trick you, to lure you in, so it's very important that you resist whatever it is they offer. Don't make any sudden movements, and don't get too close."

A group of Summoners passed by, then, each levitating a different object over their heads as if they were balancing buckets. One of them did a double take at the sight of us standing in his sector, and the pitcher that had been floating over his head gave a violent tremor and clanged to the ground.

An instructor screeched out a reprimand. Mr. Conine waited until the boy had picked up his pitcher with his invisible Summoning hands and moved on with the rest of his class before resuming his instructions.

"Your job today is to find a black mamba and trick them into leaving the Esholian Institute. Lie, cheat, steal—I am giving you permission to be the worst kind of person possible when it comes to them. Because trust me—they will see through your lies, but they will commend you for the attempt, and respect you enough to leave. But by the orchid and the owl, class, do *not* get close enough to touch."

With that, we all broke apart. Gileon and Nuisance went one way and Rodhi and Emelle went another, so I plunged toward the back of the Summoning sector, where mossy, overhanging branches soon dampened any sound and the wood of the classrooms began to rot.

A tingle climbed up the back of my neck, merging with the constant ache in my head. It was so silent here—besides the low humming of trees—that I looked over my shoulder more than once for signs of any flesh-eating plants swaying nearby.

Nothing. Nothing besides these derelict classrooms with moss-cloaked windowpanes and caved-in roofs. Too familiar. As if I'd been here in a dream or another life.

Just as I was eyeing a broken door with bloodstains splattered on its surface, a high, hissing voice said, "*Looking for someone, girl?*"

I almost whirled, but stopped myself. *Do not make any sudden movements*, Mr. Conine had said. So I turned slowly instead.

A pale gray snake, long and slender, had lifted its head from a chipped wooden porch, where it sunbathed in a single strip of light that had broken through the upper canopies. Its scales weren't black, but I was sure the roof of its mouth would be.

Not that I'd want to get close enough to find out.

"No," I lied. "Just taking a stroll. What about you?"

The mamba blinked: the only sign it was surprised that I had understood its hissing. That I wasn't a Summoner who could expel it with invisible hands, but a Wild Whisperer who could talk back.

"*You smell like you're troubled,*" it said, its tongue flicking out to taste the air. "*And slightly sad. Almost as if you are in a constant state of pain.*"

"How astute of you." I backed up a pace as it slithered down the sagging steps and re-coiled itself on the ground before me.

"*But you do not taste scared,*" the mamba said. "*Why is that?*"

Because I trusted my knife hand. Because I could feel the antler handle pressed firmly against my thigh, ready for me to wield it.

But I said, "You've had your fill of poor, innocent mice, I hear." Now, more than ever, I was glad I always snuck Willa bits of cheese. She'd never have to worry about venturing out into snake territory for a meal. "Why would I be afraid of you eating *me?*"

The mamba seemed to smile, its mouth opening at a slanted angle to reveal two delicate, needle-like fangs.

"*Indeed, I have had my fill, but not of mice. Would you like me to tell you about my latest meal?*" The mamba didn't wait for me to respond. "*It was a red-sided opossum who'd fallen from a tree nearby. She was wounded, just as you are, and begged me for a dose of my venom to take the pain away. It was a mercy.*"

"Is that so?" I tried not to sound too interested, willing the throbbing in my head to go away for one damned second so I could focus. Bored. I had to keep my face bored and disinterested.

The mamba coiled tighter, gathering itself.

"*Oh yes. My venom has a soothing property that works so quickly, it'll be like floating among the clouds and stars within seconds. Tell me, girl—how long has it been since you've felt pleasure?*"

Never, it seemed. It was as if I'd spent my whole life sleeping up until three months ago, when I'd opened my eyes to haze and coldness. To emptiness and pain that only grew and grew and grew.

The tears in my throat rose up to nip at my nose, my eyes.

Clouds and stars. That sounded nice. That sounded *good*. I *belonged* up in the clouds, between stars and beneath the moon.

But—I shook my head and stumbled back a step—I had to help the Good Council catch Steeler on Sunday.

My vision seemed to clear. I found the mamba's slitted gaze.

"I know of something even better than clouds and stars."

It paused. Flicked its tongue once.

"*Oh?*"

"Yes," I said, determination hardening in my bones. "Yes. It's far away from here, on the other end of the island, where there are no other snakes to compete with. Only endless food and endless sun."

It was my biggest lie yet, of course. Nobody knew what lay within the boundary of the Uninhabitable Zone on the other end of the island. The one time I'd seen it from a flying carriage, it had been nothing but swirling, milky mist that *definitely* wouldn't let any sunlight through.

Still, the mamba seemed to consider my words with a tilt of its coffin-shaped head.

"*And you would forego sweet, dark oblivion for this place of endless light?*"

What had Jagaros told me last night? *Everything will come to light soon enough. And this time, that light will be permanent.*

To me, it didn't matter if that light came from warm, buttery sunlight or the fiercest blaze of wildfire or the stroke of a moonbeam on a dark, misty night. I just needed something, *anything*, to shed a glimmer onto the dark, frosty thing I'd become inside.

"Light is light," I answered. "If I had to choose, I would take that over darkness any day. As should you."

The mamba was silent for so long I wondered if it had gone to sleep. Then it bowed its head ever so slightly.

"*Perhaps I shall go find this faraway place, then.*"

It saw through my deception, as Mr. Conine had predicted. Saw through my deception and respected it. With a swift jerk of its glistening gray head, it slithered away until the last of it had disappeared.

Leaving me with that single question: how long had it been since I'd felt pleasure? Or anything besides a throbbing head and a wall of ice?

Maybe Emelle was right—maybe it was time to go to a party for *real.* To break my no-drinking rule for a night and flirt and dance.

And shake away the weight of Steeler's body in that alleyway, warm and hard and electric where it had pressed against mine.

CHAPTER

12

That Friday, I stepped inside Lander's brick mansion for the first time ever. As dark and cozy as it was on the outside, it was just as stuffy and chaotic on the inside—at least at the present moment.

Groups of girls danced with colorful gills or seashells growing from their bodies like ornaments, boys played mini pentaball with what I could have sworn were classmates-turned-into-balls, and an assortment of couples lounged on couches with drinks in their hands.

Deep, thumping music poured from Shifters who'd basically turned themselves into walking drums. I let the bass of it pound through my ribcage as Emelle led me into the throng.

"Rayna!" Lander seemed to materialize from thin air and gathered me in a one-armed hug, his free hand balancing a drink of clear, sloshing liquid. "I haven't seen you all week! How do you like your new classes?" He lowered his voice, and I had to lean in to hear him through the noise surrounding us. "Melle says you have a... bad new instructor."

Indeed, Mrs. Smetlar hadn't let our second class with her go by without highlighting, once again, how much she'd enjoy watching the Good Council exile so many of us in four years' time.

"Let's just say that she doesn't like her students talking back," I said grimly—which was true. Rodhi had learned that the hard way when she'd made him polish some eyeballs after he'd questioned her primary sources yesterday. "Or her animals," I added as an afterthought.

I would never be able to stop shuddering when I walked in that classroom and had to sit beneath literal corpses.

Emelle started to say something, but just as I leaned forward to try to hear her better, I felt a tug on my sleeve and looked down to find a toddler gaping up at me, his thick blonde curls as wild as mine.

"Mommy," the toddler squeaked.

"Get *out* of here, man," Lander said.

The toddler popped back up into a young man with ginger hair and a sloppy grin. Winking at me, the Shifter turned on a heel and disappeared into the crowd, as if what he'd just done was a normal part of his Friday night.

"Okay," I said, feeling faint now, "I think the Shape Shifting sector is officially the weirdest one."

Lander laughed, the sound rich and—well, heartwarming. My memories of last year might have been foggy, but I could at least remember the way he'd once shied away from the idea of pure, undiluted joy. Now, with Emelle at his side, smiling up at him...

He looked so much more confident, more at ease in his own body, than I'd ever seen him.

At that moment, a Shifter struck up a catchy beat with his half-drum body, and Emelle tugged on Lander's sleeve with a gasp.

"This is the same one they played the other day, remember, Land? C'mon, Rayna, come dance with us! This beat is *everything*."

She was already swaying her hips, drawing Lander's eyes to her curves. I raised my palms, shaking my head.

"I think I'm going to get a drink first, actually." If I was actually going to loosen up, I'd have to break the no-drinking rule I'd given myself. Surely, one night couldn't make my head any worse than it already was. "You two go on without me. I'll catch up in a bit."

"You sure?" Emelle stopped swaying to narrow her focus on me.

"Positive."

"Well, then," Lander said, passing me the drink in his hand, "you can start with this one."

Taking the cup, I only hesitated for a second longer before I knocked it back, draining what was left in one swift gulp. The burn slid down my throat and settled like a brewing fire in my stomach.

I wiped my mouth with the sleeve of my dress. "Thanks. I'll come find you both when the ceiling starts to spin a little."

Fun. I could have *fun*. I could find pleasure for just one night.

Apparently satisfied that I meant it, Emelle dragged Lander into the fray of bodies, and I exhaled a long breath as the blissful heat of the drink started to spread through me like reaching roots.

Something tweaked in my chest, but I ignored it. Where was Rodhi? Wren and Gileon had decided to stay in and play board games tonight, but Rodhi had promised he was going to show up after he took care of some personal business. Whatever that meant.

"Rayna."

I jumped and almost dropped my empty glass to find Wilder standing right behind me, his hands stuffed in his pocket.

"Wilder!" Maybe the drink was already rooting itself into my system, because I felt the words slip out more easily than I could have possibly expected. "I've been meaning to reach out to you to talk about the other day. I hope you know I didn't mean it when I said we weren't friends. It's just that Kitterfol Lexington is—"

"I know who Kitterfol Lexington is," Wilder interrupted with a half-smile. "He's sort of the most famous alumni in my sector—and the most prying, I've learned since then. So I get it. I wouldn't want him rooting around in my brain any more than necessary either."

At the slight squint of Wilder's eyes... he was curious, I realized, curious to know why Lexington had been cornering me in the first place. Scrambling for another topic so that my thoughts wouldn't stray into dangerous territory, I asked, "So what are you doing in the Shifter house? I thought the Mind Manipulator parties were all the buzz."

Although, come to think of it, maybe Steeler's former position as the Manipulator prince had really put a damper on the whole sector—finding out their class royal had been a spy and traitor all along probably hadn't been the greatest morale boost of all time. And I still couldn't comprehend how much other people remembered of him. From the sounds of it, he'd been like a ghost waltzing along the periphery of everyone else's memories. Nothing substantial to grasp onto.

Wilder jerked a thumb over his shoulder, toward the group of Shifters playing mini-pentaball.

"I met that middle guy—the one with the green ball—right before the Branding. He became a Shifter and invited me over."

"Oh, cool. How was—"

"My first week?" Again, that half-smile seemed to weigh on his mouth. "Sorry, still getting used to the whole mind-reading thing."

"Must be an overwhelming magic," I said, trying not to let him catch my thoughts about his family and how disappointed they would be when—if—he came back without Wild Whispering abilities. I took a quick sip to try to stifle the thought—only to remember that my glass was empty. Shit, my tongue already felt sloppy.

Wilder didn't see, though. He was gazing sideways, as if he couldn't bear to make eye contact. "It gets easier every day. And besides, it has its uses. Like for instance..." He paused, his eyes swinging back to my face. "I was coming over to tell you how beautiful you look tonight, but I can tell by your outer thoughts that you're not interested in me in that way anymore."

I cringed. It was true, even if I hadn't come to that conclusion myself. "I'm sorry, I just—"

"Hey." Wilder placed a brief touch on my shoulder. "Don't ever apologize for how you feel or don't feel, okay? It's the one thing we can't control, even as Mind Manipulators." He sucked in a breath as if to say goodbye, then did a double take. "Quinn?"

My head cranked sideways way faster than it should have. A sheet of ruby-red hair paused among two grinding couples. Then turned.

Quinn Balkersaff slowly pivoted to face us.

"Wilder. Rayna," she said in a flat, empty voice that filled me with chills. "How adorable that you two are back together again."

"We're not," Wilder said before I could, his voice speeding up... as if Quinn's appearance was a welcome escape from the topic we'd just broached together. "But it's nice to see you again, too!" He looked back and forth between us. "How often do you two get to hang out, being in different sectors and all?"

I tried to stomp on his foot to get him to change the subject, but missed and ended up stumbling over mine. Quinn just studied him, her hair falling to the side with the catlike tilt of her head.

"I don't see why I should even answer that out loud," she said finally. "You can pick out anything you want from here, can't you?" She tapped her own head.

Wilder's face fell as he no doubt *did* read everything emanating from her blazing mind.

"Oh. Yeah, yeah, I can. Well..." He dragged a hand through his hair and scratched the top of his head. "I'll see you two later."

And without another word, he turned to stride back to his penta-ball friends, his hands shoved back into his pockets.

Glaring, Quinn twirled to leave, too.

"Quinn," I started, reaching out with a single hand.

But she was already gone. *Okay*, then. Maybe that should have hurt me more than it did, but at this point I was used to my ex-best friend avoiding me at all costs... and I knew if I kept pursuing her, it would just end up being harassment on my part.

Plus, the alcohol helped.

Sighing, I started spinning in a tight circle, craning my neck for Rodhi again, when a deep, deep voice said, "You want another one? Or are you just going to keep holding an empty glass?"

I looked up... and up and up... to find a man of nothing but sculpted abs, golden skin, and wavy blonde hair smiling down at me, holding out a new glass of that wonderful liquid with a bulging arm.

"Thanks," I said, taking it from him. And gulped that one, too.

The man moved closer. "Do you want to dance?"

I found myself face-to-face with his eight-pack. I had no doubt the man was a Shifter and didn't actually look like this without all his magic jacking him up, but after that shipwreck of a conversation with Wilder and Quinn... "Sure," I said again.

Because the ceiling was starting to spin.

An hour later, our teeth were clacking together.

I hadn't been able to find Emelle or Lander again, but I'd finally managed to let loose with the blonde Shape Shifter.

Now, his hands gripped either side of my waist, tugging me toward his body that didn't feel like a body at all. There was pressure in all the right spots, feeding the fire that had traveled to that spot between my legs, but my mouth—

I tried to break from the kissing, the sucking and squelching sounds of his lips around my tongue. We'd stumbled into this vacant room a while ago, but now the spinning had paused long enough for me to realize how cold and wet his mouth was. How clammy his hands were as they gripped me like vises. How his armpit areas had bloomed with dark sweat.

"Slow down," I panted, coming up for air.

The Shifter just tugged me toward him again, mashing his mouth so hard against mine it felt like my lips would bruise. I yanked back.

"Okay, stop."

"What's wrong?" He was murmuring the words into my neck now, sucking on patches of my skin in a downward trail.

"I just..." I tried to lean back even more, realizing I was straddling him on a random bed—with both our clothes still on, thank the God of the Cosmos. "I need a break for a second." Or maybe for more than a second.

Finally, the Shifter removed his mouth long enough to look at me.

"Are you fucking kidding?" His golden face crinkled into something ugly. "You're not getting cold feet on me, are you?"

That put the fire out between my legs. I scrambled off his lap and slipped onto the floor, not even bothering to turn to face him.

"So what if I am? I'm allowed to change my mind."

I made to go, but a bubbling movement caught the corner of my eye. I turned just in time to see the Shifter shrink back into his regular self—a slug-shaped boy with a neck that seemed to melt from his head to his rounded shoulders—and pop up onto his own feet.

"Oh, no, no, no." He actually laughed, though the sound did nothing to warm the room. "You came to *my* house, sweetheart. You pressed your ass against *my* dick when we were dancing out there."

I backed up a step, too stunned to so much as scowl. I remembered dancing, remembered having fun, but that didn't mean...

"I just need a couple of pumps," the Shifter said, "and then—"

"Not interested anymore," I spat, and rushed for the door, my hand jerking at the doorknob...

His flabby arm lengthened itself into something long and noodle-like, his hand shooting past me to palm the door shut.

For a splinter of time, I blinked and thought I saw him: the silhouette of Coen Steeler gathering in the corner of the room. Raw, warm power seemed to ripple off him as he stepped forward, murder etched all over his face.

I didn't wait long enough to blink again. I just whipped my crescent knife from the sheath beneath my rumpled dress, raised it high above my head, and brought the blade back down.

Right through the Shifter's hand still pressed against the door.

He howled in agony, and his hand snapped back toward him—or, most of it did.

The three fingers I'd sliced off at the tips thudded to the carpet in puddles of their own blood.

When I turned back to that corner, breathing heavily, the silhouette of Coen Steeler was gone. As was that electric, murderous power that had emanated from it.

"You bitch!" the sluggish boy wailed, cradling his dripping hand. "You ruined me! You hurt me! I'm going to tell the Good Council!"

For a second, my blood froze in my veins at the thought. The last thing I needed was more of the Good Council in my life.

Then I remembered that Dyonisia had given me this knife sheath. Surely, she wouldn't punish me for using it...even if I hadn't cut into quite the right target.

"You're a big Shifter," I said, my voice shaking. "You can grow it back."

Without waiting for a response, I opened the door and whisked away.

CHAPTER

13

Are you okay?

The dark, fathomless presence filled my mind the moment I stumbled out of the Shifter house—still no sign of Emelle or Lander—and out onto Bascite Boulevard. All the houses had calmed down now, but I couldn't tell what time it was. Not when a heavy film of clouds slathered the sky and sent warm rain streaking down all around me.

Oh, so you were *watching all that like a creeper, then*, I spat into my own mind, each of my footsteps splashing angrily through puddles of water as I staggered home. *I was beginning to wonder if I'd imagined you standing in the corner.*

Not that I knew how Steeler had done it. Because how the hell did *Mind Manipulating* make someone invisible? Unless he'd commanded both the Shifter and me to simply... unsee him.

At that thought, I made a full circle in the middle of the road, squinting through the rain for any signs of someone stalking me.

Nothing. Nobody was out at the moment.

Nobody I could see, at least.

Steeler's voice dropped a shade lower. *As much as I'd love to, Rayna, I can't spy on you 24/7 or I'd lose my mind in yours. And I'd never willingly stand there and watch you touch another man.*

I bristled at the pure possessiveness in that voice, the dominance on the brink of a frenzy. But he went on before I could come up with a response scathing enough to bite.

When I sensed that man trying to touch you against your will, though... let's just say I got there as fast as I could. But it looked like you had the situation handled all on your own, didn't you?

And now there was pride—actual *pride*—in his voice. As if the thought of me slicing off someone's fingertips thrilled him.

Hypocritical, coming from you, I scoffed, resuming my lumbering path toward the Wild Whisperer house...but still keeping half an eye out for any human-shaped movement in the dark. If Steeler had truly been in that room just five minutes ago, I had no doubt he was watching me now, following me this very instant. I cleared my throat. *As if you didn't do the same thing to me last year.*

Steeler's presence in my head seemed to hold its breath, then let it out in one long, slow exhale. It was worse than if he'd been breathing in my ear. He was breathing *inside* me. *Within* me.

I made a careless mistake in letting Kitterfol Lexington keep that particular memory, he said finally. *Not a day goes by where I don't curse myself for forgetting he had it.*

I'd made it to the double doors of my own house, but now I stopped on the front steps, letting the rain soak my tangle of curls.

That's what you curse yourself for? My whole body trembled with rage at the audacity, something in my chest shifting like a mamba trying to strike through the bars of its prison. *You're not ashamed of the things you did to me in that memory, but for failing to erase the evidence of it?* I wrenched open the doors and barged into the foyer, laughing humorlessly again. *Maybe if you weren't so obsessed with me, you would've remembered to mess up other people's minds, too.*

Oh, trust me, Steeler said without hesitation. Without shame. *Obsessing over you has put a wrench in all of my plans. You are the most distracting, most devastating addiction I've ever known.*

Chills grazed down the back of my neck as I lurched up the stairs. To the second-year floor. Down the dark, quiet hall. *Predators can't stay away from their prey,* Dyonisia had said. If I'd truly put a wrench in Steeler's plans, then... then he was admitting the same thing now. He actually *wanted* to stay away, to leave me alone—but couldn't.

Each step seemed to pull the air from my lungs, and the walls wavered. Maybe my intoxication had never cleared after all.

It wasn't until I'd made it to my own door that I was able to dredge up any kind of coherent response.

If you're so addicted to me, then why don't you come out from wherever you're hiding and face me again? I'd love to reenact what I just did to that Shifter with you.

Not the horrible, clammy kissing, obviously. But the slicing.

A dark chuckle rumbled through my mind.

As tempting as that is, little hurricane, it's not Sunday night yet. But until then—a gentle caress against the walls of my mind—*sweetest dreams.*

And then he was gone.

"Where'd you go?" I called into the darkness of my room. "Come back here right now. I'm not finished with this conversation."

But the voice that answered wasn't Steeler's.

"Rayna? Who are you talking—oh."

A lantern flickered to life across the room. Neither Emelle nor Cilia had made it back yet, but Dazmine's face flared into stark relief as she pressed her fiercest glower onto me, her fingertips drumming against her crossed arms. Even through my haze, I could see the pin-pricks all over her arms—as if she'd been spending her free time practicing with the sundew.

"You're drunk, aren't you? I can smell you from here."

"Not drunk," I muttered. By the orchid and the owl, I sounded stupid even to my own ears. "Just a little tipsy."

Dazmine raised her eyebrows.

"You going to cut my throat with that, or are you going to put it away?" She nodded at my raised hand, and I startled at the sight of my knife still in my fist, the blade glimmering with blood.

I fumbled with my dress for a moment before sliding it back into the sheath around my thigh. I'd clean it tomorrow.

"Sorry about that." My body seemed to lurch for my bed of its own accord. I fell on top of my covers and pressed my face into my pillow, moaning sideways, "My life is so messed up, Daz."

Dazmine looked at me like I was a pile of Willa's droppings.

"One, I literally don't care, and two, never call me Daz again." It looked like she was about to turn off her lantern and climb back into bed, but she paused long enough to wrinkle her nose at me again. "For God's sake, you could at least wash your face before you fall asleep."

My eyes fluttered shut. "Probably," I muttered.

For a microsecond, the start of a dream tried to tug me away... but then a cold, dripping washcloth was slapping me back awake, with Dazmine's look of pure contempt staring down at me.

"There. It looks like you have... is that *blood* splattered all over your cheeks?" After a few shocked blinks, she shook her head and turned back toward her own bed. "I don't even want to know—unless you've murdered a classmate again or something."

The tone was sarcastic, but such sorrow edged her voice that as soon as I was done scrubbing my face, I whispered, "It's not me who killed Fergus. And it wasn't Jenia either."

Dazmine twisted back around, her braids flying.

"But you know who did? He's really..." Her voice wobbled, just for a second. "Fergus is really dead?"

"Yes." If Coen's *killing that kid was all me* claim was true. My eyes were closing again against my will as I sank my head back into my pillow and let the washcloth drop to the floor.

"Well then you need to tell the Good Council!" Dazmine's voice seemed to echo from far, far away. "Maybe they'll bring Jenia back if there's proof that she didn't hurt him—"

"No," I breathed. "They won't bring her back. The pirates aren't the good guys, Dazmine, but neither is anyone on the Good Council. No one is good." Another dream tugged at me. "No one's good."

My last thought before drifting away was that *I* wanted to be good. But after what I'd done to that Shifter's fingers, after how quickly I'd resorted to violence without considering any other options...

I didn't know if it was possible for me to ever be good again.

" *Wake up, sleepyhead.*"

A little wet nose sniffled against my chin, and I peeled my eyes open to find Willa in my face, sunlight fissuring in through gaps in the vine-smothered window behind her.

" *There's a bird pecking on your window,* " she said, " *and I don't have the hissing skills to scare it away. Or the hands to strangle it.*"

No sooner had she said it than a sharp *tap, tap, tap* sounded against the glass, and I blinked at the bright blue cotinga visible through a small gap in the foliage curtain. On either side of the room, Emelle and Dazmine's beds were empty—Dazmine's crisply made as if she'd never slept in it at all—but Cilia was drooling into her arm across from me, reeking of the same kind of hangover weighing *me* down right now. She must have stumbled in last night after I'd passed out.

Moaning, I rolled out of bed and just barely managed to catch myself before crashing to the floor. I dragged my footsteps to the window, opened it a crack, and rubbed my eyes against the whoosh of a warm morning breeze.

"Hello?"

"*Hi! Hi! Hi!*" The cotinga hopped inside. "*Are you Emelle's friend?*"

"Yes." My heartbeat spiked. "Is she okay? What happened?"

Emelle spent the night with Lander a few times a week, so I hadn't even thought to worry about her whereabouts, but...

"*Oh yes, she's fine, fine, fine!*" cheeped the cotinga. "*She's at the Shape Shifter house. She just asked me to make sure you'd made it safely to your room.*" It twitched, fluffing up its feathers. "*So did you make it safely to your room? Did you? Did you?*"

"Um." I glanced around at my room. "Yes, I believe I did."

"*Great! I'll tell her! Bye, bye, bye!*"

The cotinga fluttered to Emelle's bedside table, pecked at the bird-feeder half-filled with various kinds of seeds and nuts, and flapped off again with a happy chirp.

I shut the window, just as Willa scurried up to the ledge where the bird had perched and rolled her beady black eyes.

"*I think I need some coffee after hearing that thing talk. Shall we go to the dining hall for some breakfast?*" She paused to study me long enough for Cilia to break the silence with a snore. "*I'm sure you're starving after mincing up some good old-fashioned fingertips.*"

"Shit." I groaned into my hands. "Does everyone know?"

"*No.*" Willa continued to study me. "*Nobody besides us mice knows anything. My cousins say the Shifter cried and raged and did some very gross things to himself that involved his good hand... but he didn't tell another soul. And by the time he passed out, they say he'd regrown them. The fingers, I mean.*"

"See," I muttered. "Knew he could do it."

But I finally forced myself to meet Willa's eyes, and found a peculiar blazing expression reflected in them, one that made her whiskers twitch. My gentle little mouse friend was... was *glad* I'd done it, I realized with a jolt, *glad* I'd defended myself in this way. And that small bit of curdling shame in the pit of my stomach seemed to dissolve.

Willa smiled with her two front teeth.

"*Just wash your knife before you cut my cheese with it, okay?*"

Half an hour later, after a quick bath and change of clothes (I did, indeed, wash my knife in the bathing chamber sink, thankful that no one else was around to watch the blood swirl down the drain), I made my way down to the dining hall with Willa on my shoulder.

Only a few Wild Whisperers were up so early on the first weekend of the new year, so there wasn't even a line to the kitchen counter. After I grabbed a parfait and a side of cheese, I turned to realize I'd missed Rodhi, sitting at a table in the corner all by himself, nursing a mug of coffee as if his life depended on it.

"Hey." I went over and sat down next to him. "You okay?"

Rodhi jumped, blinking at me rapidly before his face relaxed again. "Oh, hey, darling. Hey, cutie."

He nodded at Willa, who actually batted her eyelashes at that. I wrinkled my nose at her, and she stuck out her tongue before scurrying down my arm and onto the table to start nibbling at her piece of cheese.

"Yeah, m'alright," Rodhi said, uncharacteristically oblivious of all this as he sighed into his coffee. "Just had a long night is all."

"Oh?" Usually when Rodhi said he had a long night, it involved his flask and a couple of girls—or sometimes even boys—and an after-morning glow. Not now, though. Now he truly did look tired. I picked at a few blackberries sprinkled over my parfait and said carefully, "I never saw you at Lander's party." Not that I'd been in the right mind to keep track of everyone for the majority of it, but still. Rodhi made his presence known wherever he went. "Where were you?"

Rodhi's answer was a little too hasty.

"I had some stuff come up and couldn't make it." Before I could so much as raise my eyebrows at him, he turned his earnest expression toward me. "It wasn't *too* boring without me there, was it? I mean, I know I'm the life of the party, but hopefully I've imparted *some* of my gregarious wisdom onto—"

He snapped his mouth shut, released his coffee as if it had electrocuted him, scooched his chair back, and... just walked away.

"Uh, Rodhi, what—?"

But I knew before I even turned around. Knew from the slimy, oily presence that had just wormed its way into the dining hall, from the way everyone around me had all jerked their gazes away, as if yanked by puppet strings. And not the Object Summoning kind. The Mind Manipulating kind.

The kind that directed brains instead of bones.

"Hello," I said stiffly as Kitterfol Lexington sat in Rodhi's vacant spot. Rodhi himself had already lumbered out the door, and Willa had stopped nibbling her cheese to gape upward with her two front teeth.

"Shoo," Lexington said to her.

Willa squeaked and ran off, spiraling down one of the legs of the table, her tail flying behind her.

I wanted to punch him in the pockmarked face for that, but I supposed I should be grateful he hadn't punched *her* and left her a furry, twitching mess. Yes, it was better that Rodhi and Willa were gone for this.

Lexington didn't wait for my permission before he turned his cold, pale eyes onto mine and plunged into my mind.

I felt every thought and memory waft to the surface of my mind as he touched them, leaving his slimy residue behind in reverse order: there was me last night, chopping a guy's fingers off, and the two of us grinding beforehand. There was the black mamba and the sundew and the fire ants.

And then there was *him*. Steeler. Besting me in the alleyway. Anchoring my wrists over my head.

Take this pill and I won't bury this memory of us. You can show it to the Good Council—how you nicked me.

Well, Lexington was watching me nick him now. Through a hazy kind of film, I watched the color leak from his face—but only for a second. By the time he pulled himself out of my mind, his sneering composure was back.

"You let him go."

"Not on purpose, obviously." I steeled myself to say what I had to say, but Lexington cut me off.

"What did that pill do to you?"

"I don't know."

111

And you know *I don't know,* I couldn't stop myself from thinking. *I can't hide anything from your oily worms.*

Lexington's face twitched once. Before he could lecture me, I continued, "As you heard Steeler say, he'll be back tomorrow night at the same time to give me another pill, and I can't... I don't think I can debilitate him, not by myself. So I need—"

"No."

Lexington picked up Rodhi's abandoned mug and drained its contents in one gulp. Then he leaned back in his chair to cross his arms.

I stared at him.

"What?"

"No," Lexington repeated, his jaw ticking. "We can't help you."

I looked around the room to make sure I wasn't hallucinating this entire conversation. Every Wild Whisperer in here was still craning their necks, forced to look away.

"But the pirate breaches. The attacks. The danger to—"

Lexington wiped his mouth with the edge of his cloak.

"Listen, you idiot girl. If it were up to me, I wouldn't have hired you to perform this task in the first place. But as it is, our leader—" Something flashed in his eyes at that "—well, she is the only woman on this island more powerful than me. Too powerful for me to influence."

He flexed his fingers, and I suddenly *knew,* as if the residue of him in my mind had let it slip, that Kitterfol Lexington had tried to take Dyonisia to bed. And failed. And every time he spied on something intimate, every time he creeped and crawled over someone else's private moments, he was imagining himself doing those things to *her.*

The next second, Lexington closed his fingers into a fist and wrenched that residue of himself out of my mind.

"As I was saying," he said coldly, "our leader believes you are capable all by yourself. And she has ordered for none of us to intervene. You are to bring Coen Steeler to us *without* help."

I was sure my face had gone slack from the shock as all thoughts about Lexington's personal love crisis faded in comparison to this news.

Dyonisia Reeve had ordered the Good Council to... to stay out of this? I'd been so sure I was simply the bait, the temptation to lure Steeler in... but what if I wasn't? What if this was all just a test?

It's a thigh sheath. I had the best of my blacksmiths in Belliview tailor it especially for that knife of yours. So that when you do *meet up with Coen Steeler, your weapon of choice will already be on you.*

And:

A well-aimed blow—perhaps to his undeserving brand... it might hinder his magic as well as his strength.

Was Dyonisia, perhaps, trying to test out her mutilated brand theory with Steeler and me? If so, why couldn't she just cut up someone else's brand herself and see what happened? It would be cruel, yes, but... well, she *was* cruel.

It didn't make sense for her to use such a serious mission as this one to experiment with the destruction of magic.

Lexington, of course, heard every one of those thoughts as they darted across my mind. And I was sure he felt the accompanying pain throb in the back of my skull, because his lips curled in a hideous smile.

"Whatever her reasoning," he said, leaning forward again, "I can assure you that she has infinitely more patience than I do. She might be okay with sitting around for another few months and watching you fail miserably, but *I* am growing bored of you and your cold, empty mind."

He didn't say his next words out loud. *Those* I heard in my head.

Punish yourself.

My hands flew up to my own neck and clamped tight.

I gagged soundlessly, but couldn't budge them. Couldn't—

Tighter.

Now my hands pushed in treacherously, digging into my wind-pipe until bright spots dappled my vision, and everyone was *still* looking away, and the pain in my head flared with heat.

Tighter.

No, please, no. He couldn't do this. He couldn't—

"That's enough."

Lexington stood with a graceful flourish of his cloak, smiling as I broke into frantic gasps.

This was worse than the almost-drowning incident with the octo-pus—worse because even my knife, strapped to my thigh this time, wouldn't have been able to save me anyways.

"Find out what those pills are for," Lexington said before striding away, his boots clicking against the polished dining room floor. He looked over his shoulder once. "And next time you decide to mutilate someone, make sure it's an actual traitor, not an innocent Esholian boy."

As soon as he left the room, everyone's rigid postures deflated. A few Wild Whisperers blinked down at their breakfasts, obviously con-fused, but I didn't wait to explain or make sure they were okay.

I was already running, leaving my parfait behind, up the stairs and out onto Bascite Boulevard. Toward the Wild Whisperer sector and past the arboretum, where the jungle fell into eerie silence.

Dazmine was right where I thought she'd be—not sleeping in like everyone else, but talking to the sundews. Stroking their curled, sticky-ended heads as if they were cute domesticated pets and not giant man-eating traps.

The moment I broke into the clearing, however, she withdrew her hand and whipped around to face me.

"What the hell, Rayna? Why are you *everywhere*?"

Behind her, the sundew uncurled themselves. Poised. Waiting to strike on command.

Every breath burned in my throat as I winced at the girl who hated me and said, "I need your help."

CHAPTER

14

"Let me get this straight."

Dazmine and I were facing each other behind an old classroom in the back of the Wild Whisperer sector. The sundew had started lunging for me before I could properly explain, so we'd chosen this less... *carnivorous* location to talk. The only drawback was all these damn insects buzzing around without those stalks of flesh-eating plants to nab them out of the air.

"That rumor about pirates breaching the shield last year is actually true," Dazmine said now, crossing her arms. "And one of the pirate spies was, like, in love with you."

"No, no, no. Not in love, just—"

Dazmine shushed me with a flap of her hand. "And Dyonisia Reeve, the *founder of this island*, wants *you* to bring him down single-handedly with just a little piece of steel and... what? A love for mice?"

I didn't stop myself from glaring at her as I waved away a lantern-fly. "Thanks for the vote of confidence, Dazmine."

She didn't appear to hear me. "And this same pirate killed Fergus, got Jenia exiled, and has access to the ship she's probably on right now? And his people are succeeding in attacking *our* people?"

"Pretty much," I muttered. The only thing I hadn't told her about was the pill. And Steeler's unnerving speed. And the way he and I sometimes talked mind-to-mind. And how he'd bloomed into being in the corner of a Shape Shifter's room, as if he'd been on the verge of murdering another man for touching me.

Okay, so I hadn't told her the half of it. But telling anyone about Steeler at all felt like a huge dam cracking through my internal ice. Relieving me of some of the pressure but also...also...

It felt like everything was rushing fiercely outside of my control.

Dazmine frowned. A cloud of gnats circled her head like a halo, but she ignored them.

"Dyonisia Reeve is testing your loyalty. There's no other explanation." She looked back up at me, her eyes hard and calculating. "Reeve wants to make sure you're on *her* side, not the pirates'. Because if that Coen Steeler was as smitten with you as you claim... well, it *does* make one wonder if you were perhaps a traitor yourself. If you helped them spy and murder and escape."

She said it without any restraint, without hiding her own suspicion. I made myself meet her stare without flinching this time.

"Are you going to help me or not? As you said, I don't have much besides a bit of steel and my so-called love for mice."

If I was going to keep someone as fast and strong as Steeler immobile long enough to stab him, I needed something stronger, thicker, and more violent than vines.

Dazmine didn't remove her attention from my face. "Why me?"

"Because you're the best with the sundews and all the other trapper plants in Mrs. Wildenberg's class," I answered right away. Like she'd said the other day, I really sucked at getting those sundews to do anything more than snap at me, and I didn't have time to perfect my relationship with them.

Dazmine scoffed. "Right. It has nothing to do with the fact that you don't give two shits about me, right? Because I don't see your bestie Emelle anywhere around here, do I? Nor do I see any of your other little friends. You don't want *them* around these pirates because what you're doing is dangerous, but me?" She laughed without smiling. "You don't care if I live or die, do you?"

I closed my eyes against a particularly nasty throb in my head. Right. Dazmine was right, and maybe that made me the worst person on the face of this island, to ask her to help despite the potential consequences. To let her in on this side of my wall, where everything was cold and dark and deadly. But...

"I have one request," Dazmine said.

I opened my eyes.

"I trap this Coen Steeler dude for you," she continued, "and you have to catch me another pirate. Someone I can use for ransom."

I blinked at her. I knew what she was thinking—hold a pirate hostage until the others decided to give Jenia back—but the idea was absurd. And not just because we didn't even know which of the ships *had* Jenia now.

"By the orchid and the owl, Dazmine, it'll be hard enough to catch Steeler himself. Pirates aren't like tadpoles I can just scoop up with a net. They're murderous monsters with fangs and—"

"Fangs?" Dazmine snorted.

"Steeler's teeth were really pointy when he cornered me in the alley," I murmured. "Just like those bedtime stories claim."

Don used to tell me such stories while Fabian listened in the doorway, folding his arms in silent disapproval. For good reason, too. I

118

definitely remembered pissing myself one time when Don whispered theatrically that the pirate captain was a vampire who would suck every last drop of blood from my body if I ever ventured too close to Eshol's shield. Just a warning to discourage kids from wandering off, but...

A jolt of horror cut through me at the thought that Steeler might be a vampire himself—assuming such creatures were real, of course. Could supernatural lineage explain his pointed canines? Or his unreal speed? Or the way power and rage seemed to ripple off him?

"No extra pirate man with fangs, no deal," Dazmine said now.

I massaged my temples, already regretting telling her anything. Of *course* Dazmine Temperton wouldn't just help me out of her own good volition. Of *course* she'd find a way to use this to her own advantage.

And really... could I blame her? Wouldn't I have done the same thing if Emelle or Lander or any of the others had been taken?

"Fine," I said through my teeth. Once I had Coen by the throat and negated his power, I'd... I'd demand him to hand over one of his friends. And if he refused—well, I could start with his fingers. "One scary pirate man coming right up," I said, offering my hand. "Do you prefer medium or rare?"

Dazmine didn't smile, but I could have sworn something in her eyes flickered with approval as she stuck out her own hand to shake mine.

The next night, I found myself in the boys' Wild Whisperer house across the street, trying to ignore the nerves writhing in my gut long enough to focus on a game of mini pentaball:

Wren, Gileon, Lander, Emelle and me versus Cilia, Mitzi Hodges, Norman Pollard, Pierson Kaddor... and Rodhi, who hadn't mentioned his abrupt departure in the dining hall the morning before. As if he didn't remember talking to me at all before Lexington's arrival.

"I don't know how it's possible, darling, but you seem to be getting worse every time you play," he said brightly after I tried—and failed—to bounce my mini pentaball across the game table into the disc on the opposite side. My team had lost three times in a row now, and I knew it had a lot to do with the trembling in my hands.

Hands that would be wrapping around the strong column of a tan throat in about twenty minutes if everything went to plan.

"Well, *some* of us spend our free time practicing our *actual* magic rather than playing a bouncy ball game," Wren quipped as Norman stepped up to the table—her way of defending me, I knew, and I shot her my best smile in thanks. "I mean, I don't know why you're allowed to use magic in regular pentaball but not mini pentaball."

"Magic and mini pentaball don't mix if you want to keep your dick on straight. Or whatever parts you value," Rodhi added with a half-glance at Wren, who wrinkled her nose back at him. "There's simply not enough space indoors for all our competitive magic to mix together. You would know that if you'd ever deigned to play with us before now."

It was true that Wren had never played pentaball before—regular or mini. Only after I'd pleaded with her and Gileon to join us about two dozen times did she finally relent with a skeptical frown.

But I'd had to ensure that all my friends—and Cilia—would be thoroughly distracted when Steeler showed up tonight. That nobody would notice my absence and come looking for me.

"Everyone shut up so I can focus."

That was Norman. He lobbed his ball with a lazy flick of his wrist, and we all watched its neat, bouncing trek into the opposing disc.

Lander groaned. Wren cursed. Mitzi and Cilia cheered, and Rodhi high-fived Norman with a sloppy grin on his face.

Well, at least he was in better spirits than yesterday morning.

"Now you're all just getting cocky," Lander grumbled, stepping up to the table himself. Neither he nor Emelle had mentioned anything about the incident at the Shape Shifting party... which told me slug boy truly *hadn't* told anyone about what I'd done to him.

Good.

I didn't have the mental capacity to deal with any rumors or allegations right now. Not when the pounding in my head kept increasing in tempo as the seconds ticked by.

Lander was just about to shoot his shot when a dry, curt voice cut through the midst of our game.

"Rayna? Your little pest wanted me to tell you she needs you."

It was Dazmine, right on time, appearing like a ghost on the platform between staircases.

All heads swiveled toward her, where she stood there with crossed arms, as if *we* were the ones who had interrupted *her*.

I broke the silence with a well-rehearsed, "Oh no! What's wrong? Is Willa okay?" and a hand pressed against my heart.

God of the Cosmos, I could never be an actress—my voice sounded way too high-pitched to be believable. But only Emelle cocked her eyebrow at me as Dazmine waved a dismissive hand.

"I'm sure she's fine. Just something about a stomach ulcer and wanting you to grab her some apples instead of cheese tonight. Which sounds to me like you're some kind of mouse servant, but okay."

Dazmine, on the other hand, *could* be an actress. Even though we'd planned every word of this conversation, the utter contempt coating her voice almost made me believe Willa really *was* sick and in need of my servitude.

"I'll come with you," Emelle started, but I raised a hand.

"No, no, you guys keep playing. Here—Dazmine will take my place."

I was already at the staircases, prodding Dazmine toward the group. When Cilia clapped her hands and squealed, "Ooh, you're actually going to hang out with us? Yay!" Dazmine threw a death glare over her shoulder at me.

But to her credit, she wafted toward them anyway.

Leaving me to trot down the boys' staircase, through the dining hall that connected our two houses, and back up my own stairs to my house's empty parlor.

Nobody saw me sneak out the front door and slip down Bascite Boulevard, undetectable in the thick fog that had settled over campus.

Willa, I knew, didn't have stomach ulcers, and she wasn't waiting on my bed for me to deliver apples. But it was a reasonable enough excuse to explain my disappearance... not to our room, as Emelle and the others had believed, but to one of the old Wild Whisperer storage buildings in the back of our sector, where Mr. Conine kept an assortment of animal enclosures he hadn't touched in years.

I knew what was coming, but I still gasped when I creaked open the storage door and beheld the elaborate trap Dazmine had weaved throughout the spare tanks, hutches, and crates.

Potted sundew lined either side of the doorway, their stalks bowed over the room with twitching bristles. Nepenthes creepers stretched from one wall to the other, their cupped petals already brimming with poison, and flytraps dangled from the arched ceiling.

As soon as I stepped inside, the sundew jerked toward me, like cats ready to pounce—then jolted back just as suddenly. Probably realizing I wasn't the chosen victim.

"Hello," I told them nervously, then stepped carefully over the stretch of nepenthes creepers. The flytraps clamped their jaws threateningly, but didn't attack as I moved beneath them and finally made it to the one empty space in the middle of the room.

Now, whether Steeler came in through the doorway or the opaque window on the other side of the building, he wouldn't make it anywhere near me without *something* holding him back. All I needed was a couple of seconds to throw my knife, but...

What if his speed was so insane that he still managed to rip through the plants and get away? Or what if he'd already made himself invisible and was watching me from a corner of the room right now?

I slid my knife from its sheath and held it up, my heart pounding nails into my ribcage.

Maybe he wouldn't show. Or maybe he'd already force-fed me that pill and erased my memory of it. Maybe Dazmine was secretly working with him and this was all a trap for *me*—

I couldn't help myself from turning in violent circles, facing the door, then the window, then the door again, until...

The pressure in my head dissolved so suddenly, I knew he'd arrived even before his dark, sculpted figure bloomed into existence in the corner of the room.

Coen Steeler didn't even get a chance to look me in the eyes before the sundew struck.

Those bristled stalks wrapped around both his arms and yanked tight. He tried to twist, shock flitting over his features, but the string of nepenthes bucked forward and splashed their poison onto him, sending him to his knees in a hiss of pain.

The flytraps lowered themselves until they were snapping just over his head, ensuring he didn't get up again.

It was only when Steeler raised his gaze back to mine that I realized he was shirtless, every one of his muscles taut and flexing as Dazmine's trap held him in place.

He was also... shaggier. I almost blinked in surprise at the shadow of facial hair and the longer locks of dark brown hair curling past his ears.

Whatever he'd been doing over this last week—stalking, murdering, or anything else his kind liked to do for fun—a razor sure as hell hadn't been included in those activities.

Steeler finally ripped his eyes away from mine to survey the intricate tangle of carnivorous plants around the room.

Then his lips tilted into an absurd smile—revealing those canines again. I'd swear they were even sharper than last week.

"Clever," he said finally.

Remembering myself, I stalked forward to fit the curved blade of my knife under his chin. On his knees like this, his head came right to my chest, and he had to lift that chin to meet my gaze again.

"Unfortunately," I said, "I can't take the credit."

Steeler didn't flinch. He didn't do anything besides let his eyes devour every inch of my face until I couldn't bear the weight of his attention anymore.

I shifted my focus downward, to that scarred engraving of a bulbed, encircled star on his shoulder. So raw and exposed without a shirt to cover it. One slice, and he'd be powerless. Defenseless.

Finally, I was the predator.

Finally, he was the prey.

But my stupid hands wouldn't budge, wouldn't move the knife away from Steeler's throat to do the deed as he drawled, "You can't take the credit, yet it was you who asked for help, wasn't it?" A brush of dark, fathomless energy against my mind told me he'd just discovered Dazmine's involvement for himself. Shit. "You shoved down all your pride to do what you thought was right."

And why did *he* look proud of that fact? Why was there actual *admiration* gleaming in those cruel, smoky brown eyes?

I let my wall of ice surge forward a bit. Just enough to harden my eyes and calm the shake of my hand. "Pride has no place in a situation where innocent civilians are involved."

A beat of silence. Then—"Innocent civilians?"

"You know." I pressed the knife deeper into his neck, and a single bead of blood swelled from beneath the blade and rolled down to his bulging chest. Damn the sundew for making him strain. For making him flex. "The innocent civilians you and your fellow pirates attacked a few months ago? The ones you're still trying to attack as if you don't get enough magical scraps from our annual offering of exiles?" I pushed out as much sarcasm as I could in those words, hating Steeler, but hating Dyonisia just as much for giving him and his fellow pirates the people she deemed unworthy. "Or do you deny the attacks?"

Here I was, once again giving this man an opportunity to explain. To reject what the Good Council had told me.

But Steeler just said, without removing his eyes from my face, "I don't deny the attacks, but they're not what you think... I can explain more if you put your knife back in that neat little sheath of yours—" His eyes finally dipped to my waist, my thighs. "—and come with me."

I gave a scowl so scathing that Wren would have been proud.

"*Come with you?* I'm not going *anywhere* with you. And I'm not taking any more of those damned pills or letting you wipe my memory ever again."

One slice. One measly little slice over his brand, and—

"No," Steeler agreed. "I don't have to wipe your memory ever again. Because I've found an alternative. If you'll just come with me..."

"You've found an alternative to drugging me?" I threw up an empty laugh. "An alternative to stealing bits of my literal *mind*? How charming of you. But I'm not interested in your Plan A *or* Plan B."

Even on his knees, tied up and stretched taut with a blade beneath his chin, Steeler managed to cock his head.

"Then what *are* you interested in, Rayna?"

My name on his tongue did it for me. A dark thrill erupted in my belly at the soft, sensual way he said it.

"This," I said.

And moved my knife in one slashing motion, swiping it across his brand. Cutting through that scarred circle of flesh that matched the scars on mine.

Steeler sucked in a breath. His lips curled up in a flicker of fury, revealing those fangs in full. Oh God, I'd actually, truly pissed him off for the first time since he'd started stalking me, it seemed. If Dyonisia was wrong...

But no. No dark, fathomless energy seized my mind when Steeler craned his neck to look back up at me, all traces of that smug playfulness drained away. Blood trickled like crimson tears from the cut on his shoulder.

"Well," he rasped, "that wasn't very nice of you, was it?"

I didn't get a chance to respond. Didn't get a chance, because one second, I was staring down at him, and the next he was—gone.

Just gone.

The sundew whipped this way and that, screeching their confusion. The flytraps shot downward, snapping at nothing but air. The nepenthes jiggled, suddenly howling with fury at their lost prey.

126

A pair of sturdy hands grabbed me from behind, ripping my knife from my grip and flinging it across the room.

"But I think this will be punishment enough," Steeler whispered through my hair.

And ribbons of darkness seemed to tug on me from every direction as he dragged me into a rich, inky expanse of nothing.

CHAPTER

15

It was like no darkness I'd ever experienced.

Not like the cloak of nighttime or the bottom of a lake or even the pitch-black of dreamless sleep. It was pulsing and whirling, yet empty and endless at the same time. Filled with far-off lights that didn't quite reach us—wherever we were. Wherever we were going.

Because as much as I twisted and thrashed in Steeler's grip, he was definitely succeeding in taking me *somewhere*. I felt the world whiz by with each step, and nausea clamped down tight in the base of my throat as if we were whooshing through the air in a carriage.

And suddenly, *I* was clinging to *him*, terrified he'd drop me into this abyss. Terrified this had just been an elaborate way of murdering me, of dumping me in a wasteland of darkness so that nobody would ever find my body.

A whimper actually left my mouth—

Just as Steeler wrenched us through a hole in the darkness and I landed on my hands and knees on solid ground.

It was still dark here, but... stars. God, yes, those were stars winking through gaps in the clouds above us.

Rain pattered my head, and waves of smooth gray pebbles stretched in every direction beneath me. The crash of the ocean pulsed to my right, where a single abandoned lighthouse climbed toward the sky at its edge. To my left, I could just barely make out the hazy outline of a jungle towering on a far-off cliff.

"Where are we?" I panted.

As soon as the words left my lips, however, I folded over and began to retch.

From the corner of my eye, I saw Steeler lurch toward me with his hand outstretched. I flinched, and he yanked himself back. Waiting. Wary. As if I were some kind of wounded animal.

Which, maybe I was. Because I couldn't stop dry heaving until Steeler murmured, "Breathe in and out. The nausea will pass—"

"Don't you dare tell me what to do," I spat over my shoulder.

The idea that he was trying to console me after dragging me through... through whatever torment *that* had been—it seemed to snap my body out of it. I scrambled up to face him fully, a stark breeze from the ocean lifting up the hem of my dress.

Steeler raised his palms. That cut I'd made on his shoulder was still oozing blood, and now that we weren't in a dark room, I could make out the pinprick wounds all over his wrists and hands, and the holes in his pants where the nepenthes had drenched him with poison. The burnt skin beneath.

Yet he didn't seem worried about himself. He was still observing me as if I were wounded and depraved, and he answered my question with words as smooth as the pebbles beneath our feet.

"We're still on Eshol. Just a little bit north of Hallow's Perch."

"North of Hallow's Perch," I repeated, feeling my jaw drop for a second before I snapped it shut again. I didn't doubt that we were still on the island—past the lighthouse and horizon of seafoam, I could see the faint shimmer of Eshol's protective dome. But...

If we were truly this far north... well, Hallow's Perch, I knew, was about three hundred miles from the Esholian Institute. And by the angle of the moon slathered in a thin film of rainclouds overhead, I knew it wasn't even half an hour past the time I'd been in the boys' Wild Whisperer parlor, playing mini pentaball with my friends.

Which meant we'd traveled hundreds of miles in minutes. Seconds, maybe.

"That's not possible," I got out. "What—how—"

I expected Steeler to make up more excuses, more nonsensical allusions that would leave me in a state of feeling crazy.

Instead, he dragged in a deep breath and said, "I'm a faerie."

I stared at him. A flash of lightning forked between clouds in the distance. The wind seemed to howl and tug at my dress even harder.

"I'm a faerie," Steeler continued, still holding up his palms, "the same as the ones of old, and I'm... maturing." Here, his jaw twitched in... annoyance? Anger? I couldn't tell, but I definitely wasn't moving, wasn't even *breathing*, as he said, "Which means I get a shiny new power of my own."

I tried to find the twitch of his lips or that deadly glimmer of humor in his eyes to indicate he was joking, but... nothing.

And now I took a step back, my feet clinking over pebbles, as the full weight of what he was saying slammed into me.

"Faeries are extinct."

Now Steeler pretended to examine himself, his pricked hands, slashed brand, and bare chest rolling with beads of rain.

"Are we? I feel alive enough. Although I suppose you could have actually killed me back there and I could be hallucinating all of this."

Through the trembling in my bones, I willed myself to stop and think, stop and think, stop and *think*. For the first time, Coen Steeler had told me something of value. Something substantial.

"And your power is—what?" I asked hesitantly. "Ultra speed?"

Because how else would we have traveled from one place to another so quickly? How else would he have escaped the sundew in less than the blink of an eye?

Steeler dropped his palms, something like relief flickering over his eyes before hardening again into that smoky quartz.

"Not speed, necessarily. But... I can cut through space to get from one point to another. Location hopping, if you will. It's convenient, I'll admit, but it's still really new, and it *does* tend to give you the worst motion sickness." He didn't chuckle, but I could hear one brimming in his voice, and it made me remember that wicked laugh of his in the alleyway moments before I'd whirled to face him for the first time. He'd... he'd disappeared and reappeared so fast so many times that...

Yes, location hopping would explain everything. The way he moved from one point to another within less than a blink of a second. The way he'd materialized in the Shape Shifter's room, dripping with wrath.

But for some reason my brain wasn't catching up to the reality of what that truly meant.

Steeler surveyed me carefully now, as if waiting for some kind of explosive reaction. When my face remained immobile, that wall of ice wrapping even tighter around me, he sighed and pushed aside his rain-drenched, overgrown hair to reveal...

Ears. *Sharpened* ears. As sharp as his canines had become.

Now my knees hollowed out. I stumbled sideways before catching myself again.

Neither Mr. Fenway nor Mrs. Smetlar had ever described a faerie formally, but I *had* heard the rumors of those pointy ears back in Alderwick. How faerie children used to look like humans, but when they had fully matured sometime in their twenties, all their features had become sharper. Wickeder. Stronger.

Almost like a vampire's.

I couldn't allow myself to wallow in this new information, however. Couldn't try to piece together what it all meant if I wanted to get out of here. Because *here* was a place no one could hear me scream. *Here* was a place Steeler could still dump my body or keep me locked away or...

"Why did you bring me here?" I asked to keep my thoughts on track, trying to keep my voice as steady as his.

"I told you." Steeler took a single, casual step toward me. "I've found an alternative to the weekly memory wipe. But you have to come inside with me." He nodded over his shoulder at the lighthouse. "And you have to choose it for yourself."

I let my eyes flick toward the lighthouse again, this time soaking in more of its details.

It sat on a mound of boulders, a column of gray stone that nearly blended in with the mist itself. The cupola was dark, but small lights flickered in the windows of a keeper's cottage attached to the base. Two separate stone staircases wound up to different doors, one leading to the lighthouse base, the other to the cottage's wraparound porch.

"Is this some kind of ambush?" I asked... for I could have sworn several shadows moved beyond those lit windows. Another thought ignited in my chest. "Are you using your power to help the pirates breach the dome?"

Steeler hesitated for only a moment.

"I can use my power to surpass the dome, yes. And I can take others with me, just like I took you. But we're not breaching it in the way you think. And if this *was* an ambush, I would've Walked you straight inside."

Walked. All my life, society had revolved around the five different types of magic. Now Coen Steeler was obviously carrying around a sixth one—as fully formed as all the others, and just as powerful. Maybe even more so.

I clawed a drenched curl away from my face impatiently. "Why not Walk me straight inside anyway?"

"Because, as I said…" Steeler's voice held nothing *but* patience, the bastard. "You have to choose this for yourself. But if you don't…" And now he winced as a forked tongue of lightning struck the sealine behind him. "I'll have to take your memories of the pills again. I don't think I'm currently capable of it—" A glance down at his oozing cut. "But give me a few hours, and I think it'll heal."

Was he admitting that his Mind Manipulating had been wounded but not fully destroyed? I folded my arms, holding back a shiver.

"What, no third option? Just this mysterious alternative or continue to endure your constant mind invasions?"

Steeler winced again, but this time it was gone so fast, I almost wondered if I'd imagined it. A smirk pulled up one of his cheeks.

"I suppose I could also just lock you up here forever."

Exactly what I had suspected. I stomped past him, toward the lighthouse, willing myself not to lean toward him when I passed close enough to smell that rich, earthy scent of black bamboo.

"Then you aren't giving me a true choice after all, are you?"

As much as I wanted to be the one to wrench open the door and face whatever—or *whoever*—waited for me inside all by myself, Steeler beat me to it.

In a heartbeat, he reemerged on the wraparound porch ahead of me, opening the door and holding it for me.

Biting back a grumble, I picked my way up the stone staircase and through the rickety doorway. He could act like a gentleman all he liked, but it wouldn't erase the hundred or so reasons I had to hate him. Or the fact that he was a faerie—a *faerie*—and could literally splinter all of my bones like a pile of kindling.

As soon as I made it into the entryway, however, I stopped.

Those moving shadows I'd glimpsed through the windows—they *were* people. Four of them, all standing and murmuring to each other until this exact moment.

Now they froze and swiveled toward me: two identical women with the deepest, richest skin I'd ever seen; a man with grizzly red hair and more facial hair than Steeler himself; and a thinner man with a pointy chin, who stopped stroking his mustache to study me with wary eyes.

"Rayna!"

Before my heart could even lurch, one of the women had sprung toward me and twined her arms around my neck.

I shifted backward on instinct. The woman released me with a watery smile, wiping her nose with the edge of a sleeve.

"Sorry. I—I know you don't remember me. But I missed you."

Remember her? Missed me? Something in my chest shuddered at the realization that... that *these* were the pirates who'd breached the dome with Steeler last year. *This* was the whole group of spies Dyonisia was after. Right within my grasp.

Which seemed like a pretty big breach of the dome to me.

The cottage door snapped shut behind us, cutting off the howling sound of wind and waves. Steeler moved further into the room, where light from a billowing fireplace danced over a threadbare rug.

"Rayna, this is Sylvie, and her twin, Sasha." He nodded at the identical sister still loitering a few steps away; she jerked her head at me in greeting. "They're both Summoners. And this is Terrin, an Element Wielder—" He gestured at the grizzly-haired man with his good arm. "And Garvis, a Mind Manipulator like me."

As soon as Steeler finished his last words, every eye in the room seemed to flick toward his brand—and the slash over it.

"She actually cut you?" Sasha piped up from behind her twin. "Did it work? Is your mind power gone?"

Her tone didn't sound accusatory or shocked or anything other than curious.

And it was then that I knew *Steeler* knew. He knew why I'd cut his brand and what it was supposed to do to him... because he'd picked that information from my brain without my permission? Or because the pirates were already aware of this phenomenon?

"Not gone," Steeler answered, massaging one of his bare pectoral muscles. I looked away pointedly. "Just... damaged. Like the window through which it sees the world is suddenly cracked." A pause, and I felt a quivering wave of dark energy brush against my mind, then retreat just as quickly. "I can still hear all your thoughts, but they're choppy."

So a single slice hadn't been enough to destroy his magic completely, after all. But—later. I tucked away that information for later.

For now, I forced myself to face this group of traitors and—

"*Coco? Is the talking human here?*"

From the shadows of a side hallway, a scuffling figure bounded forward on rail-thin arms, its tail whipping and curling as it came to a halt at my feet.

I gaped down at the awe-struck face of a monkey. A young female, probably equivalent to a teenager judging from the lighter, pinker hue of her nose and the smaller row of teeth she flashed up at me in a smile.

"*Oh, it is you,*" she trilled, and clambered up my legs until she was hanging off my shoulder with one hand and inspecting one of my curls with her other. "*You're just as beautiful as he's described. Is it true that you can understand what I'm saying right now? I'm Felicity, by the way.*"

"H-hi, Felicity. I can hear you." I glanced from her bright, fuzz-filled face to Steeler's observing gaze and whispered, "What are you doing here so far away from the jungle?" *Did he kidnap you, too?* I meant to convey.

The monkey sighed, dropped my curl, and turned mud-brown eyes onto me.

"*My family banished me from their tribe because I'm not...*" She lowered her voice, even though I was the only one in the room who'd be able to understand her. "*I'm not very good at telling jokes. For instance...*" She cleared her throat importantly. "*Why did the orangutan divorce the chimp four weeks after he married her? This is the joke that got me disowned, by the way.*"

I could feel the others' eyes on us, and tried to imagine what they must be hearing: a lot of grunting, cooing, and barking.

"I don't know," I relented, the tiniest seed of amusement breaking through every other frenzied feeling inside me. "Why did he?"

"*Because there was a thirty-day monkey-back guarantee!*" When I snorted, the monkey—Felicity—said, "*My family ripped me apart for* using chimp and monkey interchangeably. If there's one thing they value, it's that we don't have opposable thumbs or use human tools."

"Oh. That's... not very progressive."

Dammit. That was definitely the wrong thing to say. Mr. Conine would have given me a big fat fail for that one.

But the monkey just beamed at me and clung tighter. "*That's what I think, too! I've always wanted to learn how to use human tools and do human things. I want to be a cook and a hairdresser and a candlemaker and so much more. So when I fled to the edge of the jungle and saw Coco digging for clams on the beach...*"

She nodded over her shoulder, and my gaze whipped to Steeler's. Coco? Coco as in *Coen*? By the orchid and the owl.

"*He couldn't understand me like* you *do,*" the monkey continued happily, "*but two lonely outcasts should stick together, don't you think? So I've been here, teaching myself how to cook and build things and even cut his hair ever since. Well, I usually cut his hair.*" She tossed a glare at Steeler. "*He's been so busy the past few days that he hasn't had time for his weekly trim. Which offends me, by the way.*"

I didn't have a reply to that. My body had resumed shivering against my will—from confusion or shock or residual nausea, I couldn't tell. Faeries and lighthouses and monkeys... it was all too much.

Steeler seemed to track each shudder that wracked through me and said in a measured voice, "I think this would be easier if we all take a seat."

A few plush armchairs and loveseats were crammed by the fireplace, and at his words, the others drifted toward them.

I stood rooted to the spot, though, as Felicity clambered down and bounded off to the small stretch of kitchen counter beneath a window overlooking the ocean. Lightning still flickered out there, flaring up the horizon with each strike. No pirate ships, which meant...

"You never left the island?" I asked Steeler, who was the only one still standing... waiting for me to take a seat first, it seemed. "You didn't actually breach the dome last year?"

And because the monkey Felicity was already clattering around on the kitchen counter, grabbing mugs and teabags, I forced myself to go claim the last available armchair next to Sylvie. Sinking into its cushioned frame, I let the warmth of the fire wash away the chills still crawling over my skin. For the monkey, I told myself. Because she was obviously eager to make me feel... at home. In an abandoned lighthouse. With five of the island's most wanted fugitives.

God of the Cosmos.

Finally, Steeler followed. He didn't sit, though. He loomed over us all with his hands shoved behind his back, the firelight illuminating every scar and burn I'd inflicted upon his body tonight.

"No, Rayna," he said at last. "I left the island. We all did." He gestured at the others, who shifted uncomfortably in their seats. "But as soon as we made it to the ships, I... well, the maturing process started for me." Here, something stiffened in his voice. "In the turmoil, I forgot to take my suppressant pill, and I suddenly found myself in that darkness you just experienced. When I finally clawed my way out, I was back on the island." A shrug, as if the idea of slipping through holes in space was no big deal. "So I found this abandoned lighthouse—pretty sure it was used for spying on pirates once upon a time, until our fleets decided to move more southward—and decided to stay. But this is the first time the others have come back since they left."

A hundred different questions should have been rattling around inside my head, but the only phrase that echoed back was—

"Suppressant pill?" I repeated.

Every bit of fidgeting from the others froze. The only movement came from Felicity, who was humming obliviously and transporting drinks to the grill over the fireplace to heat up.

Finally, Sylvie spoke up beside me.

"We all took the pills while we were on the island," she said softly, the onyx of her eyes warping with tears. "Even Coen used to, before his own power broke free. They kept our natural faerie magic stifled while allowing the branded magic—" She nodded down at her shoulder "—to thrive."

For the first time since Steeler and his bamboo scent had materialized in my room, my head jolted with a throb of pain. As if it *knew*.

"That's ridiculous," I choked out. "You can't possibly be insinuating that I'm a..."

I couldn't get that final word out, though. As insane as it was to suggest Steeler was a faerie, as ludicrous as it was to believe that all his fellow pirates were faeries too, it was even worse to think that *I* could ever be one, that *I* would need a power inhibitor. There were no signs, no underlying magical urges—

Because Steeler had been smothering them all along.

Find out what those pills are for, Lexington had ordered me.

Oh, they're to hide every last trace of an extinct lineage in my blood, I imagined reporting back.

Could I really expect the Good Council's most ruthless Mind Manipulator to just smile and call it a job well done and leave me alone after *that*?

No. I knew, as if something inside me had snapped the truth into place, that the Good Council wouldn't take kindly to power they couldn't control. Wouldn't take kindly to creatures that might grow stronger than them, that might wield the ability to overpower them.

No. This all had to be a mistake. Maybe Steeler had targeted the wrong victim, fed me pills that didn't actually do *anything* to me because there was no faerie blood in my veins to begin with. The memory of Lexington forcing my hands to ram themselves against my own throat... he would do so, so much worse, I knew, if he found out I wasn't even fully human, and—

Across from me, Steeler's eyes suddenly flew wide open. His hands whipped out from behind his back, rolling into fists.

"That son of a *bitch*!"

Garvis was up in an instant, followed by Terrin, who cried, "What's wrong?" just as the twins echoed the same.

"Coen saw a memory of Lexington hurting Rayna through his fractured Mind Manipulating lens," Garvis explained immediately, panting with the effort it took to hold onto Steeler—to stop him from using his new Walking power, I realized with a jolt. Although... where the hell would he be wanting to whisk away to?

My answer came a moment later when Terrin growled, "Stop, brother. He's Dyonisia Reeve's favorite weapon. Killing him now will just kickstart a bigger war you're not ready to fight yet." He tugged on Steeler's arm again. "This is why you wanted to give Rayna a second option, remember? So that she can protect herself from stuff like *that*."

At the sound of my name, Steeler's shoulders deflated. His cut had ripped open again, and small bulbs of blood welled from the clots.

As much as I didn't want to feel an ounce of pity for the male who had stalked and kidnapped me, the sight of that blood made the knots in my stomach twist with something like guilt.

Shaking that feeling away, I stood and forced my way through Garvis's and Terrin's frames until I was crossing my arms in the space of Steeler's body heat, the fire casting his form in a flickering orange outline.

Let him think me fearless. Let him think me brave. Anything to get the most important answer out of him.

"Tell me, Steeler. Why did you bring me here?"

His eyes flashed at the use of his surname—with surprise first, then with something that seemed to match the knots in my stomach. But what did he want me to call him? Coco?

"Your mind holds sensitive information... *Drey.*" I didn't miss the mocking way he said *my* surname. Nor did I miss how every other emotion seemed to dissolve in his voice in an instant, leaving nothing but those clipped, impassive words. "Our faerie blood is just one secret that could get us all killed. And since I can't be around you one hundred percent of the time to guard your mind, I'm offering you the ability to guard yourself."

Far-off thunder rolled through the floor in tiny vibrations. Lightning flashed outside those windows again, ferocious clashes of light and cloud and sea that reminded me how very far away from the Esholian Institute I was now. Only Dazmine would know who I'd marched outside to face, and even she would never be able to guess where Steeler had dragged me to.

But... guard myself? Of all the things Steeler could have kidnapped me for, offering me the ability to guard myself had not been on my list of potential torture techniques I'd have to endure.

"I don't understand," I began slowly. I had my knife and Wild Whispering, but how could anyone expect me to protect my *mind*? From Kitterfol Lexington? I couldn't even stop Wilder from listening in on my thoughts.

Steeler bared his fangs again, this time in a genuine grin.

"How would you like to become a Mind Manipulator, Drey?"

CHAPTER

16

"That's not possible."

It really wasn't. The Branding activation was random, with each inductee having an equal chance of acquiring any of the five magics when that stamp of bascite met our skin—a phrase that had been drilled into my subconscious since before grade school.

Before Steeler could respond, however, Felicity chippered, "*Drinks are ready!*" and bounded forward with mugs of steaming peppermint tea: two in each hand, one balanced on her head, and a sixth looped tightly through her tail.

I accepted mine with a mumbled thanks and waited until the monkey had deposited drinks to the others before continuing.

"The magic chooses which shape it'll take when it merges with our blood." *That* quote had come directly from Mr. Conine on my first official day at the Institute. "The magic's already chosen to make me a Wild Whisperer. I can't become a Mind Manipulator."

"Yes, you can," Steeler said simply.

"The Good Council—" I started.

"The Good Council is lying about that, as they do about many things." His grip tightened on his mug, the veins in his hands bulging with the movement. "The Branding activation is *not* random, and the magic doesn't choose which form it'll take in your blood—*they* do."

I had just started to take a sip of my tea, but now I tried not to splutter against the scalding pain of it against my lips.

"Explain."

Steeler clucked his tongue, a hint of humor playing in his eyes.

"So demanding, per usual." A pause, during which he took a sip of his own. "It might be... hard to take in."

"Try me."

But it was Terrin who leaned forward in his armchair to my left, a competitive glint in his eyes, and said, "Oh, I've got this one, brother."

He turned that glint onto me, but I had a feeling that he was just sparing Steeler from having to say something hard.

"Okay, Rayna, so you know how bascite comes from the blood of a mature faerie, right?"

"Yeah?" I tried not to glance at Steeler.

"Well, that's technically true. But the Good Council didn't just happen to find all that faerie metal at the top of the highest Esholian peak. They..." Here Terrin scratched his beard with his mug-free hand. "They kidnapped the faeries and have kept them locked up on Bascite Mountain for hundreds of years now. Forcing them to give away the magic in their bloodstream again and again every year."

Now my mug slipped from my grasp. Hot tea splashed forward between Steeler and me, and I retreated a few steps until my ass hit the arm of my chair.

"They're... they're alive? The faeries?"

Last year, Mr. Fenway had told us that bascite came from faerie blood, yes, but he'd described it as the last remnants of a long-decomposed pile of corpses. Which was morbid enough.

To think that the bascite came from *living* faeries...

"Only five of them," Steeler clarified, clearing his throat. "It's true that there used to be a whole indigenous clan of faeries on the island before Dyonisia Reeve arrived to... colonize it." His lips pulled up in distaste at that. "But we don't know where that clan of faeries disappeared to. The five she is holding prisoner, on the other hand—they are the original Good Council of the court of Sorronia." When I furrowed my brows, he added, "The faerie continent all of us are from."

I didn't dare ask if I was included in that. I still couldn't wrap any part of my head around the idea that *I* might be the same kind of monster *he* was. That one day, I might grow fangs, too.

But never mind any of that right now. What Steeler was telling me—that the icy-eyed woman who had given me the sheath still strapped to my thigh... that *she* was keeping kidnapped faeries from another continent like some kind of cattle, milking their magic every year to give more power to her own people...

"So there are five faeries locked away up there," I said slowly, "each with one of the five magics."

Steeler nodded. "Magics are like fingerprints—completely unique for each individual. Nobody was ever meant to have the same powers, but Dyonisia found a way to harvest them, strengthen them, clone them, and give the same ones to her own people. Not randomly, but of her own choosing. She even sends files to Mr. Gleekle detailing every student's information and power to be given."

For some reason, I looked at the twins for confirmation, forgetting, for a moment, that they were anything other than fellow women.

Sylvie nodded. Sasha said in a low voice, "*We* didn't even know all this until we got back to the main ship. The faerie fleet is here to get the blood that is rightfully theirs—the original *Good Council*—back..." She glanced at Steeler. "When the time is right."

I followed her glance and felt my eyebrows furrow. Something didn't add up. One disjointed piece failed to fit in with the rest of it.

"You're lying," I said to him. "You have to be. If you really wanted to get your original Good Council out of that prison, you would've just used your new power to Walk right in there, grab them, and set them free."

Steeler cocked his head at me.

"You're right, I would have. Unfortunately, my power won't let me access the prison. It's like a giant rectangular blind spot—I can't get in no matter how hard I try to dig through."

I blinked at him. "You've already tried?"

"Yes. I'm assuming whatever's keeping those prisoners subdued in there is the same thing keeping me out." His lips tugged upward. "Any more accusations you want to hurl at me tonight, Drey?

A blush climbed up my throat, threatening to warm up my cheeks. I raised a shaking hand to my mouth and drained the rest of my tea in an attempt to wash it back down. Despite how much I wanted to find more holes in Steeler's story, it all made sense in a twisted, vile sort of way.

Why else would there be such a uniform number of new inductees in each sector? Why else would the Good Council use individual brands to grant us magic? Lander had once joked that it was to be sanitary, but now I realized it had been because each brand was *different*. Infused with a different type of bascite. A different magic.

"You must trust me a lot to tell me all of this."

Perhaps that was the wrong thing to say, but it was true. I'd never heard anyone even mention the *possibility* of faeries still existing anywhere near the island. Vampires and sea monsters and other threats lurked in bedtime stories, yes—but never faeries.

Which meant it was a secret Dyonisia Reeve would kill to keep. Because if the villages of Eshol found out... well, I, for one, would protest the Branding and the Esholian Institute, and I knew in my furiously thumping heart that Fabian and Don would, too.

At the thought of Fabian and Don—at the thought that Dyonisia Reeve knew their names and where they lived and didn't seem to care whether they lived or died so long as my worry for them kept me under control—my body snapped to attention.

I shot forward in an instant, clutching my empty mug to my chest like a shield as I made my rounds around the periphery of the cottage.

"What is she—?" someone started to ask, but Steeler must have shushed them with a shake of his head, because their words trailed off a moment later.

I pressed my ear against various parts of the stone walls, peered over dusty shelves, ran my fingers along the baseboards of the side hallway where a closet and bedroom door both stood slightly ajar.

If any of the Good Council's spiders were hiding within these walls, eavesdropping on the conversation...

But nothing clicked or scuttled between floorboards or in the cracks of the stone walls. Nothing seemed to hulk behind the chipped trinkets or empty vases lining the shelves, nor the ticking clock on the fireplace mantle.

My Wild Whispering magic, so well-attuned to the presence of other creatures, sensed... nothing.

There was no plant, animal, or insect in the room besides Felicity.

I turned back to the others and coughed out, a little embarrassed, "All clear."

"Like I said." Steeler continued as if my episode of frenzy hadn't halted our conversation at all, "I can continue hiding away all the sensitive information your mind contains... or you can become a Mind Manipulator and safeguard it yourself."

My eyes roamed back to that dark hallway. The cracked doors and whatever lay beyond them.

"Are you trying to tell me you stole the Mind Manipulator faerie from Dyonisia and have them locked away in that closet or something?"

A beat of silence.

Then Terrin threw back his shaggy head and brayed with laughter. Even Steeler let his lips twitch, just for a second, but *I* thought it was a valid question. How else was I supposed to get the right kind of bascite otherwise? It wasn't like there were a bunch of spare brands lying around.

"No, Drey," Steeler said finally, his mouth still fighting off a smile over his fangs, "if we ever break the original Mind Manipulating faerie out of prison, I can assure you we wouldn't lock him in a closet just to force him to give even more of his magic. But *I* have enough of the right bascite in my system to share with you."

My eyes snapped away from the hallway, back toward him again. From somewhere to my right, a clang echoed from the kitchen as Felicity dropped a pan, but I couldn't tear myself away to look.

"You would be willing to give me some of your power?"

I didn't know how it would be possible, anyway, for him to share what I'd wounded. But just the fact that he was offering it...

No part of Steeler stuttered or hesitated as he said, "I would be willing to give you the world."

Something curled in the bottom of my belly at those words. For the first time in days, the giant octopus's words floated back to the surface of my mind.

You took a midnight swim with that lover of yours.

If I really could become a Mind Manipulator, I'd be able to remember that swim. I could assess every missing piece of memory for myself instead of trying to string together what everyone else remembered and claimed about my past.

And as much as I loathed Steeler for what he'd done to me—for taking so many vital pieces of me away—he was offering to hand me the very weapon I needed to defeat him. Him *and* Dyonisia.

No one is good, I had told Dazmine the other night.

But could *I* be good, if I had the right tools?

As if I needed more persuading, Steeler said, "You've already hindered my ability to use Mind Manipulating anyway." A wry smile as he gestured at his chest. "And it's not always... fun to have to juggle two powers at once. I'd rather be able to perfect my Walking."

"But if I become a Mind Manipulator..." I started slowly, a small trickle of hope deflating. "*I'll* be juggling two powers at once."

"Yes."

Here, Steeler's eyes strayed to his feet, just for a second, as if he couldn't bear to look at me anymore. A muscle throbbed in his jaw. In the twirling firelight, I saw the faint scar of where I'd nicked him a week ago. God of the Cosmos, I'd given this man—this *faerie*— nearly as many physical wounds as the emotional ones he'd given me.

And I tried, tried, tried to make myself feel smug about that.

Steeler cleared his throat.

"Two powers at once—and a third lurking beneath the surface, inhibited by those pills—it's a risk, Drey. That's why it... why it wasn't until you told me about your headaches that I thought it might be a risk worth taking."

Okay, now *that* pissed me off. Who was he to decide what I should risk or not?

"So you've known about this alternative all along," I said, my voice dropping just as cold as my mug had become. "Yet you didn't think to ask me what hardship I'd be willing to try to handle? You just thought you could choose that all on your own, did you?"

The closest twin, Sylvie, dropped a hand on my arm.

"Everything Coen's done this last year has been for you, Rayna."

I almost snorted at that. *Everything Coen's done...* if everything he'd done had been for me, he would have included me in all his plans. Not ripped me away from them and loitered in the shadows of my reality to talk to me when and where he pleased.

No, I didn't believe he'd done any of this for me one bit. And as much as I didn't want to hurt Sylvie's feelings—pirate or no pirate—I ignored her and bit out, "What's the risk if I do this, then?"

An unnatural paleness had washed over Steeler's face. He seemed to be scraping in deep, slow breaths.

It was Garvis who answered in his stead, setting his mug down on a side table with a small *clink* and speaking in a wispy, mild voice.

"Lunacy, mainly. Neither humans nor faeries are meant to handle more than one type of bascite at a time. The more magics you have, the greater the symptoms of paranoia, anxiety, confusion, incoherency... For many, it only takes two powers to drive them mad. Some can handle up to three. Four is when it always gets bad."

He made it sound like this happened all the time. And suddenly, my thoughts snapped to Jenia Leake, screaming on her hands and knees.

What if I'd truly seen a second brand on her arm? And what if that brand hadn't increased her Wild Whispering abilities at all, but given her a *second* power? Those butterflies that had been circling her head, for instance—they'd moved as if compelled to flutter faster and harder than their wings could physically handle.

As if she had been able to talk to them *and* control them.

I didn't know why or how Jenia could have been branded with Mind Manipulating, but it was another twisted, vile thing that seemed to click into place inside me.

"You don't have to decide right away," Steeler said, his voice raspier, more gravelly than before. "You can—"

"Let you wipe my memory until next week, when you propose this to me all over again? No, thanks." A pause hung on my lips, but only for a moment. "I'll do it. I'll take the Mind Manipulating."

Silence.

"Are you sure?"

"Yes."

More silence, this time swollen with all the sounds I hadn't been able to fully hear since my Branding: the constant grumble of thunder, the smashing and clashing of the ocean, the snapping of fire and screeching of wind against the windowpanes. All of that had been overpowered by the music of the jungle or the babble of animals over the last year.

But here, in this cottage, there was no jungle, no animals except Felicity—who had finally quit fiddling with pots and pans to lope forward with a tin container rattling with objects.

"*Coco asked me to collect some metal pieces for you to choose from if you said yes,*" she said now, holding the container out to me. "*I've sterilized all of them with witch hazel, by the way.*"

When I only stared down at the tin, she rattled it again.

"Go ahead! You said yes, right? Pick the shape of your new brand."

Gingerly, I reached out and took the container, sifting through the items inside: a bent spoon, a copper coin, an old key, a broken bell.

"What's this?" I asked, lifting a pendant by its chain, letting the firelight wink against its intricate engravings. Swirls and loops and lines.

Steeler's hand jerked forward, surprise lighting up his face, just as Felicity said nonchalantly, *"I stole it from Coco's underwear drawer."*

He dropped his hand, his expression dwindling into unreadable hardness again. I raised my eyebrow at him.

"It's just a little something my mother left for me. She died before I could remember her," he added with a shrug before I could ask, "so it's not sentimental or anything. You're welcome to use it if you want."

I rubbed the pendant between my fingers, studying the engravings—words, it seemed, in another language. Bordering the words were the silhouettes of three female faeries wearing crowns. Princesses, maybe?

"What does it say?" I asked before I could stop myself.

"It's Sorronian for 'the heart does not falter.'"

The heart does not falter. Such a beautiful saying coming from such a heartless man's lips. I flicked a look at those lips once before blurting out, "You're sure you're okay with me using it?"

Why? Why did I have to give him a splinter of... of anything other than hatred when he was the one who'd brought me here against my will? When he still hadn't denied the single memory I had of him?

"Of course you can use it," Steeler answered immediately, either oblivious of my thoughts or choosing to ignore them. "It would probably look better than a spoon. Not that we'll brand you where anybody can see it, of course."

There was something about the way his eyes dipped down my body, as if imagining all the places a forbidden brand could hide, that made that damn *feeling* flop in my belly again.

But then he was asking the others "Ready?" and when they all nodded, clambering to their feet, I didn't have time to try to push the feeling away.

Steeler turned to retrieve something from the mantle behind him.

When he pivoted back, two things were flashing in his hands: a pair of tongs and a crude, pointed knife even smaller than the extra ones in my sheath.

Quick as the lightning that blazed outside, he pressed this knife against the underside of his arm, took a quick breath, and—

"What are you—?" I jolted forward.

—sliced.

Blood gushed from the wound. Steeler refocused his gaze on the twins beside me, who stood in peculiar offensive stances.

"Remember," he told them, hardly even panting. "Just the Mind Manipulating bascite. Don't let her have an ounce of the other kind."

I was too bewildered to even take offense to that. For some reason, when he'd said he could share his Mind Manipulating power with me, it had never occurred to me that there would be blood. Lots of it, more than when I'd nicked his jaw or cut his shoulder—splashing onto the rug at our feet where that tea had splashed minutes earlier.

Sasha and Sylvie were already focusing, their hands outstretched, eyes closed. From the lifetime I'd spent growing up with Fabian and Don's Summoning magic, I knew it usually didn't require this type of concentration. This... this was advanced magic.

I stayed silent, hardly daring to exhale...

As something rose from Steeler's wound: a whirlwind of what looked like sparkling, silver dust.

Bascite.

From the original Mind Manipulating faerie who was still alive and locked up under Dyonisia's rule.

I begged myself not to faint, not to let my knees tremble, as the twins sent that cloud of bascite straight into the pendant in my hands, merging the two metals together with a flash of silver.

And now Terrin stalked toward me, holding out his own hands.

"May I?"

I passed him the pendant as if it would burn me—which it would have, because a second later, violet flames burst from Terrin's hands, swallowing the pendant in a ball of fire.

"That should do it," he said rather cheerfully for the occasion.

As soon as his flames died into a glowing orange, Steeler took the pendant—the *brand*—from his friend with those tongs and faced me once more, ignoring the way his newest injury still pulsed with blood.

"Time to turn around, Drey."

"W-What?"

"We can't let anyone see this mark I'm about to make on you. But I think all that hair of yours will hide it if we put it on the back of your neck, don't you?"

A flush washed over my chest at the realization that Steeler would actually have to *touch* me to brand me. That he'd lay a finger on me.

I should kick him in one of his wounds. I should barge out of this cottage and run. I should flee to the nearest village and cry for help.

But I couldn't.

I couldn't keep floating around in this constant haze. Couldn't keep feeling as if the right version of me was somewhere beyond my grasp, forever dancing just out of reach. I'd told Willa I wouldn't be able to find myself again until Coen Steeler was dead, and that was still true. He'd taken too much of me, kept too much *from* me.

153

So now I would take from him.

I turned.

Steeler prowled toward me until his body was hovering just behind mine. Large, calloused fingers shifted aside my weight of hair with painstaking gentleness, scraping the nape of my neck nevertheless.

"Just a pinch, little hurricane," he whispered against my ear.

And as lightning flared outside, as Felicity and the others watched on, he pressed the scorching heat of the pendant to my skin.

CHAPTER

17

A quick flash of pain seemed to lock its jaws around my throat.

Then I was on my knees as a myriad of different voices slammed into me from everywhere all at once.

Oh, shit.

She fell down.

Is she okay?

Nope, not okay.

This was a bad idea.

Coen's going to go berserk.

Should we help her up?

Oh no, now she's screaming.

Sure enough, I *was* screaming—screaming and slapping my hands over my ears as if both things at once might drown out the voices that were whipping me in the face left and right.

It wasn't just the sheer *number* of voices, but the screeching cacophony their overlapping made in my ears. The way they seemed to crawl and writhe over each other until I couldn't distinguish my own thoughts from the alien probing of others.

Then a voice cut through the onslaught with a growl that I thought might be real, not just in my head.

"Put up the blockade for her, Garvis. Please. Do it now."

Instantly, the voices seemed to slam against an invisible wall hovering inches from either side of my head.

Still on my knees, I removed my hands from my ears and cranked my head up, panting, to lock eyes with Steeler. His lips opened, but—

Poor thing is still so pale. I hope she's not going to upchuck.

Now my head whipped toward the corner of the room, where Felicity was wringing her tail in her hands on the sofa's armrest.

Her thoughts. Those had definitely been her thoughts, shooting right through the blockade Garvis had wrapped around me.

But now that it was only her, it wasn't so...screechy. In fact, her mental voice sounded sweet and crystal clear, like she'd actually spoken the words out loud.

"I'm not going to upchuck," I said to the monkey, still breathing heavily. "I'm..." I trembled to a stand. "I'm okay now."

Steeler's gaze whipped between Felicity and me, something like surprise widening the unyielding hardness in his pupils.

"You can hear what she's thinking?"

I rubbed the dizziness from my eyes. "More clearly than everyone else." I paused. "That's not normal, is it?"

Even though I'd always known Mind Manipulators could *control* animals, I'd never known of one to actually talk to any animal mind-to-mind. In fact, I didn't even know how Steeler had been able to communicate with Felicity to offer her a place here in the lighthouse.

Every part of Steeler's body seemed to be relaxing as the seconds ticked by and Garvis's blockade held firm—at least from the humans

156

in the room. Clearly, my screaming had grated on his eardrums because he'd looked ready to burst out of his skin when those shrieks had first ripped out of my throat.

Now that I was calm, a sense of shame was creeping up my cheeks. Had I really just been on my knees screaming? At Coen Steeler's goddamned feet?

"No," Steeler said eventually, massaging his jaw over the spot where I'd nicked him last week. "Usually, animal minds are muddy, hard for us to wade through. There are very few animals who have mental images and words clear enough for us to understand."

Sasha cocked her head at me, clearly intrigued.

"Sounds like her magics are working together, not clashing."

From her tone of voice, I felt like the implication of that statement held a lot more weight than I was currently able to understand, but...

My memories. That's why I'd agreed to this whole ordeal in the first place: to be able to get my own memories back and guard myself from my enemies.

I gathered a shaky breath and leveled a stare back at Steeler.

"Okay, it worked." The fact that this meant the Good Council *had* been lying to us about the Branding process... another thing I didn't have the mental capacity to think about right now. So I only said, in my most commanding tone yet in the hopes that my new Mind Manipulating power would force him to obey, "Now give me my memories back."

From the corner of my eye, I saw Terrin raise his eyebrows, Garvis shift on his feet, and the twins exchange glances. Felicity's thoughts flitted out to me, soft and bright as moth wings in the moonlight.

Uh oh, this isn't going to go over well.

Steeler didn't obey. He just crossed his arms over his chest—still stupidly bare—and clucked his tongue.

"I never said I'd give your memories back if you did this, Drey. Just that I would stop burying your new ones every week."

A molten wave of rage flowed from my head to my fingertips.

Before I knew it, one of those fingers was flying forward, jabbing him right between his annoying pectoral muscles.

"Are you *kidding* me, Steeler? You claim you've been stalking me, drugging me, invading my mind, and now kidnapping me for *months* all to hide secrets even more detrimental than the fact that we're both faeries or that Dyonisia is keeping five of our kind imprisoned at the top of Bascite Mountain." I couldn't even rake in a deep enough breath, my lungs were so filled to the brim with rage. "If that's all true—if you *haven't* been doing this all to me just because you're a sadistic monster—then you'd give me my entire mind back now that I can protect those secrets myself."

"Oh, look," Terrin said suddenly. "The fire's getting low."

He looked pointedly at the twins, who jerked their heads at the pile of logs nearby and sent them soaring into the hearth over the bed of simmering coals. Terrin busied himself with stoking the flames, though I was sure he could ignite a wildfire within seconds if he wanted to.

I, on the other hand, kept my eyes glued to Steeler's face and my finger glued to his chest, glad for the bit of privacy everyone else was momentarily giving us.

"Garvis." Steeler didn't even glance down at that single point of contact between us. "Remove the barrier again."

"Coen, she's—"

"Remove it."

I bristled at the way he spoke to his so-called friends, but then—then the protective wall around my head melted away.

The cacophony of voices pounded into me again as Terrin, Sasha, and Sylvie whirled around to gape.

He's pushing her too hard.

We should've never agreed to this.

Aaaand she's on her knees again.

Damn, that girl can scream.

It's way too late for this kind of shit.

A nod from Steeler and Garvis wrapped the barrier back around me, cutting off the voices.

I sat there, hunched over on the rug, breathing through the panic that seemed to scrape jagged fingers down the back of my neck where my new brand still burned.

Steeler lowered himself to a crouch right in front of me and grabbed my chin, forcing me to look up at him.

I didn't have the strength or the willpower to wrench myself away.

"The only thing that comes naturally about Mind Manipulating are those voices in your head," he said, his lips moving a breath away. "Eavesdropping on inner thoughts, commanding actions, stealing or guarding memories—that all takes work. And your new power, Drey, needs a *lot* of work before I can trust you to protect yourself."

Before he could trust me? Trust *me?* I would never be able to scowl enough to properly convey how I felt just then.

"What do you expect me to do?" I half-laughed up at him. "Waltz right into the Mind Manipulator classes and announce myself as a new student?" I dredged up as much sarcasm as I could muster in my current state. "*Hey Wilder, I'm in your sector now. Just got a second power from the person I'm supposed to be handing over to the Good Council. No big deal. Oh, and the Good Council isn't actually good.*"

Steeler's eyes shuttered once before he released my face and stood with surprising swiftness and grace.

"Of course I don't expect you to do that. That's why you'll be coming over here every Sunday to the lighthouse. To train."

"If you think I'm willing to spend another *second* with you—" I started, scrambling to my feet for the second time tonight.

"Not with me," Steeler interrupted. "With Garvis."

That made me clamp my mouth shut. If Steeler was as obsessed with me as Dyonisia and he himself claimed, shouldn't he want to force me into spending every single second with him?

Garvis spoke up before I could piece these words together.

"I'm not so sure the fleet will be happy if—"

"—the Fated General lets you leave the ship for a measly few hours once a week?" Steeler interrupted, and I felt my eyebrows furrow. The Fated General? Was that some fancy name for the captain of their ship? Steeler continued before I could think too hard about it. "That's hardly long enough to make anyone look twice." After a pause, in which he and Garvis seemed to engage in a short but intense staring contest, he added, "I can't bear to be in her mind that much anyway. Not right now."

Once again, my eyes were drawn to his mutilated brand, the cut I had inflicted. It was already healing, but suddenly a treacherous part of me was itching to tell him to go put some salve on it in case it got infected. The same for the clotting wound on his arm, too. Both injuries had drastically hindered his Mind Manipulating power tonight—one by limiting his ability to use it, and the other by giving most of it away.

Garvis swiveled his gaze to me now.

"Are you okay with me training you, Rayna?"

"Yes," I said before I could think twice. Regardless of what he was, his eyes were just too sad and gentle not to trust.

Garvis bowed his head.

160

"Okay, we'll start right now, then. So you can function without my blockade when you go back to the Institute in the morning."

In the morning. I rubbed my eyes again and glanced at the clock above the mantelpiece. Its twitching hands told me it was already a little past midnight: only seven hours until Ms. Pincette's class. Dazmine, Emelle, and Cilia would have turned in for bed by now and discovered my absence.

But Garvis was right. He wouldn't be there tomorrow to shield me against the onslaught of voices, and on campus there would be *thousands* to wade past, not just five. I needed his instruction.

"I'll take the others back to the ship," Steeler began.

"Wait."

I winced as they all paused to stare at me.

"I, uh..." I cleared my throat, refusing to meet Steeler's curious gaze. "I sort of promised one of my classmates that I'd bring her back another pirate so that she can... do some blackmailing or whatever." The words sounded even more ridiculous out in the open than they had in my head, so I decided to add some more accusation in there. "Her friend, Jenia Leake, was just exiled, and she wants her back."

I expected to witness a few exchanged glances at that. Some kind of admission of guilt in these pirates' eyes that might indicate they knew exactly where Jenia was tied up—or worse.

Instead, Sasha's face cracked into a shocked grin.

"Are you seriously just asking us politely if we'll give ourselves up for ransom? To a *second-year*?"

"Well...yes?"

Oh, Dazmine was going to be *pissed* when I returned empty-handed.

But Terrin snapped his fingers. "Wait. Jenia Leake's friend... are you talking about the hot one with the braids? What's her name again?"

I folded my arms, refusing to answer. Even if Dazmine and I would never be on fabulous terms, I wasn't just going to throw her name into dangerous territory if I could help it.

Terrin shrugged anyway. "I'll do it. What?" he added when Sasha and Sylvie gaped at him. "I'd like to see a girl like her try to take me for ransom. And it sounds like she's having a hard time. If it would make her feel better to cuff me for a bit..."

"Terrin." Garvis pinched the bridge of his nose.

"That's the worst idea you've ever had," Sylvie said.

"And you've had a lot of bad ideas," Sasha added.

To my shock—and to the others', it seemed—Steeler didn't immediately shut down the idea even though *I* had to admit it was absurd.

"It does sound like she's emotionally charged and dead-set on investigating Jenia's disappearance," he mused, curiosity still dancing behind his contemplative expression. "And since Drey has already involved her, we either have to wipe her memories—"

"Not going to happen," I countered.

"—or involve her under her own terms before she gets desperate," Steeler finished firmly. "But we can talk more about the logistics on the ship." He tossed a look to Garvis. "I'll be back by the time you're finished with your first lesson."

The others reached out to grab hold of him. Right before he made them all melt away into nothingness, he looked back at me with another flash of his fangs.

"I've told you before, and I'll tell you again, Drey. Your memories are still in your mind, just hidden where no one else but you *can* find them. You want them back? You can go get them yourself."

And with that, he and the others vanished.

"Asshole," I muttered under my breath.

Now that I was alone with Garvis and Felicity, I realized the storm outside had ceased. Lazy fingers of rain trailed down the windowpanes, but nothing flashed or thundered out at sea anymore.

In the crackling firelight, I turned to the monkey.

"You said you had witch hazel?"

"*Yes.*" Yes. Her thought echoed her voice, creating a strange but somewhat pleasant harmony in my ears. *Why?*

I wished I could plant my own thoughts within *her* mind so that Garvis didn't have to hear what I said next... but I didn't know how to do that yet. So I mumbled through my teeth, "When he comes back, can you make sure to disinfect those wretched wounds of his?"

"*Oh, of course!* Why didn't I think of that?"

Garvis raised a thin eyebrow at me.

"What?" I threw up my hands. "I can't throttle him if he's already dead of a fever."

The amusement didn't leave Garvis's face, but he just said, "Coen probably doesn't need sterilization. Mature faeries heal a lot faster than their previous selves, but—whatever you say, Rayna. Now, are you ready for your first Mind Manipulating lesson?"

I nodded, twisting my fingers together nervously.

"Good. Because it won't be fun, so you might want to sit down."

"Oh. Okay."

I followed his lead, settling into a cross-legged position on the rug while Felicity went back to fiddling with cupboards and drawers in the kitchen, chittering under her breath. This close, I could see the faint line of kohl smudged under Garvis's eyes—a pirate indeed.

"Do you mind if we hold hands?" he asked awkwardly. "It's tradition. Usually it's a bigger circle, but under the circumstances..."

"Uh, sure."

I let him take my hands and tried to relax into them. They were so much softer and leaner than Steeler's, reminding me painfully of Fabian and the way he used to stroke my hair to sleep.

"Okay, now I want you to close your eyes."

I closed my eyes.

"Focus on your outermost thought. Go ahead and tell me what it is. I can't hear it right now because I have my own personal blockade up."

The words slipped out before I could stop them.

"Why do you let Steeler speak so...rudely to you?"

Garvis gave a soft snort. "He's not usually like that. He's in pain, and he's a maturing faerie with a lot of new... sensations to deal with." Before I could ask more about that, he said, "Now go a layer deeper. What's your second most outer thought?"

I sighed and squeezed my eyes even tighter, trying to concentrate on digging through all the questions.

"What did he mean when he said he can't bear to be in my mind right now?" Originally, I'd thought it had to do with his mutilated brand, but the more I thought about the wording...

Garvis didn't answer this time. When I peeked open an eye, he had his own closed and appeared to be breathing deeply.

"Now go a layer deeper," was all he said.

A rattle in the kitchen made me think *I'm surprised about Felicity. That she lives with him here in the lighthouse. That she trusts him enough to call him Coco.* But I didn't say that part out loud.

"Go a layer deeper," Garvis ordered, the sound of his voice mingling with the crackling fire, soothing and hypnotizing.

I don't blame Steeler for doing everything in his power to keep these kinds of secrets confidential... even if it means Manipulating me.

Wait—what? Why had I just told myself I didn't blame the faerie who'd dragged me into this mess? Of course I blamed him, I...

"Deeper," Garvis interrupted, and that single word seemed to push me back until I was sinking into the next thought.

I liked the feel of Steeler's fingers moving aside my hair.

"Deeper," Garvis ordered before I could even process what I'd just admitted to myself.

I wanted so badly for him to deny chaining me up.

"Deeper."

I loathe myself for hurting him.

"Deeper."

"I can't," I gasped out loud. "I..."

I almost opened my eyes, but something was reeling me backward, in, in, in, and Garvis clutched my hands tighter and said, "Deeper."

My entire mind fell backward, flailing through what felt like infinite sky, until suddenly I was...

I was on solid ground again. Solid... powdery ground?

I opened my eyes, raking my fingers through the ground. Snow.

When I looked up, it was to find myself in an entirely new world, with a wall of ice looming overhead.

CHAPTER

18

A thud to my left told me Garvis had fallen in here with me.

"Where are we?" I asked him immediately, scrambling to a stand and brushing snow off my legs as I gazed around the entire space.

My breath fogged out in front of me. Wherever it was, it felt like an Element Wielder had cast a spell over the whole damn place. The wall ahead of us glimmered with impenetrable blue, coated in ice that barely revealed what lay underneath: an arched gateway made of gnarled wood.

And the sky... a hazy pink blob smeared the far side of it, while the patch directly ahead of us winked with a crescent light so much like the shape of my knife—as if both sun and moon had tried to rise or sink and found themselves caught up in all the mist.

Behind us lay nothing but a frozen wasteland that melted into a horizon as black as the Cosmos itself.

"This," Garvis said as he lifted himself to my side, "is your mind."

"*My* mind?"

I stared at the wall in front of us again, gaping. How many times had I felt as if ice coated my veins, filling my very heart? And here, all along, my mind...

"Has it always been like this?" I breathed.

"No." Garvis didn't turn to look at me, but a tinge to his voice made me glance sideways at him. "I've only ever been in your mind once before, back when it was still frosting over, but Coen..." He coughed into a fist. "Coen's told me it was once a lively place."

I ignored the jolt that last part sent through me—the idea that Steeler had once known my mind intimately enough to describe it in detail to a friend. "You've been in my mind once before now?"

"Yes."

Finally, Garvis turned to look at me, and I startled at the sight of a single tear frozen in the crook of his eye, hanging there like a crystalized diamond.

"Before we begin, I need you to know something." Garvis took a long breath. "It was I who buried your relationship with Coen last year. I buried every memory he was involved in beyond the moment you first laid eyes on him... as well as any memory that could've landed you in trouble with the Good Council. Coen's done all the meddling since then, but I... I hid the heart of it all. I took it from you."

I blinked at him. At the guilt etched all over his face.

"But then..." The snow beneath our feet seemed to wake with a grumbling quake. "Then you can retrieve them again."

Garvis was already shaking his head.

"I hid them so well that Lexington would have never been able to find them, and buried them so deep that they're long frozen over. I'm afraid Coen's right, Rayna. *You* have to be the one to retrieve them. I can't melt all of this even if I wanted to."

Diamonds were crystallizing on my lashes now, but I didn't bother wiping them away as I trudged toward the wall of ice and said over my shoulder in as bright a voice as I could manage, "Well, then, I guess I'd better start trying, huh?"

Garvis followed me to the frozen gateway, where I leaned in closer to find—

"Look. Somebody's already broken in."

Indeed, deep gouges in the ice had carved an opening to the brass handle, and when I looked down, two very separate tracks had been embedded in the snow beneath the door: what looked like large, normal footprints, and something thick and tubular, like a long body had slid through.

"Steeler and Lexington," I murmured, disgusted at that second wormlike track. I looked up at Garvis. "Why is it...?"

"Lesson number one: the longer you loiter in someone else's mind, the more your intrusive consciousness morphs into a shape that reflects its true intent," Garvis answered grimly. "Kitterfol seems to enjoy snooping in your mind, no matter what else he might claim— which is evident in these tracks."

A worm. Lexington literally became a worm, a parasite, when he invaded my brain every weekend.

Holding back a shudder, I nodded down at Steeler's footprints.

"He's in my mind every week, too. How come he's not...?"

"A monster?" Garvis smiled wryly. "I think you know why, deep down." He didn't even give me any time to process that statement. "Now, are you ready to go inside?"

"Ready as I'll ever be, I guess."

I still couldn't believe that I was a *Mind Manipulator* now. That I'd sunk into my own consciousness, that I was staring down my too-familiar wall of ice in the flesh.

Rubbing my palms together, I stole a deep breath of frigid air before pulling on the handle and stepping through.

It was a maze.

I knew that even before I'd let my gaze sweep over every winding pathway sprouting from the main walkway, each wall coated in such a thick layer of ice that I couldn't tell what lay underneath, wood or marble or something else entirely. There seemed to be no end in sight no matter which way I turned, and nothing stirred within the mist that clung to every edge like ancient cobwebs.

"What happened to me?" I whispered.

Garvis simply said, "Come on. Let's go find a random memory."

He started down the main walkway, the only path that didn't curve or bend at odd angles. I followed until he stopped abruptly and turned toward a pathway that split off in a sharp zigzag, where we rounded a corner to find a condensed pocket of swirling mist.

As soon as we laid eyes on it, the mist burst into shape and sound—an echoing, familiar whoop.

"Is that Rodhi?" I gasped, incredulous.

Yes, that was definitely a ghostly version of Rodhi, butt-naked and balls swinging as he streaked down Bascite Boulevard at two in the morning after he'd chugged a quadruple shot from a pelican's beak—a memory from last year that I'd tried very hard to forget. Apparently, I hadn't managed to stifle it properly, because now that I was watching the mist replay it over and over, I doubted I'd ever forget it again.

Garvis chuckled. "He was always a strange kid, wasn't he? Tell me—where'd he get the pelican? I've never seen one on campus. And how did he convince it to hold still long enough for him to fill its pouch with that much alcohol?"

"The pelican was a migratory guest he coaxed in from the beach, and I don't know how Rodhi does what he does. Or why," I added as an afterthought. "Okay, so these are what memories look like? And in theory I could—"

"Bury it," Garvis said, nodding at the snow-packed ground, "which would prevent you from remembering on a conscious level. You could also destroy it completely, which would make it impossible for that memory to ever be recalled. Or you could alter it, maybe give the guy some clothes. But those things all take complicated skill, whereas hiding it within an internal blockade... I could probably teach you how to do that tonight."

"An internal blockade?"

"Yes. It would... camouflage the memory so that other Mind Manipulators like Lexington would have a harder time finding it, but *you* would still be able to remember it on a conscious level. Not as foolproof as burying or destroying sensitive information, but a whole lot easier. And what we're doing now takes hardly any skill at all."

I arched a brow at him mid-shiver. "What are we doing now?"

"Shedding light onto the memory simply by observing." Garvis gazed upward. "See how your moon has shifted its focus, how it's beaming down on this spot now?"

I did. Whereas before a misty darkness had filled this pocket of the maze, now moonlight bathed it in a milky yellow glow.

Illuminating Rodhi's bare asscheeks.

Fantastic.

"Maybe another memory?" I suggested weakly.

Garvis gestured for me to go on. "Lead the way."

We followed path after path, twisting and doubling back and reaching dead ends but finding a new memory around every corner. There was me, arriving at the Esholian Institute for the first time. Emelle and I first saying hi while Jenia and Dazmine sneered at our backs. Mr. Conine's lesson with crocodiles, where Fergus Bilderas had insulted one of the females. Parties, classes, and tests that all played like misty, moving pictures.

Nothing of Steeler, though. Nothing of a midnight swim in the Element Wielder lake or any of the other times he'd forced me to take a pill these last few months.

"Every mind is like this?" I asked eventually, after a particularly heartfelt memory of Fabian and Don making me some midnight soup when I couldn't sleep a few years before the Esholian Institute. Funnily enough, rewatching it made me notice new details I hadn't before with that moonlight illuminating every angle: how Don's Summoning magic did most of the vegetable chopping, for instance, while Fabian's dealt with the mixing and the seasoning.

"Not exactly." Garvis stroked his mustache. "The substance of the walls always varies from person to person, as does the climate. But there is always a maze of thoughts—a twisting of neurons that we get to view in its personified form. There is always mist to make memories and moonlight to help guide our way." He paused, as if weighing whether or not to continue. "And a subconscious in the center of it all."

"A subconscious?" For some reason, my stomach swooped. "Aren't... aren't I my own subconscious right now?"

"No. You are your *outer* consciousness right now. But the deeper you explore your own maze, the closer you get to her—and the more in-tune with yourself you'll become. Would you like to meet her?"

Her. As if my subconscious were an entirely different being.

I shrugged, trying to hide the sudden chill that had trickled down my spine by crossing my arms. "Sure."

We made it back to the main pathway and trudged through the snow, heading straight into the center of the maze. I tried to keep track of how many different winding pathways we passed, but eventually

171

lost track after fifty. It seemed that the further we traveled, the lower the temperature dropped.

"Almost there," Garvis said, his teeth chattering.

I squinted into the mist, where a dark, rounded shadow was slowly taking shape up ahead. For a second, I wondered if my subconscious self had seriously decided to take the form of an umbrella... but then we were stepping into a rounded courtyard, where a marble gazebo sat cold and impassive in the center like a dome-crowned shrine.

And in that gazebo, sitting on what looked like a frosted throne...

Was *me*.

I stared at myself.

She stared back, her head turning with creaking slowness to meet my gaze straight on.

Her hair—as wild and curly as mine—had stiffened into place. Snowflakes patterned her clothing like lace. Every bare inch of skin—her neck, her arms, her hands—appeared as cold and white and hard as the marble of the shrine itself.

My feet stumbled backward of their own accord.

"*Go ahead*," my subconscious said airily, her breath forming a swirling fog that reached out with beckoning fingers. "*Ask me anything.*"

My face. *My* voice. And yet I'd never felt less familiar with myself than I did now. As if I'd looked into a warped, alternate mirror.

"N-no, thanks. I'm good." I turned to Garvis. "Can we go?"

Perhaps a shade of disappointment flitted across his expression, but he bowed his head and took my hand in his own.

"It can be hard at first, I know. But you will get better and braver the more you revisit her. Now." He smiled. "Before we go back, it's tradition to give you the sector motto."

And suddenly it wasn't just his voice pitching into a chant, but the entire world—the frozen, far-off sunrise and icy walls and eerie subconscious in her shrine, as if Garvis had planted the words into my brain:

> We, the captains of the mind,
> Welcome all who've heard
> The discordance of voices
> And triumphantly endured.
> For if a web of thought is tangled,
> Who but us untwines?
> If a memory is fading,
> Who but us revives?
> So we cast our rays of light
> Onto what's broken and amiss.
> We fix and care, this we swear,

"By the moonbeam and the mist," I whispered with the world, wrapping my arms around myself.

I was cold—much too cold in this space within me. A deep tremor was wrapping around my ribcage, shaking me from the toes upward, and my subconscious was *still staring at me* with too-green eyes, and I just... needed to get out of my own head.

"Okay, Rayna." Even Garvis's lips were turning blue. "All you need to do is reach for your surface. Imagine yourself rising, climbing up through the mist, using the moon as a footstool to leap up and away."

I tried to do as he said, even raising a hand to scrabble at the sky, but...

Nothing happened. Snowflakes settled in my hair, and my subconscious continued to stare at me, and the mist just swirled and swirled and swirled.

Panic sliced through my every breath at the thought that I couldn't defy gravity. I might be trapped within the confines of my own mind if I couldn't find a good foothold on the—

"Don't worry, Drey," a voice drawled beside me. "I've got you."

My eyes flew open to find that Steeler had arrived on my other side and already clamped a firm hand on my elbow.

A *tug* from him, and we were soaring upward, through the mist, past the streak of moonlight.

My eyes flew open *again*—this time to the real world.

To find that I'd collapsed right against his chest.

CHAPTER

19

I righted myself instantly, stumbling back a few paces away.

Garvis, it seemed, had managed to stay upright the whole time he'd been in my mind with me, because he was observing us with quiet calculation on his own two feet as if nothing had happened.

"You shaved" fell out of my mouth as I took in Steeler's appearance.

God of the Cosmos, that was such a stupidly obvious thing to say. But he *had*, and his hair was cut back to its original length, revealing those sharp, elongated ears while a crisp, long-sleeved tunic covered all his muscles and scars.

Steeler blinked at me, then shrugged. "Felicity wouldn't quit chasing me around with her scissors and razor until I sat down."

I glanced over his shoulder at the monkey, who paused from scratching her armpits long enough to say, "*I also got him with the witch hazel just like you asked. He whimpered like a baby, by the way.*"

A snort escaped me at the thought of Coen Steeler whimpering like a baby, and Felicity gave me an appreciative flash of her teeth.

Steeler quirked a brow and breathed into my mind, *I take it you didn't get a chance to practice blockading?*

I swatted at my ear, startled.

How are you—?

Apparently, the witch hazel healed my ability to use whatever Mind Manipulating power I have left... which is why I was able to go in and save you.

I felt every inch of me bristle at the implication that he'd heard my fears of being stranded in my own mind.

"Get out of my head," I snapped out loud.

Steeler crossed his arms and smiled. "Make me."

I resisted the urge to stomp a foot. "You are so..."

His eyes tracked the twitch in my leg, as if knowing exactly what I'd been itching to do. "I'm so *what*, Drey?"

Full of yourself. Infuriating. Annoyingly capable of getting under my skin. I couldn't pick out of the tangled insults, so I just turned to Garvis instead.

"Can you teach me how to blockade? Right now?"

"Yeah, but..." Garvis glanced at Steeler over my head. "We were in your mind for two hours, Rayna. Are you sure you don't want to rest a little bit first? Usually, inductees go to bed after their first—"

"Two *hours*?"

I gaped at the clock on the mantlepiece. Sure enough, those ticking hands were now indicating it was two in the morning. Five hours until my Spiders, Worms, & Insects class.

There was no way I was getting a wink of sleep tonight, but adrenaline had revamped the energy in my veins anyways.

"Yes, I'm sure. I need to be able to block out pesky voices—" I flung a glare at Steeler, which he returned with a smirk. "—by the time I get back." A sudden question bubbled in my empty stomach. "You *will* be taking me back, right?"

Steeler shrugged with way too much grace for that smug look crawling all over his face. "Unless you beg me to keep you. I don't think I could say no a second time if you did."

I rolled my eyes harder than I ever had in my life and turned back to Garvis. "I'm ready. If you're not too tired," I added awkwardly, suddenly realizing how smudged his kohl liner had become.

"Oh no, I'll be fine. I've had later nights than these." Garvis sighed at the ceiling for a second, then said to Steeler, "But I think *you* need to leave again, Coen. Whatever's happening between you two is way too distracting for me to work with."

Steeler and I, both on the verge of saying something, snapped our mouths shut in unison, looked at each other, and looked away again.

"Fine," he finally said curtly. "I need to go hunt for some breakfast anyway. Felicity, you coming?"

The monkey bounded off the kitchen countertop, her tail flying behind her as she said to no one in particular, "*Gladly.*" Then her thoughts added: *Coco and Raynie hiss and sneer at each other more than two baboons fighting over the same coconut.*

As the cottage door swung shut behind them, I puffed out a sigh. Apparently, I was Raynie now.

The next few hours passed in a sickening blur, but by the time the first blotches of dawn graced the horizon outside the lighthouse windows, I could do it: sink into my own mind, gather the ghostly essence of my internal wall, and push it out, out, out like icy vapor, until it wrapped around my entire body. It wouldn't keep a Mind Manipulator out, necessarily, but it would keep all the unwanted voices from crashing into me. And it would keep my own thoughts from floating outward to anyone else.

Hiding individual memories was harder. Garvis and I spent our last bit of time packing snow into blocks of ice and building them up around the misty replays of the events this weekend, blocking off that part of the maze. That way *I* would know they were there, *I* could access them, but as long as Lexington didn't know to look past innocent-looking dead ends...

Hopefully, he would never find them.

"Eventually you'll be able to Manipulate your own mind with more ease," Garvis said at last, collapsing on one of the sofas as the first seagulls began cawing outside. "You won't have to use your hands to build internal blockades or move memories around—you'll just be able to do it with half a thought. But *that* requires getting to know your subconscious better... which most Mind Manipulators don't do until their second or third year."

Yeah, a friendship with my eerie subconscious clone wasn't happening anytime soon. I'd just have to be content with the archaic way of Mind Manipulating for now.

I collapsed in the armchair beside Garvis, daydreaming about a bath, just in time for the cottage door to fly open again.

My body jolted upright, but it was just Steeler stomping in with Felicity on his heels—not with a bucket of dead mollusks like I'd been expecting, but with a basket of fruits: papaya and mango and what looked like maracuya from the reddish coating of the smaller ones.

"What, did all the clams sleep in today?" I asked with a bit more attitude than I'd intended. My mouth had started watering at the sweet and tangy smell of all the fruit after so many hours of Mind Manipulating on an empty stomach.

"No, but I felt you cringe when I mentioned hunting for food. I know you wouldn't want to eat something you might've once conversed with—even if they are just clams."

Steeler began unloading the fruit onto the kitchen counter and slicing them up with a kitchen knife while Felicity dropped a lumpy sack of something else next to him. I didn't really know how to respond as I watched them. It was strangely... considerate of him to keep my food preferences in mind. I'd eaten meat my whole life until the day I'd become a Wild Whisperer, when our house cook had begun making my every meal using the fruits and vegetables and seeds the jungle willingly gave. It was like an unspoken rule to avoid meat in our house, one that I hadn't even thought much about until now.

Perhaps it was the realization I was about to tell Coen Steeler *thank you* that made me say, "Well, I'm not hungry anyway."

"Yes, you are, Drey." When I opened my mouth to argue, Steeler said, "I've got shiny new faerie ears, remember? I can *hear* your stomach grumbling. And Mind Manipulating requires lots of fuel."

Shit. He was right. My stomach gave a particularly aching lurch as Steeler slid all that colorful array of fruit onto four separate plates from the dusty cupboards, and Felicity opened her sack to scoop out handfuls of macadamia nuts beside each helping. Maybe a few bites wouldn't hurt before we returned to the Institute...

Steeler dragged a chair back and gestured for me to sit in it.

"Eat. You too, Garvis."

Hesitantly, I took my seat, holding back the second *thank you* ready to spill out of my mouth. As soon as Felicity and Garvis picked up their utensils and started eating, my restraint broke.

I gorged myself.

And I didn't care that Steeler was watching me every time I licked the sticky juice off my fingers, didn't care that his pupils followed the bob of my throat each time I swallowed. He could stare all he liked, but I wasn't going to show any manners after the twenty-four hours I'd just endured: dragged through space, told I was a different species, branded with Mind Manipulating, and facing my literal subconscious without any kind of reprieve. Until now.

Now I was content to stay silent and listen to Garvis make small talk with Steeler, flexing my new Manipulating blockade around me as if it was the thinnest film of malleable ice.

"—everyone made it back to the ship okay?" Garvis was asking.

"Yes. Nara says hi."

"What about Barberro?"

"I believe *togu vi fyka arana* were his exact words."

Garvis gave a small chuckle and wiped his mouth.

"And the Fated General—"

"—will punish anyone who tries to stop you from leaving with me once a week," Steeler interrupted firmly, his own smile fading. "Trust me."

The wording of that seemed strange, somehow. I stopped flexing my blockade around me to listen to him a little more intently—only to find him already fixated on me.

He plunked a gray pill onto the patch of table before me.

"We have an issue regarding *this*, though, I'm afraid."

Ah, yes. The suppressant pill that supposedly stifled my natural, faerie power... although, come to think of it, Steeler hadn't provided any proof that I even *was* a faerie. But I decided to humor him anyway.

"Oh? What's the issue?"

"Lexington's going to be expecting an explanation for the pills next week, and I know *you* know you can't tell him it's a way to hide your forbidden power. Of course, I could just kill him..." Steeler seemed to lose himself in some kind of sick murder fantasy, but Garvis cleared his throat and he shook himself back to the present. "But Dyonisia has a dozen other Mind Manipulator elites at her disposal to replace him with, so that would just be a temporary solution anyways."

I chewed on my lip.

"Are you saying you're going to plant a false memory in my brain? One that lies about what the pills truly do?"

"Oh, no." Steeler pushed back his bowl. "I promised myself I'd never plant a false memory in your head again." Before I could mull that over, he leaned forward onto his elbows and said, "But we could... reenact the moment I told you about them, if you're comfortable with it. That way you can keep the truth hidden within your internal blockades while Lexington observes the reenactment instead."

My frown only deepened.

"But if we reenact that moment, what would you say the pills even *do*? No matter what, Lexington will want me to get him one so that he can study it. Figure out how it works. Use it to his advantage."

Over the last several months, I'd felt Lexington in my mind so often that I was beginning to sense his motivations, his desires, his need for control. I knew he didn't care about me catching Steeler the same way Dyonisia seemed to. He worshiped his ruler but wanted to dominate her at the same time. And if there was a single Mind Manipulating trick that he didn't understand, even if it was in drug form...

Steeler furrowed his brows, leaned back, and crossed his arms.

"Killing him is sounding better and better every—"

"But maybe we could flip the table on him," I interrupted. When Steeler gestured at me to go on, curiosity evident in the way his brows unfurled, I cleared my throat. "What if we dangled it over Lexington's head—something he wanted so desperately he'd do anything to obtain it? Even if it meant he had to play the game on our terms. Even if it meant he'd go behind Dyonisia's back to get it."

Steeler glanced at Garvis, who shrugged and nodded. Felicity beamed and clapped her hands.

Steeler himself leaned back in his chair again, a surprised smile lifting up one side of his mouth.

"I think you're more devious than I give you credit for, Drey."

CHAPTER

20

"Do I really have to touch your hand to do this?"

Steeler had Walked Garvis back to the ship and I'd bid farewell to Felicity moments before she'd clambered up to the rafters in the kitchen and fallen asleep with her tail wrapped around herself.

Now, the two of us stood in the middle of the pebbled beach, the sharp sting of salty breath from the ocean playing with my curls.

With his hand outstretched, Steeler gave me that smile I'd grown accustomed to in the last day—wide and full of teeth.

"You can touch other parts of me if you want, Drey. Any part you'd like."

Of course he'd say that. "No, thanks."

Gritting my teeth, I placed my hand on top of his, and felt a yank of what seemed like electricity before the world dissolved and we were back in that darkness full of far-off lights and dense, inky blackness.

A space between stars. Between worlds.

I clung to Steeler's hand, the sole warm, textured thing in this darkness, and only let go after we fell into a very familiar classroom still filled with crates and hutches and my fallen knife and...

The sundew snapped around Steeler's arms as soon as we'd fully materialized, screeching with triumph.

At the same moment, the string of nepenthes bucked and splashed more poison at him, while the flytraps lowered themselves to a snapping stance over his head. From the sounds of their shrieks and growls, it seemed like they'd been in a state of indignation all night, just waiting for their chosen victim to return so they could disable him again.

Well, Steeler had returned, alright. And in a matter of two seconds, he was back in the same exact position he'd been in merely twelve hours ago: on his knees, arms splayed wide by the stalks of sundew, completely at my mercy. Even the low lighting made it seem like it could still be nighttime, what with the cluster of trees blocking any morning light from streaming through the opaque window.

But now... now Steeler's shirt was covering every scar, his face and hair were groomed, and I wasn't scared anymore.

I'd already scooped up my crescent knife from where Steeler had flung it to the ground by the door. I stalked forward and pointed the curved blade at his branded shoulder, just as we'd planned. As if we'd rewound time and started this whole scene over.

"Answer my questions, or I'll mutilate your magic."

Steeler's eyes dipped to my knife hand, pretending to flare in fear.

"What is this?" I reached forward with my free hand and dug in his front shirt pocket to bring out the pill. "What does it *do* to me every week? Why do you make me take it?"

My blockade was up, but I still felt that dark, fathomless energy of his brush up against it as he said, in his Mind Manipulating tone, "Swallow it first, little hurricane, and then I'll tell you."

I pretended I'd fallen prey to his command. I sheathed my knife, pushed the pill between my lips, and forced it down.

One side of Steeler's lip curled up. "Good. Now come closer, and listen very carefully."

I stepped forward, supposedly on command, until my lower half was pressed against Steeler's upper half. His eyes right in line with my breasts.

"It's a new stimulator I came up with," he said finally, smirking up at me. "To control you from afar. To make you *want* me even when you're the only damned woman who's never wanted me before."

A performance. This was all just a performance. Because what Lexington wanted most, I was sure, was a way to force Dyonisia to love him back. To control the most powerful being on this island who seemed immune to the normal influences of the five magics. Steeler wasn't truly talking to me this way right now. It was an act.

But I still felt a deep, curling shock when Steeler strained against the sundew stalks like he wanted to tackle me to the ground.

"A stimulator? Is that so?" I forced myself to ask.

Steeler nodded. "From the moment it kicks in until the moment it fades, you will think of me. And every time you think of me, you'll crave the feel of my body against yours."

As if to stop myself from leaning in, I pressed my blade harder against his shoulder, but he didn't even wince.

"And every time you *do* feel my body pressed against yours," he continued, the words slow and steady, as if he wanted to savor them on his tongue, "your legs will beg you to let them spread for me."

No, no, no. They were getting to me, those words. A low, simmering sort of fire seemed to be building in my core. I—

"And every time you spread your legs, Rayna, even if you're alone in your room trying to pleasure yourself, it'll be *my* cock you think of. *My* cock you want buried so deep inside you that you'll never be able to escape. Do you understand? Say you understand."

"I understand," I gasped.

I could have sworn Steeler's nostrils flared, just for a second, as his eyes swept down my body and back up in a blink. Then—

"Okay, that should do it. You can ease up on the knife now."

I stared at him, trying to clamp my legs together without him noticing, anything to smother the heat that made me want to slide a finger through the slit in my dress and give pressure to the ache.

"Drey?"

"Oh, right."

I removed my knife from his shoulder and stepped back, surveying him still on his knees with his arms spread. I had class in twenty minutes, and he should be Walking back to the lighthouse by now, but suddenly I was straining to keep certain images from flashing through my mind: me, unbuttoning Steeler's pants, rediscovering just how big he really was underneath...

"How long?" I blurted in an attempt to distract my mind from the filthy direction it was heading. "How long do full-blooded faeries typically live for?"

Steeler's nostrils flared again, and his pupils were spreading as his eyes grazed down me again. "More than a thousand years."

"And... half-faeries?"

I'd purposely avoided thinking about the logistics of my supposed faerie heritage, but it was obvious that Fabian was human, that it would have had to be my mysterious, unknown mother who'd been one...

"It depends on the specific percentage, but... anywhere from six to seven hundred, I'd say." Steeler was still on his knees, still strung up, still entangled by growling plants leaching onto him, but he didn't look like he'd rather be anywhere else as he cocked his head and whispered, "Any more questions, little hurricane?"

Oh, yes, a million of them. But I knew my Mind Manipulating wasn't strong enough to hide the most earth-shattering answers from Lexington yet, so I'd have to choose carefully. Pick the questions that would matter the least to anyone but me.

"Why do you call me that?"

"What?

"Little hurricane."

Something seemed to be happening to his body now—a kind of tense quivering, as if he truly *did* have to restrain himself from ripping through his makeshift chains and pouncing on me.

"Because of what you do to me... among other reasons."

I stiffened and looked away, suddenly hearing the mist in my mind replaying certain scenes.

You took a midnight swim with that lover of yours, the octopus said with his tentacles.

You were just one of his oblivious pets that he liked to use and abuse, Lexington said with his oily smile.

I made a careless mistake in letting Kitterfol Lexington keep that particular memory, Steeler said with his mental voice. *Not a day goes by where I don't curse myself for forgetting he had it.*

And what had he said back at the lighthouse? *I promised myself I'd never plant a false memory in your head again.*

My eyes opened again to find that Steeler, in the here and now, was surveying me with concern warring with raw, savage hunger in the smoky quartz of his eyes.

"Was that memory—the one with the chains..." I sucked in a gulp of air. "Was that something like this one?" *Fake? Fabricated?*

Steeler's eyes didn't move from my face.

"Yes."

I looked away again, feeling my blockade of ice slip like a torn cloak.

I was starting to see hazy edges of the full picture form around me even without having obtained my old memories again. And there was something in Steeler's voice that told me the truth: he wanted me to hate him, *needed* me to hate him, until I could fully protect myself. Because if any part of Lexington suspected I *didn't* hate him...

Dazmine had been right. This was all just a way to test my loyalty to Dyonisia, and my loathing, my anger toward Steeler, kept me safe from any chance that she'd exile or even execute me as a traitor. I couldn't love him, couldn't want him, so he'd been playing the part this whole time.

But it didn't change the fact that he'd lied to me.

It didn't change the fact that he'd abandoned me.

It didn't change the fact that he'd tried to protect me without my input, without my discretion, without my consent.

Coen Steeler had played the part too well.

So if he had given me the gift of Mind Manipulating as a peace offering or a way to get me to fall back in love with him, it was pointless. My body could burn for him all it wanted in a purely physical way—that didn't mean my heart would ever melt for him again.

I turned toward the door without another word, intending to leave him to get himself out of the sundews' prison.

188

Steeler reappeared in front of me, blocking my path in the one empty space of the room where none of the thrashing sundew or snapping flytraps or bucking nepenthes could reach him.

"You never said it last year, you know."

I crossed my arms. "What?"

"You never said you loved me," he half-whispered. "You never said those words. I'm not under any assumption that you'd *ever* say them after what I've done to you."

I couldn't help the flicker of surprise from crossing my face.

"Then why are you doing this? Why are you helping me?"

He leaned forward with his hand outstretched, sending a wave of unwanted warmth down my body again. "Because *I* can't help still being in love with *you*—and that's not transactional. Here," he added before I could dredge up a response. "You forgot this." He opened his fingers, revealing the little black pearl that sat on his bed of callouses. "If you want it, of course."

After a moment of consideration, I plucked it from his palm and slid it down my cleavage just like last time.

The smallest shiver of triumph passed through me at the way those dilated pupils tracked the progress down. At the way a hint of shock finally sliced through his usually smirking exterior.

"For my tally," I said. "To keep track of how many reasons I still have to kill you at the end of this."

Then I shoved past him and out the door.

CHAPTER

21

I had to run to make it to Ms. Pincette's class on time, my dress flailing behind me, all the thorny, grisly underbrush politely jostling out of my way just in time to avoid scratching my ankles.

When I finally slid into my seat next to Emelle and Gileon, trying desperately to suppress the urge to pant, Ms. Pincette began her lecture of the day right away. Guess I'd made it with seconds to spare.

"Today, we deal with bullet ants, the most pompous of the hive mind—and the most likely to attack if you so much as breathe on them the wrong way."

She unveiled five glass containers to reveal a single reddish black ant prowling in circles at the bottom of each.

"As I've mentioned in passing, a single sting can leave one paralyzed with pain for hours, so it's crucial that we know how to offer the respect their kind demands in face-to-face situations. Eventually, you should be able to hold one on your palm without incident. For right now, though, we'll keep them in these jars as we practice pleasantries."

After a few seconds of mentally patting my blockade, making sure it still fit tight around me, I let myself glance at Emelle.

No suspicious frown. No urgent widening of her eyes, wondering where I'd been all night. She just gave me a small, side-eyed smile back, then resumed listening to Ms. Pincette talk about bullet ant etiquette.

And Dazmine... from across the room, Dazmine wasn't looking at me at all, her posture at rigid attention in her chair, her gaze locked intently on the head of the classroom.

Had my absence really gone unnoticed? Maybe Emelle had stayed the night with Lander, Cilia had stayed with Mitzi, and Dazmine had thought good riddance?

It wasn't until Ms. Pincette released us to practice in groups that Emelle turned to me and whispered, "Did you have a fun night?"

The mischievous sheen in her eyes confused me at first, but then she went on as Gileon went to fetch a bullet ant from Ms. Pincette, his rhino beetle making nervous swirls around his neck.

"Willa said you went off with some guy." Emelle wiggled a brow at my unruly hair and rumpled dress. "She looked a lot better, by the way. Well, I didn't see her sick with the stomach ulcer, but the apples must have really helped because she looked just as lively as ever when we finally came to bed."

A breath whooshed out of me as I realized that Willa, that wonderful, smart little creature, had saved my ass with her quick thinking even though I hadn't told her a thing about my plans last night. Except now I had to follow that storyline, too.

"I, uhh... yeah, I did." The blush that seeped down my neck didn't feel entirely forced. "He's a Mind Manipulator—not my ex from back home," I added quickly, "someone I met on the night of the Branding."

I didn't want to outright lie to Emelle, so I figured it would be best to stick with vague truths. That this particular Mind Manipulator had pinned me up against an alleyway and called me a good girl within minutes of our little "meeting" didn't seem like details I wanted to share just yet.

But when that gleam in Emelle's eyes seemed to flicker, I let my blockade fall around me for just a fraction of a second.

Amid the cacophony of thoughts that flooded in, burying me in their crescendo, I thought I could pick out hers.

What are you not telling me? Are you sick? Pregnant? Is someone hurting you? Who is this guy? What did I do to lose your trust?

I felt a wince sprout on my face as I snapped my blockade back around me in a vice-like cocoon. She was still hurting over this, and I... I still wasn't willing to risk her safety like I was willing to risk Dazmine's. Still wasn't willing to let her all the way in.

Oh God, I was getting as bad as Steeler. What could I give Emelle that was real that wouldn't put her in danger?

I let my smile drop and said in an even lower voice, "I'll tell you more about him if it turns into anything, okay?" *Not that that'll ever happen again.* "But I kind of want to keep it on the downlow for right now." I cleared my throat with a hoarse laugh. "To be honest, I'm still kind of traumatized by something that happened at that party on Friday night."

Emelle's eyes went wide. "What happened on Friday night?"

In a whisper, I told her about the Shape Shifter who hadn't wanted to respect my no, watching Emelle's normally sweet, innocent face become more and more patched with rage until her hands curled into fists.

"By the orchid and the owl, Rayna, please tell me he didn't force you..."

"No, no." I shook my head. "I, uh... I managed to get away." My knife flashed in my mind, but I didn't think a Spiders, Worms, & Insects class was the best place to shout about how I'd chopped someone's fingers off. Still, the thought that I couldn't even tell Emelle about *this* left my stomach in sour knots. The secrets I had to keep were bleeding into too many areas of my life to count.

Emelle's fists were still shaking. "Who was it? Lander would kick his ass for you, and I'd help."

"Oh, no, it's okay. It's over and done with." The idea of Emelle hurling herself at a Shape Shifter who could grow an eight-pack... I didn't know if that was funny or terrifying. Or both. "Where did you and Lander run off to, anyway?" I asked slyly, trying to turn the conversation back onto her.

Her hands relaxing slightly, Emelle told me about her night in as vague of a manner as I had told her about mine. I listened until it was her turn to take the glass container from Gileon. Then I watched as she bowed her head at the bullet ant inside.

It paused for a few seconds to survey her, using its forelegs to wipe at its compound eyes.

Finally, the ant seemed to decide something and flicked its antennas back. Not like a returned bow, but a nod. An acceptance.

Looking pleased, Emelle lifted her head back up and whispered from the corner of her lips, "Was the Mind Manipulator better than the Shape Shifter, at least?" She handed me the jar with steady hands.

I couldn't stop the memory of Steeler's voice from leaking in.

Every time you spread your legs, Rayna, even if you're alone in your room trying to pleasure yourself, it'll be my *cock you think of. My cock you want buried so deep inside you that you'll never be able to—*

193

No. Hard stop. I squirmed in my seat, trying to stifle the warmth that my body was letting creep back in like the traitor it was.

"It... we didn't go that far." *And we never will.*

I bowed my own head at the ant in the glass, who—to my delight—dipped his antennas back immediately.

It was only when I passed the glass carefully back to Gileon that I whipped toward the empty seat beside me with a frown.

"Wait. Where's Rodhi?"

How could I have forgotten about him? Nobody ever missed class unless they were on their literal deathbed in the sick bay, and Rodhi wouldn't miss *this* class even if he was.

Emelle's frown mirrored mine.

"I have no idea. To be honest, when both of you were late, I started to assume maybe *he* was the guy you ran off with. But—"

"Ugh, no!" I shook my head so violently, our ant started prowling in agitated circles again. "I love Rodhi to pieces, but... not in that way."

"Well, Ms. Pincette doesn't seem to have noticed he's gone."

I glanced at our teacher, currently parading up and down the aisles to monitor each group's progress. I was sure nothing got past her, least of all the boy who'd been obsessed with her for a year failing to arrive at a government-sanctioned lesson he was required to attend.

"Nuisance says Rodhi's off on a high-stakes adventure," Gileon piped up, his rhino beetle indeed buzzing incessantly in his ear, "battling deadly foe and winning armies to his name. Maybe Ms. Pincette is okay with us skipping class if we're winning armies to our name."

"I'm *okay* with you bowing to your bullet ant," came a sharp reply behind our shoulders, and Gileon jumped so high off his seat that it made a sharp *cricking* sound when he came back down.

Ms. Pincette came to a towering halt over our sitting positions.

"Do you know how hard it was to find bullet ants to agree to hang out in what they perceive as see-through *coffins* for a day? I had to offer their colony a month's worth of nectar. And here you three are, yapping about stomach ulcers and high-stakes adventures instead of giving your ant the respect it deserves. Now bow."

Quicker than the whip of the sundew, all three of us bowed.

After our last class of the day, I told Emelle I was going to change and wash up before dinner while she and Gileon waited for Wren in our parlor.

I was looking forward to some stillness and silence. Ten minutes of alone time to fully process the brand hidden beneath my hair on the back of my neck and Steeler's pearl still beaded in between my breasts.

But when I opened my door, it was to find that Dazmine had beat me here, facing me with a glare glued on her face, and—

Willa, of all creatures, perched on the palm of an upturned hand.

"What," Dazmine began with a hiss.

"*Happened?*" Willa finished with a squeak.

I slammed the door behind me and toggled back and forth between their pairs of eyes: Dazmine's slitted with cool animosity and Willa's wide with gleaming worry.

"Since when did *you* two start ganging up on me?"

"*Since you used me as an excuse to sneak out without even telling me about it,*" Willa said. "*I had to find out I had stomach ulcers through Barty, who heard it from Gerald, who heard it through the wall. Thankfully, Dazmine ended up filling me in.*"

Dazmine flung back my glare with one of her own.

"What? You employed my help, made me listen to Mitzi and Cilia squeal like bellbirds all night, then *never came back*. What was I supposed to do, just go to sleep?"

I started to say yes, but she plunged on.

"So I had to tell Willa everything to get her to *lie* to Emelle and Cilia for you. Then I went looking for you at three in the goddamned *morning*. And you know what I found when I got to that abandoned classroom, Rayna? Nothing but a roomful of pissed off plants that told me you'd disappeared into thin air with the very man I'd asked them to trap!"

Dazmine's chest was heaving, her nostrils flaring, and a sudden surge of guilt wound its way around my ribs at the thought that *I'd* caused this: more panic and stress in her life after Jenia's exile.

Perhaps she saw that regret solidify in my eyes, because the next second she huffed out a laugh.

"Oh, no. You're not keeping this from me. Not after I had to listen to Norman Pollard burp his way through a drunken victory song when he won *another* round of mini pentaball. That shit was scarring."

Willa's whiskers twitched with a sigh.

"*She's right, unfortunately. We deserve to know.*"

Dazmine wrinkled her nose down at the mouse. "What do you mean *unfortunately*? I thought we were supposed to be ganging up on her together?"

"*We are. And that's rather unfortunate given your previous attitude toward my favorite cheese-providing human.*"

"I have *not* had an attitude—"

"Okay, okay." I tried to massage that growing heaviness from my eyes. I glanced at the walls. "Is the coast clear, Willa?"

The mouse nodded. "*I already checked for spiders before you got here. There's nothing but a colony of termites next door. And my whole family is in the dining hall begging for crumbs like the desperate vagabonds they are.*" She sniffled in distaste.

"Okay," I said again, this time in resignation.

If I refused to tell Dazmine what had happened after she'd helped me, I had no doubt she'd only become even more suspicious of my motives and make each of my days a living hell—maybe even report those suspicions to the Good Council. Besides, now that I understood more about Mind Manipulating, I knew that even Lexington wouldn't be able to walk around without a blockade to keep all those thoughts from pouring in. He wouldn't have a reason to lower his and invade her mind. She was just a random classmate of mine as far as he was concerned.

I turned to slip my pearl into my nightstand drawer, where it clinked against the others, and began to quietly describe that space between stars that Steeler had dragged me through. Landing on the pebbled beach by the old lighthouse. Steeler's fangs and ears. The faerie blood he claimed ran through both our veins. The four other faeries waiting inside. Felicity and her tea. Each little bit felt like a weight easing off my chest.

By the time I got to the part about the pendant and the makeshift Branding, Dazmine broke her silence with a sharp, "Let me see it."

I hesitated for a few seconds before swiping away my mass of hair and turning around, letting her and Willa take in the faerie insignia burned against my skin: *the heart does not falter,* apparently.

Willa whistled through her two front teeth.

"Prove it," Dazmine said when I turned back around.

"Prove that I'm part-faerie? I can't. I don't even know if—"

197

"No, no." Dazmine waved a hand as if my supposed faerie heritage couldn't matter less to her. "Prove you can read my mind. What number am I thinking of?"

After a moment's pause, in which I realized she was dead serious, I sighed and lowered my blockade.

Her mental voice blared outward immediately, strong and tinged with that faint, echoing screech, while Willa's thoughts flowed toward me like a smaller, clearer stream. Their overlapping still created a cacophony that made my head start to spin, but it was easier to untangle their mental voices when there were only two of them.

"Seventeen," I told Dazmine.

She narrowed her eyes. "Color?"

"Teal."

She widened them. "Animal?"

"A satanic leaf-tailed gecko."

Now she almost dropped Willa in her shock.

"Holy shit, you really *are* a Mind Manipulator."

"And a Wild Whisperer," I made sure to add, wrapping my blockade back around myself to block out the harsh overlapping her words and thoughts made with Willa's. To my pleasant surprise, the head spinning stopped at once. And come to think of it, none of those paranoia symptoms that Garvis had warned about seemed to be taking root inside my head. A dull ache *had* returned to the base of my skull after leaving Steeler's bamboo scent, but it seemed...

Lighter. More like the ghost of a throb than pain itself.

I didn't feel anything like Jenia Leake had looked in that courtyard, screaming and spitting on her hands and knees.

"Dazmine," I started hesitantly, because I knew we had to get going within the next two minutes and I wasn't sure I wanted to start this conversation now. But if she knew about *my* second brand... "Did you ever see another burn mark like this on Jenia, before she was exiled? Maybe... maybe under her arm?"

Dazmine's head snapped up, confusion creasing her forehead.

"No. Not before the... the incident, at least. After the incident, she was always draped in so many sheets that I never saw anything but her mutilated eyes. But..." The crease of Dazmine's forehead deepened. "She *did* come to visit Jenia in the sick bay, Dyonisia Reeve did, along with a posse of her Good Council elites. She ordered me out and wouldn't let me back in until hours later, just as they were finally leaving." A stiff pause. "Are you telling me you think...?"

That Dyonisia had secretly branded Jenia with Mind Manipulating bascite while she lay there half-delirious? Yes, yes I did.

But before I could say that or elaborate on *why*, a frantic set of footsteps thumped its way toward us from the hallway outside, and I sucked my breath back in as the door burst open to reveal—

Wren?

I stared at the image of her panting in the entrance, my stomach dropping when her wide, frantic eyes bypassed Dazmine and Willa completely and landed on mine. The fact that she appeared to have sprinted here meant something was wrong. Wren didn't *run*.

"Rayna. Come quickly. It's Emelle."

My heart shriveled and exploded all at the same time, flooding me with a fear so potent it seemed to scramble up my lungs.

"What's wrong? Is she okay? Where is she?"

I had just seen her merely twenty minutes ago. If something had happened to her in that measly time fame...

I was already lurching forward, my blockade wavering and my hand reaching for my knife, when Wren shook her head.

"She's safe in the parlor. But a bird just arrived with news about her home village, Merkwell—it's under attack."

CHAPTER

22

I flew downstairs faster than my breath could catch up with me, Wren right on my heels.

As soon as we made it to the parlor, I spotted Emelle bowed over on one of the sofas, surrounded by Cilia, Mitzi, and a small mob of other Wild Whisperers who were all pelting her with questions. Above their heads, a vaguely familiar blue cotinga spiraled in quick, fluttering flurries like a moving fluorescent halo.

"Melle?"

As soon as she looked up and saw me—her eyes rimmed with red—I shouldered my way through the other women and dropped to my knees in front of her to gather her into a hug.

"I'm here," I said into her hair. "What happened?"

I'd heard Wren, of course, and Dyonisia had told me about the pirate attacks on seaside villages last year in the Testing Center, but...

What had Steeler said to me right before he'd Walked me to the lighthouse? *I don't deny the attacks, but they're not what you think.*

And I'd been so overwhelmed with everything afterward that I'd forgotten to ask him to elaborate later.

"I..." Emelle started in a shuddery whisper, "...I made friends with Pedwill last year right after our first quarterly test."

She nodded up at the blue cotinga still zipping in circles over her head, and I suddenly remembered where I'd seen it before. It had been the bird tapping on my window the morning after Lander's party. The one Willa had wanted to strangle.

"My grandpa was sick when I left Merkwell for the Esholian Institute a year ago," Emelle continued, each of her syllables shivering like fracturing glass, "so Pedwill has been flying back and forth, giving me periodic updates on his health."

Emelle's grandpa was sick? She'd never said, never told me. And...

Pedwill. The name of a bird I'd never even *heard* of until now.

My stomach clenched with the realization that Emelle had been keeping secrets of her own... for even though it wasn't strictly *forbidden* to communicate with family back at home, it broke one of the many unspoken rules that always seemed to loom over us alongside the domed shield arching across our sky. Keeping us small. Contained.

Emelle pulled back to look at me, a silent plea swimming in her eyes—a plea to not question it right now.

"I wasn't expecting Pedwill today, but he showed up right after Mrs. Wildenberg's class to tell me that some...some..."

Just as I was wondering if I should drop my blockade to try to access the thoughts that seemed stuck in her throat, her blue cotinga chirped in her stead, " *Those monsters breached the shield and started ravaging the town with Magic! Magic I've never seen before! The villagers tried to defend themselves, but by the time I left to tell Emelle, half the town was already burnt to a crisp! Or torn to pieces!* "

My heart seemed to stall, then pick up again with a resounding beat against my ribs, pumping the first surges of rage through my heart.

Because *burnt to a crisp* and *torn to pieces* sounded *exactly* like what Dyonisia had described in the Testing Center all those months ago.

"Your family?" I managed to breathe.

Emelle shook her head, and Pedwill chimed in again.

"*I couldn't spot them in the chaos!*"

God of the Cosmos. Emelle didn't know if her family was dead or alive. When would the attack end so she could find out? I knew the pirates—faeries—wanted to break their original Good Council out of prison, but Merkwell was at least a hundred miles south of Bascite Mountain. If they'd managed another breach, why the *hell* would they destroy an innocent village on their way? Just to get Dyonisia's attention?

My hands twitched around Emelle's neck, itching to drag my fingernails down Steeler's treacherous face. Who else could have helped the pirates bypass the shield besides someone with the literal power to surpass space itself? If he'd been directly involved in this attack, I would *not* hesitate again before shoving my knife straight between his clavicles.

"Where's Lander?" I asked, pulling back from my hug with Emelle before she could feel the hateful quiver traveling up my legs.

Wren answered from behind my shoulder.

"Gileon went to fetch him."

Okay.

Okay.

All I had to do was wait until Lander arrived before I let that pumping rage propel me into action, spur me forward, and—

Lander came sprinting through the open doorway on elongated legs mere seconds later, surging through everyone to scoop Emelle up against his chest.

As soon as I heard Emelle's muffled sobs finally unleash themselves against his shirt, I scrambled to my feet, hurrying for that doorway just as Gileon came lumbering in with Rodhi following closely behind.

"What'd I miss?" Rodhi asked, panting.

"*Everything*," Wren spat. "Where have you *been*?"

"That's a private matter, darling, but I appreciate your interest." Rodhi blinked at the blue cotinga zipping around Lander and Emelle's conjoined form. "Is this a new mating ritual, or something?"

I didn't wait to hear Wren's outburst to that.

I was already out the door, sprinting across the estuary bridge and through the Wild Whisperer sector until I crashed into the jungle, letting all the leaves and bristles and branches reel me in.

"Jagaros?" I called.

The trees hummed. The thistles at my feet nudged my ankles. Some nearby monkeys giggled as they peeked at me through the leaves. But not a single sarcastic growl ripped through the wildlife.

Of course not. I'd told him to not bother coming back. Jagaros was probably on the other end of the island by now, and honestly good for him. Because the accusations I wanted to scream at him would make even the top of the food chain cower and curl their tail.

But I still pushed myself forward until I was sandwiched between two colossal surface roots of a nearby tree and pressed my forehead against its moss-slick trunk, inhaling the heavy, sappy scent of it.

"Is Jagaros nearby?" I breathed into it.

The tree's humming intensified, springing into a chaotic melody that told me *yes*, Jagaros was, however inexplicably, nearby.

"Where?" I asked.

Again, that humming increased its tempo, and suddenly a branch was curling around my waist, another one wrapping around my legs.

And hoisting me up.

Through snarled limbs and vines that parted a path for me, past lizards freezing on bark, snakes looped lazily around boughs, frogs, monkeys, and even a singular sloth dripping with moss.

My stomach bottomed out as the branches fed me to a neighboring tree that grabbed me with stiffer, clawlike limbs and passed me to *another* tree. And another and another.

Deeper and deeper, the jungle carried me along its braided chain.

Until it finally plopped me down gently on a bed of branches somewhere in the upper half of the canopy, where waxy leaves the size of my face cradled either side of me and a pair of fierce yellow eyes fixed onto mine.

"*Interesting,*" Jagaros said, uncrossing his paws.

He appeared to have been lounging in a flattened fork in the tree, but now his ears pricked on high alert as I readjusted myself, straddling one branch while I gripped another one with a tight fist.

"Hello," I forced myself to say. For manners' sake.

"*I thought you no longer wished to talk to me.*" Jagaros's pupils had gone arrow-straight as they focused on my face. "*Or are you done throwing a temper tantrum like you're three years old again?*"

"That depends." I blew away a hawk moth fluttering near my face. "Are you going to give me one straightforward answer this time?"

"*That depends,*" Jagaros retorted. "*Are you going to ask questions that won't jeopardize all of our safety while you're still learning to protect the secrets in your mind?*"

No. The answer to that was no. This time, I planned to ask him all the questions I wanted and eavesdrop on the hidden thoughts simmering right behind that feline skull. It definitely felt like a massive invasion of his privacy, but if Emelle's village had been attacked by pirates and Jagaros was working with them...

I let it dissolve around me, my blockade.

Then I said, "I *knew* you were working with Steeler this whole time. You sound just like him."

There. Let him deny it out loud but confirm it mentally.

But when Jagaros spoke, his outer thoughts matched his verbal growls so precisely, the two sounds merged into one.

"*I'll take that as a compliment, Rayna Drey, given Coen Steeler's the only one I approve of for you.*"

I was too stuffed full of shocked rage to even scoff at that.

"Okay, one, you're not either of my dads."

I pushed down the urge to think of Fabian and Don right now. I missed them hard enough to hurt, and the idea that *they* might be next, that Alderwick might suffer the same attack as Merkwell...

"Two," I pushed on, "*I* don't approve of Steeler for me. Did you know that his precious pirate family just demolished most of Emelle's village? That her family might be *dead* because of him?"

I could feel the quivering take over my entire body now, and the branch I straddled actually seemed to be tensing, as if preparing for me to fall or lunge toward Jagaros and claw his eyes out.

But Jagaros didn't even blink.

"*Those monsters weren't pirates that attacked Merkwell.*"

My quivering stopped. My very heartbeat stopped.

"What? How do you know? What were they, then?"

Once again, Jagaros's mental and verbal words merged into one, his stark honesty evident in the absence of even the faintest echo.

"*Something far more unstable and dangerous. I do not know any more than that.*"

He paused as that sunk into my gut like a vise clamping down.

Steeler hadn't been involved in the attack today.

None of the pirates had.

I don't deny the attacks, but they're not what you think—Steeler hadn't been lying when he'd said those words to me on his knees.

When Jagaros eyed me now, his pupils softened.

"*You are correct in your assumption that I have been working with Coen Steeler. Not often, I might add, but whenever it is necessary for your protection. His mind called out to mine when he left you all those months ago, asking me to take care of you. His mind called out to mine again merely a week ago, telling me his plan to offer you Mind Manipulating power.*"

So he knew. Jagaros knew I could read his outer thoughts right now, even if I hadn't yet learned to dive into his mind to access his inner ones.

My lungs twisted in my chest as I raked in a breath and let it out again on a question that seemed to hover uncertainly between us. A question that had been hovering uncertainly between us for a while.

"And why *are* you protecting me, Jagaros? What am I to you?" I almost stopped there, but if I was expecting honesty from him, I knew I'd better deliver my own, even in the way I shaped my questions. "Why are you so invested in my safety, but no one else's? Why are you comfortable talking to me, but no other Wild Whisperer?"

This time, Jagaros kept his maw shut.

But I heard every desperate thought break free from his constraint of silence anyway.

Once upon a time, it was I who ruled this island in a different body. I was the faerie king of old, in harmony with my people... until she came and conquered.

I knew who *she* was even though his mind couldn't seem to conjure her image without clamming up. Dyonisia, of course.

I froze in my position in the tree, reeling in every unspoken word.

She conquered, and I could do nothing to protect my people, not truly, not as a rightful king should have. But you, Rayna Drey... Pain and regret and something even more ancient swelled in the cracks of his thoughts. *You are a faerie born on this island, just as my people were. So maybe I can save you in ways I couldn't save them.*

A lump burned its way up my throat.

Perhaps I had known, deep down, that when Steeler had said Dyonisia swept away the indigenous clan of faeries, he'd been talking about *Jagaros's* clan. But that didn't make the lump burn any less.

"I'm sorry, Jagaros. For everything you lost." I reached out and placed my hand over his paw. When he didn't move away from me, I said carefully, "Does this mean I need to bow to you?"

Jagaros gave a snarling laugh that lightened some of the density in his eyes.

"*No. What you need to do is focus on your Mind Manipulating lessons with Steeler. And keep practicing defending yourself with that knife in case you're ever in a position where either of your magics are nullified.*" He placed his other paw on top of my hand for a brief moment before hefting himself up. "*And no, Coen Steeler didn't ask me to train you with the knife. That was my idea... perhaps born of my frustration that I don't currently have proper hands of my own.*"

I furrowed my eyebrows at that.

Why *didn't* Jagaros have hands of his own? If he'd once ruled the island in a different body—a faerie body, I assumed—did that mean he was a Shape Shifter who'd become stuck in this alternate form? Or had Dyonisia cursed him, somehow?

It wasn't in me to pry even further, however. Not when Jagaros had already given me the one truth that mattered most:

I truly was a faerie born on this island. Which meant Dyonisia was not my only ruler—*he* was, too.

And for now, that ruler wanted me to train.

I pulled my blockade back over myself like a shroud.

"Well, if I'm going to focus on Mind Manipulating and defense, I need to get Kitterfol Lexington's weekly interrogations out of my way."

CHAPTER

23

On the morning Lexington was due to arrive, I woke up to meager veins of sunlight straining through our window's foliage and felt my heart sink at the sight of them landing on Emelle's empty bed.

Over the last five days, the news about Merkwell had spread across campus in both whispers and wails. The older Wild Whisperers had sent some other birds back to the village to check for survivors, but the birds had yet to return, and none of our instructors seemed to want to address it—except Mrs. Smetlar, who'd given a smug, "See? This is what happens when you don't have enough control of your magic to ward off outside threats" during Tuesday's class.

To which Rodhi had called her an ugly old bogsucker.

To which Mrs. Smetlar had slapped him across the face with a stuffed iguana and assigned him more after-class eyeball polishing.

Emelle had stayed quiet through it all, a ghostly paleness permanently stamped over her face. The birdfeeder on her bedside table was empty, save for a few cracked shells, and she hadn't made any moves to refill it. She spent every free moment outside of class—including nights—with Lander, and...

Guilt nipped at me, to be honest. All of my masks and shields and secrets had kept me from being the person who could hold her together when she was falling apart.

I'd have to think about that later. For now, I had a sadistic, too-powerful Good Council elite to scare off.

Just as I was pushing back my covers to try to slip out of bed without waking Cilia or Dazmine, a dark, fathomless presence pushed against my blockade.

I sucked in a string of curses and fell backward into my own mind, landing on that snowy patch of ground with the ice-slathered wall before me, the vast expanse of nothingness behind me, and...

Steeler leaning casually against my wall.

"Knock, knock."

"What are you *doing* here?" I stomped over to him in the spotlight of the crescent moon.

In the real world, I could feel my body still lying in bed, eyes closed and heart battering furiously. In here, though, my eyes had to have been *blazing* and my heart was hulking down like a tiger, poised to attack this... this *intruder*.

I had to call him an intruder or else my hypocritical, devious mind might forget that he wasn't just a finely cut male pinning me with beautiful eyes that dared to blaze back.

"Well, I was hoping you'd let me in," Steeler drawled, nodding at my colossal gateway. "So that I could test out all your internal blockades, make sure all your sensitive memories of last weekend are still hidden before Lexington interrogates you today."

I stared at him, caught between telling him to get the hell out and finding it kind of... thoughtful that he hadn't just forced his way in. I knew I wasn't yet a strong enough Mind Manipulator to keep that gate locked and secured if he—

No. I shook my head. Him asking my permission was the bare minimum. Just because he'd barged his way in before didn't mean I should start drooling over the fact that he'd waited long enough to ask me this time.

"Go ahead," I said dryly. "But I doubt you'll even find them."

Indeed, I'd spent the last few nights lying in bed just exploring my own mind before I fell asleep, continuing to pack in the walls of ice around my forbidden memories until that part of the maze completely blended in with its surroundings—the swirling mist of it muffled behind another frozen part of me. I'd even hidden my conversations with Jagaros and Dazmine as best as I could.

Steeler was gone in a blink. When he returned merely thirty seconds later, I blurted, "You can Walk inside my own mind?"

"The benefits of having two powers that merge," he said, leaning against my wall as if he'd never left. "Well, I've got to say, Drey—you were right. I couldn't find a single memory of last weekend. Of course I didn't look for long, but unless Lexington plans to do another full-scale investigation today and knock down every wall in sight..." His lip curled up at that. "... I don't think he'll ever know."

"Great," I bit out. "Thank you for the maintenance check. Now go back—" I pushed against his chest. "—to your lighthouse before Lexington finds traces of you in here."

Steeler caught my hands over his chest and held them there, all the smugness draining away as his expression hardened into stone.

"I've kept my distance during his interrogations with you until now, Drey, but if you think I'm going to leave you alone after knowing that he actually *hurt* you..."

"Let me guess," I said mockingly. "I'm an even bigger fool than you thought?"

"... then I haven't made it clear enough I'm never leaving you alone with him again," Steeler finished firmly.

Oh. Well, I couldn't tell if that was a promise or a threat.

"It would be my fucking *pleasure* to kickstart an even bigger war with Dyonisia if he does it again," Steeler continued, lips mashing together—to hold back a snarl or something else, I couldn't tell. "So no, I'm not going back to that lighthouse yet, especially not while you're attempting to trick the most powerful Mind Manipulator on the island."

For a moment, I forgot to try to tug my hands away, so overcome by the wicked promise glittering in his eyes.

Then I remembered Emelle and the empty bed next to mine.

"Maybe you should start a war over whatever dangerous, unstable things are attacking Esholian villages." I ripped myself out of his grasp. "Do you have any idea what they might be if they're not pirates? Your pal Jagaros wouldn't tell me."

To my surprise, Steeler flinched as if I'd delivered a blow. He glanced sideways, toward that large expanse of nothingness circling my mind, and dragged a hand through his hair.

"I don't know exactly who—or what—is attacking the villages either," he sighed, apparently deciding to ignore the sarcasm I'd used in reference to Jagaros. "Whatever they are, they *are* dangerous, they *are* unstable, and I *would* dispatch a fleet to annihilate them if I could."

The way he scowled at that last part made me feel like I was missing another chunk of context. And also made me want to put my fingers on his face, to smooth out the sudden harsh lines creasing his features.

I refrained, of course, and when I didn't ask any more questions, Steeler hefted himself off my wall to loom over me.

"I will be right outside that same classroom where you first held a knife against my throat, little hurricane. If our plan goes sideways, if Lexington so much as makes your heartbeat falter..." He reached out and brushed his thumb right over the pulse that would be fluttering beneath my neck in real life before removing it again faster than I could strike him away. "...I'll be there to end his before he can take another breath."

My enemy. Coen Steeler was my Good Council-declared enemy who definitely didn't have a strong jawline clenching with a kind of violence I found attractive. He definitely wasn't staring at me as if *I* was the thing his world revolved around. And his thumb *definitely* hadn't sparked electricity against my throat when he'd—

God of the Cosmos, it was so much harder to control my thoughts in my own mind than it was in the outside world where I could distract myself with classes or conversations.

I clenched my own jaw and leaned closer to him, looking up into the smoky quartz of his eyes that could probably devour me whole if I drank them in for long enough. But I wanted Steeler to *feel* exactly how steady and controlled my breath was against his lips.

I wanted him to know I could handle this all on my own.

"My heartbeat will not falter."

Twenty minutes later, I was in the dining hall, asking the house cook for two plates of breakfasts—battered toast sprinkled with cinnamon and coconut flakes this morning.

I sat down, but didn't touch my food, even when other Wild Whisperers filtered in with yawns and curious expressions shot my way. Some of them waved, but when I waved back, I made sure to do it with a grimace before throwing my head back into my hands and massaging my temples—the Esholian Institute sign for *I'm messed up right now so please leave me alone.*

I simply waited.

And waited.

And waited.

Finally, I felt the air in the room stir as everyone was forced to look away. Felt the slimy presence of Lexington stride into the room, where he blinked down at the second plate of breakfast before me.

"What is this?"

Hurriedly, I dropped my blockade before he could sense even the thinnest veil of Mind Manipulating magic from me, expecting the thoughts of everyone else in the room to come rushing into my head.

Instead, I was greeted with silence. As if Lexington had smothered everyone's thoughts as well as forced them to turn their heads away.

Trying not to look shocked, I pushed the second plate toward him, nodding at the chair across from me.

"You're late. Better eat before it gets even colder."

Lexington had always managed to catch me off guard before now. Now, I wanted him to know I'd been *awaiting* him. That I had the upper hand here.

Eyes slitting with suspicion, Lexington dragged the chair back, sat, and dove into my mind without further ado. As usual.

But this time... this time...

I tried so hard not to gasp.

Because I could *see* it this time. The outside world was a hazy film in the background, while this internal one was where Lexington's monstrous form fell with a thud against my snowy ground.

He was ten times bigger than a black mamba but without the face or tail of one. Tiny bristles along his slick, fleshy body propelled him forward as he plunged through the gateway that led to my maze.

I refrained from sprinting after him and forced myself to stand perfectly still in the snow.

Garvis had told me Lexington wouldn't notice anything strange about my internal presence as long as I didn't do anything out of the ordinary in here—like look him in the eye or run after him. The only difference now that I was a Mind Manipulator was that instead of a vague understanding of which memories he was observing, I could *hear* them play for him as he dug deeper into my mind. The sounds floated over my walls in tendrils of mist.

I shall be glad to watch the Good Council throw many more of you to sea after you fail your Final Tests, Mrs. Smetlar said.

You are adults, and it's your own lives at stake if you don't take this class seriously, Ms. Pincette said.

What use do we have for our carnivorous friends? Mrs. Wildenberg asked.

Your job today is to find a black mamba and trick them into leaving the Esholian Institute, Mr. Conine said.

You bitch! the sluggish boy wailed in the distance. *You ruined me! You hurt me! I'm going to tell the Good Council!*

I felt Kitterfol Lexington pause at that one, amused and smug—just as I'd hoped. With him so thoroughly distracted, he didn't notice any holes in any of the memories: no Dazmine, no Jagaros, no Walking. No lighthouse or Felicity or secret Branding. No Steeler.

Until he came to our reenactment, of course.

Then, the creak of me opening that abandoned classroom door on Sunday night and the stomp of my footsteps as I stalked toward him with my knife on Monday morning blended into one, as if nothing between those two moments had ever happened.

Answer my questions, or I'll mutilate your magic, I said. *What is this?* I could practically see myself reaching forward with my free hand and digging in his front shirt pocket to bring out the pill. *What does it do to me every week? Why do you make me take it?*

And then, after he'd forced me to swallow it, Lexington heard Steeler say, *It's a new stimulator I came up with. To control you from afar. To make you want me even when you're the only damned woman who's never wanted me before... From the moment it kicks in until the moment it fades, you will think of me.*

Among those other things that I refused to let get to me again.

As soon as Lexington withdrew himself from my mind, the mists dissolved. The background film of reality snapped back into place.

"You *have* to get one of those pills for me, girl."

I tried not to smirk at the way his eyes were popping. How his reaction played right into my hands.

Lifting my fork, I popped a square of toast into my mouth and chewed slowly, pretending to savor it.

Lexington watched me, veins straining beneath the skin of his forehead. "You better not be mocking—"

I swallowed and smacked my lips.

"What do you want me to do, sir? Puke up my next pill and try to give you its vomity remains? Or..." I dared to lean forward onto my elbows, even though every ounce of me wanted to cringe away. "Do you want me to find Steeler's entire stash of pills, figure out how they're made, and steal a whole supply of them for you?"

Lexington's eyes flashed with surprise, and I knew I almost had him snared. All I had to do was plough on.

"I know I won't be able to think straight while the pills are in my system, but you heard Steeler in the memory," I said. "The effects eventually fade. So if I can just get close enough to him, earn his trust back, then I can strike right between the fading and the next dose when my head clears."

I could see the realization spread across Lexington's pocked face. That for the first time since Dyonisia's initial meeting with me in the Testing Center, he might need me for his own private gain rather than hers.

He leaned back and stroked the ball of his throat.

"The pills work, then? You truly feel drawn to Coen Steeler when they're active in your system? Never mind." He waved a hand. "I can see it etched all over your barren little mind."

I forced my mouth to smile even when it wanted to snarl.

"Yes. But I won't be able to get close enough to him to steal those pills for you unless you give me space for a while. Let me pretend to... submit. To stop fighting him every second. Because *that* coupled with your weekly visits are keeping him dancing just out of reach." I stabbed my fork into my toast. "So I don't care what you tell Dyonisia Reeve—whether you pretend to keep checking up on me or not—if you want those pills, you need to. Leave. Me. *Alone.*"

Once again, Lexington's monstrous form dropped into my mind with that oily precision, until I found myself face-to-face with his giant worm. Staring at him from both within my mind and outside it.

Are you lying to me? the worm asked from a gaping mouth bursting with sharp teeth: Lexington's voice in my head, personified.

I froze, feeling the truth bubble in my mental mouth, feeling the shadow of a dark, fathomless energy hover as if prepared to pounce down on the invasion in my mind. Then—

No, I'm not, I said clearly.

Well, damn. I guess I *could* lie now that I was a Mind Manipulator of my own.

Lexington withdrew again. I blinked at him as if nothing out of the ordinary had happened—as if he'd simply demanded the truth from an innocent Wild Whisperer's head and nothing more.

"Get me those pills, girl," he said finally, standing with a swish of his cloak and a tap of his finger against his brand, "and I'll get you a seat on the Good Council... if you pass your Final Test, that is."

I watched him go, the short burst of elation at my success quickly washed away by the realization of what he'd just offered me at the end of all this.

CHAPTER

24

I expected Steeler to spring back into my mind as soon as Lexington left.

He didn't. It was only when afternoon brought a warm gush of rain over campus that I heard his voice in my head, but it had nothing to do with Lexington.

Bring Dazmine Temperton into the jungle tomorrow morning. Terrin's keeping his word.

As his voice faded, I felt the first nips of agitation crawling through my veins.

All that talk about starting wars for me and he wasn't even going to give me a "good job" when I succeeded at a dangerous task all on my own? Had he truly just loitered on campus long enough to make sure I was alive, then Walked away without asking me for any of the details? I had actually lied to an accomplished Mind Manipulator, for God's sake! Surely, that was worth noting since I hadn't even had a full week to develop my new power yet?

Whatever. I didn't care, I didn't care, I didn't *care*. I hadn't been expecting him this morning anyway, so any kind of congratulations afterward would have just been excessive.

By Sunday, though, my teeth were still grinding together while I ran various errands on campus: washing my dresses and nightgowns in the house laundry room by the dining hall; sending a letter to Fabian and Don via crow, telling them to be prepared for any kind of emergency; leaving another note for Dazmine before I left to go forage in the jungle for seeds to refill Emelle's birdfeeder for her.

It was just as I was rubbing the last of the seeds from the safflower heads that a chorus of low voices permeated the dense foliage.

I turned, pushing a branch aside and squinting through the murk of muggy air and swirling gnats.

Mr. Gleekle? Yes, that was definitely the institute president traipsing through the jungle, his glasses and cheeks sparkling with condensation and sweat while seven or eight students followed closely behind him.

What sector were they from? Did Mr. Gleekle even teach any classes? I'd always suspected he was an Element Wielder based on the way he sent an unnatural wind to carry his voice during ceremonies and games, but I couldn't see why he'd be teaching on a weekend.

I stepped closer, my foot cracking through a half-disintegrated log...

"Rayna."

A hand touched me on the back of my shoulder and I whirled, dropping my basket of seeds to brandish my knife.

A familiar pair of scornful eyes squinted at the tip of the blade near her nose.

"Dazmine," I breathed out, slipping the knife back into its sheath immediately and cursing under my breath at all the spilled birdseed scattered around my feet on the jungle floor. "You shouldn't just go around spooking people like that."

Dazmine scoffed. "And you shouldn't go around waving a murder weapon in someone's face just because you're apparently too deaf to hear them walk up to you. *You* asked *me* to meet you here, remember?" She glanced over my shoulder. "What were you looking at, anyway?"

"I... I'm not sure." I peered back through the gaps in the foliage, but Mr. Gleekle and his posse of students had moved on. "Probably nothing."

Dazmine planted her hands on her hips, apparently uninterested in *probably nothing*. "We never finished our conversation earlier this week. About Dyonisia giving Jenia a second brand after the incident."

Right. Because one of our island's villages had fallen prey to monstrous attacks that no one seemed to know anything about. Bending to scoop handfuls of the salvageable seeds and nuts back into the basket, I motioned for her to continue.

"I've been thinking back," she said, "trying to remember details about little odd comments Jenia would make about this or that, hints that she might have dropped long before the incident itself."

I straightened again to face her.

"And?"

It didn't make sense. How could Jenia have possibly known about the possibility of her second Branding before it even happened?

Dazmine yanked in a deep breath. "And she mentioned that her sister... knew things. Secrets. About the Good Council. About the island itself. And about *you*, Rayna."

"Me? What secrets could Kimber Leake have known about *me*?"

Of course, I'd had plenty of secrets to snatch last year, from the sounds of it. But if the Good Council hadn't become suspicious enough to investigate until the very end, I didn't know why or how the princess of our house would have been prattling about my forbidden faerie blood to her younger sister.

"Jenia liked to... dangle information just out of people's reach," Dazmine admitted quietly. "Not to keep others safe, like you do, but to keep them constantly in... want of her." A grimace twisted her face, but Dazmine hurried on. "So Jenia never specified what she was actually talking about. But she seemed to think *you* were a danger to the entire island. And that if she could help get rid of you, using Fergus's wounded pride as a way to get him to do the dirty work for her, she'd be given the same special privileges as her sister."

My frown deepened as I mulled over every one of those absurd statements.

"She thought she'd be given special privileges like a princess title if she *killed* me? That literally goes against one of the only three rules here at the Esholian Institute."

"I don't know. I'm not even sure she meant the princess title at all." Dazmine hesitated, chewing on the inside of her cheek. "But if Jenia knew there was a possibility she could get a second brand—a second *magic*—she would have done anything to achieve that goal."

We both stood there in a state of troubled contemplation, letting the buzzing and humming of insects and plant life wash over us, until Dazmine seemed to shake herself from her reverie with a shake of her head.

"Regardless, Jenia didn't actually kill you *or* Fergus. And she shouldn't be exiled for a murder your boyfriend committed. So I'm still waiting for you to fulfill your end of the bargain by—"

"Hold up." In my jolt of disbelief, I almost dropped the damn basket of birdfeed again. "One, Steeler is *not* my boyfriend. Two, I *did* fulfill my end of the bargain even though it was an absolutely ludicrous thing to ask of me. That's why I told you to meet me here."

Dazmine pretended to survey our surroundings.

"Really? You brought me back a pirate? That's funny, I don't see any of them around, but perhaps they're experts in the art of camouflage."

"Nah," came a vaguely familiar voice from behind us, each of his words brimming with laughter that seemed to rumble the earth beneath our feet, "you're just not looking hard enough."

Dazmine twirled with her fists extended.

A breath later, Steeler emerged casually from the foliage, his Element Wielder friend with the grizzled red hair stepping out beside him.

Terrin grinned at Dazmine.

"I heard you wanted to hold me hostage."

CHAPTER

25

Dazmine struck.

With a violent whistle through her teeth, the bulbous roots of a nearby tree came lashing out toward Terrin like a whip.

Only to meet a sudden gust of muggy wind that pushed it back.

"Oh, you want to play first?" Terrin tilted his head.

Dazmine didn't answer. She was already crouching with a hum, telling the ferns and hawthorns to lasso his ankles and pull him down.

As soon as they did, Terrin sent a tornado of soil shooting upward, ripping through the shrubs and propelling him back to his feet.

Which prompted Dazmine to send a horde of mosquitos at him.

Which prompted Terrin to fling a cloud of smoke at the horde to suffocate them in midair.

Before I could get pummeled with either one of their magics, I sidled off to where Steeler was leaning against a tree, observing the proceedings with a mix of amusement and exasperation.

"How long do you think they'll go at it?" he asked without looking my way.

Well, if he wasn't going to turn to face me, I wouldn't so much as glance at him either.

"Knowing Dazmine... a while," I admitted.

Steeler snorted. "Knowing Terrin, they'll be at it all night. I'll give them a few more minutes before I Walk them both to the lighthouse where they can battle it out there instead of where someone might hear us."

Not that it was unusual for random bursts of magic to rattle various parts of the jungle on the weekends as students practiced, but I could see his point: if anyone actually saw *who* was rattling this part of the jungle, they might recognize Terrin as someone who didn't belong to the Esholian Institute—or the island at all anymore.

"I'm shocked you actually brought him here," I said.

And okay, maybe my tone was a bit snippy, but Steeler *still wouldn't look at me*. He *always* looked at me. Too much looking, in fact. And yet now that I'd succeeded in warding off one of my greatest threats for the time being, he wasn't going to spare a single glance in my direction?

"Like I've said before, Drey, you've already involved her." Out of the corner of my eye, I saw him cross his arms over his chest, his sharp ears poking through his hair with the movement. "And from my experience, if we don't give someone the answers they're seeking, they'll just start meddling. Which would cause a bigger problem for all of us."

"How pragmatic of you."

We both resumed watching Terrin and Dazmine throw Element Wielding against Wild Whispering, earth and wind and fire and air against all the insects and plant life in the vicinity.

I had to admit, Dazmine was... good at talking to the jungle. It followed her hums and whistles like war cries, reacting to her voice with passion and violence as opposed to the usual gentleness it offered me.

But soon enough, a whisper pushed against my blockade—like thoughts floating on a muffled wind—and I knew instinctually that a group of people were moving closer to our location.

Perhaps Mr. Gleekle and his mysterious posse of students were coming back, or maybe it was just a group of friends passing by, messing around during their free time...

Either way, I wasn't surprised when Steeler disappeared in a flash, reappearing right between Dazmine and Terrin only long enough to let his eyes land on mine from across the trampled, battered space of jungle between us.

Then he reached out to grab them both, and they all three blinked out of existence. Leaving me alone.

I cringed at the thought of Dazmine experiencing that dragging darkness for herself. But if she was going to make such a ruckus in response to her wish coming true exactly as she'd asked for it...

Quietly, I crooned to the roots and vines and ferns, urging them to retreat back into their original positions. I couldn't do anything about the pile of ashes littered here and there or the various holes in the ground that Terrin had made, but soon the undergrowth swallowed up any evidence of his magic as it regrouped itself in response to my voice.

"You're good at that, you know."

Steeler had returned.

I kept my back to him, bending to stroke the safflowers on their quivering, serrated leaves.

"Good at what?"

"Good at encouraging. At healing. At growing."

I snorted. "Maybe the right version of me is, but this is the wrong version of me, so no, I'm not good at *healing* or *growing* right now." I clutched my basket harder. "I can barely manage to keep my best friend's birdfeeder full for her. But you know what I *am* good at, Steeler?"

When he didn't answer right away, I couldn't handle it any longer—I straightened and rounded on him.

A jolt ran down my body, right to my toes, when I discovered how close he'd truly been lurking behind me.

"What else are you good at, little hurricane?" Steeler whispered.

I wiggled my toes to try to stop them from tingling. "Lying to Kitterfol Lexington."

"Oh, I know. I was watching the whole thing. You did lovelier than I could have ever dreamed of—and I dream of you quite a bit." He paused, his attention roving over every curve and dip of my face. "Is that what you wanted to hear, Drey? That you did lovely?"

By the orchid and the owl, I would *not* blush for this man.

"Or," Steeler pressed on, eroding the distance between us with half a stride, "did you want to hear that I was going out of my God-forsaken mind while you faced that monster alone? That it *killed* me to simply hover and wait while he barged through the mist of your mind?"

"I—that's not—"

I stumbled back.

His hand shot out and caught me by the small of my back.

"*Or* did you want to hear that I was so sure our plan would fail, so sure a Mind Manipulator in her first week couldn't conceal memories from a Mind Manipulator in his fifteenth *year* that I had my fucking sleeves already rolled up, ready to progress the course of fate

227

faster than intended? That when you stepped away victorious, I couldn't bear to face you because I knew if I did, I would grab you and pull you in close and never let you go again?"

He *was* pulling me in close now, my breasts curving into the hollow beneath his chest. The tingling in my toes hadn't gone away—it had traveled upward again, swirling around the warm pressure of his hand against my back.

"What I want," I breathed up at him, "is to go check on Dazmine and learn some new Mind Manipulating tricks from Garvis. That's it."

Lies, lies, lies.

But with my blockade up, my thoughts wouldn't be floating out to him right now, and I could tell he hadn't lunged into my own mind for a taste of that subconscious truth that sat in its regal shrine.

"Well, good," Steeler finally said on a stiff exhale, "because Garvis spent all week preparing his lesson plan for you, and Felicity's currently destroying the kitchen in her attempts to make a three-course meal."

"Well, good. Let's go, then."

"Fine."

"Fine."

There was no need for me to grab his hand this time. Not with his arm still locked tight around me.

The darkness simply picked us up and carried us away.

After Walking me to my room—empty, thank God—so that I could dump my remaining birdseed into Emelle's feeder, Steeler whisked us straight into the lighthouse itself.

Here, Dazmine was glaring at Terrin from where she stood against the edge of the room, her body tense and ready to spring into action at any moment, like a rabid animal backed into a corner.

In the kitchen, Felicity clattered through the cupboards, singing a jaunty tune about a homeless sea monster amid boiling pots and sizzling pans. Next to the fireplace, Garvis gave me an awkward wave.

"Well, this is probably the most conflicting atmosphere I've ever witnessed," Steeler muttered, withdrawing himself from me.

I ignored how his absence lingered around me like a cold sheet as Felicity spotted me, swung off the countertop, and leapt into my arms.

"*Raynie! You're here! I can't wait for you to try my chickpea stew. Coco and I spent the week gathering herbs and spices for it, and I even nabbed a handful of peanuts for garnish.*"

"Sounds like it'll be delicious." I made a show of inhaling the swirling scents of oregano and cumin before glancing over at Dazmine and lowering my voice. "How is she holding up?"

The monkey's face turned solemn. "*Not well. She dry-heaved for a good few minutes, then tried to get me to bite* his *head off as soon as she recovered.*" Felicity nodded at Terrin. "*Which is gross, by the way. I don't eat heads.*"

"I can hear you both, you know," Dazmine intoned, sending the briefest glance my way. "And I just think it's funny that I asked *for* a hostage, not to be *taken* hostage."

For once, Terrin's smile was faltering.

"What more do you want from me, woman? I literally risked my life to come tell you the truth about your friend's exile. But you tried to decapitate me before I could do so." His non-smile turned into a downright glare. "So yeah, we had to bring you here where no one can hear me scream if you continue to try to decapitate me."

"*I'd* hear you scream," Steeler remarked, snatching a peanut from Felicity's stock on the counter and popping it in his mouth before the monkey could beat his hand away.

"As would I," said Garvis from the fireplace.

I winced but raised a hand. "As would I."

"Truly, a male's dreamiest end," Terrin remarked without taking his eyes off Dazmine. "To bellow, not into a void, but straight into his friends' ears."

For the strangest slice of a second, a ripple of warmth went through me at the thought that Terrin might consider me a friend even though I didn't remember a single interaction before last week.

Then Dazmine was turning all her spiteful, spitting rage onto Steeler.

"Brave of you to joke, when you're the one who killed Fergus."

The temperature in the room seemed to flake away. Even the flames behind Garvis fluttered, as if caught in all of our inhales.

"Do you deny it?" Dazmine asked, nostrils flaring, and even I cringed internally at the brazen way she faced him, her hands curled.

"No, I don't deny it," Steeler said finally, his posture tightening. "You want to know why?" When Dazmine didn't answer, he hissed, "Because that little asshole was about to fill *her* body with rot..." He didn't have to point at me for everyone in the room to know who he was referring to. "Just like he did to your good old Mr. Fenway last year."

Dazmine's eyes widened at the same time mine did. Steeler took the opportunity to let out a mirthless laugh that rippled down my spine.

"You didn't know about that? You didn't know that he used his weird obsession with fungus to murder one of your instructors and was planning on doing the same to your classmate? Well, guess what?

Jenia Leake *did*. She was *in* on it. So maybe it's a good thing she's in prison, huh?"

With that, Steeler stomped toward the cottage door, wrenched it open, and slammed it shut again behind him.

In the ringing silence that followed, Dazmine's shoulders sagged.

"Prison?" she whispered.

Terrin turned toward her, something keen and inquisitive in the way he observed the pinch of her eyebrows.

He jerked his head at the kitchen table.

"Why don't you sit down like a good human, and I can tell you everything?"

For a moment, it looked as if Dazmine was contemplating being a very *bad* human. She glanced at the knife block behind Felicity, then at Terrin's throat. Terrin responded by blowing her a kiss of smoke.

Finally, Dazmine gritted her teeth and stomped over to the table.

Five minutes later, with steaming bowls of chickpea stew in front of everyone—save for Steeler, who still hadn't returned—Terrin and Garvis told us everything about the exiled ones. How they weren't thrown out to sea like we'd always been told, but hauled up to Bascite Mountain and experimented on. Tortured. Locked away alongside the original five members of the Sorronian Good Council. The information sounded vaguely familiar, as if it had been uprooted from a dream in the frigid foundation of my mind.

When they were done explaining, Dazmine was silent for a long time.

Terrin tracked the way she gnawed on her lip, deep in thought.

Finally, Dazmine looked up, not at Terrin, but at me.

"I will never forgive Jenia for what she tried to do... but nobody deserves torture. Not her, and certainly not all the other exiled ones that have been brought up there over the last five centuries."

I nodded. The shock of re-learning what my previous classmates had planned to do to me tasted acrid in my mouth, like I'd swallowed a memory too fast. But Dazmine was right—nobody deserved what loomed over the island at the top of Bascite Mountain.

Apparently satisfied that I understood her sentiment, Dazmine swung her gaze back to Terrin, and they clashed like blades. One expression dry and unforgiving, the other glinting with sparks.

"I want to help," she said. "I want to help break everyone out of that prison."

Garvis and I exchanged surprised glances. Terrin's mouth slashed into his widest grin yet.

"Welcome to the pirate side, Temperton."

When Garvis suggested we take our Mind Manipulating lesson outside, I didn't hesitate before agreeing.

Mostly, I wanted to escape the tension bursting in the cottage now that I was sure Dazmine and Terrin weren't going to slit each other's throats. But a quiet, sly part of me also wanted to catch a glimpse of Steeler—to see where he'd stomped off to. To find out if his mood had calmed.

Only, Steeler wasn't outside at all. There wasn't even a distant figure on the beach to indicate he'd gone on a long walk. He must have used his power to leave this part of the island entirely.

Which made that quiet, sly part of me wilt with the smallest sliver of disappointment.

The view was beautiful, though. The faintest beginnings of a sunset were just barely skimming over the water, turning the foamy shoreline a murky pink. Seagulls picked their way across the rocks, yelling at each other over who had claimed which crustacean, but not in an unpleasant way. The soft pulse of an ocean breeze swished fresh, salty air across my face.

After Garvis and I were both sitting cross-legged next to the dark imprint of the tideline, I smiled at him.

"So Steeler told me you made an entire lesson plan for me today. Do I finally get to learn how to control people?"

Not that I wanted to control anyone, necessarily. But if Lexington ever told me to choke myself again, it would be nice to throw a little of his own Mind Manipulating games back at him.

Garvis only shook his head.

"Not quite. I'm afraid that controlling somebody else's actions is usually a fifth-year thing. But even so, we'll be skipping several months of normal Mind Manipulating lessons to start working on one I'm hoping would benefit you the most right now."

The sound of the sea beating against the island seemed to pick up speed.

"Oh?"

"Yes." Garvis smiled. "I think it's time we start the hunt for your missing memories."

CHAPTER

26

Back in the maze of my mind, Garvis and I had just meandered down another twisting alleyway where ice towered over either side of us when he flung out an arm.

"There. See that little memory tucked away in the corner?"

I squinted at the moving mist in a nook of an alleyway. It appeared to depict Emelle and me walking arm in arm down a crowded Esholian Institute square.

"Yes, I see it. It looks normal to—"

"Watch again."

Frowning, I moved closer until I could clearly hear the echo of my past conversation with Emelle, both of us chattering away as we wove a path through all the Cardina peddlers from last year, occasionally stopping to inspect various bits of merchandise.

Right after I brought out a little copper coin to pay for two chocolate truffles—one for Emelle and one for me—the memory made a sharp V turn. Now, the two of us were heading toward Grandma

Gretel's gown tent near the fountain, our expressions... tighter than they had been a few moments earlier.

As if something invisible had happened to us between the abrupt change in our direction.

"It's a blip," Garvis said.

I couldn't look away from the memory of Emelle and me—so happy and close back then. So trusting of each other.

"Are you telling me," I started slowly, "that one of my missing memories used to be imbedded within *this* one? And you... buried it?"

"Yes." Every syllable in Garvis's voice whispered with shame. "I ripped the mist apart and stuffed it beneath the foundation of your mind. You were already... frosty back then. But nothing like this."

My gaze snapped to the perfect, untrampled swath of snow beneath the memory's feet and the thick ground of solid ice that surely loitered beneath. If neither Garvis nor Steeler could melt it...

No. I shook away the surge of hopelessness. This was *my* mind. I had control over it.

I clapped my hands together.

"Okay. How do I melt it?"

Garvis eyed me warily, but just blew out a clouded breath and said, "I want you to focus on the details of the memory you *do* have intact. Think of how those details made you feel at the time. Joyful? Hopeless? It doesn't matter, so long as you allow yourself to feel *something*."

Because all this ice served as a preservation of my emotions, I was guessing. And it wasn't going away unless I let that preservation dissolve, fully dived into my own insecurities... and whatever else lay within me.

Reconsidering the moving mist of Emelle and me arm in arm, I watched our faces go from smiling and carefree in the first half of the memory to rigid and pursed in the second.

I moved closer.

This time, I could make out the tears glittering in Emelle's lashes like ice crystals in the second half of the memory. I watched my free hand shake, each finger trembling like icicles poised to fall off.

I cleared my throat.

"I was definitely happy at the time—at least in the beginning of this memory. I felt like I belonged, like I'd finally found my own family here at the Esholian Institute. I felt... amused at Rodhi and Gileon, how they both rushed off to find gifts for their crushes. And I felt grateful that Emelle chose to stick by my side."

Garvis nodded gently. "Anything else?"

No. I didn't want to say anything else.

I swallowed a lungful of biting cold and did anyway.

"I felt a little overwhelmed, I think. There were so many people around, so much going on. And..."

"Yes?"

"I was apprehensive," I blurted. "I was waiting for something. Or someone." I could see that in the periodic shift of my attention over all the tents and booths and haggling vendors, as if my eyes were hoping to snag onto... what? I wasn't sure. Couldn't remember.

Garvis persisted.

"And how does all this make you feel now that you're remembering it? Or at least remembering part of it?"

I bit my lip, wishing I could keep it all in, not let the dam break. But...

"Nostalgic," I blurted out. "For the moments when I felt like I fit in last year. For the moments when I felt... worthy. Of friendship. Of belonging. And now I'm... I'm sad that it's gone, Garvis. I miss Emelle, miss feeling close to her..."

"Keep going. But now put your hand on the ground."

Trying to sniff up the burn in my nose, I bent and planted my palms into the snow beneath the swirling mist, letting the crunch of ice crystals envelop the lingering warmth within me.

"I'm worried that I can't keep a friend." The words were rushing out, tumbling over my tongue, falling over this frozen bit of ground. "I'm worried I'm not *worth* permanent friendship because my whole life seems to be one giant ball of secrets and I can't be completely honest about who I am."

The ground seemed to be thumping, like a drum trying to beat its way out of the ice below us.

"I don't think I'll ever find someone as sweet and kind as Emelle again. I hate that I have to keep my distance and push her away. I wish—"

A *crack* fractured the ground beneath my palms, parting the snow until it fell away...

And mist rose from the crevice in the ground.

It merged with the mist of Emelle and me, twirling and dancing with its missing counterpart like long-lost lovers.

Gaping, I scrambled to my feet and watched the memory reform itself, swelling in size so that I had to take a few steps back.

Emelle and I didn't just turn right around to go visit Grandma Gretel's Gowns. A blanket peddler stopped us to give me a letter from *Fabian*.

A letter that told me to follow it.

And as my crescent moon beamed upon this first missing memory, I watched the whole thing play out like an unearthed dream. Starting with that abandoned classroom in the Element Wielder sector—the very same one I'd seen and recognized on my first day of class when I'd been talking to the black mamba. I just hadn't realized *why* I'd recognized it.

I listened to Lord Arad and Velika tell me about my mother and Fabian's love story. How she'd wanted to give me to the pirates. How he'd kidnapped me and stolen her knife—*my* knife now—too.

I saw Jagaros arrive to save Emelle and me when those tomb bats began morphing into their mutant vampire selves...

But then Garvis was pointing at a hole in the mist, frowning.

"Something is missing there." He turned to me with furrowed brows. "Did you ever rip the mist? Hide part of it elsewhere?"

I shook my head, bewildered.

"N-no. I would have known if I'd done that, wouldn't I?"

Garvis stroked his mustache. "Yes, you would have. That's... strange."

As I returned my gaze to that hole in the mist, the rest of the memory eddying and churning around it, I couldn't help but feel as if its darkness matched the dense, fathomless darkness of Steeler's Walking magic. Like once upon a time, *he* had filled that gaping absence.

For better or for worse.

Throughout the next few Sundays, Garvis and I kept searching for the rest of my buried memories.

We found the moment my innate faerie power had exploded with Rodhi in the tent. The moment I dry-swallowed my first pill while I sat nervously next to Lander right before the Branding. All the forbidden conversations between Ms. Pincette and me in the Testing Center

238

and in her classroom. Every wretched thing Fergus had ever done to me and Gileon and Mr. Fenway.

But the memories almost always cut short as the mist formed a gaping hole.

A very distinctly Steeler-sized hole.

I couldn't find the first time he'd given me that pill. Couldn't find a single exchange between the two of us, a single touch or midnight swim in the Element Wielder lake. It was as if I truly *had* somehow ripped my recollection of him away from everything else—and perhaps destroyed it.

"We've just got to keep looking," Garvis said three weeks into it, both of us once again sitting cross-legged on the beach. Firelight flickered from inside the lighthouse, where I could hear the rumble of faerie, monkey, and human voices alike.

Although we made a point to never speak in public at the Esholian Institute, Dazmine had been sneaking into the jungle with me every Sunday so that Steeler could take her to the lighthouse, too. There, she and Terrin sat hunched over the kitchen table, scribbling out various break-in plans that they always crumpled up and threw in the fire by the end of the night.

I wasn't surprised they hadn't come up with anything solid yet. The faerie fleet had been loitering outside the dome for five hundred years, unable to figure out how to break into that prison to get their Good Council back. I doubted a nineteen-year-old human and twenty-year-old faerie would be able to make much of a difference.

But Dazmine was determined, and I wasn't about to break over the fervor that had twined around her over the last few weeks.

My Mind Manipulating power, on the other hand, needed a break.

"Maybe my mind doesn't *want* me to keep looking," I finally sighed at Garvis as a nearby seagull squawked at its mate about a slug that it had just found in the rocks.

This last week, Mr. Conine had been teaching my Wild Whispering class about the birds of the island and their mating habits, so I knew by now that gulls were monogamous creatures with low rates of divorce. If only my own not-love life could be just as straightforward.

"Do you..." I resumed hesitantly. "Are you really so sure my past relationship with Steeler was a good one?"

I couldn't deny we'd had *some* kind of relationship last year. The way he looked at me and the way I felt around him must have had something to do with the history there. Whatever it was.

Garvis's eyes landed on the pair of seagulls hopping over to us. He didn't say anything for a long time, so I let him mull it over, watching as the male seagull began preening his female counterpart with gentle pecks.

Finally, Garvis craned his neck up to look at the sky.

"For my entire life, I've always been... *desperate* to find that one spark that lights up my whole world. I knew it existed, the spark. I saw it in some older faerie couples on the ship where I was raised. I saw it in my adoptive parents in Hallow's Perch. But I was beginning to lose faith in its existence, much as you might begin to lose faith in the sun if it were to fail to rise for several years... until you and Coen."

I sucked in a breath, letting the salted air swell inside my lungs.

This wasn't what I had been expecting from Garvis at all. I didn't know much about him or his mind, despite the fact that he had to be *sick* of my mind and its frostbitten chill by now.

"Whether your relationship with Coen was a good one or not isn't for me to decide," Garvis continued, still examining the sky. "But I could see the spark between you even from a mile away—it lit up

240

both your minds like lightning whenever you were around each other."

I considered that. The cold, reserved thing that was my mind... could it have once been as bright and wild as my Whispering magic? Could it ever return to that?

"A spark doesn't necessarily mean what Steeler and I had was good," I started, even though I knew I *wanted* it to mean that.

Garvis moved his gaze to mine until I saw the sadness loitering within his kohl-lined eyes.

"No, it doesn't, Rayna. What determines whether it was good or not is your choice to keep *feeding* the spark. To give and take fuel when needed. To blow on the embers when they're dying. To never give up on the light, no matter how distracted or numb or cold you become. It is your choice that matters. And you have one now... whether you find your missing pieces or not."

Garvis lifted his eyes, then, to a spot just over my head. As if a certain someone had just materialized right behind me.

I twirled to a stand, already reaching for my knife instinctually.

Merely five paces away, bathed in the shadows of a raincloud that had rolled in from the ocean, Steeler tracked that movement of my hand with a raised eyebrow.

"Were you eavesdropping on us?" I hissed, already removing my hand from the slit in my dress—and maybe feeling a little smug at the way he stared at the visible part of my thigh beneath.

"I wish I *had* been, judging by the look on your face, Drey. Were you talking about me or something?"

"Unfortunately."

I had to admit, I'd been a little sour since he'd stomped off all those weeks ago. Ever since then, it seemed he'd been keeping his distance, sending frustration pounding through my veins whenever I thought of him... which was often, dammit. Way too often. But since I couldn't quite grasp him in my memories *or* reality, it left my fingertips itching for something they always failed to reach.

Steeler scrutinized my stance, a trace of curiosity following my crossed arms. "As much as I would love to ask you what kind of compliments you were showering me with behind my back, I came to ask you a question."

"Oh? Let's hear it."

I was ninety-nine percent sure I was going to say no, but...

"I've got to go to Alderwick," Steeler said, "and I was wondering if you'd want to come with me."

I uncrossed my arms. Blinked at him.

"*My* Alderwick?"

"Is there another village of that name?" Before I could smack him, he added, "We can't let ourselves be seen, of course, since I'm supposed to be a pirate on a ship and you're supposed to be a student at the Institute, but I'm looking for something that I think might be there, and I—" He raked a hand through his hair, as if suddenly nervous. "I thought you might want to join me."

I was still blinking stupidly at him.

"You need my help finding something in Alderwick?"

"No, I don't need any help at all. But considering that you only found out recently that I'm *not* the monster attacking villages, I figured you'd want to be there to see with your own eyes that I mean no harm."

Confusion was only settling deeper and heavier into my chest.

"But you could have just gone and not told me," I said slowly. He had his Walking power. I hardly ever saw him anyways. I would have never known.

"And how would I have earned your trust back that way?" Steeler asked.

Earned my trust back. The confession that he was trying to do exactly that rippled in the air between us, and I suddenly didn't know what to do with my hands. Maybe he didn't have hope I'd ever fall in love with him, but he had hope that he could repair some semblance of trust between us—and I wasn't sure I wanted to douse that.

I glanced at Garvis. He gave a shrug with just the *tiniest* hint of a coy smile.

Spark, I could practically hear him saying.

"Yes," I told Steeler. "I would like to go with you."

The lighthouse windows were still flickering with shadows of Terrin, Dazmine, and Felicity behind us, but when he followed my gaze, Steeler said, "Don't worry. It shouldn't take too long. We'll be back before moonrise."

I didn't allow myself to think on it anymore.

After taking his hand and allowing him to pull me through that gut-wrenching darkness, I stood to face my home village for the first time in more than a year.

CHAPTER

27

Alderwick looked the same as I'd remembered it from afar.

A wide dirt street split the many cottages and shops, leading to a village square that more closely resembled a lopsided circle. The jungle was thick here, blocking our view of the clouds and the sky above it, but all the windows down below twinkled as merrily as stars. Smoke twirled from a few chimneys—including my own.

Steeler had dropped us off at the top of a slope overlooking my old house. Even though I was sure nobody would see our silhouettes melting into the darkness of the trees up here, I could easily see the shape of the cottage I'd grown up in surrounded by all those lights down there.

My heart tugged violently as a figure flitted within my old kitchen window—stumpy and flat-footed, that had to have been Don.

And following him a second later, more slender and graceful... Fabian.

Homesickness welled in my throat. My fathers were so close. *So* close, and I couldn't go down and talk to them. Couldn't knock on the door or let them know I was here, watching them putter throughout the house I missed with every aching heartstring. My Wild Whispering power didn't sense any spiders scuttling along the many branches and leaves surrounding us, but there were other ways for the Good Council to spy on its citizens.

Beside me, Steeler leaned against the trunk of a kapok tree and folded his arms, staring down at the village below.

I cleared away the burn in my throat.

"What are you looking for?"

"I'll let you know when I find it."

Judging from the way he closed his eyes, a deep furrow wrinkling the space between his brows, I was willing to bet he wasn't looking for anything physical—he was looking for something in somebody's *mind.*

Fine by me. As long as he wasn't taking or harming, only looking, I was content to stand there and squint at my old house for more signs of my fathers.

Smaller objects were whizzing through the kitchen now, spoons and spatulas and baking sheets. I could practically smell the cookies they were baking together, and the pang of homesickness became so strong that I had to look away before the tears in my lashes could spill.

Steeler's eyes were still closed, his brow still furrowed, but he seemed to sense my attention anyway.

"Don't judge me, Drey. I used to be able to do this kind of thing in a few seconds flat. Now..."

Now I'd scarred the use of his Mind Manipulating magic and taken half of it for myself. It was no wonder he had to concentrate so much harder. Still, I shot a glance behind us as an owl screeched in the distance and something else rustled in the foliage much closer.

"Not judging you this time," I said, "but it might not be a good idea to stand in the middle of the jungle with your eyes closed nearing nighttime. There could be any number of predators nearby."

"Good thing I have a Wild Whisperer to guard my back, then."

I stared at the wry smile picking up his lips, even as he kept his eyes closed. My knives were still buckled to my thigh, yet he didn't seem the slightest bit concerned that I might slice open his throat while he stood there unguarded.

Can you stop looking at me? he asked suddenly, his voice crashing through my blockade. *The weight of your gaze is utterly distracting.*

How can you tell I'm looking at you with your eyes closed?

Let's call it a sixth sense, little hurricane.

Biting down on a smile, I jerked my gaze away, and decided to train it on the jungle behind us rather than the village and my fathers down below. The croaks, hoots, and screeches of nighttime were beginning to roll in, but a certain stillness within the darkness beyond my vision had the Wild Whispering part of me stilling as well.

Something was quiet—much too quiet—amid all the noise.

As my eyes adjusted to the darkness, they picked up on the reddish tint of a pair of feline eyes trained on Steeler as he continued to lean against the kapok.

"Hey!" I called out, just as I sensed the large cat lowering itself into a crouch.

It was smaller than Jagaros, but still lethal enough to do some serious damage with those claws if it pounced—probably a leopard. Which meant it would be territorial over any potential meal. Which meant I had to play its game.

When the leopard's red-tinted eyes flicked over to me in surprise, I hissed, "Back off. He's *my* prey."

"*Yours?*"

The leopard slunk forward just enough for me to know I was in deep shit if I couldn't convince it of my superiority in the next thirty seconds. It had obviously taken one glance at me and figured I was the smaller, weaker one of the two.

"*Mine*," I repeated firmly, hand floating to my sheath.

I shifted my body until I was between the leopard's line of vision and Steeler himself—Steeler, who hadn't moved an inch from his position against the goddamned tree, as if he didn't know or care that he'd just become a wild cat's next hopeful snack.

"*If he is yours*," the leopard purred, "*then why haven't you sunk your claws into him yet?*"

I hesitated, hit hard with the question, and that single pause was my downfall.

"*Oh, that's right. You don't have claws.*"

And it pounced.

Not at Steeler. At me.

I was already ducking and twisting, a knife in each hand. I dragged each one down the leopard's backside in two quick slashes, mimicking claw marks—not deep enough to seriously maim, but just enough to sting a little. To warn away.

When the cat screeched, rolling over the foliage and slamming into a protruding tree root, I snarled, "No, but I have these."

It wasn't just me who brandished my knives now, though. The jungle itself, vines and branches I'd hummed out to, hoisted up each of my blades that I'd asked them to pluck from my sheath within the span of a few seconds.

247

The leopard took one look at all those shiny claws pointed in its direction and scrambled up and away, yowling as it went.

"Thank you," I muttered to the trees, sending out another hum.

As quickly as they'd snatched my knives, the vines and branches deposited them back, and soon I was staring at Steeler as he finally opened his eyes and turned to face me.

"So." A smug smile twisted his mouth. "I'm your prey, huh?"

I couldn't believe he was just standing there, completely at ease, after what had just happened. He'd *heard* me talk to that cat, even if he couldn't hear the cat's responses, and he hadn't twitched a single sculpted muscle.

"So what if you are?" I dared ask.

"Well, does that mean you want to pounce on me, too?"

Yes. "Only to wipe that smirk off your face."

The way he cocked his head at me, a single lock of deepest brown hair falling over his forehead, made me suddenly want to squirm... as if I weren't the predator, after all.

"And how are you planning on doing that? Because trust me, Drey—if you laid a single hand on me, I think I'd only be smirking harder."

My blood pulsed in my ears. "Maybe I'd take your whole head."

"Hopefully you're on your knees when you do."

I almost *did* fall to my knees at those words, purely from shock. But I managed to keep most of my face impassive and leaned in to whisper back, "I'm surprised you'd let my teeth near anything so precious."

The breath of his sudden laugh tickled against my face, mellow and sweet. "Now you're calling me precious, Drey? I don't know what to do with all this flattery."

Fortunately for the flush that had ridden up my entire body, a light flickered off down below, and both of our heads swung toward the village that had once been my home. I needed to get my imagination away from images of me on my knees, gripping Steeler's thighs, before I melted into a puddle on the jungle floor.

"Did you find what you were looking for?"

To my surprise, that furrow between his eyebrows returned. When Steeler glanced back at me, all the mischief and light in his eyes had faded away.

"No," he said. "I didn't find anything at all."

After my lesson with Garvis the next Sunday, I still hadn't found anything either—no mist in my mind that could fill the gaps in any of my unearthed memories.

Dazmine and Terrin were doing just as abysmally. As Felicity clattered about in the kitchen, I watched Dazmine pace around the living room, spouting off her frustrations regarding all those crumpled plans of theirs turned to ash in the fireplace.

"So Steeler can't Walk us straight into the prison, because there's some kind of power suppressor infusing the whole place. An Object Summoner wouldn't be able to lockpick the front door for the same reason. And even if we got a Shifter to turn one of us into an elite so that we could gain entry that way, there's no guaranteeing they'd be able to maintain our altered appearance once we made it through."

Felicity paused in the middle of kneading some type of dough on the counter, each of her long fingers clumped with goo.

"*Monkeys wouldn't bother with such subtlety, you know. We'd just storm the prison with sticks and stones. Sharpened, by the way.*"

"What's she saying?" Terrin asked Dazmine.

"Basically, that we should just get a whole army of your faerie pirate friends to help us outright attack Bascite Mountain until they hand the prisoners over."

Terrin coughed out a humorless laugh.

"And we could do that, if *someone* would just decide to lead the attack..."

Steeler's gaze shot up to land on me, as if sensing the way all of this strategy talk made my brain buzz with exhaustion. After another week of nonstop Wild Whispering lessons followed by a Mind Manipulating one, I felt like I needed a break from my own magic. From my own mind. Even for five minutes.

"Hey, Drey," he called, hoisting himself up, "have you ever been inside a lighthouse?"

I wrinkled my brow, gesturing around us.

"No, not the keeper's cottage. The actual lighthouse."

He jerked his head upward, toward the darkened tower that loomed over the cottage. An invitation, I realized. To get away to somewhere quieter. If I accepted it, though, I'd be putting myself in a room alone with Steeler for the first time since we'd reenacted the scene with the sundew, and I wasn't sure I'd be able to hold myself back from the desires that had been swishing low in my belly ever since.

"Okay," I heard myself say anyway.

I could feel everyone's smirks follow us as we made our way out the door, closing it behind us and starting toward the other set of crumbling steps that led to the tower.

Inside, it was nothing but cold, wet stone—lichen drooping from the cracks—and a metal staircase that wound up and up and up, so tightly we'd have to go one at a time. When Steeler gestured for me to

250

go first, I could practically feel the burn of his attention on my ass as I began the climb. That burn seemed to settle right between my thighs, until I couldn't resist swinging my hips a little more than necessary, relishing the sound of him sucking in a breath from behind me.

When we finally neared the top, I stepped up into a pentagonal room bordered by nothing but fogged glass, handrails bordering each of the five sides, and an enormous dead brazier squatting in the middle of it all.

I drifted to one of the handrails, resting my fingertips on it and squinting through the fog to find the horizon of the ocean in the distance. I definitely felt like I could see further than I ever had before up here.

"It's a nice view."

"Yes," Steeler said without taking his eyes off me, "it is."

"Who do you think built it?"

"My guess is the first humans who came to the island after Dyonisia conquered it...but not to find ships in a benevolent way. I think it was probably more of a warning to stay away."

I turned back toward him. When he took a step toward me, everything around us—the brazier, the glass walls, even the ocean beyond—seemed to dissolve like melted snow.

"I know you've warned me to stay away, little hurricane. But I'm not warning *you* to stay away. My own memories are very much intact, and now that you're a Mind Manipulator..."

The blood in my veins froze with rigid intensity as I stared at Steeler, my eyes rooted to the curve of his jaw and the way it was so close to giving that familiar smug smile with a hint of a challenge.

Now that I was a Mind Manipulator, I didn't even *need* to find my own memories of our moments together. I could access Steeler's.

Could judge our past relationship for myself from the formation of *his* mist.

"Of course, you'd have to get past my gate." Steeler gave a skeptical wrinkle of his nose. "Which I doubt you could do, but..."

"You're on."

The words were out before I could rein them in. That glittering amusement in Steeler's eyes—I wanted to rise up to the challenge. I would get past his damned gate and watch all the mist I wanted even if it was the last Mind Manipulating thing I did.

"Just tell me how to... how to dive," I said, tasting that phrase in my mouth for the first time and intuitively knowing it was the right one.

"You're sure? You truly want to see what lies within me—for better or for worse?"

I found my gaze tracing the dark brown locks of his hair, the shape of his nose, the point of his ears and fangs. Finding new parts about him that I hadn't let myself notice before. How one eyebrow tilted up ever so slightly at the end while the other tilted down. How a splash of smile lines creased the side of his mouth that smirked the most. How a single freckle dotted his right cheekbone.

He might be the most perfect-looking male specimen from a distance, but up close, Coen Steeler had all these crooked little flaws that made me yearn to dive beneath his skin and discover more.

I made sure my voice rang loud and clear.

"I want to see everything."

CHAPTER

28

"The first thing you need to do is lower your blockade," Steeler said.

The two of us were standing so close, our chests were grazing. As if I were shedding a layer, I let my blockade wither away around me.

"Now, I want you to try to grab onto my outermost thought. Use your mental hand—the one that pushes your blockade out."

I waited until Steeler's thoughts hit me...

You look especially beautiful whenever you're determined like this.

...and *snatched* at it.

The thought flowed through my mental fingers like the light of a sunset.

"Dammit," I hissed.

"Try again."

Now his internal thoughts came at me louder, a chuckle rumbling throughout the dark, fathomless texture of them.

Look at that little pout.

I snatched and missed again.

Pushing out your lip just because you didn't get what you wanted the first time. That's so cute.

Oh, hell no.

I struck, pinning that thought between both my mental palms like a trapped mouse. It wiggled and squirmed, but I held tight.

Steeler cleared his throat. "Now use my chain of thoughts like a rope to pull yourself toward me. Grab at each thought the deeper you go."

I pulled myself forward, my physical body still standing at the top of the lighthouse while my mind dove inward and latched onto...

God of the Cosmos, Coen was thinking beneath the surface, *she's scary good at this for her first time.*

I pulled myself forward again, feeling as if I was actually floating toward those eyes of smoky quartz even though my feet were still firmly planted on the floor.

This isn't normal, came his next thought beneath that one, tinged with awe and maybe a little worry. *This isn't normal for her to be so stellar at a second power so soon.*

I pulled myself forward, deeper and deeper into a darkness so alive and rich that I almost forgot to breathe, until I felt the layers of it give way around me and I was clutching onto a final thought of his.

She's the one.

Then my mind broke into his, and I landed with a thump onto the moon.

Or, at least, that's what it looked like: glowing and bone-white.

When I planted my hands against the ground, though, it felt smoother and warmer than I would have imagined the surface of one to be. And an *actual* moon floated overhead, filled to the brim with light that illuminated Steeler's mind—the void circling it, and the colossal marble gate guarding the maze that stretched before me.

There was no sunrise here. Only distant stars.

"Like what you see?"

Steeler had appeared in front of his gate, arms crossed and eyes narrowed as he watched me make a slow, unfaltering stand.

"I can't say I'm surprised." I smoothed out the wrinkles in my dress. "Of course your mind would mimic your innate magic."

For that's what this place reminded me of: the darkness Steeler dragged me through every time he Walked. A void he managed to breathe energy and life and stars into.

I took a step toward him. Toward his gate and the mist beyond.

"How do I get through?"

Steeler adjusted his stance, as if preparing to chase me away.

"First thing to know about breaking into someone's mind, Drey. Their consciousness is the key. Literally. Non-Mind Manipulators don't even know how to lock their own gates, so you'd be able to slip inside without lifting a finger. Me, on the other hand..." He shrugged, such a nonchalant gesture in contrast to the determination settling on his face. "As long as I keep focusing on that gate, it will never break for you."

I glanced at the elegant silver door handle and the lock on the top half of the plate. I had a sneaking suspicion Steeler thought I would try tugging on it or lockpicking it or even climbing that vast marble wall.

But none of those things would work, I was sure.

If Steeler was the key, and his focus kept it locked...

"How am I supposed to break your focus?" I asked, taking a slow, calculating step toward him.

Another shrug, this one less casual than before. "The Mind Manipulating instructors at the Institute would tell you to fight me. Overpower me. Get me to yield."

I liked that thought—getting him to yield. But I didn't have my knife in here, and a deep, humming part of me wanted to overpower him in a different way.

Removing my attention from the gate, I latched it onto Steeler instead. His predatory stance. His tunic. His pants.

What had he said all those weeks ago when I'd asked if I had to touch his hand in order for him to Walk me back to the Institute? *You can touch other parts of me if you want, Drey. Any part you'd like.* And then right outside Alderwick, he'd said, *I hope you're on your knees when you do.*

I treaded toward him until I was close enough to do exactly that. To touch.

But I didn't yet. I cocked my head to the side again, finally letting my eyes devour the lower half of him, the half I'd been avoiding until this very moment. Even in here, in this internal space between stars, his pants strained with the outline of—

"What are you doing?" Steeler's voice came out as a growl.

"I'm just wondering," I mused, grudgingly looking back up, "what would happen if I put my hands on you in here? Would it be real?"

Suspicion hardened every line of Steeler's face.

"What do *you* think, Drey? Does any of this feel real to you?"

I didn't answer. I wouldn't have an answer unless I actually touched him.

Feeling as if the world around us was simultaneously slowing down and speeding up, I reached out and let my hand land upon his chest.

It was hard. Solid. Warm. I could feel the drumming of his heart beneath my fingertips, just as I imagined my own heart was pounding in the outside world. And when I brought my fingers down, cresting and falling over the ridges of his abs beneath his shirt, I felt his body tense as surely as if he was holding his breath.

"Yes," I said, looking back up from his abdomen to meet his gaze that brewed with an undeniably hungry ache. "It feels very real to me."

But it wasn't. I'd learned by now that the mist of our minds didn't form memories based on mental interactions. If I did what I burned to do, there would be no tangible record of it. It might *feel* real, but any action in here was just a thought.

If I touched him in here, it would be nothing more than finally letting my imagination run wild.

Steeler's eyes had drifted shut at my touch, but they flew open again when my hands closed around two fistfuls of his shirt. I shocked myself by pulling him a half-stagger closer—a display of confidence I hadn't even realized I was capable of. As if in here, there weren't any self-doubts to hold me back.

"Can I still touch any part of you I'd like to, Steeler?"

His mouth opened, caught in a surprised breath. He glanced over his shoulder, which told me he was still aware of the gate. Was aware of my scheming. And yet...

"I will never say no to a single touch from you, little hurricane."

His gaze dipped to my lips, but I didn't lean in to kiss him. I trailed a thumb against his neck, ran my fingers down the bulges of his arms, and swept my touch back to his pelvis. Then, unable to stop the direction of my filthy thoughts and the reality they were creating in Steeler's mind, I lowered my hands to the buttons of his pants.

Where I took my time undoing them.

Maybe in another life, my fingers would have been trembling, my heart racing, my head spinning. In here, though, the richness of this universe alongside the mellow scent of black bamboo that seemed to spill from nowhere and everywhere all at once—it made my hands work steadily. My heart went still as I finally got the buttons undone and tugged down all the fabric in my way.

Coen Steeler's cock sprang free, longer and thicker than my imagination had ever suspected beneath all my self-denial.

God. I couldn't blame my past self for falling for his charms. This right here had to be the culprit.

"Rayna." My name was a whisper on Steeler's tongue.

"What?" I asked rather impatiently. "Do you want me to stop?"

His eyes flashed open in alarm. "Fuck no."

"Good. Then shut up and let me do what I want."

Steeler bit into his lip, as if he had to actually anchor his mouth shut with those fangs.

Telling myself it didn't really count because it was mental rather than physical, I finally let myself do what I'd secretly wanted to do since the moment he'd pulled me out of my own mind. I traced the glorious length of him with my fingertips, along the shaft to the head, until a deep shuddering rose from the moon-like ground.

"No wonder you're so cocky," I whispered. "Look at you."

"Can't," he gritted out. "I'm too busy looking at *you* all the damn time."

"Well, then..." I ignored the fluttering rush of what those words meant to me and released my hold on him to palm his chest, pushing against him. Just like I wanted, Steeler stumbled backward until he was flush against his gate, his chest rising and falling in rapid succession. "I guess you'll have to busy yourself with looking at what I do to you."

At the pained groan that fell from his mouth, a smile tugged at my mouth. I stepped forward and sank to my knees before him until my face hovered inches away.

Slowly, with painstaking gentleness despite my desire to lunge, I wrapped my hand around the base.

My fingers could barely manage to fit around the whole circumference even as I tightened my grip. I could feel the hungry blood thumping beneath my palm, could feel the tremor of the ground rise up into his legs, until his entire body vibrated with restraint.

"You're... you don't have to..." Steeler's words came out in rugged pants. "Why are you going..."

"So far?" I finished for him, breathless. "I told you. Because I want to." And it was the truth, dammit. I didn't just want to distract him—I wanted to taste him, too. I could lie to Steeler's face, but not to his mind. "I could go even further, if you'd like." And I licked along the underside of his length, from the bottom to the tip.

"*Shit*." He jolted, his eyes flaring. "Yes."

A smirk puckered my lips. Maybe it was because we were in his mind, and his mind wanted me to do this just as much as I did, but it felt like the center of gravity in here was *him*.

It was as effortless and thrilling as a freefall for me to slide my entire mouth around the hardest part of him.

He tasted silky and almost sweet, the size of him filling me all the way to the back of my throat and causing tears to spring into my eyes.

Fine by me. Tears were good. They meant I was feeling *something* of my own accord—even if that feeling was pure, carnal pleasure at the knowledge that I had the male I should despise by the literal cock.

"Rayna."

Now Steeler's voice came out as a desperate plea, his hands digging into my hair, clutching my curls like reins. I knew from the way those hands trembled against my head that he wanted to tug me in, to force me to move and give him that friction he now needed.

I also knew he wouldn't do that. Not yet. Not while he was still trying to maintain his focus on that stupid locked gate behind him.

So I removed my mouth from around him and took my time playing with the one thing I couldn't deny I wanted any longer. Licking him up and down. Swirling my tongue along the tip.

"Fuck, Rayna." Each of his breaths sounded strained to the point of pain. "You're going to be the death of me."

I shot him an upward grin. "That's the plan."

Then I took him into my mouth again, gripping his hips for support, and *moved.*

Steeler's grip tightened in my hair. I dared a glance up to find—

Yes. A ravenous haze was swirling in his eyes, as if the longer he watched me take him, the more his focus was moving away from the gate to hone in on me. My mouth. My throat. My tears.

"This," he rasped, "is the only reason I ever want to see you cry, little hurricane. Such pretty tears." He untangled one of his hands from my hair to swipe his thumb along my cheek, brushing away a trickle of moisture before rubbing his fingers together. "I wish I could feel how wet the rest of you is right now."

My core fluttered with heat in response. With need.

No. I couldn't lose control. Couldn't lose the thrill of victory that had started to build inside me.

With renewed determination, I took him even deeper and deeper, gagging myself on his length until his restraint broke free. Until *he* was thrusting himself into me with each pump, that groan finally rumbling out of his chest. And...

Now. Steeler's focus was gone. I could remove myself now.

But I didn't want to stop. Couldn't find it in me to quit sucking and tasting and letting the enormity that was *him* slam into my mouth again and again, until that burn in my core swelled and hummed.

My eyes snapped upward to lock with his.

As soon as our gazes slammed into each other, he erupted.

His release poured into my mouth, so much of it that even as I gulped some of it down, more just spilled out of the sides of my lips.

At the same time, the entire world trembled with every word Steeler couldn't manage to say through the groans of his climax.

Rayna. Rayna. Rayna. You're here. You're divine. You're everything.

Oh, God. No. I couldn't allow my pleasure to grow any longer. If I did, I was sure Steeler would return the favor, and then *I'd* be the one trapped here for eternity, and I'd forget about his memories entirely.

With my heart thundering as surely as if I'd truly just sucked Steeler dry in real life, I ripped myself away, jumped up, and lunged around him, my hand already outstretched.

The door of his gate sprung open for me as soon as my palm pressed against it—unlocked now that his focus had burst through his grasp.

And resisting the urge to look over my shoulder to catch sight of Steeler's reaction, I launched myself through the gateway.

Right into the maze of his mind.

CHAPTER

29

Steeler's maze wasn't a tangle of alleyways like mine.

It was more like a multilayered spiral.

Those marble walls curved and curved as I ran, other spiraled paths sprouting off the main one and herding me continuously inward. There was no snow to muffle my footsteps here, so each one of them clacked against the moonstone as I took one of those side paths and—

Steeler appeared in front of me between blinks.

He'd buttoned his pants back up, and there wasn't a single tussled part of his hair or flush in his cheeks to indicate that I'd just sucked the life out of him. Even so, the smoky quartz of his eyes glittered with... something.

I didn't halt long enough to figure it out.

Pivoting on a heel, I took another pathway, cursing those walls that only ever curved with smooth precision. Noise bubbled from a patch of mist up ahead, sounding a lot like my laughter used to...

But then Steeler appeared in front of me *again*, blocking my path forward.

A scream of frustration ripped out of me. I turned and sprinted back to the main pathway, aiming for another pocket of noisy mist that echoed from the entrance to a smaller path up ahead.

Only for Steeler to appear in front of me again.

And again.

And again.

But I wouldn't quit perusing his mind until I'd found one. Just *one single memory* that didn't seem to exist within me anymore. Just *one damned explanation* for the yearning I couldn't shake off when I looked into his eyes and saw entire galaxies swirling within.

Finally, one of the pathways came to a tapered end, where a memory was replaying with a fluidity that made me think Steeler had mulled this particular one over again and again, smoothing out the details until it resembled an actual moving picture.

When he didn't materialize in front of me to ward me off, I stopped to watch, even though I knew, deep down, that I was not a part of this memory. That this memory came way before me.

A group of children—six of them—stood in a line on a swaying deck bordered with polished wooden guardrails. I recognized five of them immediately, even though they couldn't have been older than nine or ten: Steeler, Garvis, Terrin, Sasha, and Sylvie.

I didn't recognize the sixth one, though, a boy with sand-colored hair and thick conglomerations of freckles running down his arms.

As I squinted at this one, a new figure of mist stepped up to the children, arms behind her back—and now my spine scurried with tingles, because I *did* recognize her.

She'd been in that vision I'd had to endure in my first hour at the Esholian Institute, the one where I'd fallen into the thrashing waves of the sea and climbed aboard a ship to meet a four-fingered pirate and the sting of her sharp slap across my face.

Now, that same pirate was staring down at the line of children in this tangible memory. The only difference between then and now were her sharpened ears and elongated canines that marked her as a faerie.

"The queen has requested that you get to know our enemy on a more... intimate level."

Her voice was as coarse and gravelly as I remembered it, although now, with the moonbeam illuminating the entire memory, I could see more details: the tattoo crawling up her neck, for instance, toward her rough crop of hair. The ink formed a circle at the top, almost like a badge of honor that shot more prickles down my spine.

The Fated General. This female had to be the mysterious Fated General that Steeler had been whispering about. There was an air of authority about her and that tattoo on her neck that made me want to snap to attention.

The Fated General removed her hands from behind her back and examined the stump where her fifth finger would be, its clump of skin like an outgrown socket, before continuing.

"You will all be shipped through the dome tomorrow morning to spend the rest of your adolescent years on the island."

The children glanced at each other.

"But won't we die if we pass through it?" Sylvie piped up, raising a little hand. "Like those faeries on that ship that approached the dome when we first got here? Everyone on board just collapsed into dust as soon as they touched the mist!"

The Fated General chuckled without a stitch of real humor. "And eyes like yours are exactly why you'll make great spies. It is true that when a fully-matured faerie touches the dome, the venom within its substance targets the power in their blood and stifles it so viciously that every bit of their body disintegrates, too. But because *your* powers are still shapeless, child, that venom cannot latch onto it well enough to stifle it, so you are immune to these catastrophic effects. You will only feel a small tingle as you go through, my sources say."

My sources say. Even though this was only a memory, my blood boiled at the implication that the Fated General must have tested out said *catastrophic effects* on other children before this moment. And from the slight twisting of young Steeler's face...

He'd been astute, I realized, even as a young boy. Astute enough to have plenty of questions brewing behind his little eyes.

"Madam Loressa has used her magic to inspire some coastal families to find the idea of adopting a welcome one," the Fated General went on. "When you arrive on the island, you will tell these families you were sent through as a distraction so that our fleets can attempt to breach the dome. You will not tell anyone you are spies. That is an order."

Every single child in the memory straightened their spine, as if they'd been conditioned—cruelly—to always obey.

"And are you actually going to try to breach the dome?"

That came from young Steeler himself, in a voice that shocked the hell out of me: much too hard and cold for such a small child.

The Fated General leaned over him, and now something caught my attention from the stump of her finger: the socket seemed to flex moments before a silver finger shot out from the smooth patch of skin...

And *kept* shooting out. Longer and longer and longer the finger stretched, until it curled like a metal hook and lifted young Steeler's chin. Apparently, the Fated General's innate power was the ability to grow literal weapons from her body.

"You know as well as I do that when the time comes for the dome to break, it will not be me who shatters it, boy."

The mist changed.

Now Steeler and his friends sat in a circle on fallen, moss-eaten logs outside a flickering village—older and more carefree than they'd been on the ship. The dense line of jungle in the distance told me they were indeed on the island, just as their Fated General had planned.

The bottle they were passing in circles, however, told me they weren't taking their jobs as spies too seriously for the time being.

"Oh, come on, let me have another go."

It was the sandy-haired boy, the freckles on his arms faded now that he'd been living within the shaded foliage of the jungle for the last ten or so years. He held out a hand toward Steeler and eagerly wiggled his fingers, wagging his brows along with them.

"Don't be greedy, Mattheus," Sasha snorted from across their circle. "Wasn't it enough when you blew steam out of your ears a moment ago?"

The boy named Mattheus shook his head with a too-serious expression stamped over his face. "Until I can blow steam out of my asshole, too, I will never be satisfied."

Sasha tutted and Terrin punched him in the shoulder.

Groaning, Steeler passed over the bottle of what must have been bascale, filled with several particles of the five different types of bascite all mixed together. Rodhi had once claimed the effects were random, that our powers just didn't know what shape to take until the actual Branding, but now I knew: with so many separate magics swimming in that liquid, the blood probably reacted to the strongest one in each individual swallow.

I held my breath, a chill of familiarity sweeping over me as the scene played out almost exactly like mine had in the tent with Rodhi.

266

Like me, these teenagers had shapeless power lurking in their blood, easily triggered by the drink. But unlike me, none of them had exploded upon their first gulp. Now, though...

Mattheus chugged the remains, coughed, and wiped his mouth with his wrist. The others leaned in.

His eyes glazed over.

A shiver wracked his body.

Then it burst from him: not any of the five sanctioned magics, but his *own* magic, formless and raw and unending.

Steeler and Garvis, Terrin and the twins—they all flew backward off their logs, their backs slamming into the ground. Wails and moans rose from the five of them while Mattheus scrabbled at his chest, trying to contain the energy that was pouring out of him.

But he couldn't. And where my recollection of my own memory had stopped abruptly after a few seconds, this one kept going.

And going.

And going.

Neither Steeler nor his friends could get up against the surge of power. They couldn't do anything besides cower and cover their heads and wait for several adult figures to come sprinting toward them from the village, shouting out questions.

The mist changed.

Mattheus stood limply in the village square, each of his arms chained to a post behind him. I wanted to scream at him to run when Kitterfol Lexington strode up to him with a leather whip in his fist.

And a grin on his face.

"Ladies and gentlemen." Lexington turned to address the crowd of villagers all smashed together behind a long line of Good Council elites. His braids were shorter in this memory, but only slightly. "This is what happens when our blood cannot handle the magic we are gifted." He swept a hand toward Mattheus behind him. "Chaos and destruction that threatens the safety of the entire island. This boy was not yet Branded, but he did steal a small amount of bascite and proved himself unworthy of even that. And such danger to our community will not be tolerated."

When the whipping began, I turned away. I didn't want to see.

But I heard each slap of leather against skin, heard the mutters and screams of onlookers fill the square until my eyes locked on young Steeler—how he strained and pushed against an older man's arms, sobbing, reaching out for his friend he could not help.

And maybe it was because I was in Steeler's mind and could taste his thoughts and knowledge like fog settling on my tongue, but I knew the man was his adoptive father, knew this adoptive father was a branded Mind Manipulator and had wiped Mattheus's memories... when I chanced the smallest glance upward to inspect the teenage boy on the stake again, I realized his eyes had smoothed over with glossy nothingness. He was already mentally gone.

Even as his skin hung in bloody strips over his bones.

With a guttural scream that tore through my chest, Steeler ripped through his father's arms.

Only to collapse to the cobblestone a second later.

Another thing I knew instinctively: his father had just ordered him to go to sleep so that he could not interfere. Could not get hurt.

The mist changed.

Teenage Steeler was on a boat by himself, an oar clutched in each hand. The churning milkiness of the dome hovered just ahead of him, where another vessel bobbed toward him from the other side.

Was it the Fated General? I couldn't tell, but whoever it was, they must have chosen to meet Steeler on a night when the ocean rose and fell in waves soft enough for the both of them to row themselves out here without magic.

Finally, this other vessel stopped right before the border. It wasn't the Fated General, after all, but a beautiful, silver-haired faerie in a rowboat on the other side of the shield.

"You came," Steeler called through the dome.

Something fundamental had broken in his voice. It was no longer hard and cold, but... fractured.

"Barberro and I promised you that if you ever needed anything, all you'd have to do is call." This faerie's voice was smooth and soft, like strips of fluttering satin. "Still," she said, "we were shocked when a seagull dropped a letter from *you* right into my lap. How did you convince a Wild Whisperer to help you fraternize with your supposed enemy?"

Steeler's shoulders tensed.

"M-Mattheus's adoptive mother... she's great with birds, and wanted to help me in whatever way she could because... well, it doesn't matter. I need you to make me something with your Alchemy magic. A way to hide our immature power."

The silver-haired faerie narrowed her eyes at him. I didn't know what the conversion from human to faerie years was, but in the sudden spill of moonlight that highlighted the faintest lines around her eyes as some clouds shifted overhead, she looked like a late-thirty-year-old. Delicate lines of ink spiraled around her neck and up her jaw to the tips of her ears.

"What happened to Mattheus?"

Steeler gave her a few surprised blinks.

"I know grief when I see it," the faerie said quietly.

Steeler exhaled, nodded, and relayed what had happened to his friend in the quietest of shaking murmurs. "So when we go to the

Institute next year," he finished, "it will happen to all of us when we are Branded. And I cannot..." He swallowed thickly. "I cannot lose another one."

The faerie stared at him through the dome for several long minutes, and I found myself wanting to *change* the mist. To make her simply drag Steeler back through, return him and his remaining friends to the ships where they could forgo the Esholian Institute entirely.

But she only said in a voice as soft as a falling feather, "The only thing that can suppress power is power. You know that, Coen."

"Please, Nara." He gripped his oars in tighter fists. "I don't care how you do it. Please find a way. Or convince the queen to let the others come back before it's too late. I can stay here, but let them go."

The faerie named Nara sighed and stared up the arc of the dome, the tips of her tattooed ears reflecting its milky glow.

"I will do my best. Meet me back here in a week."

The mist didn't change, but the tension in the air did.

It was a week later. Nara was holding out a tin canister... which Steeler reached through the dome to take. Nothing but the smallest of winces passed over his face when he did so. Truly just a tingle, then.

"Pills?" he asked, screwing open the lid to survey the small heap of pearl-like capsules inside.

Nara nodded and seemed to hold her breath.

She let it out again in a tone that sounded a lot like admittance.

"I took a microscopic amount of substance from the dome itself. Don't worry," she added when Steeler's eyes flashed open. "There is not enough in each pill to disintegrate anyone, least of all yourselves. But there *will* be enough to subdue any magic if something were to cause a flare-up again. I altered the chemical composition of it so that it will latch onto shapeless power as well as formed power."

"But…" Steeler's frown was as deep as my own right now. "When the time comes for our Branding, won't it subdue the Good Council-given magic, too, then? I don't think they'd be too happy if we didn't react during their precious ceremony."

Enough ire simmered in his voice for me to know that he did more than loathe the Good Council now. He wanted to destroy them. For what they'd done to Mattheus.

Nara closed her eyes for a brief moment.

When she opened them again, a decision seemed to settle over her face.

"I'm going to tell you a little secret they don't want you to know about, Coen." She leaned in dangerously close to the milky substance that would kill her on contact. "This dome is… conscious. Or, rather, it stems from a *consciousness*."

Both Steeler and I froze. Both of us seemed to arrive at the same conclusion, judging from the taste of inherent knowledge on my tongue. There was only one consciousness who could control the dome, and she lived within it.

Dyonisia Reeve.

But that meant… that meant the leader of the island was a faerie.

Of *course* she was a faerie. I should have known from the beginning.

Dyonisia didn't have any of the five powers branded on her shoulder because she had a power of her own. The dome itself. And she wasn't immortal because of some Shape Shifter renewal magic. She was immortal because she wasn't *human*. Her ears and *fangs* were what Shape Shifter elites probably controlled—hid—with their magic.

The taste of mist on my tongue told me Steeler had known all of these revelations all along.

What this young teenage version of Steeler didn't understand, however, was the nature of her power.

"What do you mean Dyonisia's magic is conscious?" he asked slowly, holding the canister of pills in a vice-like grip.

"I mean," Nara sighed out, "that her dome will disintegrate any full-fledged faeries with powers of their own, yes... but she does not seem to want to hurt the humans of this island with their Branded magic. Anyone with Wild Whispering, Mind Manipulating, Element Wielding, Shape Shifting, or Object Summoning can go in and out of the dome without harm."

I felt my heart begin to hammer somewhere in my real body in the outside world, because this... this didn't make any sense. Dyonisia Reeve was keeping the original Good Council locked away in here. Why would she grant *their* magic—or clones of it—immunity?

"But that means that any of the Branded humans could leave this island with their children if they choose to," Steeler said slowly.

Nara dipped her head.

"Indeed. In fact, there have been a few families over the years who have escaped unharmed—and not because they were exiled, but of their own free will. We picked them up and had Old Veracious scan them to test their true identities, of course, make sure they weren't Dyonisia or her elites in disguise... but then we let them go."

Let them go. My head reeled at the thought that some Esholian families had fled the island on boat, encountered the pirates they'd always been taught to fear, and been released again—only to face what? An endless expanse of ocean and no idea of where to go from there?

I could only hope they'd found land before they perished.

Nara pointed at the canister in Steeler's hand.

"You and the others will need to take those pills once a week. They will not touch your Branded magic; they will simply prevent your

272

innate faerie power from bursting into shape. But be warned..." She leaned forward. "There is a price to pay for such a thing."

Steeler stiffened. "I'll pay you anything you ask. I can get—"

Nara shook her head. "I'm not talking about coin." Here, her gaze lowered as if ashamed. "If we are to keep meeting each other in secret so that I can give you a new stash every month, you must give me inside information about the island. Those are the stipulations I was given. I am not allowed to help you for free."

"Oh." Steeler blew out a disgusted breath, one that I echoed at the thought of the Fated General holding something like a life-saving medication over his head like this. "Well, I assumed she'd find a way to make sure I followed through with my spying anyway. It's a deal."

Nara nodded, but then her gaze lifted again.

"You must remember that these pills are only temporary, Coen. You and the others can't take them forever. As soon as you graduate from that wretched Institute, I want you to come back, okay?" A hidden message seemed to be lurking beneath her words. "I want you to come back and let yourself *explode*."

The mist changed.

Steeler was older, lined with the muscles I'd grown accustomed to, patrolling the pentaball arena with his hands behind his back.

It was strange to see him walking so openly about campus, no stalking or sneaking or Walking required.

And even stranger when I heard my own scream pierce through one of the tents a few rows down from him.

The sound of Mattheus's scream from so long ago seemed to fill his ears... and suddenly he was sprinting toward me, ripping open the tent flaps, finding me surrounded by my new friends on their backs. He recognized me as the girl with the beautiful mind—the one he had wanted to sink into and lose himself within upon my arrival at the Esholian Institute earlier that day.

This was where my own memory cut off. I had no recollection of looking up to find the prince of the Mind Manipulators gaping at me.

In Steeler's memory, though, I watched him throw me over his shoulder and haul me to that alleyway between our sectors' houses. I heard everything he said to me, felt his confusion about the possibility of me, his desperation to save me from the same fate as Mattheus, the savage possessiveness that slammed into him from the moment I lifted my chin and repeated my name, loud and clear.

"Rayna Drey."

"I see. Rainy Days doesn't make much sense anyway, does it? You're not a soft little drizzle." His lips tilted up, although now, from this angle, I saw it for what it was: a frantic attempt to hide the snarling rage he already felt at the thought of a whip striking against any part of my body. "You're more like a raging hurricane."

She has to be, he thought. *She has to be, or she will not survive this.*

The mist changed.

Steeler was seated at the front row of the Mind Manipulator section in the stadiums during the Branding, looking bored out of his mind.

Until my name was called.

Then, every fiber of his body perked up as my figure made its way onto the stage where Mr. Gleekle stood with his poker and brand. Now I knew that particular brand had always been infused with Wild Whispering, but at the time, I'd had no idea which magic would erupt from me when it pressed its scorching kiss against my skin. I hadn't even known if *any* magic would erupt, considering I'd just dry-swallowed Steeler's pill moments earlier.

Neither, it seemed, did Steeler. Despite everything Nara had told him about the nature of the pills and the dome, he seemed to be caught in an inhale as he watched Mr. Gleekle stamp that brand to my shoulder...

Only for nothing to happen.

Nothing, nothing, nothing.

Steeler's hands curled into fists. He was already half-rising, his eyes on the back of Kitterfol Lexington's neck, preparing to fight him mind-to-mind if Lexington so much as *sniffed* at my thoughts.

But then Jagaros came.

Jagaros came, and everyone's heads twisted amid shocked gasps to watch his sleek, stealthy trek to the stage, and Steeler's face broke into a beam as he finally ripped his eyes from Lexington and found me again.

The mist changed.

Now he was stomping down the staircase in the Mind Manipulator house with the twins trailing behind him.

"Wait!" Sylvie reached out with a hand that barely managed to scrape against his shoulder. "You broke up?"

"I don't want to talk about it." When Steeler reached his room, he closed the door behind him without looking back.

The twins just used their Summoning powers to unlock it.

"What are you going to do at the end of the year, then?" Sasha hissed as she trudged through his doorway, and I heard her throw her thoughts out for Steeler to catch. *Kidnap her? What if she doesn't want to leave the island with us now that you're not together anymore?*

Steeler replied by shooting his own thoughts into her head.

We're not taking Rayna with us.

Excuse me? Sasha stared at him, livid. *You said she wouldn't be safe on the island without us. And while her innate power is still shapeless, the dome won't hurt her. Now's her chance to leave.*

"Some new information has come to light," Steeler said out loud, in a tone edged with enough authority that it made the hairs on the back of my neck bristle. "We're not taking Rayna with us."

The mist changed.

Now a memory-version of me was watching Steeler pack up his things with burning intensity. As soon as he stilled, this Rayna said "I'm coming with you."

"Rayna." Steeler's voice was hoarse, but his face... his face filled with enough self-loathing to shatter it. "You can't. Dyonisia doesn't know what you are, so your safest bet is to stay here and—"

"If this is about the shield, then I'm willing to test it," memory-Rayna said. "Maybe I'm immune, too."

And now I knew I *was* immune. Not because of any special reason, but simply because my own power hadn't developed yet, and the dome wouldn't touch my Wild Whispering magic.

But Steeler laughed dryly, finally turning toward me.

"I've seen faeries disintegrate on the spot just from grazing the shield. It's not a physical barrier, Rayna. It's an anti-power that targets the magic in your blood and strikes."

Not a lie. Not a lie, and yet...

Not the whole truth. He was *one* breath away from telling me that anti-power *wouldn't* target the magic in my blood as of now.

But he didn't.

He didn't.

And the mist changed.

Now I watched, horror-struck, as my past self writhed and flailed in Steeler's grip, screaming at him to let me keep my memories.

"*Let me go! Don't touch me! Don't you dare!*"

Steeler only bowed over me, his body like its own dome shielding mine from Dyonisia's spitting, venomous anti-power overhead, and commanded me to breathe.

But I wouldn't. Couldn't. It was so obvious in this memory that I might never be able to breathe properly again. And despite all that, Steeler was saying, "I *will* come back for you. I will make you pick up my pieces. And I will pick up yours."

Instead of replaying itself from the beginning, the mist faded as soon as he lowered his mouth to mine and muffled my sobs with a trembling kiss.

Then silence.

Such endless, echoing silence.

A single exhale behind me made me whip around.

Steeler—the real one, the one who had chased me all throughout his own maze—straightened from where he'd been leaning against the nearest curving marble wall, watching *me* watch it all.

He'd been watching me take in these memories the whole time.

Memories he'd woven together like braids of steam. Memories he'd *herded* me toward so that I would stumble across this darkest truth.

He took a half step toward me, his foot falling into a sliver of moonlight pouring down into this pathway, his mouth opening to say something.

"You bastard," I said before he could.

Steeler stopped.

Every part of my body had gone still besides my fingers—*those* were itching to grab a knife that didn't exist in this mental space.

"I could have gone with you," I whispered. "But you left me anyway."

"I know, Rayna."

No sooner had my name left his lips than I hissed, "Don't you *dare* call me that. The girl you knew by that name was in love with you, but you left her anyway."

It felt like an anchor falling off from the center of my chest, admitting that. I couldn't deny it anymore. My past self had been hopelessly, ridiculously in love with the male who stood before me. And maybe we'd had a good time together. Maybe we'd made each other happy for a finite space of time.

But in the end, it hadn't mattered. In the end, he'd hacked right through that love until I'd had to freeze everything within me to preserve it. To keep it from further mutilation.

Steeler opened his mouth again, every shade of pain imaginable swimming through his eyes. "There was—"

"No reason!" I shouted, and now I was the one taking steps forward despite my better judgment, filling the sliver of moonlight with the darkest, most quivering part of me. "You *left* me!" I shoved against his chest. "You *abandoned* me." I shoved again, hating that he wouldn't budge, also hating that he didn't try to defend himself. "You kissed my lips and turned your *back* on me." I pummeled the heel of my palms against his chest again and again, wanting so viciously to shove him to the ground the way he'd shoved me to the ground and left me there to rot. "You told me you loved me and then walked *away*. You—"

"It was to keep you *safe*!" he cut in, finally grabbing my wrists. Holding them back. "Everything I *do* is to keep you safe, Rayna!"

A shriek snapped out of me. "Stop CALLING me that!"

"No! I will not stop! I will not call you by your surname anymore as if you mean nothing to me when you mean *everything* to me!" Steeler tightened his grip on my wrists. "I don't *care* if you hate me for the rest of your life, Rayna, I don't *care* if you never forgive me, I don't *care* if my heart wants to fucking die whenever I look into your eyes and see the reflection of the monster I've become."

I stopped struggling for just a moment as his own eyes shimmered with a reflection of its own: my face, looking up at him. Me, and only me, like a pale imitation in dark water.

"I don't care," Steeler continued, "because I cared with Mattheus. I cared what he thought of me. I cared that he'd be mad at me for not passing him the damn bottle, so you know what I did, Rayna? I passed him the damn bottle. *I* did that. *I* gave him what he wanted, and he is *dead* because of me. And I will never get him back."

He stood there, panting so raggedly I wanted to patch up the holes that had obviously punctured him in every place that mattered.

Instead, I simply dragged in a deep breath of my own.

"How were you keeping me safe by leaving me here? The dome—"

"—might not have killed you, no," he said on a shuttering exhale. "But every tattooed faerie on that ship is oath-bound to kill Dyonisia Reeve upon sight—or anyone who belongs to her by blood."

I shook my head. "I don't belong to Dyonisia, Steeler." And maybe that made him flinch, to hear his surname still coming from my mouth, but I ignored the twinge of guilt beneath all the layers of rage and sorrow I'd become. "Just because she gave me orders and a sheath doesn't mean I belong to her."

Steeler slid his hold on my wrists down to my elbows, as if to steady me during what he had to say next.

"Under Sorronian law, it would if she was your mother."

CHAPTER

30

"No."

I tugged myself out of Steeler's mind to find that we were pressed together in real life, too. The sound of distant crashing waves beyond the lighthouse glass filled my ears once more as I took a few hasty steps back.

"No." I shook my head. "There's no way."

And because my mind had just done so much running without my body, it was like the excess energy exploded beneath my skin.

I took off down the spiral staircase until I hit the beach, sprinting along the pebbled shore while a low-pitched wind came rattling in from the ocean. It was nearing nighttime now, the sky darkening to a bruised purple, the water streaked with the setting sun.

I didn't know where I was going. I knew it was stupid to run. But my limbs were screaming to move as fast as my brain was, so I didn't stop until the lighthouse was the size of an upright thumb behind me.

Only when my lungs burned with the smell of salt and seaweed did I slow to a walk and think about what Steeler had just claimed.

If she was your mother...

Well, Dyonisia Reeve *couldn't* be my mother. I'd found my memory of Lord Arad, so I knew the bats' description matched fairly well—*hair dark as shadows but skin that glowed like honey*—but they'd called her a lady from the *sea*, and Dyonisia Reeve wasn't a lady from the sea. She was from the top of Bascite Mountain, the cold center of it all. She wouldn't have hidden in an abandoned Object Summoning classroom nearly five hundred years into her reign, and she definitely *wouldn't* have fallen in love with Fabian. Somebody would have noticed her pregnancy. Fabian himself would have told me.

Why, then, would Steeler think there was a chance?

My eyes absentmindedly fell upon a nearby seagull, who was hopping toward me with something clamped in its beak. When it was close enough for me to see the yellow rings around its pupils, it dropped its prey at my feet with a shy bow of its head.

"*Will you be my mate?*"

"Oh." I glanced at the crushed snail on the rocks, ripping myself out of the flurry of thoughts in my head. "I'm sorry, but no thank you." I pointed at another seagull picking through the rocks closer to the water. "That one looks like a nice option, though."

The seagull didn't even sound surprised to hear that I had talked back. It gave a sad, cawing laugh.

"*I've already asked her. She said my wingspan isn't big enough.*"

I chewed on my lip, eyeing the seagull's feathers. "Well, I think your wingspan is just fine."

"That may be one of the strangest compliments I've ever heard," drawled a familiar voice as Steeler materialized in front of me. The seagull squawked in shock, its wings bursting open on impulse. "But I'll take whatever I can get from you."

I glared at him. "I was talking to the bird... which you've scared away," I added as the seagull grabbed the snail with its beak and took off with a flap of gray wings.

Steeler surveyed me, his arms folded, a shadow falling over him as a storm cloud drifted overhead. "Did you blow off enough steam? Or do you need to punch something, too?"

"I don't know, your face *does* look pretty appealing right about now."

In more ways than one, but I wasn't going to clarify that. Not as Steeler gave me the smallest of smiles and dug into his pants pocket, bringing out a folded piece of parchment that he handed out to me.

"What is this?"

He waited until I'd grabbed it between my fingers before saying, "You know how I told you that Mr. Gleekle has an office filled with the files of all his students? After I heard that bat's description of your mother, I... became curious and *may* or may not have commanded an Object Summoner to lockpick his office door, conjure your file for me, and forget about the entire ordeal immediately afterward."

I didn't even have it in me to glare at him again. My fingers had gone numb against the paper in my hands as I realized what it was.

My file.

"Go ahead," Steeler said gently. "It's your right to know."

Trying not to tremble, I unfolded the piece of parchment and found another, smaller piece of paper inside, which I read first:

To Stanley Gleekle – CONFIDENTIAL

The conquered has insisted he has a right to claim her as his own, and unfortunately, he is right. The oath dictates that I must uphold my end of the bargain in that regard. Therefore, you shall give her his requested power when she arrives.

But, Stanley, I am warning you—no one must know who she is until the time is right. You must call her by her lesser name, and if you so much as look her in the eyes for too long, I will skin you alive and rip the meat off your weak human bones.

Sincerely,
DR

Now my whole *body* was trembling as I lifted this paper to read the thicker, more formal ink beneath it:

Subject: #580,945
Status: Alive
Birth Year: 482 AF
Home Village: Alderwick
Power TBG: Wild Whispering
Name: Rayna Reeve

"After I found it, I tried to get into Mr. Gleekle's mind," Steeler was whispering, "but every bit of information regarding you appeared to be locked up tight by another Mind Manipulator."

I wasn't listening. A numb sort of buzzing had started to twist around my bones at the sight of that last name.

It wasn't possible. I was Rayna Drey. I'd always been Rayna Drey and I always would be. Fabian Drey was my father by blood. He—

My blockade must have slipped, because Steeler said gently, almost cautiously, "In Sorronia, the females pass their surnames down, not the males."

I curled my fingernails into my palms in an attempt to pierce through the numbness rising to the surface of my skin. There was so much I didn't know about Sorronia and why Dyonisia had left it.

If only I could strangle the information out of Steeler's throat, since I obviously didn't have the ability to navigate his maze yet.

At that thought, Steeler's eyes flashed with a spark of something darker and grittier than amusement.

"No need to strangle it out of me, little hurricane. I'll just tell you ... after you come inside and eat something for me, that is. You need the nourishment, and Felicity will be pissed if we skip dinner."

"Felicity's as bossy as you are," I muttered before pushing the papers back to him. I didn't want to touch those words any longer than I had to. They felt like poison leaking onto my fingerprints.

I watched Steeler pocket them carefully again, then turned on a heel to march my way back to the lighthouse.

Back to whatever answers I was finally going to get.

Sure enough, Felicity jumped up from where she appeared to have been pestering Garvis, Terrin, and Dazmine with napkins, trying to tuck them into their shirts like bibs, as soon as Steeler and I made it through the front cottage door.

"*Coco! Raynie! What took you so long? The food's getting cold!*"

"Sorry." I sat down before an immense platter of dumplings in the center of the table, golden brown and perfectly crimped at the edges. I ignored Dazmine's raised eyebrows, Garvis's inquisitive glance, and

Terrin's muffled chuckle. "Steeler was about to start telling me a story."

Just as I'd planned, Felicity clapped her hands together, the irritation on her face widening into a sharp-toothed smile.

"*Ooh, I love a good story! Tell Coco to start from the beginning.*"

Steeler was lowering himself slowly into a chair opposite of me, every one of his muscles on edge as he realized what trap I'd set for him.

There would be no explanation of Dyonisia's origins *after* dinner. There would be an explanation *now.*

I pinned him with my best expression of fearlessness. "Felicity wants you to start from the beginning."

And so did I. No more holes. No more gaps or half-truths or missing pieces. If I was going to peer into the monstrous possibility that Dyonisia Reeve might have given life to me—that the knife she'd made a sheath for had been hers from the very beginning... well, I needed to know everything.

When Steeler made the smallest of glances toward Dazmine, who had lowered herself into the seat beside me, I nodded. She was already involved, already formulating plans to get Jenia back from Dyonisia whether any of us liked it or not. No hiding the truth from her, either.

Steeler nodded back and cleared his throat.

"Okay, then. I'll start with once upon a time, when there were three faerie sisters with powers that marked them as royals."

Terrin paused with a mouthful of dumpling already in his mouth. Garvis scrunched his eyebrows. Obviously, the two of them knew where this was headed with just those few words. My own thoughts flashed back to Steeler's pendant with the engraving of the Sorronian words and the three female faeries wearing crowns.

"The eldest sister," Steeler continued, eyes tacked to mine, "could steal anyone else's faerie magic with a single glance and keep it for herself to wield forevermore." His jaw twitched, as if such a thing disgusted him. "Her name was Mydusia, and she became queen when their mother grew to a weary age and passed her the crown during a symbolic duel."

"A symbolic duel?" Dazmine tilted her head.

Terrin was the one who answered her, forcing himself to swallow his forkful of dumpling with a thump to his chest.

"According to Sorronian tradition, any female can claim the throne so long as they challenge the existing queen to an official duel—and win, of course."

Dazmine raised her eyebrows at him. No matter how many weeks had passed since their first encounter in the jungle, she always looked half inclined to eat him alive.

"This Mydusia person is still the queen of your realm?"

"Yes," Terrin said.

"And in theory, any one of us females in this room could challenge her to a duel and take her place? Even Felicity?"

"*Oh, I like that,*" Felicity piped up. "*I would be a good queen.*"

Terrin boomed out a harsh laugh. "Millenia's worth of powerful faeries with astounding innate magic have continuously challenged our current queen, and they've all ended up in pieces. The monkey wouldn't come out of it with half a tail left."

Although Felicity's face fell, I couldn't say I was surprised.

If the current queen could actually *steal* other faerie magic with a single glance and wield it for herself... well, nobody she faced would prove a threat to her. She could render her opponent completely magic-less, then simply use their own power to destroy them.

"What about the other two sisters?" I prodded. "What were their powers?"

"The youngest, Chrysanthia, had the power of Camouflage," Steeler answered with a more relaxed jaw now. "Much like her older sister, she could mimic the magics around her... but more as a mirror, a reflection, nothing she could keep forever. She was gentle, aloof, and perhaps a touch mad—but welcomed and loved throughout the queendom despite this."

The power of Camouflage. I wondered what that would be like, to be able to echo every power around you. To be able to hear the song of the jungle, the cacophony of minds, the pull of objects, the morphing of skin and bone, and the call of the elements all at once.

"What about the middle sister?" I asked, dreading the answer but knowing what it was deep in my coiling gut.

Steeler closed his eyes. Garvis tensed beside him.

"The middle sister, Dyonisia, could suppress other faerie powers with a misty, milky magic I am sure you are all well familiar with."

Dazmine sucked in a sharp breath and Felicity made a small, "*Oh!*" while my heart only curled into a tighter ball.

Dyonisia Reeve wasn't just a faerie. She was a faerie... princess? Or, at least, the younger sister of the queen of Sorronia. A royal.

Steeler opened his eyes again, meeting mine.

"Dyonisia was rebellious and wild-spirited from the day she took her first breath, they say. And yet the three sisters remained close for hundreds of years—until Princess Chrysanthia went missing."

I blinked. That wasn't what I had been expecting at all.

"The youngest sister went missing? Why? How?"

Steeler didn't answer right away. His gaze lowered to my shaking hands, then to my uneaten dinner, the look on his face so pointed and commanding that I didn't need Mind Manipulating to interpret the words behind the gesture.

No more answers until you take a bite of your food, little hurricane.

My belly clenched as I heeded him despite my every instinct to resist the temptation. I shoveled a bite of food into my mouth, letting the blend of flavors explode across my tongue. Then another, and another, each mouthful as savory as the last.

"This is delicious, Felicity," I said through a warm, muffled bite.

As if that had popped a bubble over the table, everyone else began eating again, too. Everyone besides Steeler, who merely resumed his story, apparently satisfied that I was getting something down.

"Nobody knows how or why Princess Chrysanthia disappeared despite door-to-door investigations across the queendom. But after she did, Dyonisia began pointing fingers at the queen, claiming their youngest sister's disappearance was *her* fault—a treasonous statement, as you can imagine." His jaw twitched again. "It got to a point where the queen was about to throw her only remaining sister in prison when Dyonisia challenged her to a duel for the crown."

Dazmine glanced at me, her confusion echoing mine.

If Dyonisia could *smother* other faerie magic but her older sister could *steal* it, who would have had the upper hand in such a fight?

"And?" I asked.

"And Dyonisia lost." Steeler shrugged. "According to those who were alive to see it, it was over quickly. But the queen didn't kill her sister, even though she killed every other faerie who dared challenge her—nor did she steal her magic. With her final death blow hovering right over Dyonisia's head, Her Majesty withdrew and ordered her sister into exile."

288

Those words painted shivers up and down my neck. Not only because a wild, possessive energy beneath my skin wanted to snap at the way he'd said *Her Majesty*, but because Dyonisia... she'd already been through the worst thing she inflicted upon her own people.

Exile.

"That bitch." Dazmine had stiffened next to me, obviously of the same mind. "Obsessed with exiling others all because it happened to her. Except instead of actually kicking her throwaways out to sea, she's *hoarding* them."

Steeler nodded. "Along with the entire council of the queen's most trusted advisors, all of whom she managed to steal before she fled. And for this added insult—for kidnapping the queen's personal Good Council after she spared her life—Her Majesty has ordered her military that if they are to see Dyonisia in the flesh ever again, they are to kill her on sight... along with any offspring she might have produced in her hundreds of years playing queen on this island."

Well, there it was. A segway back to what he'd told me in his mind. *The tattooed faeries on that ship are all oath-bound to kill Dyonisia Reeve or anyone who belongs to her by blood.*

"Does the queen... *expect* Dyonisia to have produced offspring?" I asked, chewing each word carefully as I tried to figure out how to phrase it. For whatever reason, Steeler seemed to be hiding his suspicion from the others—and as much as I hated the sneaking and scheming, this *was* about me. Nobody else but me. I didn't want to share it with anyone else either, not until I understood it completely. "I mean, why would the queen even fear such a thing?"

Why would she want to have me killed for the misdeeds of a mother I've never even known until last year?

Steeler seemed to read the real question in the purse of my lips.

"Faerie children are becoming increasingly rare. So rare, in fact, that our queendom has begun to consider any offspring divine gifts of Fate." Steeler glanced at Garvis and Terrin. "And Her Majesty has been unsuccessful at producing a potential heir of her own, a female to one day pass her crown to in a symbolic duel. So if Dyonisia had... involved a human to make a conception more likely, and if that child just so *happened* to inherit the type of antipower that would mark her as part of the ancient Reeve dynasty..."

I swept away the furious upsurge of revenge that wanted to rise inside me at the thought that Dyonisia might have somehow manipulated Fabian into... being with her in that way. Sweet, gentle Fabian, who'd only ever been in love with Don, who would have never chosen such a cold, brutal woman to sleep with and meet up with in secret of his own accord.

For now, revenge could wait. Because I'd just realized—

"Dyonisia's not just playing queen," I whispered. "She's creating an army, isn't she? An army she can perfect over the centuries until she decides it's the right time to..."

I couldn't even get out the rest of the words.

"To try to take over the throne she fumbled five hundred years ago," Steeler finished for me. "To redo the duel with a new race of magic wielders—and an heir of her own—by her side. Yes. That's what we think, too."

God of the Cosmos. I couldn't imagine the villagers of Alderwick forced to face this *Majesty* figure who could suck out each of their powers like sardines from a jar. My own innate power hadn't even developed yet. To think that the queen could steal it from me before I had the chance to find out what form it might take...

A soft pressure against my blockade had me cracking open for Steeler. Letting him slide inside so that he could hear my thoughts.

It still doesn't feel right, the idea of Dyonisia being my mother, I said. *Why would she have manipulated Fabian, out of all people, into falling in love with her? There's no way she would have ever actually loved him. They wouldn't have had any compatibility whatsoever.*

At that thought, another one struck me.

Why don't you Walk us to Alderwick and get the truth directly from Fabian's mind? He doesn't even have to know we're there...

The thought of violating my father's privacy like that made me feel sick to my stomach, but what if it was the only way?

We already did that, little hurricane. That's what I was searching for in Alderwick: the truth from your father's memories.

I stared at him.

You entered Fabian's mind?

You saw with your own eyes that I didn't harm him.

I had. Based on how he'd been making cookies with Don, unperturbed, I doubted he'd even known a Mind Manipulator was sneaking into his head at all. I bit back the reprimand I had no right giving him after I'd suggested doing exactly that.

What did you find?

Nothing.

Across the table, Steeler's face didn't so much as twitch to indicate that he was currently in my mind, but his consciousness beneath my blockade had settled into a deep frown.

That whole part of your father's life is gone until the moment he stole you away from the abandoned classroom in the Object Summoner sector. He knows that he kidnapped you and nicked that knife from your mother, but nothing more. Nothing before that. Even his knowledge that he was in love with your mother... it doesn't have any kind of face or emotion attached to it. It's just a dry fact.

Someone had erased it from him, then. Fabian hadn't purposely kept my mother from me, after all—he hadn't known how I came to be all along.

The realization loosened something vital in my chest. That letter he'd written to me last year must have been his way of sharing the only thing he knew about the incident. That he'd come from that abandoned classroom. That he'd stolen a baby from a female he'd had no recollection of ever seeing.

There's a way to find out for sure, Steeler said.

Is there? My heart began hammering against my chest.

Yes. Two ways, actually. The first one isn't really an option, though. We'd have to put you in front of Old Veracious—a sword on the main ship that tells its handler the absolute truth about the person before it. It's how we verify the identities of anyone new who boards the ship, make sure they're not enemies in disguise.

I shuddered.

So if I had come with you all those months ago, if I had boarded the ship, they would have put this sword in front of me—

—and discovered if you were Dyonisia's daughter for themselves right then and there.

And if I *was* Dyonisia's daughter, they would have killed me immediately with that same sword: an act Steeler would have had to watch, maybe even partake in, because of that creepy oath-bound shit.

No. A growl had erupted in my mind, and even the others at the table paused as Steeler seemed to bristle in his chair. *I am not an official part of the queen's military yet, and as for the others...* He flexed his fingers against the table. *They might have* tried *to kill you, but I wouldn't have let them. Keeping you from that ship was more for their sake than yours.*

A cold, creeping calm had trickled down his face.

You mean....?

I would have had to turn them into piles of bones and guts, of course. And then the queen would have put a target on both of our backs. Not a situation I wanted to put you in.

I found myself swallowing thickly.

Okay, so Old Veracious isn't an option. What's the second one?

I needed to know. Needed to finally have that truth about my birth and purpose in my hands. Needed to have an idea of what my innate magic might be once it finally exploded into form.

I have an older friend on the ship, Steeler started haltingly. *He's... very close to Nara, the one who makes the pills for us. In fact, he helps her formulate a variety of medicines with his power of Magnification—an ability to see the very smallest of details down to their chains of chemical compositions.*

Sounds fancy. That wasn't even sarcasm. The more I learned about other types of powers out there, the more intrigued I became about the seemingly endless possibilities. *What would he do, look at Dyonisia and me side by side and tell us if we're related just by our... our particles?*

Steeler leaned back with folded arms, obviously impressed.

That's exactly what he'd do. Except you don't need all of Dyonisia by your side. If you can just steal one of the hairs on her head...

My mouth fell open. Was Steeler actually asking me to pluck a perfect, glistening hair off of our Good Council leader's *scalp?*

I'd do it myself, he said casually, *but even if I could Walk straight into that prison—which I can't—I think it would be a bit problematic if I just appeared right in front of her face, don't you?*

My heart sank a notch. He was right. If Dyonisia found out about his Walking power, then it put our entire situation in jeopardy. It was our one secret from her, the only thing that gave us the upper hand.

Plus, for some reason, I didn't really like the idea of him anywhere near someone who wanted him dead—especially someone who would wrap him up in a web of her antipower as soon as she saw him.

Steeler's eyebrows shot up. *I'm around you all the time, and you want me dead.*

That's different, I snapped, annoyed that he'd heard that little slip-up in my thoughts.

Oh? His lips quirked. *How so?*

I can want you dead, alright? But nobody else can.

The declaration was as ridiculous as it sounded, but Steeler nodded with those damned lips of his still twitching.

I'm your prey, no one else's. Got it.

"Are you two done with your silent conversation now?" Dazmine asked. "Or are you going to sit here and suckle each other's eyes for another few minutes? Because if so, we can give you privacy..."

Garvis choked on his bite of dumpling. I stomped on Dazmine's foot beneath the table.

Smirking, she stomped back.

"Women," Terrin muttered.

"*Are fabulous*," Felicity sang even though he couldn't understand her. She put her hand over her mouth and whispered to Dazmine and me through hairy fingers, "*He's just jealous because he's not the one touching Dazmine's feet.*"

A laugh bubbled out of me even as Dazmine rolled her eyes, but it was short-lived when Steeler propped up an eyebrow and I remembered what *I'd* touched in his mind merely an hour ago.

It didn't count, I tried to convince myself. *It was technically just our imaginations running a little wild together, that's all. Almost like a dream.*

If that's the case, it was the best wet dream I've *ever had,* Steeler joked in my head.

I scowled at him.

Are you always eavesdropping on people's most intimate thoughts and feelings, or just mine?

Just yours. They happen to be unnaturally interesting, after all.

Dazmine was right. I definitely needed to shove Steeler out of my head before my hackles actually rose like a hissing cat's.

I just had one more question for him before I did.

How am I supposed to get one of... of Dyonisia's hairs? I refused to call her my mother until we were absolutely certain. *It's not like she hangs out around campus. And I don't think it would go over well if I left the Institute to go knocking on her door at Bascite Mountain either.*

Steeler's smile—both in the outside world and inside my mind—jolted right through me with its intensity. With its vicious humor.

Like I've said before, little hurricane, you're more devious than I ever imagined possible. He passed me a mental image of his finger flicking my nose. *Go figure it out.*

CHAPTER

31

Go figure it out.

I was still seething over that on Wednesday during a particularly laborious lesson of Predators & Prey.

Mr. Conine had been leading us up the slope of the jungle mountain for the last forty-five minutes, until we'd surpassed the furthest point we'd ever gone and the upward angle of our trek had risen into a vertical mossy cliff.

Now, we were all dragging ourselves upward rock by rock, foothold by foothold, the mixture of our panting and humming bleeding into the song of the jungle. Perhaps before becoming Wild Whisperers, a few of us would have fallen to a skull-crushing death by now—but whenever someone's foot slipped on the silky surface of moss, a bramble or branch would jut out to catch them.

"You've got it," Gileon called from where Emelle and I were climbing side by side. "Nuisance says we're almost there."

I glanced upward to find the bumbling dot of his beetle friend hovering near what looked like an edge, which Mr. Conine himself was about to reach with a few more pulls upward. As was Rodhi—the fastest climber of everyone in the class, apparently. Sweat sparkled on Emelle's face as she forced out a laugh.

"I'm not sure I even *want* to get there if this is just the beginning of the lesson."

She'd been more morose than ever the few times I got to see her during classes. The news of her village had dwindled away to nothing over the last few weeks, so I couldn't blame her for the darkened edge to her voice, but still... I wished I could do something, say something, to put a smile back on her face.

"Maybe Mr. Conine has a picnic waiting for us at the top," I panted, my muscles straining as I pulled myself upward, "and we'll simply get to eat it while we overlook the entire Institute."

I was wrong, though. As soon as everyone in the class had reached the top, Mr. Conine only led us onward, through thickets so dense that it would have been impossible to push through the crisscrossed branches if we were in any other sector.

As it was, Mr. Conine himself sent out a humming song that had this upper part of the jungle parting for us, until it all opened up to—

"Welcome," he said finally, spreading his arms wide, "to the southeast end of the Esholian river system."

We all lined the bank of a massive stretch of murky, slow-moving water that spread as far as we could see from one direction to another in snaking twists and turns. Edging closer, I had the distinct impression that hundreds of reptiles and fish were observing us quietly from its depths.

"This river system spreads across the entire island," Mr. Conine resumed, "making it the perfect travel system for those less inclined to take carriage by air. Now, while Element Wielders might simply control the speed and direction of the water and Object Summoners might propel boats in whichever direction they choose, we Wild Whisperers must rely on aquatic creatures to carry us to our destination." He turned to face us, a smile wrinkling his leathery skin. "Can anyone guess which water creatures might be willing to pull a Wild Whisperer across the island if only we are devoted enough friends?"

Rodhi bounced on the balls of his feet, but didn't say anything. On his other side, Dazmine wrinkled her nose at him as if she'd found herself next to an overactive toddler who might wipe boogers on her at any moment.

I snapped my gaze back toward Mr. Conine as he waited for someone to answer. It was best not to make eye contact with Dazmine, not to reveal that we were anything more than unfriendly peers.

"Crocodiles?" Mitzi Hodges guessed after a few seconds of buzzing silence. "They're probably strong enough to pull us."

Mr. Conine shook his head. "Too proud."

Norman Pollard raised a finger. "Giant turtles?"

"Too slow."

"Frogs?" Gileon asked.

"Um." Mr. Conine scratched his sideburns awkwardly. "I think frogs are a little too small. Anyone else?"

Finally, Rodhi burst out with, "Dolphins, of course."

"There you go."

Mr. Conine snapped his fingers in Rodhi's direction, to which Emelle and I exchanged startled glances. Since when had Rodhi become an expert in Predators & Prey? Although, come to think of it, *I* should have known that answer, too—I vaguely remembered a local fisherman talking about a family of dolphins that kept stealing his nets in the part of the river that flowed near Alderwick a few years ago.

Mr. Conine nodded at the general air of awe and excitement. "The river dolphins live in families of three or four throughout the entirety of the river system, and they're always curious to meet you. If you can coax them out of hiding, that is… for they are also much shyer than their saltwater counterparts."

He waited. After a few seconds of everyone standing stock-still, the class burst into motion and sound, some people calling for the dolphins in high-pitched voices, others getting on their hands and knees on the bank and swishing palms throughout the water.

Maybe it made me a massive cheat, but curiosity had me instinctually pushing open my blockade like the hinges of a shutter, funneling that opening toward the river.

To my surprise, it worked. The cacophony of my classmates hit the sides of my blockade, but I could suddenly pinpoint several dozen thoughts lurking within the river.

Hulking within the seaweed of the silty riverbed, a crocodile was debating whether or not it could stuff down another catfish.

A female turtle was having a nightmare about cracked eggs.

A male poison dart frog, hidden within the weeds by the bank, was desperately trying to get the attention of a nearby female by swelling up his throat to twice its usual size.

And bubbling up to the surface, four slippery, mischievous thoughts flowed from the depths in front of Mitzi and Norman:

He brought friends!

Look at those flat foreheads.

Oh, I better get the cute one with the button nose.

Ugh, fingers are so creepy.

I couldn't help myself. I grabbed onto that last thought with my mental fingers, reeling myself inward until my internal voice hovered right outside the dolphin's mind.

Why don't you come out and play? I whispered into its... ear? The dent on the side of its slippery head?

The dolphin shrieked and flipped, sending its companions into utter chaos until...

"They're pink!" Cilia shrieked as the four of them jumped out of the water and twisted in midair, their giggles more like clicking cackles when Norman got a violent splash of water to his face.

"*Of course we're pink.*" One of them resurfaced with its elongated mouth full of smiling teeth. "*What were you expecting? That dreadfully drab gray of those sea-dwellers?*"

"N-no." Cilia blinked. "I think your coloring is quite lovely."

"*Well, of course you do. A pretty thing like you knows everyone looks better in pink.*"

Cilia's blush matched the sunburnt shade of its skin.

Over the next hour, Mr. Conine had us take turns wading into the river, playing with the dolphins who took flirting to an entirely new level—especially when Rodhi dove into the languid current.

Emelle sidled up to me as I watched him on the bank, my curls still heavy and dripping from my own time riding up and down the river on the back of one of them, clutching its dorsal fin like a lifeline. Her clothes, too, clung to her body like a sopping second skin.

"At least he's interested in something else other than Spiders, Worms, & Insects?" Despite her attempt at conversation, her voice still held a... weight to it. Like an anchor had dragged it down an octave.

"Well, I imagine Rodhi and these dolphins have lots in common."

Emelle turned to me with a squint. "Such as?"

I counted on my fingers. "Coy. Cocky. Social, yet constantly disappearing." Even as I said that, all four dolphins plunged back under the surface, taking Rodhi with them for a moment before they flipped back into the air with those clicking cackles.

Emelle was still squinting at me.

"What?"

"Your head," she said. "You're not constantly massaging it any-more. Have your headaches gone away?"

My smile dropped. Come to think of it, I *hadn't* felt even the ghostly remnants of pain in the last several weeks. Maybe Steeler's lack of meddling truly was mending the fractures in my mind despite my inability to find any of those crucial memories that involved him.

Or maybe it was the fact that the smell of his black bamboo seemed to cling to me wherever I went, soothing every treacherous part of my body.

"Yeah." How to tell the truth without revealing anything of importance? "I... I found a medicine that works, I think."

A medicine that involved a lighthouse, a monkey, and a male faerie that was an absolute pain in my ass. *Go figure it out.* As if stealing a hair from an exiled Sorronian princess with murder in her veins was just a fun little side adventure.

Emelle's mouth opened to say something, but a violent flurry of cheeping and squawking overhead had us both looking skyward through the strip of jungle parted by the river.

Birds—a flock of all shapes and sizes—swarmed us with eager pelts of news, Emelle's blue cotinga fluttering in their midst.

" *They're alive! Your family is alive!*"

" *We found some survivors shielded within a burrow!*"

"*The monsters are gone!*"

"*The village is being rebuilt!*"

Tears flooded Emelle's eyes, and I grabbed her into a fierce hug before Mr. Conine and the rest of the class streamed over to hear the news for themselves. Nobody else had been from Merkwell, but the fact that the birds had returned at all had the class breaking out into excited chatter. Even Mr. Conine himself sighed in relief, despite his refusal to acknowledge the attack a few weeks ago.

Stepping away from the commotion so that Emelle could receive embraces from Gileon and Cilia and Mitzi, I eyed Rodhi as he slid off the back of a dolphin and trudged to shore, dripping with seaweed.

An idea had itched in the back of my brain at the sight of Mr. Conine's obvious relief. An idea that involved *another* instructor who seemed too frightened to speak out against the Good Council in public but who, according to my unearthed memories, liked to sneak in tiny moments of resistance behind their backs.

"Did you enjoy your ride?" I asked Rodhi.

"Oh, yeah." He winked at the dolphins still poking their elongated mouths out of the water. "I'll see *you* four later."

They gave final clicking cackles and slid back under the surface, and his eyes slipped to the flurry of birds surrounding Emelle.

"I'm guessing it's good news by the look on her face?"

"Yeah, good news." I steeled myself to keep talking naturally. To loosen my shoulders and pop out a hip as if this abrupt turn in conversation I was about to make wasn't anything out of the ordinary. "So... you know how you're obsessed with Ms. Pincette?"

Rodhi's eyebrows shot up.

"Well aware, darling, well aware."

"Do you, like, know where she lives?" If I was going to employ Ms. Pincette's help again, I wanted to ask her in the privacy of her own home, not a classroom where anyone could hear us.

Rodhi's eyebrows couldn't have gone any higher.

"Do you mean to tell me you've lived on this campus for a year and half and you've never wondered where our instructors sleep at night?"

He waited. I didn't answer, because no, I hadn't. Not until now, when my mind was imagining cold dungeons dug into the ground beneath the Testing Center.

"They live in their sectors, of course!" Rodhi had never given me such a look of exasperation before. "For instance, you know that tall building with the sharp, curved roof and the gangly drainage pipes between Mr. Conine's classroom and the arboretum?"

"Yeah?"

"That's Mrs. Smetlar's house."

I blinked. I'd thought that building was just another classroom, perhaps for upperclassmen to practice advanced magic in.

"Are you telling me you know where every instructor lives, Rodhi?"

He shrugged. "Just the ones I love or hate. Love Ms. Pincette. Hate Mrs. Smetlar."

"She is pretty horrible, isn't she?" Just this Monday, she'd made us feed the rotting carcasses of animals to a family of vultures, telling us that those carcasses would be us if we didn't pass our Final Tests. "Okay, so which building is Ms. Pincette's?"

Rodhi narrowed his eyes at me.

"You're not trying to win over her romantic affections, right?"

"What the hell! No! One, I'm not into women." Though it would probably make life easier if I was. "Two, she's an *instructor*, Rodhi."

Rodhi shook his head, his voice dropping into a silky quiet despite the squawking, cheeping cloud of birds still surrounding our classmates up ahead. "Oh, but she's so much more than an instructor. Okay, so here's where you're going to go."

Up the stone staircase, through the alleyway where crab-eating racoons liked to loiter, and down the cobblestone lane cracked with moss, I finally found Ms. Pincette's house crammed against a jutting piece of mountainside.

Cottony white cobwebs clung to the windows like exterior curtains. Moths perched on the roof like fluttering shingles. Cracks in the stone walls crawled with ants carrying leaves up and down. I couldn't say I was surprised, but the sight of it all gave me the feeling that I was intruding upon a space that wanted to blend in.

When I moved to step up to the door, something silky and thin tickled against my chest.

"What...?"

I looked down and swiped away a single strand of silk.

Weird.

Trying not to get spooked before I'd even knocked on the door, I stepped forward again, but another tickle against my arms and legs had me scrabbling at the rest of me, too. Then something brushed against my neck, and I clawed at it to rip away a braid of silk nearly as thick as a noose—just as more flung around my body and I finally saw the culprits flying past my eyesight from every direction.

Spiders.

"Hey, stop."

I ripped away handfuls of thickening cobwebs as they wound tighter and tighter around me, but the spiders didn't answer me. More and more came flying from the trees, from Ms. Pincette's rooftop, from nowhere and everywhere all at once, until I couldn't tear their strands off fast enough.

"*Stop*," I said again. "I'm not going to hurt you!"

Even before I'd finished that last word, though, I was ripping out my crescent knife to hack at the ropes of webs careening around me, and the spiders hissed in unison. They spiraled around me so fast I could barely keep track of them, pinning my arms to my sides until I dropped my knife.

Oh, I was going to kill Rodhi for not warning me about this.

I tried to backtrack, figuring I'd talk to Ms. Pincette another time, but my foot caught on a gnarled root and I fell, landing with a painful thump on my ass. Heart thumping, I looked down to find my body completely encased in a web so tight around my ribs that I could barely scrape in deep enough breaths. Several dozen spiders scurried up to where I had fallen, still attached to their strings and ranging in size from a marble to a dinner plate.

The largest of them, a birdeater, rubbed its hind legs against its abdomen in a hissing rattle.

"Who are you and what do you want?"

"Well, you could have asked that *before* you tied me up!" I cried. The birdeater hissed again, and I amended quickly, "I'm Rayna. Rayna Drey—" My mind tickled with the thought that according to Dyonisia, I was Rayna *Reeve*... but I wasn't going to accept that as reality until it was proven.

"Tessa wasn't expecting a visitor of that name," the birdeater said, *"so why are you here? To spy on her? Kidnap her? Kill her?"*

"What? No! I'm her student! I just wanted to talk about...an assignment."

"Lies. You brought weapons."

"Yeah, in case stuff like *this* happens." I could feel the rest of my knife handles pressing against my thigh in the suffocating cocoon around me, and wished for the first time in my life that I had the power of Object Summoning to conjure them out of their sheath.

The spiders were crawling closer, their hundreds of eyes reflecting my terrified face, and I sucked in a breath to send a cry of help to the jungle.

"Leave her be."

I could have cried in relief at the sound of Ms. Pincette's voice.

My Spiders, Worms, & Insects instructor had appeared in her doorway, folding her arms across her chest.

"Leave her be," she repeated. "She is not here to spy, kidnap, or kill me. Though I am certainly interested to hear why she *is* here," she added, arching an eyebrow at me.

Reluctantly, the spiders unwound their webs from around me. As soon as it was thin enough, I ripped my way out and scooped up my crescent knife, locking it in a tight fist until the last of them had scurried away.

Finally, I sheathed it and returned my gaze to Ms. Pincette.

"To what do I owe this very unexpected visit?" she asked, lips pursed.

I hesitated, still trying to gather my breath. Knowing that the jungle would have helped me get out of that predicament didn't stop my skin from prickling all over as if in preparation for spider venom.

"Ms. Drey?"

I unleashed a breath and asked, "May I come in?"

Just because I'd seen what Ms. Pincette had done for me in my memories didn't mean she'd be willing to help me again, especially now that she knew Dyonisia had a closer eye on me. Plus, her own memories had been wiped clean by Steeler last year and she didn't have her own recollection of any type of past relationship with me. But unless there were more vicious spiders inside her home, it wouldn't hurt to ask—even if I was ninety-nine percent sure she was going to say no after what had just happened.

To my surprise, Ms. Pincette only glanced over my shoulder once before swinging open the door and ushering me in.

"Come in, then."

Trying not to appear too shocked, I followed.

The interior of her home couldn't have been more different than the outside. Neat, polished bookcases lined the walls. Two identical loveseats glimmered with velvety sheens. Flickering candles filled the space with warm, buttery light that revealed clean, dust-less air.

Not a hint of a single insect inside.

"Apologies for the spiderweb thing," Ms. Pincette said, shutting the door behind us and striding into a small kitchen around the corner. "It's just a precaution. I usually don't take visitors—especially students—but I can see by your face that this must be something serious." Her voice carried to me even after she'd disappeared from sight. "Would you like a muffin?"

"Oh." I startled. "Oh, no thank you."

"Good." Ms. Pincette reappeared with drinks with lemon wedges stuck on the rims. "Because they are stale and I am not the best at making muffins." She handed me a glass. "What seems to be the matter?"

I sat in one of those velvet loveseats and clutched the glass in two tight hands, hoping the cold bite of the drink would prevent them from sweating. "The first quarterly test of the year is next week..."

Even saying that out loud felt sour on my tongue. To think that we all existed in a bubble of an exiled princess's wrath and were still being made to take tests like the experimentation subjects we were...

"Go on, Ms. Drey. Surely, you are not here to remind me that a test *I* have to give you is right around the corner."

I cleared my throat. "Right. You have to give it. Which is why I was wondering if you can get Dyonisia Reeve to assess my Spiders,

Worms, & Insects portion. Tell her that my power is suspicious, that I'm exhibiting too much of it, to get her to come observe."

Now that I knew how much interest Dyonisia held for me, I doubted she'd kill me over a secret piece of information she already probably suspected—whether she was my mother or not. Like Dazmine had said earlier, I'd already be exiled by now if she didn't have other plans for me. Whatever they were.

Ms. Pincette straightened her spine for a moment before sinking into the armchair opposite me and leaning forward with flared nostrils.

"Any attention from Dyonisia Reeve is too much attention, Ms. Drey." She brushed her free hand over her stomach absentmindedly, shuddering at the touch. "Why would you possibly be wanting more of it?"

I held her gaze, refusing to break.

"You were there in the Testing Center last year. You handed her the spider that helped the pirates escape by forewarning them of her plan to trap them. You know that my memory was severely altered after that occasion—and I suspect you know yours was, too."

Ms. Pincette didn't break my gaze either.

"What are you trying to get at, Rayna?"

She'd never said my first name like that before. I glanced at the locked door and shut windows draped in cobwebs from the outside. Then leaned forward.

"What would you say if I told you that you and I used to be closer than we are now? That you helped hide some of my more... concerning characteristics from the Good Council?"

Silence.

Then—

"Go on" was all Ms. Pincette said.

"And what would you say if I need that same level of... help from you because I..." My throat stuck on a lump as dry as the pills Steeler still gave me every weekend. "Because I have found some of my memories since that day in the Testing Center, and all is not what it seemed back then."

"Go on."

"And what would you say if one of those things that is not what it seems requires some further digging that involves me getting as close to Dyonisia Reeve as physically possible... sooner rather than later?"

Ms. Pincette leaned back. She sipped on her drink, seeming to mull over all my questions with each one. A steady pitter-patter on her roof told me it had started to rain and drip through the canopy.

Finally, Ms. Pincette lowered her glass.

"What I would *say* to all of that is that I do indeed have holes in my memory, and I am not surprised to hear that you may have once filled them. I would also say that rebellion is dangerous and often leads to senseless tragedies, tragedies that could have been avoided if the rebel had just kept their head down... unless they play it smart. And I would ask if *this*—whatever this may be—is truly the only path forward for you."

Now it was my turn to mull it all over.

Was this the only path forward?

No. I could choose to forget what Steeler had told me in the lighthouse, could choose to pretend that Dyonisia Reeve was not the mother I'd always craved to know. I could refrain from investigating, live in ignorance, know I could never step foot on Steeler's ship because his Fated General could very well use Old Veracious to slice through my neck if the truth-telling sword saw through the lies.

Maybe by telling me to go figure it out, Steeler had been giving me that choice. *Go figure out if you really want this or not.*

309

I nodded at Ms. Pincette and lifted my chin.

"It is the path I would like to choose."

She gave the barest hint of a smile.

"You know, I do remember one thing very clearly about you from last year, Ms. Drey: you were abysmal at talking to insects. They simply wouldn't respond to you no matter how hard you tried." She stood and tucked a strand of chestnut hair neatly behind her ear. "So imagine my surprise when you walked into your first day of second-year class and demonstrated perfectly average insect communication? As if the thing—or person—who held you back last year is now gone?"

Kimber Leake. The person who had held me back last year was Kimber Leake, by commanding all the insects to cease all communication with me. I could feel that little piece of memory dislodge itself from the ice of my foundation with little effort on my part. Maybe my mind was beginning to melt of its own accord.

"Nevertheless," Ms. Pincette continued with a sigh, "I will send a message to Dyonisia Reeve saying that her most... suspicious student is still performing abysmally and needs further assessment."

I blew out a breath. "Thank you, Ms. Pincette."

She inclined her head. "I hope you find what you're looking for, Ms. Drey. Now please leave before someone discovers you here."

I was halfway to the door, leaving my glass on a sparkling glass coffee table, when I paused with my back turned to her.

"You didn't say 'leave us'."

"Come again?"

I half-turned to her, my hand floating to the doorknob as those cobwebs outside her window darkened with trickles of rain.

"Those spiders back there—they're the first ones I've seen on campus in six months. You would think they'd be eavesdropping on us right now, ready to turn us in. You would think you'd have to tell them to leave us for a conversation as forbidden as this one."

Ms. Pincette's eyes glimmered with something restrained and muffled. Something that hinted of a layer she'd long ago buried.

"You would think."

CHAPTER

32

The first quarterly test started the same way it had last year.

All the second-years swarmed the outside of the domed building until the third-years were finished and Mr. Gleekle ushered us inside.

Each sector streamed to their own archway crowned with the respective mottos. I felt the hidden brand on the back of my neck tingle as I passed BY THE MOONBEAM AND THE MIST on my way to the Wild Whisperer one.

What would it be like to take those tests instead of the ones I was supposed to? Would I pass them, or would my weekend lessons with Garvis amount to nothing compared to the daily classes other Mind Manipulators got?

A pair of cool blue eyes in the center of the room flicked toward me, and I froze. Mr. Gleekle, with his shiny, tightened smile permanently stamped on his face, had caught me looking at the wrong archway.

Shit. I bowed my head and let the crowd sweep me onward, where I clambered up my own staircase and sat in the waiting room outside the first Wild Whisperer testing door next to Emelle, Rodhi, and Gileon. My heart was pounding in my ears at that eye contact Mr. Gleekle and I had just made; he knew me as Rayna Reeve, and now he'd just seen me staring at the Mind Manipulator archway with—I couldn't deny it—longing on my face.

Thankfully for my nerves, it didn't take long for Mrs. Smetlar to appear from behind that first door.

"In, in, in," she said with a clap for each word. "Or do none of you think that the History of the Esholian Biome matters?"

"Not really, no," Rodhi muttered a little too loudly.

Mrs. Smetlar's glower couldn't have oozed with more hatred as we took our seats in a neat row of desks topped with papers and pens.

"There will be no talking unless you want a fail." She lowered herself into the bloodred armchair at the head of the classroom. "There will be no peeking over at your neighbor's paper unless you want a fail. There will be no bouncing of knees or fidgeting unless you want a fail."

That last one had been directed at Rodhi, I was sure. His whole body stilled in his seat at those words, and another surge of rage rushed up my throat at the small ways she managed to be cruel to my friends.

"Begin," Mrs. Smetlar said.

We flipped the paper over. I squinted down at the first question.

In 215 AF, a rogue Shape Shifter turned a lizard into a dragon. How did Wild Whisperers of the time calm the dragon before elite Shape Shifters could turn the beast back into its original state?

My neck muscles burned with the effort it took not to peek over at Emelle beside me, but I saw from my periphery that she was wrinkling her nose in confusion, too. Dragons were one of those legendary creatures in bedtime stories that Esholian adults used to warn children off from bad behavior... alongside vampires. I'd never even *heard* Mrs. Smetlar mention the existence of a dragon on the actual island—even if it had started out as a simple lizard.

I moved to the next question.

In 427 AF, a Good Council elite was attacked by a silverback on his trek from one village to another. Which Wild Whisperer was behind the attack, and what did the Good Council do to punish him?

What the hell? I'd never heard of a silverback attack either.

Once again, the brand on the back of my neck seemed to tingle. Surely, this wouldn't be the time to use my Mind Manipulating power, not when a hundred other Mind Manipulators were demonstrating their magic somewhere on another floor in this building.

But despite Mrs. Smetlar's earlier warnings, the sound of rustling rose as more and more classmates scratched their heads, bit their pens, scrunched their eyebrows. From the edge of my vision, I could see a smile slowly raising Mrs. Smetlar's sharpened cheekbones.

It couldn't hurt to open up my blockade for a *second*.

I funneled the opening toward her just like I had with the dolphins until her harsh, raspy thoughts filled my head.

Fools. Utter fools. I'm such a good teacher, and they don't even appreciate me. If any of them had been paying attention, they'd know I've never taught them any of this. Just proves that they're all going to fail their Final Test no matter how great I am at my job.

Thickened rage boiled in my blood. None of us could remember these questions because Mrs. Smetlar was testing us with material she'd never taught. To make sure we failed our first quarterly test.

At that moment, she pointed a cracked yellow nail at Rodhi, who couldn't hold back any longer: his knee jiggled.

"You," she started.

I didn't hesitate to intervene.

Clinging to her outermost thoughts, I pulled myself forward until I fell into the confines of her mind, the bristled walls made of dead sticks and thorns and moldy bits of feathers.

Her consciousness was as hunched and gnarled as her body had once been, wholly focused on Rodhi and the fail she was about to give him simply because he'd fidgeted.

Do you really think that's fair? I whispered into her mind.

Mrs. Smetlar swatted at her ear. "What? Who is that? Who's talking to me?"

One by one, my classmates looked up from their papers.

Do you really want to give anyone a fail over a faulty test? I asked.

Inside her mind, that hunched consciousness still hadn't recognized me standing by her unlocked gate—and would *never* recognize me without a Mind Manipulating power of her own. Hopefully, she thought a Good Council elite was nearby, checking on proceedings by probing instructor minds from a floor above or below.

Slowly, Mrs. Smetlar dropped her hand. She narrowed her beady black eyes at Rodhi but said through mashed lips, "It seems I've accidentally given you all the wrong test. My—my apologies. I will give you all a pass this time for your... discretion."

"Well, you just made my day brighter for the first time ever." Rodhi clapped his hands together and popped up, bounding for the waiting room without a backward glance.

The rest of the class followed suit, muttering.

Hesitantly, I withdrew from that moldy nest of a mind to do the same, glancing at Mrs. Smetlar's pursed, quivering lips as I passed.

Hoping I hadn't just made things worse.

I was the last to be called back into the classroom for Mr. Conine's test, where I successfully lulled a weasel to sleep by singing it a lullaby about its favorite thing: killing frenzies in the moonlight.

Mrs. Wildenberg had nodded off against her own chest by the time I entered her testing room and passed right by all the cold cups of tea and pots of curare plants littering the table before her.

Dyonisia Reeve was waiting for me in the last testing room.

She sat in the bloodred armchair like she had during our last meeting under the dome, the perfect picture of rejected royalty. Ms. Pincette stood behind her with her hands knotted behind her back.

To their left, a tank of oily black leeches streaked the inside of the glass with a crisscrossing mess of mucus trails.

"I'm glad to see you are wearing those dresses I bought you."

I jerked my head back to the woman—faerie—in the armchair.

Dyonisia's gaze cut to the slit in my current attire, as if seeing through the fabric to the sheath dutifully strapped to my thigh. One side of her mouth squeezed up in satisfaction.

She can't be my mother. I'm nothing like her.

Now that I knew Dyonisia had to keep a harsh leash on her own power encircling the island, I didn't have to worry she had the magic of Mind Manipulating to hear my thoughts. It was a strange relief, to be able to think what I wanted without the fear that she'd overhear.

I gave a slight bow of my head.

"Thank you for the dresses, ma'am. They are very pretty."

I hate the dresses. Not because they're ugly, but because they came from you.

Dyonisia sat back, her hair shimmering with the movement.

"Lexington reports great success with your weekly check-ins. He says you are closer to capturing your target than ever before."

I didn't let a single part of me twitch as that news sunk in—that Lexington had followed through with our deal. That he'd been lying to Dyonisia every week in the hopes that I could grow closer to Steeler and steal his entire stash of Nara's pills.

Good.

"But." When Dyonisia raised her chin, I traced the ebb and flow of her hair over her shoulders. "Ms. *Pincette* reports that your power fails in the face of her class's tasks. Why do you think that is, child?"

Oh yes, she definitely knew I was part-faerie, mother or not. I could see that knowledge in the predatory tilt of her head, in the wild ice that seemed to be cracking behind her pupils as she observed me.

"I don't know, ma'am." I rubbed my chest, right where my memories had shown me my innate power stemmed from. "Sometimes it seems like something is brewing in here and wants out."

Behind Dyonisia, Ms. Pincette's eyes flew open in alarm. She gave a jerky shake of her head, but I ignored it.

Dyonisia nodded at the tank of leeches. "Let me see."

I glanced at Ms. Pincette, who cleared her throat.

"Your task today, Ms. Drey, is quite straightforward: don't lose a single drop of blood."

That seemed more like a warning than a task. I wasn't quite faking the shivers that strummed my body as I forced myself toward that wretched tank I'd come to loathe.

The leeches seeped and dribbled over each other, the faintest fizzing sound emanating from their squishy mass—whispers of half-baked thoughts, words that trailed off like mush.

When I stepped up onto the stool beside the tank, it took a surge of willpower for me to bow my head over the edge and whisper down into the squirming depths: "I'm a friend. I'm a friend. I'm a friend."

Ms. Pincette had taught us that much like worms, each segment of a leech's body had to echo information down to its other parts, so repetition with a slight fizzing, spitting of our tongues was key.

"*Frien... fr... frien...*" they whispered back.

"Yes, friend, friend, friend."

I swung a leg over the edge, feeling the ice behind Dyonisia's eyes carve glaciers into the dips of my spine. The brand on the back of my neck seemed to burn with the attention, but... *I think all that hair of yours will hide it,* Steeler had said once. I'd never been so grateful for the tangled mess of my curls that hid the truth crawling in my veins;

I was a Wild Whisperer *and* a Mind Manipulator.

And I would use these leeches to steal a hair from Dyonisia's head.

Closing my eyes, sucking in a breath, locking up my muscles...

I rolled into the tank.

The squelch of leech bodies cushioned my fall, and I winced when some of those fizzing whispers stopped abruptly. But too many more twisted toward me, anchoring onto my legs and arms with their sticky undersides.

Oh, God. A scream was running jagged fingernails inside my lungs, for I had purposely told the leeches the wrong thing. To them, a friend meant someone with good blood. What I should have said was that I was a foe and my blood was poison, but I couldn't let Dyonisia witness me excelling at this test when Ms. Pincette had given her completely opposite information. I couldn't let myself pass.

I needed to fail. Needed to fall into Dyonisia's arms begging her to let me stay on the island despite my disappointments. To have a sobbing, blubbering reason to wrap my arms around her neck and take a hair while she was too distracted by all the sucker marks on my body.

Except as the first leech latched onto me, pulling in warm mouthfuls of blood from my underarm, I felt something open an eye in my chest.

When more oily black bodies clung to me, sending pinpricks secreting up and down my limbs, I felt it *strain* against the smothering bars that contained it.

"Get off me," fell out of my lips.

Because that numbness, that *life* being sucked right out of my skin—I'd felt this way for too long. Like a buzzing husk, too full of fear to fall asleep properly, too empty of joy to wake up all the way.

I couldn't take it anymore. Ripping a leech off my forearm, then my shin, then my chest, I said it again. "Get off me. Get off me. Get off me."

The leeches didn't respond. I'd told them I was a friend, and they'd already gotten a taste of my blood.

I tried to stand, but sparkles of light jiggled in the forefront of my vision. My lungs wouldn't expand for a full enough breath. In my desperate haze, I locked eyes with Ms. Pincette, and she lurched forward, past Dyonisia, as if to help me.

Just before she reached the tank, the thing in my chest broke through the pill's suppressant.

Leeches ripped themselves off my body, flying upward in a whirlwind and splattering into each other high above my head—forming a blob of oily black goo that writhed and bubbled in midair.

Then burst.

Globs of goo sprayed in every direction, hitting the walls and ceiling and doors and floor... and Dyonisia's face.

With my heart scrambling to catch up with what the hell had just happened, I launched myself out of the tank and toward the founder of this island, who had frozen in her chair with her nails digging into its velvet arms.

"I'm so sorry, ma'am, I didn't know that was going to happen."

Truth. I could have never planned that, even though I knew it had happened with the cockroaches last year. But that *thing* in my chest that felt so wild and monstrous was already fading back to sleep, like a curtain had stifled it once more. And oh shit, shit, shit, Dyonisia's perfect, glowing face and hair was *dripping* with the leech goo.

I reached out to grab handfuls of the stuff off her head.

The movement seemed to shake Dyonisia from her furious stupor. She swatted my wrist away and rose to her feet as swift as a serpent strike.

"Stop, before you cause any more damage, you insolent child. I shall have a Summoner remove the rest."

She hooked her nose down at me, her nostrils widening as she scoured the length of my body and lingered on my shoulder brand.

"I have a great many plans for you, Ms... Drey. It's up to you whether those plans involve chains and scalpels or crowns and thrones. Do you understand?"

Yes, I understood, despite the cold pit those words dragged into my stomach. But I slid a mask of terrified ignorance over my face, curling my hands into fists.

"No, ma'am. I don't."

"You will, child. You will."

I could almost *see* steam, like the milky mist of our dome, pouring from her ears. With a swish of her dress, she turned and flowed out of the room, leaving a trail of inky black splatters behind her.

Ten seconds after the door smacked shut, Ms. Pincette and I stood side by side in utter silence.

Thirty seconds later, we were still standing side by side in silence only broken by the occasional plop of goo from ceiling to floor.

It wasn't until an entire two minutes had leaked by that my Spiders, Worms, & Insects teacher rounded on me in utter fury.

"Are you happy, Ms. Drey? Is *this* what you really wanted?"

She gestured at the splotches of leech goo still dripping from overhead, speckling the walls, puddling on the floor.

"No," I said somberly.

Then uncurled my fists and brought up the black-as-midnight strand of hair pinched between my fingers—just a little something I'd grabbed from Dyonisia's head along with the goo.

"But this is."

CHAPTER

33

I knew you could do it.

Steeler's smug voice was loitering right outside the wall of my mind by the time I got back to my room, my hands rummaging hastily through all my drawers for a bottle or container I could put Dyonisia's single strand of hair in for safekeeping.

I didn't waste time getting to the question that seared on the tip of my tongue as my fingers speared through all the little black pearls in my nightstand—Steeler continued to give me one at the end of every week, and I always accepted it. For my tally, of course.

"Why is my innate power able to surpass the effects of the pills in that Testing Center?" Nobody else was in the room at the moment, not even Willa, so I didn't care that I was speaking aloud as if to an invisible person. "Is it... is my power trying to take shape?"

A deep, sharp thrill shot through my chest at the thought that maybe this was it. Maybe, if I stopped the pills altogether, my magic would explode into form and I would finally get to find out what it *was*. Maybe even use it against Dyonisia.

Steeler's voice was hesitant in my head.

It takes a catastrophic event for a faerie's power to take shape.

I scoffed. "Falling into a bed of leeches is a catastrophic event."

No. Steeler shook his head inside mine. *Falling into a bed of leeches is triggering, sure—just like drinking bascale or getting branded is. But not enough for your power to do more than throw a tantrum. For it to actually burst into shape, you'd have to endure something traumatizing beyond repair. Something that wrenches out your lungs and heartstrings, knots them together, and stuffs them back in like a life-ending punch to the gut. One you can't straighten from unless your power springs to life and helps you back up.*

I paused with my hand still in the drawer, surrounded by pearls.

That's weirdly descriptive.

I tried to not let myself wonder about Steeler's own burst into power. How he'd said it had happened right after he'd left me on that beach...

In my mind, he gave a careful, casual shrug. *It's textbook. Some faeries in Sorronia will purposely put themselves through a catastrophe if their power hasn't matured by their mid-twenties.*

I wrinkled my nose at that thought—of someone harming themselves for power. But whatever those normal faeries did in Sorronia, it was clear I was doing the opposite here in this dome: purposely suppressing my innate power's tantrums.

Except those tantrums had broken through that suppressant every time I was in the Testing Center now. Maybe not to take shape, exactly, but to rage and kick and whirl at... something. I just didn't know what.

Steeler's voice grazed along the wall of my mind.

I was always scared that one of our powers—mine or Terrin's, Garvis's or the twins'—would break through the pill's suppressant like yours have. I always told them not to drink any alcohol, even if it wasn't bascale. Not to eat any funny foods or take any suspicious medicine in case it tipped them over the edge of what the pills can contain. But nothing ever happened to us. My fear was just paranoia—until you.

A pause that felt like a breath of star-riddled darkness.

Whatever's brewing inside, he said finally, *must be stronger than any of ours.*

I went quiet for so long that my knuckles turned white around the drawer handle.

Rayna?

"It's just that…" I straightened with the strand of hair still pinched between my fingers. "How do you stand it, not knowing what your magic will be? Isn't there some kind of… I don't know, seer faerie who could tell me?"

I didn't want to be like the queen or Dyonisia, with an antipower that stole or suppressed other magic. I wanted my power to help or uplift or even create in some way. Wanted it to help the world, not harm it.

There are plenty of seers in Sorronia, Steeler mused, *but you'd have to pay them. And cross the ocean, of course.*

"Well, couldn't you just Walk me there?"

His thoughts flashed through me: if I was Dyonisia's daughter, he wouldn't take me within a hundred miles of the faerie realm where the queen would have my head on a dinner plate.

"Right," I grumbled. "I might be the exiled princess's scary heir and all that. When can we get this hair test over with again?"

In nothing more than a stutter of shadow and light, Steeler appeared by the door with a little glass vial in his hand.

"Right now, if you'd like."

"What are you *doing*?" I tried to smooth the shock out of my features, glancing at the cracks beneath the door and between the windows. "You can't just materialize in my actual *room*, Steeler. What if someone walks right in?"

"Well, then, I supposed I'd just have to Walk right back out."

His eyes traveled the length of my body—not to appreciate my skin, I realized with a sudden surge of embarrassment, but to assess the swollen, elongated leech marks peppering my arms and legs.

A crease of worry knotted between his brows, but he didn't comment on the marks. He just uncorked the vial and held it out.

Trying to swallow that absurd sense of self-consciousness, I marched forward and dropped the midnight-black strand inside.

"Perfect. Now give me one of yours and I'll take this to Barberro right away." Steeler nodded at my mess of curls. I assumed Barberro was the faerie with the power of Magnification who would be testing the similarities between our hair strands, but something about the wording of that sentence made me pause.

"Wait a second." I stepped back, out of Steeler's reach. "I want to be there when he makes his assessment."

I needed to hear the words come from this faerie's lips. That Dyonisia was truly my mother, and that the entirety of Sorronia wanted me dead for my veins that ran with a rebel's blood.

Steeler looked at me as if I'd spoken monkey gibberish.

"Rayna, I already told you I'm not taking you onto that ship."

"Then Walk Barberro to the island just like you Walk the others," I argued, stepping even further out of his reach until we were on opposite ends of the room: him with his back still to the door and me with my back to my own bed. Not that the distance would matter in the end. If Steeler wanted to, he could materialize next to me, pluck one of my hairs off, and leave.

He tore his free hand through his hair in obvious frustration.

"Barberro is oath-bound to the queen like most of the others, Rayna. If you are Dyonisia's daughter, he will still have to try to kill you... even if he *was* the gentlest, most peaceful male alive. Which he's not." Steeler dropped his hand. "So excuse me if—"

Before he could finish that sentence, I whipped out one of my throwing knives and sent it careening through the air—right over his head, missing his scalp by half an inch...

Where it lodged into the wood of the door behind him.

Guess all of Jagaros's lessons had paid off, after all.

The smoky quartz of Steeler's eyes widened at me for just a moment.

Unable to stifle the smirk I could feel rising to my lips, I stalked forward to stand on my tiptoes, reach over his shoulder, and wrench the blade out of the wood.

"I think I can handle myself against one little faerie man whose only power is that he has really good eyesight."

Steeler didn't even glance at the knife.

His free hand shot out to clamp around my closed fist, holding the weapon in place between us while shadows dropped like curtains over his pupils and heat rose in my chest.

"And *I* think you're getting rather cocky with that thing, little hurricane."

Wrapping his arm around my backside to lock me into place, he brought our joined hands closer to my neck until I felt the cold flat of the blade lifting my chin. Forcing me to look at him.

An unnecessary act. I was *already* looking at him. Dead-on.

And I huffed out a laugh right into his face.

"You're trying to scare me into changing my mind, but guess what, Steeler?" I leaned into the knife, swelling with satisfaction when he immediately drew the blade away to avoid cutting me. "I'm not scared of you. I'm often infuriated by you, constantly frustrated with you, still angry at you, but *I'm not scared of you.* And I'm coming with you to give my own damn strand of hair to this Barberro guy because I know you won't let him hurt me."

Steeler's lips parted in surprise, and my fingers twitched with the sudden desire to touch his fangs. To trace their sharp points and perhaps imagine what they would feel like against my neck.

"*Pssst. Sorry to interrupt, but you might want to wrap up your... staring contest?*"

I jumped as something furry and gray wiggled from a crack in the baseboards.

"Willa!" I turned to the mouse, a blush squirming down into my belly at the position she'd caught me in—pressed up against Steeler with only a knife between us. "It's nice to—what did you say?"

"*You might want to wrap up your staring contest with the wanted fugitive who's definitely not supposed to be on the island, let alone this room.*" If a mouse could smirk, Willa was doing a damn good job at it: one corner of her mouth pinched upward, revealing half a bucktoothed smile as she assessed us both from head to toe. "*Because Cilia's coming upstairs with Mitzi in five, four, three...*"

I whipped my gaze back toward Steeler just as Cilia's and Mitzi's chattering voices did indeed reach us from the outside hallway.

"Don't you even *think* about leaving without me."

Something pained and strangled seem to overtake the exasperation in his expression.

"*Two,*" Willa urged. "*One...*"

Just as the doorknob began to turn, Steeler disappeared. And I disappeared along with him.

CHAPTER

34

The darkness spit us out onto a narrow valley, sandwiched between bluffs that trickled steadily with thin sheets of water in every direction.

"Where are we?"

I untangled myself from Steeler, my knife still clutched in my hand.

For some reason, I'd assumed he'd be taking us to the lighthouse, not this...oasis of sorts. Mushrooms as fat as my palm burst from the small, crisscrossing ravines running along the sides of the bluffs, and a thick carpet of liverworts gave out steady, warbling drones from underfoot. A single, dark cloud hovered overhead among a pillow of lighter, fluffier ones.

Steeler shielded his eyes to squint upward, scouring the cliff-line for signs of life or intrusion.

"We're as far from the ships as we can get without actually leaving the island—just west of Wyndrip, actually." His jaw flexed. "I'll go fetch Barberro if you wait h—"

"Steeler?"

He turned to me, that little glass vial still tight in his grip.

"Yes, Rayna?"

"Thank you. For bringing me."

My heart was still crawling up my throat from that breathless moment I'd feared he would leave me behind again.

Steeler's mouth instantly softened.

"You deserve to hear it with your own ears, Rayna—you're right about that. I just have a hard time sharing you."

I blinked. Surely, he didn't think this Barberro fellow would be interested in me... romantically?

"Sharing me? With who?"

"The world," Steeler whispered. "It's a harsh, unforgiving place full of greedy, manipulative people, and I don't trust it not to hurt someone like you."

Just like that, I felt that heat in my stomach rise up my throat in anger this time.

"Someone like me? What's that supposed to mean?"

"You know." He threw his head back. "Someone..."

"Someone *what*?" Deep in the center of my mind, I felt a creak of ice, a stirring of my subconscious. "Do you think I'm weak? Or fragile? Or breaka—"

"Kind!" Steeler burst out. "Soft-hearted. *Compassionate.*" He took a step forward, pressing the vial into my free hand, closing my fingers around the glass. "But I'm learning how to trust the other parts of you that *aren't* as soft, Rayna—your powers and your bravery and that devious little mind of yours."

A brush of dark, fathomless energy against my gate of ice had my knees turning hollow with the trail of hungry promises it seemed to leave in its wake.

"And I trust you to still be here when I get back," Steeler finished. Then he was gone.

Knees wobbling, I finally let myself collapse onto a nearby slab of mossy stone, clutching my knife in one hand and the glass vial of Dyonisia's hair in the other while the liverworts droned around me.

Kind. Soft-hearted. Compassionate.

I'd been terrified that I'd lost all those things along with my memories. Terrified that I'd never actually been kind or compassionate at all, that it had all been a ruse, a trick my mind had played on itself to hide all those darker, wilder parts within.

But maybe... maybe even if I *was* Dyonisia's daughter, it didn't mean I was destined to turn out like her: as harsh and unforgiving as the world Steeler couldn't trust. Maybe I could still be good because...

Because I was Fabian's daughter, too. And despite the fact that I hadn't seen him in a year and a half now, he was the kindest, most compassionate man I knew.

I exhaled into the space between my knees. No matter how this coupling between him and Dyonisia had happened, I could choose which parts of my parents to keep alive in my own blood.

I could *choose* to be a force of good in a world that needed so much more of that.

For the next two minutes, I sat with my eyes closed, face turned up against the warmth of soft sunlight, listening to the tinkle of water all around me. It was only when a sudden scuffle and a sharp string of foreign curses echoed through the valley that I popped them open again.

Steeler was back, this time with...

I scrambled to my feet. My mouth dropped open at the figure that had doubled over next to him, a massive fist to his gut as he retched.

"Rayna, meet Barberro," Steeler said through a smirk. "Your... what did you call him? 'Little faerie man'?"

The seven-foot male with swirling ink patterns on his bald head and glittering hoops in his pointed ears paused his retching long enough to squint at me with small, unassuming hazel eyes.

"*Little*, you say? Is that why you are staring at me like that, girl with curly hair? Because you thought I'd be *little*?"

"N-no," I said, unsure of the temperament behind those words. "I just...thought you'd have bigger eyes, given your power and all."

"Bigger eyes?" the faerie named Barberro mouthed.

Then, after a too-long beat of silence, the valley echoed with the sudden hawing boom of his laughter.

"Bigger eyes! Ha!" He looked at Steeler over his mountainous shoulder. "I like this girl already. God of Cosmos, I hope you don't belong to traitor so I don't have to kill you after this," he told me cheerfully.

Steeler was between the two of us in nothing more than a breath of wind, all traces of his earlier humor swallowed by instant rage.

"Go ahead and see what happens if you try to touch her. I fucking dare you."

Barberro blinked and took a half step backward.

"Well, this is new behavior, friend."

Steeler ignored that. "I already told you, Barberro—Rayna might be good with her knife, but she won't have to lift a *finger* if you start to attack her because I will have your mind scrambled in half a second, and you will only be able to unscramble it long after I toss your unconscious ass back onto the ship."

"*Ati, ati, ati*, I get it." Barberro raised his palms. "Try to kill girl with curly hair: maybe. Succeed at killing girl with curly hair: *never*." I tried not to gape when he untucked an entire folded table and chair set that had been hiding beneath the rippling bulge of his arm, setting it up on the flattest surface of ground he could find. "Now give me traitor's hair. This might take a bit, so make yourselves *veriga*."

Bewildered, I passed the vial over to Steeler, who passed it over to Barberro, who uncorked it expertly and laid the strand against the table with the gentleness of a nursing mother, not a fanged faerie the size of two Gileons put together.

I cleared my throat in an attempt to normalize the conversation, since tension was still emanating from Steeler in waves.

"So I hear you're close with Nara, the one who makes our pills?"

If Barberro had dissected anything from the strand of Dyonisia's hair yet, he didn't let on. He swiveled his head toward me, those unassuming hazel eyes widened with shock.

"Close? *Close?*" A gape at Steeler. "Have you told this girl nothing?" He shook his head with a sigh and returned his attention to the table. "Nara is my *vigate*."

"*Vigate?*" I repeated.

"Yes. It means..." He snapped his fingers. "Help me out here."

Steeler's shoulders had lowered a notch. In a quieter voice than I'd ever heard him use, he said, "Soulmate."

"Ahh, yes!" Barberro nodded. "Mate of the soul. Destined lovers for all eternity. Stitched together by Fate."

"Oh." I frowned at him, chewing on my lip. "Like a seagull?" When the other two blinked at me, I shook my head and directed a different question at Barberro. "Can your magic eyes detect true love at first sight, or something?"

Once again, silence shuddered from the faerie bent over the table.

Then he lifted his chin and sent a nearby flock of birds bursting from a crag with the boom of his laugh.

"Please, please, please, girl with curly hair, I am begging you with everything I have, don't be traitor's daughter. I need to have you over for dinner when this is all over. I make best *empinettes* in Sorronia."

Blowing out a sigh, Steeler said, "A soulmate is a very real—though rare and revered—thing for faeries. In Sorronia, there are temples where it is said the seamstress for the God of the Cosmos—Fate—makes it official: an eternal bond that is both more spiritual and carnal than ever before."

"Very, very carnal," added Barberro. "I can eat Nara's pussy for breakfast, lunch, dinner, and snack time. Sorry, inappropriate, I know," he said before Steeler could smack him over the back of the head. "I wouldn't say it if I didn't know Nara is laughing her voluptuous ass off back at the ship right now."

I startled.

"You can...?"

"Read her mind? Yes. Without that cloned mind magic you both have." Barberro waved a hand in our direction without looking at us. "And unlike *your* magic, I can read Nara's mind no matter how far from her I am. No matter how much world is between us. I can sense where she is at all times. I know the moment her mood turns sour because she remembers how I make better *empinettes* than her. Ahhh!" He jolted upright. "She just threw shoe at my mind."

Maybe I should have laughed at that, but something heavy had sunk deep into the pit of my stomach at those words.

"So you're telling me that... that Fate decided to pair you up together, and you just accepted it? And made it official in a temple?"

The pit in my stomach was telling me it sounded like the *opposite* of love to be bound to someone by forces outside of your control.

"Oh, no, no, no. You have it flipped around, girl with curly hair." Barberro was still squinting at the strand of midnight-black hair on

334

the table as he explained, "I met Nara through random chance. We fell in love of own free will. *Then* we went to temple to see if Fate would accept our choice and bind us together in stitches of... how do you say it? *Divine* magic. Most couples are not so lucky, but we..."

His face smoothed out into a smile.

Steeler flicked a glance back at me.

"Almost every faerie couple visits the temple to see if Fate will award them the status of soulmates," he explained in that peculiar quiet voice. "And almost every faerie couple is rejected. For a pairing to be accepted by Fate is... special. As you can probably tell by this asshole's inflated ego."

"What can I say?" Barberro sighed lovingly. "My love for my *vigate* actually made my dick grow by two sizes—how could you not get ego from that?"

I tried not to imagine how big Barberro's dick was, instead refocusing back on the concept of soulmates. *Vigates.*

"So Fate—who you're saying is a *seamstress* for the God of the Cosmos, a real entity—just...what? Gave you and Nara a holy marriage license?"

Barberro nodded, squinting downward. "A holy marriage license that tightens bond between souls into something...*radaga*. Impenetrable, that is. But like I said, Fate is picky. She doesn't approve of vast majority of requests, no matter how deep the love might appear to outsiders. So those of us who are approved to be *vigates* are usually held in high regard. You could even bow, if you'd like, girl with curly hair."

The growl that ripped out of Steeler cascaded down my spine in tingling little goosebumps.

"If anyone's bowing to anyone around here, you will do so to *her*, Barberro."

335

The giant of a faerie glanced up, a flicker of surprise lifting his eyebrows.

"When did you get so grouchy, my friend? If she is traitor's daughter, she won't be counted as legitimate—"

"I don't give a damn whose daughter she is," Steeler said, and somehow, he seemed to loom over Barberro. "Just because the rest of *you* do doesn't mean Rayna's worth anything less than absolute devotion. Now, have you studied that hair long enough?"

By the orchid and the owl. Whatever biting, snarling rage Barberro had made rise within Steeler at his little joke... I had to admit, I was glad I wasn't on the end of that withering glare even *if* the way Steeler bared his fangs made me wonder, once again, what they'd feel like against my neck, down my belly, between my—

"I have memorized genetic patterns in shaft, yes." Barberro turned to me with a little more hesitation this time, and I was glad for the abrupt change in subject to cleanse my mind. "Now give me strand of yours, girl with curly hair."

Steeler's shoulders tensed. His fingers flexed, his stance shifting into a predatory one, like Barberro might turn feral at any moment.

Slowly, I reached for a curl and separated a single hair from the rest.

This was it.

The truth about my mother, once and for all.

The lady from the sea, Velika had said in my memory, *who had hair dark as shadows but skin that glowed like honey.*

I yanked, feeling the quick sting against my scalp as I pulled the hair free and passed it to Steeler, who passed it to Barberro, who held it up.

And squinted at it.

And laid it down on the table.

And squinted at it some more.

Words clogged up my throat like rocks. I couldn't attempt a normal conversation anymore, couldn't think about what I had just learned about Fate when my *own* fate sat before me in the form of a bald giant with small, hazel eyes.

In the distance, birds called out to each other.

The water tinkled.

The liverworts droned.

I could have sworn Steeler's heartbeat was thumping in my own ears, his adrenaline seeping into the air around us like a living thing.

You are traitor's daughter, I could practically hear Barberro saying. Could practically see him pouncing on me as his oath to the faerie queen forced him into action. There would be a shout, a blur as Steeler dragged him into darkness, and then silence again. Silence where I would have to come to terms with the finality of the truth. Rayna Reeve.

At the table, Barberro's lips curled.

With painstaking slowness, he stood with the coiled strand of my hair pinched between his thumb and forefinger.

Steeler took a step toward him, his hand already raised in preparation. His body practically *vibrated* with hostility.

But Barberro just looked over his head to meet my eyes.

"Dyonisia Reeve is not your mother, girl with curly hair."

Steeler dropped his hand. I stumbled back a step, all my blood draining to my toes—in relief or shock, I couldn't tell.

"W-what?"

Barberro smiled, his fangs glinting bright in the sunlight.

"Dyonisia Reeve is not your mother... but she *is* your aunt."

" *What?* "

That came from Steeler, who furrowed his eyebrows at me, then shot his gaze back to Barberro.

"The queen hasn't left her castle in the last five hundred years. There's no way she would have snuck onto the island, got pregnant with a random Object Summoner at the Institute, had a baby, and let a human steal away her only heir."

As harsh as those words seemed, I had to admit that Steeler was right. If the queen of Sorronia was as powerful as they claimed, Fabian wouldn't have stood a *chance* in his endeavor to keep me from the faerie world outside the dome.

Barberro's smile grew wider as he cocked his head at my hair.

"Indeed. And I have seen Her Majesty's genetic material many times before—I know it by heart. She is *definitely* not mother either."

"Then what the hell do you mean Dyonisia is Rayna's *aunt?*"

Barberro only raised his eyebrows at Steeler.

And it seemed to hit both of us at the same exact moment.

"By the orchid and the owl!" I nearly yelped.

"By the moonbeam and the mist," Steeler said appraisingly, a smile slowly dawning on his face as his eyes painted me up and down with awe. "Rayna Reeve, indeed."

Yes.

Yes, I was Rayna Reeve, daughter of one of the three royal sisters. Not Dyonisia, but her sister. Not the older one, not the queen, but...

"Chrysanthia," I whispered.

And Barberro's smug nod, tipped forward as he bowed in my direction, a hand against his broad chest, told me I was right.

My mother was the lost princess of Sorronia.

CHAPTER

35

"Wait." I ignored Barberro's bow, too overcome by the rattle of truth in my bones to fully process his dipped head. "How many years ago did you say Chrysanthia disappeared again?" I asked Steeler.

He began to pace in circles around me, his forehead furrowed in concentration.

"Five hundred."

"Five hundred and seventeen, to be exact," Barberro said, straightening and raising a finger.

"So... what would it be? Four hundred and ninety-eight years after her sudden disappearance, Chrysanthia showed up here? On the island?" I glanced up, as if to make sure the dome still loomed overhead. Sure enough, the faintest shimmer stretched across the sky through spare gaps in the bulging clouds. "But how would she have made it through her sister's shield?"

"Perhaps she has been here whole time," Barberro suggested. "It would be just like traitor to blame Her Majesty for Princess's disappearance, only to have kidnapped her and brought her here herself. The wretched *fyka*."

I assumed *fyka* wasn't the nicest word in the Sorronian vocabulary, but I didn't ask what it meant. Had my mother really been locked away in the prison on Bascite Mountain for nearly five centuries before she escaped to meet Fabian and gave birth to me? Had she been caught again, lugged back like Jenia, chained up with the rest of the original Good Council? Or was she hiding somewhere in the depths of the jungle?

I shook my head. The jungle would have whispered to me about it if she was still here, hiding within its nest. And besides... "Lord Arad said my mother had come from the *sea*," I said out loud. "She must have snuck through the dome somehow..." But how? And why? I glanced down at my sheath and whipped out the knife in a sudden flurry as a thought came to me. "Were you alive when the three sisters were still united?" I asked Barberro.

"Whoa there." Barberro went cross-eyed in his attempt to track the knife. "I was boy, yes. Ten years of age when Princess disappeared. I lived near palace, but only saw her handful of times."

So he wouldn't have developed his power of Magnification by then. But maybe he'd still noticed little details. "Did you ever see Chrysanthia carrying this around?" I brandished the knife again.

Barberro zeroed in on the curved blade, as if pinpointing and memorizing the actual elemental disposition of it.

"I'm afraid not, girl with curly hair. Your mother always seemed to float around like feather back then—she would not have let *that* weigh her down. But a lot can change in five hundred years, no?"

I supposed it could. And I supposed it didn't matter why Chrysanthia had had a knife or how she'd slipped through Dyonisia's dome all those years ago or what she'd been doing for those five hundred years of absence.

No, what mattered right now was what *I* could do with this new knowledge humming in my blood. Leave the island. Board the ship, where nobody would cut my head off with Old Veracious. Sail away and never look back.

Steeler stopped pacing to snag my gaze, as if he'd sensed exactly where my thoughts had flowed. Because he'd been there all along.

I lifted my chin at him. "What would you have me do?"

A slight cock of his head. A flare of his nostrils that was so miniscule, I might have missed it if I hadn't memorized every piece of him. "What?"

"What would you have me do right now if you could have your way?" I repeated, and I could feel my eyes blazing, cutting holes through his own. "If you didn't need anyone else's input, would you leave me here or take me with you?"

I already knew my own answer, but I needed to hear his. Out loud. Right now.

"Would I take you with me?" Steeler repeated, uncrossing his arms and forging a step closer.

The absolute disbelief etched all over his features had me thinking that I was wrong. That I'd mistaken his intentions. That he wasn't still in love with me as he'd claimed on the beach that day.

Then he came a step closer. The world shrunk into a cocoon around us, and the scent of his black bamboo filled my senses until I could feel his presence in every pore.

"Tell me the truth," I whispered up at him. Even if he didn't love me anymore, even if he didn't want me to leave the island with him— well, for some reason, that would hit me like a sucker-punch to the gut, but I could handle it. I didn't want anything less than undiluted honesty from this male ever again.

"Are you sure?" Steeler breathed down at me. "My answer isn't very... nice."

My heart dropped a fraction, but I nodded, my resolve tightening. "Don't censor it. Tell me exactly what you're thinking." *Don't keep trying to protect me from the truth—whatever that may be.*

"Fine, then." Steeler's face took on an open earnestness I'd never seen before. "If I could choose what to do with you right now, little hurricane, I wouldn't just take you away from here. I would whisk you away to some remote corner of the universe, where I would keep you all to myself forever and ever and fuck you into a whimpering puddle, until every single worry in that beautiful mind of yours melted away and pleasure was the only sensation you ever felt again. *That's* what I would do right now if I could have my way."

Oh.

My stomach thrashed with butterfly wings, and Steeler's fangs were *so close*, and my fingers were finally reaching up to touch them—

"We can go right now, yeah?" Barberro interrupted. "Then you can get own room on ship and I won't have to watch? Or do you jungle people prefer the wild? If so, interesting concept, I will have to try it with—"

"We're not going anywhere," Steeler said.

Barberro stuck a finger in his ear. "I'm sorry? I don't believe I heard you right. We just found out girl with curly hair is not traitor's daughter and you said you're..."

"Not going anywhere," Steeler confirmed, taking a step away from me and shattering the trance that seemed to grip me. "Because what *I* want to do and what Rayna wants to do are two different things."

I blinked. Reassessed my surroundings and wrenched in a sharp breath of air that scattered the wings in my belly.

For once, Steeler was right—though he must have dissected those creeping thoughts of mine before my subconscious could form them into clear shapes for me.

"I can't go," I said, turning to Barberro, if only so I wouldn't get locked in a Steeler-induced trance again. "If Dyonisia is building an army... I can't just leave my friends and family here."

For even if she didn't try to attack the queen soon—even if Fabian and Don, Emelle and Lander, and all the others could live out their lives semi-peacefully—there was always a *chance* she'd decide it was time. There was always a *chance* my fathers and the family I'd made at the Esholian Institute would find themselves facing a queen they had no hope of surviving.

And that was a chance I wasn't willing to risk.

"We could take them with us," Steeler suggested quietly. "You heard Nara in my memory. Anyone with Wild Whispering, Object Summoning, Element Wielding, Shape Shifting, or Mind Manipulating can make it through the dome just fine. And even if they couldn't, I would Walk them through—to wherever you want to put them."

The way he said that, with a hint of a cringe, made my heart pause.

"Where *would* we put them, Steeler?" Not on the ships, surely— I doubted the Fated General would want to keep a whole pack of humans onboard even *if* they passed the Old Veracious test.

Now Barberro was cringing, too.

"I don't know," Steeler answered finally, hefting up his chin with a look of defiance. *You want the truth from now on? Well here it is.* I wasn't sure if he'd grazed my mind with those words or if I could just read his expressions like a map at this point. "The human territories aren't safe—they're run over with vampires. And Sorronia is prejudiced against humans, so I don't really know of a place we could take your friends or family. But we can try to find somewhere, if you'd like."

I'd turn over the world for you, if that's what it takes.

That *was* his voice in my mind, dark and fathomless as always.

I shivered, even as an idea hacked through me.

"*Or* we could keep the island for ourselves."

Barberro crossed his arms. Steeler spiked an eyebrow.

"Go on." His lips hitched up at the corner, obviously amused by the spark I could feel flickering in my eyes.

"Think about it." I began to pace, just as he had before. "We get rid of Dyonisia, and we get rid of the whole damn system. The bubble pops. No more Branding. No more Final Tests. No more exiles or torture chambers or secret readying for war." And everyone in that prison would be set free—including my mother, if she was up there.

Steeler's attention moved with me as I paced.

"And how, Rayna, are you planning on *getting rid of* the second most powerful faerie to ever exist in Sorronian history?"

For a moment, I felt like I had my own fangs as I stopped to flash him a grin. The idea churning in my mind felt like a hurricane of hail and ice and snow and every cold, sharp thing the last six months had carved into me.

"We won't have to touch Dyonisia at all." I turned to Barberro. "If Nara can fill those pills of hers with poison and I give that stash to Kitterfol like I promised him I would..."

"...then Kitterfol will poison Dyonisia for us," Steeler murmured, "thinking he's slipping her a love potion instead. God of the Cosmos, woman. I'm actually starting to fear you."

I couldn't find it in me to smirk, because the idea was risky. But if Kitterfol was truly as power-hungry and love-crazed as I thought, he'd go to any lengths to crush up those pills and get them into Dyonisia's system—and how would he know if they were poisoned? He still didn't know I was a Mind Manipulator, and at this point I was fairly certain I could learn how to feed him those mental lies without Steeler and I having to... act out certain scenes again.

"Yes, yes." Barberro was nodding, his gaze distant as if listening to a conversation in his own head. After a few moments, his eyes refocused on me. "Nara says she can do it... but it's very hard to poison faeries, and she doesn't have right ingredients on ship."

"Well..." I gestured around us, at the liverworts and bluffs bursting with fungi and the thick overflow of foliage looming over us in every direction. "It's a good thing we live on a jungle island where ingredients aren't hard to come by, isn't it?"

I could feel Steeler's smug pride wash over me, but I chose to ignore it for now. If I was going to do this, I needed every last dreg of mental clarity... and whatever it was that always seemed to radiate from him and wrap me up in a chokehold was not helping with that.

"What does Nara need to get the job done?"

CHAPTER

36

So do you want me to call you princess now? Because I will—gladly.

Against my will, a deep thrill unfurled in my belly when Steeler's voice grazed against my wall merely twenty minutes after Walking me back to the Institute that night.

I'd just slipped into a nightgown and settled into my pillow, curling my blanket around me in the dim starlight that squeezed through the window and dappled the ground of my dorm. Knowing that he was still somewhere out there within Mind Manipulating range, lurking in the dark, maybe even watching my silhouette through the window—why did that send tiny explosions cascading through my bloodstream?

I'm not a princess, I replied, turning over in bed to hide my smile from Cilia and Dazmine. Emelle was, once again, with Lander for the night. *I'm a foreign queen's long-lost sister's estranged daughter. There's a difference, Steeler.*

A slight pause that had me shivering, waiting. *If the queen never has a child, you could very well be Sorronia's preferred heir, Rayna.*

Yeah, an heir who would have to fight for a throne I don't want and never asked for in a country I've never seen. And even if I won, which I wouldn't, and you know it, any female willing to challenge me could usurp and kill me at any time. No, thank you.

Another pause, this time deeper and more thoughtful. I wrapped my blanket tighter around me. *You wouldn't have to fight Her Majesty if she passed you the crown in a symbolic duel,* he said finally.

There it was again. A feral, possessive snapping of teeth deep inside my chest at the way he said Majesty, though I immediately stuffed it back down before it had a chance to really bite.

And do you think the queen would? Just pass me the crown?

Not that I would ever even accept it. While a part of me did yearn to see Sorronia and the rest of the world beyond this dome, the island of Eshol... it was my home, and I had a feeling I would always drift back to it if I ever did end up sailing away. But Steeler's silence inside my head was enough to confirm the assumption that had been bubbling in my periphery since Barberro's declaration: the Sorronian queen might not want my head on a dinner plate, but she'd never pass me the crown. Both Steeler and I knew it, felt it, even though there was no real proof.

That's what I thought, I told him. *So don't call me princess. Little hurricane is fine.*

I thought he would try to argue further, but his tone just turned slightly gloating instead. *Oh, so you admit it?*

What?

That you're a hurricane. In other words, absolutely devastating.

My heart fluttered again. *I didn't realize I'd wrecked you so much for you to think of me like that.*

He chuckled. *I mean, you punched me in the face once.*

I nearly gasped aloud, but managed to bury my face in my pillow. *I did not.*

Oh yeah. Gave me a black eye and everything, but don't worry. It was a sexy punch.

I squeezed my eyes shut, wishing for the hundredth time that I could remember... but every time Garvis and I tried to find those missing pieces, the mist would dissolve right as Steeler was about to come into the picture. As if my brain itself had been eating away at any moment that involved him.

Show me, I breathed out on a mental whisper before I could think better of it. *Show me from your side.*

I was almost positive he wouldn't. The only reason he'd herded me toward those other memories in his mind was to give me the truth I needed, not to let me in to the private things tucked away in the deepest parts of him.

To my surprise, a rough, calloused hand grabbed mine inside my mind as if he'd been there all along—which he had.

Come here, then, little hurricane.

He dragged me toward his mind, catching me when I nearly fell into a heap in front of his colossal moonstone gate. My nerves lit up as I remembered what my mouth had done in this exact spot... but this time, Steeler led me right through his gate without blocking my way.

Hand in hand, he led me down spirals, spin-offs, and side corridors of moonstone that towered over us until we came to a halt in front of a particularly vibrant pocket of mist, the Cosmos twinkling and swirling high, high above.

My past self was leaning against a stalk of black bamboo in this memory, closing my eyes and inhaling the scent of it. Everything was still and peaceful—until a branch creaked. Leaves swished. I turned just in time to find Steeler emerging from the depths of the grove without a single speck of wicked humor in his eyes. No, in this memory, his face only held depthless sorrow.

The first time he'd snuck back to campus to give me a pill, I realized with a jolt. One week after he'd had Garvis bury my memories. One week after he'd left me.

For a moment, my past self looked like I was about to tremble backward. The Steeler in this memory raised his palms and opened his mouth, evidently thinking I'd view him as a random stranger in the jungle, an obscure threat rather than a target I'd been ordered to capture.

Then I shrieked, rushed forward, and pummeled him right across the nose. And yeah, I kind of *did* look good doing it, even though my present self cringed at the *crack* of cartilage that followed.

"You," I shouted, punching him again, "gross," –*punch*— "monster. I'm going to—"

Steeler recovered from his shock in time to hold me away at arm's length before I could land a fourth one, scouring my mind for information about what the hell was going on. It wasn't until several seconds had passed and I'd sent a humming command to the bamboo that his eyes flared open and he muttered, "By the moonbeam and the fucking mist. I forgot about that."

The memory. The fabricated one that Lexington had given me— he could see the hatred it had given me spewing from my eyes as the nearest stalk of bamboo began to twine around his throat.

Steeler flashed out of existence before it could choke him and appeared behind me. I screamed, whirled, raised my fists again, and—

"Sleep," Steeler commanded shakily.

I slumped, but he caught me before the floor could. Hoisting me up, he cradled me against his chest, staring down at me with shock-wide pupils that actually *glistened.* Maybe it was just the condensation of the mist, but I could have sworn tears were streaking down his cheeks.

He fumbled in his pocket one-handedly and brought a pill to my lips.

"Take this. Just take it and... I'll fix this. I'll find a way to fix this."

His voice snagged on the syllables of that last word. Sleepily, my past self heeded his Mind Manipulating command. I opened my mouth for the pill and swallowed it before slumping back against his chest, my eyes rolling in their sockets.

Steeler backed up against a stalk of bamboo and just held me, rocking my sleeping body against his. He didn't move from that position for several hours, until bats began to swoop overhead, moths began to flutter around him, and a low growl sprang from the shadows.

You need to put her back before someone wonders where she is.

It was strange to hear Jagaros speak, not through my Wild Whispering magic, but through Steeler's memories that had dissected his thoughts from the dark.

"I... I can't," he breathed, not looking up from my dreaming face to pinpoint the tiger's lithe form that stalked to a halt before him. "She doesn't just remember me. She—she *hates* me. I saw it in her eyes. Felt it in her mind. I can't put her back or she'll just keep thinking of me as a goddamned villain every time I return for her."

Jagaros chuffed, his eyes gleaming like two moons in the dark. *Then be the villain, Coen Steeler. Play the part until you don't have to anymore, until you can whisk her away for good. That way you're not confusing her subconscious or pulling her mind in two different directions.*

His whiskers twitching, his tail flicking, he looked so much like a protective father figure as he let his slitted pupils flicker toward my sleeping face that a lump knotted in my throat.

When Steeler only continued to rock me, Jagaros repeated, *Be the villain—do you understand?*

This time, when Steeler looked up, I could see that dark, wicked glimmer lighting up the smoky quartz of his eyes along with the first purplish bruise of a black eye.

"Yes, I understand."

Good. Because I'm going to make sure she can do more than just throw a few punches at her enemies, so you'd better come prepared next time.

Steeler didn't wait any longer. Hoisting himself up with me still lolling against him, he whipped us away into his realm of darkness — straight into my Wild Whisperer room. The other girls were all fast asleep in their own beds, but Steeler was so quiet as he lowered me into my own that none of them so much as muttered or stirred.

When he dug into his pocket for a second time, it was to bring out one of those little black pearls that he carefully set on my nightstand: the scene I'd always imagined since the morning I'd woken up to find one next to me.

"Sleep tight, little hurricane."

His voice was little more than a sigh that might have been a gust of warm air against the windowpane.

Then he was gone.

When the mist of this memory began to replay, Steeler in real time waved it away.

I turned to him, processing the reality that I was no longer that sleeping, helpless girl in his past. I was in *his* mind now, and I could damn well do more than throw a few punches.

"I wasn't going to give you the pearl at first," Steeler said quietly, his head angled down to meet my eyes. "I found one when I was hunting for food a few days after my magic exploded and I landed up near the lighthouse. I kept it with me because it reminded me of the dress you wore when you first came over to the Mind Manipulating house." A smile lifted up one of his cheeks before a frown dropped it again. "But as soon as I realized how much this whole experience had altered your mind—and how much I would have to keep altering it—I knew I had to give it to you as a way to help your subconscious deal with the repeated memory loss. A way to prove to you that you weren't crazy, that the holes in your mind *were* there. My hope was that they would be significant to you, but not significant enough for the Good Council to pick up on it and punish you for our repeated meetings."

I could hardly get my breath to move along in my lungs after seeing all that.

"It—it worked." I rubbed a hand across my throat, trying to unclog the lump in there. "It helped me keep track of the gaps."

Among other things. Like how many times I should have driven my knife through his heart by now. But when I thought about my tally, I found something else burning in the background behind that revenge and hatred it had always stood for, too.

Something I didn't want to confront just yet.

"Rayna," Steeler began, urgency creeping over his tone, "I know you won't ever forgive me, but I want to say it anyway. I'm..." He clawed a hand through his hair. "I'm not sorry that I led you to keep believing I'm a monster, because I am. I'm not sorry that I've made some messed-up choices to keep you safe, because I'm fucking *messed up*, and I won't deny that. But I *am* sorry that I kept you locked away in my little lair of protection without ever considering the fact that keeping you in the dark was hurting you more than any outside threat.

I'm sorry I didn't trust that you're just as formidable as all the things I feared might want to snatch you away."

I'm learning how to trust the other parts of you that aren't as soft, he'd told me earlier. Which meant that even though he didn't think of himself as forgivable, he was still willing to change.

His mouth parted as if he wanted to say something, and I moved before I could think—because in here, within Steeler's mind, every action *was* a thought.

Taking a step closer, I raised my hands to his face. My thumbs found the tip of his fangs, and I sucked in a breath at the feel of those sharpened points I'd only imagined until now. Ever so slowly, I moved them up along the slopes while the rest of my fingers landed gently on his jawline to anchor myself to him.

Steeler had gone rigid, his chest frozen mid-breath, his eyes bursting with both ravenous hunger and.... confusion. Shock. Maybe even a little fear. This was different from me getting on my knees for him, somehow. I could suck his cock all I wanted and still be able to call it a release of hatred, but if I let my lips do what they truly burned to do and fit my mouth against his...

Steeler threaded one of his hands through my hair, holding the back of my neck and drawing me closer to him. So close that I could see the constellations in his eyes.

And... no.

No, no, no.

The last time I'd done this, the last time I'd let my lips get this close to him, we'd fused together only for me to open my eyes against nothing but mist and emptiness.

If I kissed him now, he could leave. If I kissed him now, I might blink awake to find myself back in my bed in my Wild Whisperer room, with nothing in my hands but a fistful of blankets.

And despite that tally, despite the ache and anger he'd left like handprints all over me, I didn't want this male to leave me again. I wouldn't be able to focus on my next task at hand with that kind of heartbreak cracking through me once more.

"Rayna..." Steeler breathed against me.

I exhaled and pulled back.

As violently as if I'd shocked him, he let go of my hair.

"So..." I said, hating the sudden wrenching feeling of separation but forcing a coy smile onto my face as if I didn't. Anything to get back to small talk, to smear that *almost* moment away. "You remember the very first dress I wore, huh?"

Hurt and shame and disappointment seemed to be rolling off him, but he just said, eyes tacked to mine, "I remember everything you've ever put on, actually." The look in his eyes told me he remembered everything I'd ever taken *off*, too, even if I couldn't.

"Good," I said, still trying to play it casual. I threw a glance up at the swirling Cosmos of his mind to reorient myself. "You know my size, then. I might have you get me some more after I have to trudge through swamps to get... what was it? Poison dart frog eggs?"

Barberro had given me a hefty list of herbs, bones, and other distinctly strange or deadly items to procure for Nara's poison concoction. And while yes, I was a Wild Whisperer, I didn't fancy the idea of trying to convince a swarm of hornets to squirt their venom into a jar for me.

Steeler gave a half-grin, apparently accepting the turn of the conversation. "Why do the dirty work when the shadiest of the Cardina peddlers do it for you?"

Ah, right. The Cardina peddlers came to the Esholian Institute at the start of every wet season, which meant they were due to arrive any day now. I lifted my eyebrows, though.

"You seriously think the *Cardina peddlers* will just happen to be carrying around ingredients to kill Dyonisia Reeve?"

Steeler shrugged. "I've seen the Cardina peddlers selling mushrooms that could keep a grown man high for two weeks straight. Plus, they don't know alchemy like Nara does. I bet they don't even know the power of what they sell. So yes, I do think they'll be carrying all the ingredients you need—in fact, I'll bet you on it." He stretched out a large, calloused hand.

I considered that hand and hated myself for immediately wishing it could be threaded through my hair again. Or somewhere—anywhere—else on my body. "What do I get if I win?"

"Whatever you want."

I squinted up at him, more than suspicious at how serious his tone sounded. "And what do you get if *you* win?"

"You'll have to wait and find out, little hurricane." He had the audacity to wink at me then. "But I promise it'll be good."

I couldn't help myself anymore.

I reached out and grabbed hold of his hand, melting into the warmth of his callouses as his fingers closed around mine.

"You're on."

CHAPTER

37

Steeler was going to win, dammit.

As I meandered through the bustling market with Emelle, Wren, and Gileon on the Friday the Cardina peddlers came to campus, I kept half an eye peeled for the items on Nara's list.

To my dismay, we passed by almost all of them—a cart of golden dewdrops for insomnia here, a booth of castor beans for constipation there—all seemingly normal supplies unless you ate too many of the dewdrop berries or actually chewed the beans. Or mixed them together to make a poison lethal enough to kill a faerie.

No matter what, buying such things in such large quantities would be a little hard to explain to my friends. I had to disentangle myself from them soon.

"I kind of want to get another tattoo," Wren mused, staring wistfully at a booth where a female Object Summoner was commanding dozens of needles to dip themselves in bottles of ink and prick the arm of her current customer over and over, forming a black glob that looked like a slowly-crystallizing hummingbird.

I eyed her in surprise. "I didn't know you already had one."

"I have two, actually." Wren smirked. "But they're not in any place you would ever see them."

Emelle and I exchanged quick, purse-lipped glances, but I recovered quickly.

"Well, what's one more then? I say go for it."

"You think?" Wren's eyes had snapped back to the Object Summoner's booth of jerking, bobbing needles.

"Oh, for sure." I nodded, perhaps a bit too vehemently. "You can never have too many snakes or crows on your ass, or whatever—"

"Skulls," Wren interrupted. "Snake and crow *skulls.* And I like your spirit today, Rayna. I think I'll add a jaguar skull today."

She patted me on the shoulder, cracked her knuckles in an outward motion, and dove through the crowd in a streak of feather-black hair.

One friend successfully preoccupied. Two more to go.

"What were you thinking about getting this year, Gil?" I asked as the three of us resumed a slow trek down the rows of carts and tents, the heat of hundreds of bodies and magic slowly blossoming into a sticky bubble around us. I had a simple satchel slung around my neck today, and the rough fabric of the strap was already digging sweat into my skin.

Gileon's brow had furrowed at my question.

"I... I can't remember, actually. Do you, Nuisance?"

The rhinoceros beetle buzzed something into his ear, shelled wings whirring.

"No, it wasn't a new pair of underwear." He scratched his head. "No, not that either. It was something important."

I frowned up at him. Last year, he'd gotten Wren a bouquet of needles, which I'd thought might have indicated some kind of romantic affection between them. I still didn't know whether their relationship was more than friendly or not, but I did feel like I knew Gileon's heart—big and always focused on other people.

He looked so sad now at the realization that he couldn't remember what he'd wanted to get today, his lip trembling, eyes glassing over, that I didn't feel a shred of guilt for funneling an opening in my blockade toward him and slinking into his mind to try to help him out.

Whoa.

My consciousness blinked against the blinding expanse of white leather that was Gileon's mind.

His walls were straight edged, perfectly uniform, and... padded, like bricks made of cushions from the most pristine of sofas.

When I whirled this way and that, it was to find that neither a gate nor Gileon's consciousness were anywhere in sight.

What the hell? I hadn't been in too many minds, but this was... strange, to say the least.

I didn't have time to dwell too hard on the phenomenon, though, as a faint, familiar voice echoed overhead.

> If only I had the right kind of pan,
> I'd bake her into a pie
> and feed her to the...
> If only I had the right kind of pan,
> I'd bake her into a pie
> and feed her to the...

It took me a solid ten seconds to realize that it was a memory of *Rodhi's* voice wafting over the padded walls—a memory of Rodhi's first declaration of hatred toward Mrs. Smetlar and her vulture-like soul.

Pulling myself out of Gileon's mind, I gave him a soft smile.

"Were you maybe looking for..." I couldn't believe I was about to say this out loud. "... a pie pan? To buy as a gift for Rodhi?"

Gileon's mouth popped open and his eyes went round as coins.

"Yes! You're a life-saver, Rayna. Thank you."

He patted me on the shoulder just as Wren had and lumbered off toward the nearest pottery cart, Nuisance still spiraling in circles around his ear.

Two friends successfully preoccupied. One to—

I turned to find Emelle folding her arms at me.

"Lucky guess." I shrugged at the question swirling in her eyes.

She didn't look convinced, but didn't argue.

Instead, she just asked quietly, but firmly, "And what are *you* hoping to find today, Rayna?"

Wishbones, snake skins, and black caiman scales. But obviously I couldn't say that or she'd *know* something was up, so I settled on another honest answer.

"I think I'd like to find a jewelry maker." A blush warmed up my cheeks against my will. "I've been wanting to have a necklace made."

I'd had the idea right before that almost-kiss in Steeler's mind— an idea that was now buried in a pocket of my satchel, along with a fat handful of coins that I'd saved up from my years growing up in Alderwick.

Emelle's mouth softened and her arms fell. Perhaps she'd seen the vulnerability of that truth in my eyes.

"Oh. I think I actually saw a jeweler on the other side of the fountain." Standing on her tiptoes, she pointed over a clump of students ogling at a shoe stand, where the cobbler had bewitched his shoes to change color at every step—nothing but a gimmick, considering the enchantment would eventually fade. "It was in that green-striped tent with the little flag," Emelle continued, "if you want to... um, can I help you?"

A Cardina man had suddenly appeared in front of her. Short, ruddy-faced, and bulbous-nosed, he was staring at Emelle's cleavage with sweat running in rivulets down his face and drool sitting in the corners of his mouth.

"What a lovely bosom you have, ma'am."

Oh, hell no. My hand had already whipped my knife out when Emelle actually *laughed.*

"Stop it, babe. I know it's you."

To my utter shock, the man didn't bubble into Lander's true form, but *shrunk*...and became a bundle of potted begonias that Emelle caught with quick hands, as if she experienced this kind of thing all the time. Only after I slipped my knife back in its sheath did Lander himself emerge from around a nearby booth.

"Did I *almost* get you, at least?"

Emelle beamed at him, hugging the pot of flowers to her chest.

"Almost. The sweat and drool were nice touches, but he had *your* eyes... and your eyes are much too beautiful to belong to that creep-face."

"Dammit," Lander swore. "I'll have to work on that. The eyes are the hardest thing to change."

I looked away as he leaned over the begonias to press his mouth against Emelle's. Not just because I didn't want to invade this brief moment of privacy, but because... holy shit. I hadn't realized Lander had become so advanced at Shape Shifting that he could turn plants and inanimate objects into walking, talking *people.* That had to be a fourth-or fifth-year thing, even if he couldn't quite get the eyes right.

Had I become so far removed from my old friends that I hadn't realized when one of them became unnaturally good at their gift?

"You could have had me fooled," I tried to say cheerfully when Lander and Emelle finally broke apart. "That was... creepy."

Lander grinned at me, his arm wrapped around Emelle.

"It's hard to maintain for long periods of time, but it comes in handy when my friends are late to class—which happens more often than you'd think in the Shifter sector. I can turn a book or a fountain pen into a replica of them until they show up."

"Wow." My jaw had actually dropped open. "That's seriously badass, Land. I never would have thought you'd cheat the system that way." No, before the Institute, Lander had always been all about diplomacy and rules and fairness. But now...

He shrugged, but that newfound glint speckled his eyes. "If you ever need help out of a tight spot like that, I've got your back."

"Noted." I forced out an easygoing laugh, then nodded toward the direction of the fountain. "I'm going to go check out that jeweler. See you at dinner?"

I was already angling away, remembering all too well what had happened last time I'd tried to sneak away during the Cardina market: Emelle had demanded to go with me.

For a split moment I thought she'd do the same now. Time seemed to waver as she sucked in a breath at me—then blew it out again. Eyes softening again, she waved. "Yeah, see you at dinner!"

She was already tilting an ear toward the begonias to focus on their faint, crooning music, a smile lighting up her face.

I turned to leave, ignoring the weight of eyes lingering on my back.

Over the next few hours, I filled my satchel with almost everything on Nara's list, slipping coins into sweaty palms and stuffing the ingredients deep into the bag, where nobody would be able to see them.

In the end, there was only one thing I couldn't find among all the carts and booths—those poisonous dart frog eggs.

I couldn't help the smile from tugging at my mouth. The Cardina market didn't have every ingredient I needed, after all. I'd won. I'd have to make a quick trek into the jungle to collect the frog eggs myself, but I'd won that bet with Steeler.

I couldn't wait to gloat in his face when we saw each other next.

First, though, I really did want to check out that green-striped tent with the little flag on top.

A golden glow was trickling through the layer of clouds overhead as I made my way toward the tent, finally pushing through the flaps and taking in the spread of gemstones and shiny metals on the table inside.

"Hello," I told the woman behind the table.

She was sitting in a whicker rocking chair, her bony fingers moving as if knitting. But instead of a needle and yarn, she worked with ropes of pure flame, shaping a glob of floating silver into a delicate ring.

"Oh." She looked up briefly, the wrinkles in her face scrunching. "Another customer." Her face had soured so viscerally that a sliver of my blockade opened again on instinct to pick up the thoughts behind that twisting expression. *Funny how you kids still want bracelets and rings and piercings when the world's about to come crashing down. But a woman's got to make money until the very end, eh?*

I stared at her, my grip on my satchel tightening. "What makes you think the world's about to come crashing down?"

The jeweler froze in her rocking chair, the ropes of fire halting in midair. "Ahhh, I see. You're a dirty, eavesdropping little Mind Manipulator, aren't you? Spying on my thoughts?"

I froze, trying to mask the mortification warming my cheeks. It had happened so casually, so easily...

"I'm sorry. I'll go."

"No, you're *not* a Mind Manipulator," she interrupted, halting my abrupt turn to leave. "Because Mind Manipulators don't admit fault to strangers. They're too proud for that. What are you, then?"

I am a Mind Manipulator and a Wild Whisperer and a faerie with an undeveloped power of my own, I wanted to say. But of course, I didn't. I bit down on my lip until the jeweler sighed and stood on a frail pair of legs.

"The wind is my friend, and it brings me the smell of death and decay from other villages. They got Gildenleaf and Eeler first. Then Sickimore. Then Merkwell. Soon, they'll be coming for Cardina and this Institute and the rest of them, too."

My blood seized up along with every muscle in my body.

"Who? Who got them? Do you know?"

The jeweler shook her head. "The wind doesn't ever give straight answers. It spirals and loops and eddies around the truth, but it tells me the attackers are pale. Damaged. Altered beyond recognition. Now, what pretty piece of jewelry would you like to wear to your deathbed, hm? I have this stunning pair of topaz studs that—"

"Actually, I'd like to give you a custom order." My stomach was curling inward at those words she'd just uttered out loud. *Pale. damaged. Altered beyond recognition.* Whatever was attacking the villages, they didn't sound human *or* faerie.

I blew a breath of air out through my teeth, and the jeweler's bony fingers twitched upward as if to catch it.

"I don't take custom orders from Esholian Institute students."

She winced and braced herself, as if... as if expecting me to use Mind Manipulating to coerce her into taking a custom order anyway. The brand on the back of my neck burned with shame as I wondered how many times someone had used that kind of magic on her. I didn't know how to make commands yet, but I wouldn't even if I could.

"Okay," I said. "Have a good day, ma'am."

She blinked, then called out just as I was turning around, "How would you expect me to get it to you anyway? Custom orders take time, you know, and I'm afraid I'll have to pack up and head home for Cardina soon, seeing as that nasty president of yours forbids us from staying any longer."

I bit my lip. This had been a stupid idea. I had frog eggs to collect and corrupt rulers to poison, not pieces of little jewelry to have made.

But the soft remnants of black bamboo that always lingered on my skin nowadays seemed to pull me back, reminding me of what lay in that pocket of my satchel.

I turned to the jeweler. "I thought you said the wind was your friend."

In response, she cracked open a smile and beckoned me back.

CHAPTER

38

Twenty minutes later, I was sneaking into the jungle behind the Wild Whisperer sector, heading toward that same cliff Mr. Conine had made us climb in our Predators & Prey class.

Now, though, I didn't bother with actual footholds. I just sent a whispering song to the jungle until vines and tree trunks curled around me, hoisting me up, up, up until I'd made it to the very top.

A reddish glow had begun to trickle through spaces in the clouds by now, but the clouds themselves were bursting with gray. It wouldn't be long before the sky pelted the canopies with rain.

I picked my way toward the river system, occasionally trading jokes with various monkeys who called out or saying hi to the birds that watched me pass. It wasn't until I actually made it to the riverbank that I felt the presence of those eyes on my back again.

"Hello?" I called. "Emelle?"

Nothing answered besides the song of the jungle.

I lowered my blockade a fraction to see if I could pick out any thoughts hiding among the trees behind me, but there were so many animals nearby that the cacophony of mental words crashed over me instantly. And I didn't know where to funnel my opening toward.

Trying to shake off the feeling, I returned my attention to the riverbank. Poison dart frogs usually laid their eggs on the moistest parts of the ground rather than the actual water itself, so I was willing to bet there would be a spawn of eggs somewhere among all these water hyacinths I now knelt in.

"It's okay, I'm not going to hurt you," I muttered when a slug froze as I pushed aside some leaves and found it hulking in the mud. "Have you seen any frog eggs around, by chance?"

God, I was going to feel awful when I picked the eggs from their nesting place and put them in a jar. Mr. Conine's old motto came to mind. *Part of being a Wild Whisperer is bearing the pain of the cycle, of balancing the love and suffering of predators and prey alike.*

In a way, I was doing that right now. Bearing the pain, the discomfort, of snatching life from the soil of Eshol in order to hunt the biggest predator on the island: Dyonisia herself.

"*Think I saw some eggs that way a few days ago,*" the slug finally said in a slow, loose voice, twisting its flexible neck to its left and nodding with tapered antennas.

"Great, thank you. Have a nice day."

I released the leaves exposing it and shuffled in the direction it had indicated for several seconds until—yes! There they were: a black cluster of the tiniest orbs resting in the crook of a giant grass blade.

As I dug through my satchel for an empty jar, I felt the weight of those eyes return to the back of my head and twisted around.

"Hello?" I called again, this time straightening and letting my fingers drift to my knife.

The trees behind me seemed to stir. Not as if a monkey was jumping from one of them or a bird was taking flight, but as if something much larger had poised to attack from within.

Narrowing my eyes, I funneled an opening in my blockade toward the trees in an attempt to catch whatever mind was pinned on me.

A resounding *crash* by the riverbank had me spinning sideways, brandishing my knife at—

"Rodhi?" I gasped.

My friend was picking himself up from the bank, dripping wet and wearing the biggest shit-eating grin I'd ever seen.

That grin faded slightly as he rubbed his eyes and blinked at me several times through the water streaking down his face.

"Rayna?"

"What are you doing here?" I asked incredulously.

Rodhi folded his arms against his drenched shirt.

"I could ask you the same thing, darling."

"I'm..." I stared down at the jar that I had dropped in the mud, my eyes flicking toward that cluster of frog eggs. Thankfully, it had gone undisturbed. "I was just paying a visit to the river dolphins."

Rodhi laughed through a smirk. "No, you weren't. I know you weren't because I just got off their backs after a nice long ride."

I blinked at him. "A nice long *ride*? From where? What have you been *up* to?" I asked, my suspicion finally brimming to the surface. "You're always sneaking off and disappearing nowadays. You missed the Cardina market..."

"Well, yeah, it's the perfect time to do super secret things while everyone is distracted by fudge pops and sex toys. As you very well know, given that you're doing something super secret right now."

Rodhi nodded at my satchel and knife with eyebrows that were much too raised for his own good.

"Oh, don't give me that look, Rayna." He waved a hand. "Anyone with two good eyes can see that you've been sneaking around yourself. So what have you been hiding? I'll spill my secret if you spill yours."

I couldn't believe this kid. I'd known something was up with him for a while now, but I hadn't thought of it as any of my business if he didn't want to share. Now, though, we were obviously locked in a stalemate—he knew I was up to no good; I knew *he* was up to no good.

It would be pointless to try to look the other way.

"Fine," I sighed, squeezing my eyes shut. How to tell him the truth in a way that didn't reveal any confidential details? "I had a boyfriend last year, but everyone's memory of his existence got erased, including mine." I opened my eyes again to find Rodhi listening intently, his eyes sparkling with utter amusement. "But I recently re-met him, and I've been meeting up with him in secret every week. Happy?"

"Extremely," Rodhi grinned. "I *told* Wren you were getting laid in secret. She owes me another thirty coppers."

"What? No, I— He and I aren't back together in that way." Every one of my nerves had perked up at the insinuation, though, so that wasn't a good sign. Trying to force my sudden blush back down, I said, "But if you tell anyone that I'm even *seeing* him, I could actually get tortured and die a very cruel and painful death, Rodhi, so... please don't tell."

It sounded dramatic, but it was true. If Dyonisia heard that I was meeting up with him so casually or if Lexington discovered that my meetings with him weren't just to try to steal that batch of pills....

To my surprise, Rodhi didn't turn that into any kind of twisted joke. In fact, his face fell with something like horrified recognition.

"*Oh*. Is your not-boyfriend the pirate fugitive who's been staying at that abandoned lighthouse north of Hallow's Perch by chance?"

I froze.

Then attacked.

Throwing my knife into the mud so that I wouldn't be tempted to use it on him, I yanked him toward me by his ear.

"What the *hell*, Rodhi? How did you *know* that?"

Something feral and monstrous had sprung alive in my chest at those words spoken aloud. If Rodhi Lockett, of all people, knew about Steeler's whereabouts, then he wasn't safe at the lighthouse anymore, and neither was Felicity. Both of them would have to—

"Calm your tits, Rayna," Rodhi hissed, wrenching himself away. "I was literally just about to tell you my secret, which would have explained everything." He rubbed at his ear with a wince. "By the orchid and the owl, your not-boyfriend's a lucky guy—that's a strong grip you've got there."

I smacked his arm, and not in an amused, playful way.

"Explain yourself."

"Okay, okay." Rodhi raised his palms. "Do you guys want to come out now?"

I stared at him, sure he'd gone crazy as he raised his hands toward the rumbling sky.

Until, that is, five or six giant fishing spiders scuttled out from beneath his sopping clothes and settled on his shoulders and arms.

"What...?" I leaned forward for a closer look. "I haven't seen any other spiders except for—"

"Ms. Pincette's?" Rodhi suggested. "Yeah, that's because they've been at war with each other for the last six months. All the spiders on campus are either guarding one of us, dead, or engaged in some other battle on another part of the island."

"Wait, *what?*"

I blinked at him, confident that I must not have heard any of that right.

Rodhi heaved a deep breath as if in an attempt to reel in patience.

"Ms. Pincette put me in charge of the rebel spiders. That's my secret. We killed every dickhead arachnid working for the Good Council on campus ages ago—" Here, he puffed out his chest, clearly proud as the giant fishing spiders on his shoulders nuzzled his cheeks with long, velvety legs "—and we've been slowly pushing our way toward Bascite Mountain ever since. Huh, guys? You've done so good, haven't you?"

I needed to sit down. Or gulp some wine.

Still not quite believing what I was hearing, I repeated, "There's a spider civil war going on?"

"Yes."

"But why?"

"Well..." Rodhi pulled a grimace. "Dyonisia Reeve *may* have squashed one of their princesses with her shoe last year. Now, granted," he hurried on as he saw my expression change, "there are about a thousand prince and princess spiders on the island, but given that there are around two hundred *million* total... it offended them, to say the least. So the ones faithful to the royal family asked Ms. Pincette for help, she organized a resistance for them, and they've been battling ever since."

One of the fishing spiders on his shoulders added in a high-pitched, clicking voice. " *We will not serve and spy for someone who would so easily murder our revered in cold blood.*"

My gut was churning. I knew exactly what spider princess Rodhi was talking about, though I'd never even asked for its name. I'd seen it in the memories I'd uncovered with Garvis, seen how it had helped me and spied for me during the short remainder of its—*her*—life.

The rest of it was clicking into place, too. Not just the absence of all the spiders and Rodhi's disappearances, but what Gileon had claimed in class that one day, too: *Nuisance says Rodhi's off on a high-stakes adventure, battling deadly foe and winning armies to his name.*

God, that had actually been true all along. And Ms. Pincette had *known*...

"She put *you* in charge of the spider resistance?" I asked, wanting to make sure I understood this completely.

"Well, yeah. You and I both know I'm the only one who would die for her. And she knew it, too."

I couldn't tell if Rodhi looked sad or upset about this fact. His face had gone slightly taut, as if trying to mask something deeper. The topic obviously wasn't something he was comfortable discussing, so I grabbed at a question that would pivot us away from Ms. Pincette.

"Does Dyonisia know?"

Rodhi's face lit up. "Oh yeah. And she's *pissed*. But her Wild Whisperers on the Good Council have no idea who's behind the resistance because... well, we've been killing their spies faster than they can scuttle back up the mountain to report it."

I stared at him, suddenly in awe.

"And you've been—what? Using the dolphins for transportation?"

It made sense why Rodhi had made such instant friends with the creatures during Mr. Conine's class. He'd *already* been friends with them. It was a wonder none of us had caught on.

Rodhi, however, was squinting as a new water spider crawled up his body and whispered something into his ear.

His eyes switched to me, then to the trees where I had heard rummaging not too long ago.

"We know you're there, Temperton!" he called out. " You don't have to hide anymore!"

My mouth popped open as a frustrated sigh came from within the trees. A few seconds later, the branches rustled and... Dazmine did indeed step out onto the riverbank, brushing mud off her shirt.

"Were you following me?" I asked her incredulously.

"Well, yeah." She didn't even have the audacity to look ashamed, though she shot a filthy glance in Rodhi's direction. "You looked really dodgy at the marketplace."

"Are you serious right now?"

Dazmine had still been coming with me to the lighthouse every Sunday, going round and round with Terrin about whether this or that plan would help break the exiled ones out of prison—which often resulted in more bickering than my ears could handle. Yet that shared secret between us, the Sundays we spent together... I'd thought it had made us, not friends, exactly, but *allies.*

"You still don't trust me?" I asked.

Rodhi was looking back and forth between us with raised brows.

"I was starting to," Dazmine said with a lift of her chin. "But then I saw you heading in the same direction as Mr. Gleekle and all those students about half an hour ago, and I wanted to see if you were going to join them." Her chin went even higher, but—

"What did you just say?"

"I was starting to trust you..."

"No. About Mr. Gleekle and a group of students? You saw them take off into the jungle?"

Dazmine nodded. "During the height of the Cardina buzz, yeah. They looked really dodgy, too. So when you headed off in the same direction..." A bit of shame finally split through the hardness in her gaze.

My heart thumping against my ribcage, I turned to Rodhi. "Do you think your spiders could find out where Mr. Gleekle is right now?"

I wasn't really sure how the spying system worked—or whether he had access to more spiders than just the ones on his shoulders—but Rodhi's mouth burst into a huge grin as soon as one of them whispered into his ear again with those velvety legs resting against his neck.

"I think they already know *exactly* where Mr. Gleekle is."

After hastily collecting the poison dart frog eggs, I had the jungle take my satchel and hide it for me—just for an hour or two, I told it.

Then Rodhi, Dazmine, and I slipped into the river and onto the backs of the dolphins that emerged shyly from the water's depths, giggling and splashing each other until Rodhi told them where to go.

I clung to the dorsal fin of mine, wrapping my legs around its slippery torso as it plunged forward through the river system.

Left, right, right, center, center left.

Rodhi's spiders whispered in his ear, telling him which direction to lead us when the river split into separate streams—sometimes against a sudden rush of current, other times up a shallow, murky waterway caked in layers of algae.

Finally, just as I was wondering if I'd ever get the taste of moss and rot out of my mouth from how many times I'd accidentally swallowed a splash of water, Rodhi looked back and put his fingers to his lips. He and his dolphin eased to the bank, and I told mine to follow. Behind me, I could hear Dazmine muttering the same to her own dolphin.

Here, the jungle was absolutely crowded with strangler figs. It even seemed to sing a different tune than it did around campus, this one a deep baritone compared to its usual sweet humming.

When Dazmine, Rodhi, and I clambered off our dolphins and onto the shore, that tune paused for a second, noting the newcomers with a hesitation that made my skin prickle.

This way, Rodhi mouthed, pointing straight ahead.

Waving goodbye to our dolphins, Dazmine and I snuck after him.

We crept forward for several minutes until the sky finally opened up overhead, sending a spray of rain down onto the fig canopies and water rolling down their twisted trunks.

Only when the rain had completely overtaken the deep tune of the jungle with its deafening drumming did Dazmine tap me on the shoulder and point to her own head.

I nodded my understanding and funneled an opening in my blockade toward her as we continued to follow Rodhi.

You've seen Mr. Gleekle with a bunch of students before? she asked.

Yes, I sent back, ducking under a gnarled fig branch. *Once. Right before that first time you met Terrin, actually. I thought it was just a strange one-time occurrence, though.*

Now that I knew about that letter Dyonisia had sent Mr. Gleekle... I couldn't let this go. He was obviously some kind of player in this game, not just a pawn. So why would he be taking groups of students into the jungle outside of regular class periods? Was he interrogating them? Testing them? Or just giving them extra help?

Do you trust him? Dazmine asked. I thought she was talking about Mr. Gleekle until she nodded forward at Rodhi's back as he hopped over a log with limber ease.

Oh. Yes. More than you trust me, apparently.

A beat later, Dazmine thought, *I'm sorry about that. I don't trust anyone or anything anymore—not since Jenia. It's nothing personal.*

I felt the tinge of her sorrow behind those words, as if maybe she wished she could change that, and I hefted my blockade back up. She'd probably claw my brain out of my skull if she knew I could sense her deeper emotions behind those carefully-controlled thoughts.

Just then, Rodhi halted in front of us. Dazmine and I snuck to either side of him, crouching and peeking through the dripping fig leaves ahead.

What I saw made my lungs twist with shock.

Embedded deep in a basin that looked like it had been carved of magic, a circular stone platform swam in shadows made of towering pillars and twisting vines. Mr. Gleekle himself stood in the center of this basin, surrounded by a circle of those same students I'd seen before and holding...

A poker.

Sucking in a breath, I strained to listen to whatever he was telling them, but it was as if an invisible film of glass separated us from the basin below. The rain splattered against the barrier and rolled off, and none of their thoughts drifted up to me either.

Dazmine craned her neck, squinting at the strange barrier and leaning forward through the fig leaves for a better look—

She hissed a curse through her teeth as Mr. Gleekle's head jerked our way.

We all ducked low.

"Do you think he saw me?" Dazmine breathed.

Rodhi shook his head when a spider whispered in his ear.

"Don't know. The spiders can't even get in to hear what they might be saying. Whatever they're doing down there, they don't want *anyone* to know about it."

375

Whatever they were doing seemed obvious to me: Mr. Gleekle was conducting his own private Branding ceremony... but with students who already *had* powers, judging by the boy with the brand on his shoulder who stepped into the center of the circle and raised his left arm, exposing the spot where I thought I'd seen a second brand on Jenia all those months ago.

Is there ever a reason someone would have two brands? I'd asked Dyonisia at the start of the year.

To which she'd only responded with a question of her own: *What reason would someone have to get a second one?*

Not a no.

Just not an explanation of *why*. Why give some students extra brands but not others?

"You were right, Rayna," Dazmine breathed. "Jenia must have—"

We all winced when Mr. Gleekle stamped the poker into the soft part of the boy's underarm.

"Damn. I'd rather have my own nipples twisted than get branded there," Rodhi murmured. "That would hurt *and* tickle."

Not even two seconds later, the air beneath that invisible film of glass appeared to *whoosh* away from the boy, knocking Mr. Gleekle and the circle of students onto their asses. One of them in particular fell into a rare stripe of sunlight, and—

Before I could inhale sharply at what I had just seen—at *who* I had just seen—the glass-like structure around them exploded.

Four or five giant fireballs burst from the newly-Branded boy, arcing high up in the air and whistling back down...

One of them toward us.

Rodhi, Dazmine, and I turned and ran just as it came crashing down where we had been moments earlier, blasting a hole into the ground with a flare of heat that singed my skin from behind.

The force sent the three of us sprawling, while the echoing boom of the rest of the fireballs landed in other areas of the jungle around us. If it wasn't pounding down rain right now, I'd probably worry about the fig trees catching on fire.

As it was, I looked over my shoulder to find the fire already sizzling out.

"Well," said Rodhi from where he lay in the mud on his stomach, "that was a little more intense than a regular Branding."

Dazmine and I exchanged glances as we got to our feet. From the sharpness in her eyes, I was pretty sure she'd seen it, too: another newcomer in whatever cult Mr. Gleekle had created.

I'd recognize that glossy sheet of ruby-red hair anywhere.

Quinn.

Raindrops rolling down her forehead, Dazmine turned to me with a glint of rage that seemed to breathe sparks onto my own ice.

"Okay, *that's* it. It's time to get that bitch to talk."

CHAPTER

39

Unfortunately, Quinn wasn't much of a talker.

Dazmine learned this the hard way when she tried knocking on the Element Wielder house door after class the next day. And the next day. And the next.

Each time, the person who answered the door simply told her that Quinn wasn't available. Just like they'd always told me.

"We're going to get her to talk," Dazmine seethed during a Language of Plants lesson where Mrs. Wildenberg had paired us up once again. "One way or another, she's going to tell us what she knows."

Last year, I might have been just as determined as Dazmine after what we'd seen, but my nerves could only seem to be directed at one thing right now: those pills.

After that fireball incident, I'd retrieved my satchel from the jungle. Steeler had arrived that night to pick up the ingredients for Nara, but apparently, she would still need four more weeks to mix and brew the poison until it was strong enough to kill a faerie. Four whole weeks of torture for me as I went to class after class, playing the part of an innocent Esholian student and trying not to wonder if Dyonisia's death would create a level of chaos that the island wasn't prepared to deal with.

I climbed sun bears in Mr. Conine's class, helped caddisflies gather sticks and stones in Ms. Pincette's, listened to Mrs. Smetlar's scowling lectures in History, and, one Sunday, found myself sitting on the beach outside the lighthouse with Garvis, finally learning the Mind Manipulating art of commands.

"So, this is what your mind is like, huh?"

I stood up outside the gate of Garvis's mind for the first time, gazing around me in awe.

His walls weren't walls at all. They were more like *curtains*, hung up by pillars and rods of stone but flowing back and forth with strips of what looked like cashmere. The result was a constant fluttering of white, as if Garvis's thoughts were wisps of the gentlest clouds.

"This is me." Garvis's consciousness turned to face me. "No need to get through someone's gate for this lesson, though. All you need to do is give me a command with as much force as you can muster."

"Oh. Okay." I tore my eyes away from the mesmerizing flow of those curtains. "Jump up and down?"

Garvis shook his head. "Not enough force. When you make a true command, you'll feel it in the form of a mist leaking out of you and latching onto your victim."

Victim. I didn't like the sounds of that, but it was accurate, and something I needed to learn *about* even if I decided to never use it on someone else.

Clenching my fists, I filled my voice with as much force as I could muster. "Jump up and down."

Like tendrils of smoke, my command flowed out of my mental body in little wiggling strings and drifted to Garvis's consciousness. Right as they tried to latch onto him, he gave a great, violent shudder... and they dissipated.

In the background film of the real world, I saw Garvis remain sitting from where we faced each other, cross-legged. "Try again," his inner self said. "Really *push* the command out."

"Okay." I flexed my mental fingers. "Jump up and down."

This time, the tendrils of mist floated out of me and latched onto Garvis's consciousness like squirming puppet strings before he could shake them off. In the real world, he scrambled to a stand and jumped twice before sitting back down.

"Oh, good!" He sounded surprised that I had caught on so quickly. "Can you do that again?"

"I don't know." I hadn't liked the feeling of those strings of mist connecting me to him, but I gave another command anyway. "Scratch your nose."

Again, that mist flowed out of me and latched onto Garvis's consciousness. Again, he heeded my command and scratched his nose.

"Tap your head," I commanded.

Garvis tapped his head.

"Wiggle your fingers."

Garvis wiggled his fingers, but frowned.

"I don't think these commands are really testing your abilities, Rayna. I have no reason to resist them. You need to tell me to do something I wouldn't want to do."

Inexplicably, my thoughts drifted to Quinn again, and how often her Mind Manipulating mother used to tell her to do something she didn't want to do. No matter what kind of person she'd turned into since our childhood, I should have stood up for her more in the face of that. I folded my arms at Garvis.

"Sorry. There's no way I'm doing that to you."

Garvis stroked his mustache with a soft smile. "While I appreciate the thoughtfulness, Rayna, this wouldn't exactly be my first time. In our very first year as Mind Manipulators, our instructors made us command each other to do unwanted things. I'm pretty sure one of my classmates actually made me shit myself during my first quarterly test."

I gaped at him, unfolding my arms. "That's horrible!" Now my thoughts drifted to Steeler in the lighthouse behind us. If that had been everyone's experience in the Mind Manipulating sector, I could only imagine what manner of classes and tests he'd had to endure over the last five years. No wonder he'd developed such a commanding presence—this power required you to control or *be* controlled. No alternatives.

"Okay," I said slowly. "How about this? What's something you've always *secretly* wanted to do that you haven't had the courage to?"

Garvis stopped stroking his mustache to peer at me.

"That's an interesting question."

I shrugged. "Seems more humane than telling you to shit your pants."

Something in Garvis's expression reminded me of a cat raising its head after a long afternoon nap. He glanced at the foundation of his mind and said, "I would want just that—to have courage."

"What?"

He sighed and looked back up.

"All my life, I've felt that I just drift wherever the tide takes me. And while that's how I prefer to go about things, I also wish, just sometimes, that I could throw myself *into* it. Meet new people, go to new places, discover new things." He smiled. "To have the courage to try something new."

I stared at him. Garvis—a Mind Manipulating pirate, one of Steeler's best friends who had been giving up his time to teach me about this power with everlasting patience—*he* felt that he lacked courage?

The look on his face was already darkening into embarrassment, so I made a quick decision before he could regret telling me.

"Jump into the ocean," I commanded. "Right now."

Those strings of mist shot out from me harder and faster than before, latching onto Garvis with shocking force. I snapped out of his mind just in time to see him begin sprinting toward the water's edge.

Laughing, I ran after him, feeling the heavy presence of a pair of watchful eyes from the lighthouse window but not looking over my shoulder to meet them. If I was going to make a friend throw himself into something like this, I was sure as hell going to join him.

We both crashed into an oncoming wave at the same time.

The biting cold of it wrapped around my ankles, and Garvis gasped beside me. I could feel the puppet strings of my command withdrawing from him, but he only shot me a rare laugh and threw himself deeper. I waded forward, too, letting the waves soak the bottom of my dress and the seaweed wrap around my ankle, until we were both chest-deep in the water, rocking back and forth with the waves.

"And to think," Garvis called over the roaring sound of it all, "that our captain always warned us against even *touching* the water lest a sea monster got us!"

I whipped my head toward him with a squint, my smile plastered on my face.

"Captain?"

"Yeah!" We bobbed up with a particularly large wave, and a splash of water salted my mouth as Garvis said, "The captain of our ship."

"Oh." Had I been mistaken about the female faerie with the tattoo on her back in Steeler's memory? Was she, perhaps, not the Fated General, but merely the captain? I didn't ask Garvis, though, not when he laughed again in the face of a wave as if he'd never truly laughed before.

We were both completely soaked by the time we trudged back up to the lighthouse to dry off.

"Well, how does it feel to have made your first official command as a Mind Manipulator?" Garvis asked.

I hesitated on the doorstop, thinking about that question while I wrung out my hair. The idea of controlling someone like that on a daily basis made actual bile pool in the base of my throat—it felt as if the more I did it, the more I'd feel those strings of mist wiggling around inside me, begging to be released.

"I don't think I want to go around making commands," I said honestly, "unless it's a life-or-death situation." Those spiders back at Ms. Pincette's swam in my mind. I wouldn't have had any problem combining my powers to tell them to get off me. Lexington, too. If he ever tried to touch one of my friends like he'd used his commands to harm me, I wouldn't think twice before shooting that mist at every inch of his consciousness I could latch onto.

But other than that? No. The Cardina jeweler's wince back in her green-striped tent was enough of a reason to stay away from this type of Mind Manipulating as much as possible. I never wanted to see anyone look at me in fear like that again.

"I think that's a good idea," said Garvis.

I nodded and pushed open the door to find that Felicity was chatting away to Dazmine and Terrin in the kitchen, despite the former looking as if she wanted to claw her ears out and the latter staring at the monkey with an utterly blank expression. The two of them had begun trying to create a blueprint of the prison at the top of Bascite Mountain based on information they'd been able to gather from the birds and the wind, but so far, that blueprint only consisted of a sad little rectangle surrounded by an iron gate crowned with spikes. Nobody who'd gone in, it seemed, ever came out—much like the Uninhabitable Zone.

It was just one more reason to kill Dyonisia. When she was gone, Dazmine and Terrin would finally get to act.

My gaze shifted to Steeler by the fireplace.

"Here," he said, moving aside. "You two look like you need the fire more than I do."

Garvis and I both hurried forward, water trailing behind us at every step. I felt every sweep of Steeler's gaze as it lingered on the dress I was wearing today. Made of a white, cottony material much like the cashmere in Garvis's mind, I could feel it clinging to every curve of my body.

When I looked down, heat rose to my cheeks as I saw how transparent it was now. My nipples were pebbling through the material—whether because of the cold water dripping off me or the dark glint in Steeler's eyes, I didn't know.

All too aware of my own body, I cracked open my blockade and shot into his mind, *Do you happen to have a change of clothes I could borrow until this dries? I seem to be getting too much attention.*

Too much? Steeler had followed my downward gaze with a flash of amusement. *I could never give those too much attention. They would always deserve more.*

I rolled my eyes, but my nipples only peaked harder against my will, and I couldn't deny that I *liked* it when he looked at them—I just didn't want the others to glance over and see how stupidly turned on I was.

Garvis just taught me how to make commands, I warned. *I could make you take off your own shirt and give it to me right now.*

Is that just a ploy to see my abs again?

Again? My lips twisted. *What makes you think I've ever looked at them before?*

Uh, I don't know. Your eyes?

Well, damn. He had me there. I tried another strategy.

I could cash in my prize for that bet I won.

Not that I actually would. When I'd told Steeler that the Cardina peddlers hadn't carried poison dart frog eggs, he'd cursed, but asked me what I wanted for winning. I'd told him I was waiting for the right moment, but the truth was I had no idea what to ask of him. He'd given me so much already: his blood, his time, his makeshift home.

Well, there *was* one thing I wanted, but that was a secret locked deep beneath my skin...

As if Steeler could scent that secret, his nostrils widened briefly before he nodded at the hallway to our right.

As much as I'd love to keep watching you blush, you're right—we wouldn't want you to catch a cold in that thing. I have some dry clothes in my room... no Mind Manipulating or cashing in bets required.

I'm not blushing, I muttered, but left Garvis and the others behind anyway and followed Steeler to that singular door in the hallway.

He opened it and led me into a small, drafty room with a rickety cot slammed against a corner next to a gnarled nightstand that looked like it had been here long before him. A flash of silver caught my eye on top of it: the pendant he had Branded me with. Next to it lay my stolen file from Mr. Gleekle's office.

I looked away from those items quickly. Despite how many times I'd been to the lighthouse by now, I'd never been in here before. Nothing about it was anywhere near as homey as the rest of the cottage, and my heart squeezed to think that this was where he slept every night.

"Felicity sometimes sleeps in the rafters up there when the wind gets bad," Steeler said, as if he could hear my rush of thoughts despite my blockade that I had closed up again. He rummaged through one of his nightstand drawers before whipping out an oversized gray shirt. "How is this? It'll probably cover about as much as those dresses of yours..."

I took the shirt from him and found myself wanting him to look at me again, but he just turned his back, blocking the crack of the door, so I took that as my cue to change.

As quickly as I could, I slipped out of the sopping dress until I was completely naked except for the sheath and all those glittering blades at my thigh. Then I paused, staring at the way Steeler's back muscles tensed and his fists flexed at his sides.

Why was I so desperately close to telling him to shut the door and turn around? So many people were in this cottage right now that the click of the lock wouldn't go unnoticed, and I'd been smothering my feelings for him fairly well over the last few weeks. Why was that control fracturing right now?

But here I was, nothing to cover me from those devouring eyes that could eat me alive if I let them. And I wanted to let them. I *ached* to let them.

Just as I found my mouth inexplicably opening, Steeler spoke up instead, his voice softer than before.

"Thank you."

"W-what?" Jolting out of my reverie, I slipped his shirt over my head and relished the smell of black bamboo that floated over me. The fabric did, indeed, fall all the way to my knees, which shouldn't have surprised me. I wasn't exactly the tiniest girl in my sector, but Steeler himself always towered over me.

"For what you did out there for Garvis," he clarified. "I haven't seen him smile like that in ages—since long before we first arrived on this island."

Finally, he turned around to face me, his fists uncurling as he took in the way my hair dripped over his shirt, something purely masculine lighting up his eyes with approval.

I forced out a shrug, still feeling the ache of my nipples against his shirt. "It was just a Mind Manipulating lesson."

"Oh, no, Rayna." He locked his gaze with mine. "It was the reason I will never find a mind as beautiful as yours—because all your thoughts come from your heart."

I opened my mouth, but didn't know how to respond... and suddenly, Dazmine was yelling my name from the kitchen before I could figure it out.

Both Steeler and I ran out of the room to find Dazmine beaming, wearing that same glittering malice I'd seen a few weeks ago in the jungle. She pointed past Felicity, locking her finger on Terrin.

" *This* guy just reminded me about his sector's annual winter formal. It'd be the perfect way to get into the Element Wielder house, don't you think?"

"I was just wondering if anybody had asked you," Terrin muttered rather grumpily, which struck me as odd. Even if he'd wanted to, he wouldn't be able to take Dazmine to a dance at the Esholian Institute. But I realized what Dazmine was implying half a second later.

Quinn couldn't hide in her own home.

Steeler had stiffened beside me, and when I glanced at him, it was to find a mask sliding over his features. I wondered if he was thinking about the last time I'd been at a party, when I'd danced and kissed that Shape Shifter. Or maybe he just wished things were different, that he could ask me to go.

Either way, I looked at Dazmine and nodded.

"I'm in."

If I had to keep playing the part of innocent Esholian student for a little while longer, I might as well go to the ball.

CHAPTER

40

The Element Wielder houses looked the same as they had last year.

Magic-induced skirts of snow frosted the edges of both alabaster mansions. Garlands bordered the widespread windows, where sheets of fire writhed freely within each double pane and fat snowflakes drifted down to the front steps before both sets of double doors.

Emelle and Lander had gone together, Cilia had run off to get ready with Mitzi, and Wren and Gileon had decided to skip it this year, so Dazmine and I approached the girls' side together.

"Are you sure you want to do this?" I muttered. "It might get ugly."

Indeed, anytime I even tried to say *hi* to Quinn in the last year, it seemed to veer on the side of ugly. I couldn't imagine anyone backing her into a corner and demanding she talk about her very obviously illicit activities.

Or...maybe not so illicit if Dyonisia knew about them, but still.

Dazmine didn't even pause.

"No. I never liked Quinn even during the rare times Jenia had the three of us hang out together. I want to be there when she cries."

Ruthless. Dazmine was ruthless, and maybe I needed a bigger dose of that for myself tonight.

I smoothed out my dress, a cardinal red flow of sequined lace with a sharp V-neck and dainty straps that revealed every inch of my brand—the one on my shoulder, at least. My hair itself was pulled back into a half knot, the rest of my curls spreading over the brand on my neck with their usual unruliness.

Dazmine herself wore her braids up in an elaborate swirl, highlighting the bronze column of her neck. I had zero doubts that in her strapless mermaid dress, she would attract a lot of attention inside. Attention she needed.

Quinn had never bowed to small or meek or *less than*, after all.

I knocked.

An Element Wielder answered the door without looking at us, her head still thrown back over her shoulder as she laughed at someone behind her.

Dazmine and I slipped inside, gave each other nods, and broke apart to begin the hunt before anyone could notice us together.

I squeezed through the mass of mingling bodies inside. Couples danced to the music of instruments that floated and played above everyone's heads on an endless loop of elaborate wind. Others lounged in chairs or on stools scattered along the edges of the room, clinking drinks together and tossing their heads back in the kind of nervous, giddy laughter reserved for more formal occasions.

Across the room, I caught sight of Wilder in a suit and tie doing exactly that.

"Hey, darling!" Rodhi pushed through the crowd to throw an arm around me. He leaned in close to my ear, his breath bordering on drunk already. "No sign of her yet."

Dammit. Even though we'd all decided it was best if Rodhi was as hands-off in this little endeavor as possible, he was the one who'd secured us these invitations, and I'd hoped he might have pinpointed Quinn's position for us.

I hugged Rodhi back. "Don't worry about it. Thanks, though."

With that, I continued to crisscross through the crowd, smiling at faces I recognized and nodding politely at ones I didn't whenever their gazes snagged on me for a little longer than would probably be considered normal. Shit. Did I look too out of place? Maybe I was walking too fast or frowning too hard.

Or maybe you're a hot girl who seems to be at a formal alone.

I wasn't even surprised that Steeler's voice caressed the walls of my mind. In fact, it filled me with something like... relief, knowing that he was somewhere within range.

Hot? I jabbed back. *You haven't even seen me yet.*

Not in person. But I may have taken a few small peeks into other people's minds to find out exactly why they're gaping at you like that.

They're not gaping, I scoffed. *They're scrutinizing.*

At that thought, I grabbed a drink from a nearby bar and pretended to take a sip, slowing my pace to a muddy crawl. No sign of ruby-red hair. No hint of Quinn's drawling voice with the slight rasp to it. It was time to go deeper.

Skimming a glance over my shoulder to make sure none of those eyes were still fastened onto me, I plunged into the shadows of a hallway and up a flight of spiral stairs. Rather than take the staircase to the famous, gated roof where braziers would be flickering beneath the starlight, I snuck down one of the side hallways to investigate the rooms.

I almost stopped in awe.

Unlike the hallways in the Wild Whisperer house, self-burning torches lined the stone walls here, while statues tinkled with water that simply floated back upward in hundreds of little droplets once they hit the floor.

Shaking my head, I crept forward. Some doors were open, and I peeked inside to find couples—or sometimes three or more—twisting and moaning together on one of the beds. In one, I accidentally caught the tail end of an orgasm that sent flurries erupting from the woman's bouncing nipples and flames erupting around the man's—

Okay, yeah, Quinn wasn't in that room.

Shut up, I told Steeler, feeling his stifled laugh echo inside me.

When I poked my head in the sixth or seventh room, a pack of upperclassmen who were smoking and playing card games looked up.

"Hey, you lost or something?"

Every one of my bones snapped to a halt. Deep within the maze of my mind, memories were swirling into frenzies, dislodging themselves until my eyes swiveled back to the group of men.

There were four of them, all unfamiliar besides...

I didn't realize I was floating forward until the one who'd asked me if I was lost smirked and jabbed his neighbor, the one I was staring at.

"My buddy here isn't really into blondes, but..." Water spurted in neat little arcs from his fingers, landing with separate *splats* at my shoes. "I can show you a thing or two about how to get *really* wet if you're up for it."

In my head, Steeler's dark, fathomless presence seemed to crouch and pulse with a territorial rage that shivered through my veins.

But my eyes couldn't unstick themselves from that so-called buddy, who finally looked up with bleary contemplation.

The Object Summoning boy.

Fergus's friend. The one who'd sent sticks to whack Gileon and stones to pummel Emelle and me.

He had been the reason for those bruises cascading up and down my body last year, not Steeler. *He* had been in on the plan to kill me along with Jenia and Quinn.

And I'd never even known his name.

Rage curdled beneath my skin, lighting adrenaline inside me until I practically vibrated with it.

I speared into his mind and rifled through the thick, gauzy material that housed his thoughts and memories and all those other vital pieces of him.

His name was Jaques. He'd grown up in Yellowseek.

He had a mommy and daddy who loved him. Who couldn't wait for him to pass his Final Test and come home.

He'd met Fergus at the Branding Ceremony. They'd caught up afterward, Fergus whining that Jaques had the cooler power, and Jaques had thrived off of that jealousy. Had sought to prove it true by doing anything Fergus asked of him, no matter the consequences to others.

And yet...

Yet...

After Fergus had died, I couldn't find a single memory of him bullying or abusing others.

No hitting or poking. No yelling or cursing.

No meeting up with Quinn, either. No attempt to revisit any of those past friendships that had goaded him into doing what he'd done.

Just this: cards, smoking, and relatively pleasant friends from a variety of sectors. It was as if Fergus had been a poison rotting his brain and heart from the inside-out, but once that poison had been re-moved...

"I..." the Object Summoner started, eyes widening in vague recognition. Even if he couldn't remember actually hurting me, I was sure he remembered planning to do so with Fergus.

"Forget it," I pushed out on a razor-sharp breath.

My fists had clenched like the rocks he'd once thrown my way, and I wanted to bash them through his skull until it splintered, until his brain oozed through my fingers, but... I also didn't. I didn't want to continue the hurt or feed the cycle of pain. Maybe, if I let it be, if he stayed away from festering friends like Fergus, Jaques wouldn't use his power for ill ever again.

I turned to leave when the first man whistled.

"What, you got a boyfriend or something?"

Something that wasn't quite *me* bristled at the tone.

"Yes," I lied. Anything to cut this conversation short and resume my search for Quinn. Anything to get away from the Object Summoner's guilt-riddled gaze through the haze of his current high.

"Oh, come on." The man squirted water playfully from his fingers again. "What's his name, then?"

"That's none of your fucking business, is it?"

I whipped around as the dark, fathomless presence in my mind solidified behind me and Steeler stepped from the shadows of the hall-way.

I'd say it is my business considering you're in my house, the man wanted to reply. I knew so because my blockade had cracked open in shock and all the thoughts in the room swept over me in the instant before I heaved it up again.

But as the man's gaze dragged up Steeler's muscled figure and up to his face—his much-too-identifiable *face*, for God's sake—that fury faded. As did the water from his fingers, which trickled down to a slow leak.

"No, I suppose it's not," he muttered finally, apparently deciding that Steeler wouldn't be a fun opponent to get into a raging fistfight with.

"Good." Steeler pressed his mouth into a rigid line that melted when he looked down at me. "Come on, beautiful."

His hand clamped possessively around my waist, twirling me around and dragging me back into the hall.

It was only when I'd picked up the pace and marched us around a corner that I let go of the hiss that had been building in my chest.

"Are you *serious* right now, Steeler?"

"Dead serious." His attention buried itself into every inch of my body, as if he'd forgotten what the moon looked like but found beams of it shining from me now. "You're the most beautiful thing I've ever seen."

I didn't let the stutter in my heart reflect as a stutter in my words.

"You just revealed yourself to *four* students."

"Yeah, and I changed their perception of my features," he murmured, absentmindedly reaching out to tuck a rogue curl back over my shoulder. The skim of his callouses against my cheek had warmth pooling in my lower belly. "They didn't see any ears or teeth. I promise."

As if it would make me feel better, he flashed those teeth now.

God of the Cosmos, what I wouldn't do to feel them drag down my neck, between my breasts, to the soft skin of my stomach and...

No. I shook my head. This smoky, sex-addled hallway was messing with my mind. I could literally *feel* it getting hazy in there, clouding my current mission.

"I don't care that there are no spiders around anymore," I whispered up at him. Even without the ears and teeth, his presence seemed to swell throughout the hall, undeniably out of place. And though those four men back there wouldn't have any memory of who he was, they were probably wondering what sector he was in, who he was, why he was here. "You can't be here at the *Element Wielder ball* where anyone could see you."

Steeler's mouth hooked up in a half-smile. "Not even for a dance?"

For a moment, the offer hung in the air above his outstretched hand. A dance. Had we ever danced? What if this was our only opportunity to ever dance again?

Then footsteps clacked around the corner of the hallway, and I pushed against the unyielding planes of his chest.

"*Go.*"

Something snapped back into place in his face, a kind of hardening that tightened every one of his features. A rough, ragged return to reality that he'd been in too much of a haze to fully grasp until the moment I'd said that word.

Go.

My hands fell through thin air as he melted away, and—

Dazmine nearly ran into me from around the corner.

"Oh." I let my hands fall. "It's you."

Dazmine blinked at me. "What are you—never mind. I was trying to find you. I did some good old-fashioned eavesdropping on a group of third-year Element Wielders and found out that Quinn went up to her room with some guy around the same time we showed up."

Right. Quinn. I squeezed my eyes shut to clear the image of Steeler's outstretched hand. "So her room is...?"

"On the third floor in the left-hand corridor, second door on the right." Dazmine's smirk broke through her continuous effort to look as if nothing and no one ever fazed her. "God, I'd make a good spy."

"Maybe Rodhi will recruit you." I opened my eyes again and almost snorted when her smirk turned to outrage at the mere idea of that. "Okay, let's go."

We stole up that spiral staircase again until we were creeping to a halt right in front of the supposed room next to a statue of a naked woman. From the other side, a mingling of deep and high-pitched noises had me wondering if Quinn was fucking or fighting with someone behind that door.

"Remember," Dazmine breathed out, "I do the talking, you do the creepy mind-reading."

"It's not creepy," I huffed. "But okay."

I sank behind the shadows of the nearby statue, pressing my back against the wall. Even with Dazmine's elegant dress, hairdo, and aura, the chances of Quinn opening up to her were low. They'd sink straight to zero if she knew I was anywhere in the vicinity.

Dazmine didn't give me time to mentally prepare—literally—for the Mind Manipulating I was about to use against my childhood friend.

She just brought her fist to the door and hammered.

CHAPTER

41

Once, when Quinn and I were nine, her mother had tasked us with spooning out the seeds from a bowl full of pomegranates for her upcoming cocktail party. To keep us busy while she cleaned, she'd said.

As soon as Quinn had started chucking spare seeds at my head in fits of giggles, however, her mother had decided that busy wasn't quite enough. She'd infiltrated Quinn's mind right then and there and commanded her to be quiet. Keep her head down. Focus on the task.

The silence had thickened over the house like a congealing shadow, filled with the ticking of the clock and the beating of my heart as I stole glances at my best friend in search of signs that she was fighting the Mind Manipulation.

Nothing. Not even a flutter of her eyelashes as she deadpanned the spooning motions over and over, going through pomegranate after pomegranate like a child made of cogs and gears.

Now, that same shadowy silence fell behind her door. As if Quinn knew that she was about to be betrayed by the one person who'd seen what her mother had done to her and how much it had affected her.

No, I reminded myself. I wasn't going to coerce her into doing anything. I was simply going to lower my blockade in her direction. And she'd betrayed me ten times over by agreeing to take part in that *prank* last year, so I—

The door opened a crack.

An inhale stung in my nose.

Through the tiniest crack behind the statue, I could see that Quinn's hair was no longer a glossy curtain of ruby red, but pale, stiff, and cropped to her shoulders. The color blended into her pallid face as she took in her visitor.

"Dazmine." Even her voice sounded more hoarse than usual. "What do you want?"

"Aww." Dazmine tilted her head. "Is that how you greet an old friend?"

"We had a mutual friend, but *we* were never really friends. And I don't think you're under any delusions that we were, so *what do you want?*"

"To talk."

Quinn puffed out a dry laugh. "No, thanks."

Just as she was slamming the door shut, Dazmine stuck out a shoe.

"Would you like to talk in your room or out here?" she asked sweetly. "I'm fine with either one... though I'd love to meet the lucky guy in there."

Pupils narrowing into lines that could cut, Quinn spared a glance over her shoulder, where I could hear the soft stirring of quiet breaths: probably whoever she'd come up with earlier. If this were any other circumstance, I'd feel horrible for interrupting them.

For a moment, sparks flared to life beneath Quinn's fingernails, as if she had half a mind to blast Dazmine out of the hallway with her magic.

Then movement behind her had a panicked look scurrying across her face. She definitely didn't want whoever was in her room to come out.

"Fine," she muttered and slipped out into the hallway, quickly clicking the door shut behind her. The sparks beneath her fingernails died. "Go ahead, then. I'll give you two damn minutes of my life."

Caging in a breath, I slowly chiseled an opening into my blockade.

"Let's start with that hair," Dazmine said. "What happened?"

"What happened?" Quinn's nostrils flared. "What *happened* is that I had a Shape Shifter dye it because I wanted a change. And why should you be inquiring about my hair, anyway?"

Lie. She'd altered her hair herself—because Mr. Gleekle had branded her with Shape Shifting weeks ago. I heard that truth burn right through me with roaring flames that nearly had me gasping for air again.

Dazmine was already ploughing on.

"Why did you go into the jungle with Jenia and Fergus that day?"

Quinn's eyes flashed in alarm at the mention of those two names. I didn't blame her, necessarily: one dead, the other exiled. They'd practically become a taboo topic.

Through gritted teeth, she said, "Last I checked, you're not on the Good Council, Dazmine. I've already explained to the real people in charge that we were just going to play a harmless little prank."

Lie. But her thoughts behind that lie were too muffled for me to pick them apart.

Dazmine drummed her fingertips over her crossed arms.

400

"Did the Good Council tell you anything else? Have you been in contact with them since that *harmless little prank*?"

The breathiest pause, then— "No."

Lie.

Of course, she was lying. What else had I expected? I let myself cling to those outermost thoughts and dug deeper, searching for the truth.

Dazmine has no right to be here right now, she was thinking beneath her hardened exterior.

But I'm surprised she didn't confront me sooner, she was thinking beneath that. And—

Rayna will never forgive me, she was thinking beneath that.

I tumbled into her mind.

When I straightened, it was to find a wall of ice so similar to mine that for a second, I thought I'd sunk backward into my own instead.

I squinted at the ice again and realized it was... opaque. Frozen walls of water drooped with icicles, their borders etched with frost. The scope of it was chillingly beautiful, but without a single sign of the raging flames I'd always associated Quinn with.

I hadn't realized until just now how dark and thick my own ice was, as if something more solid lurked beneath its frigid surface. This... this was bare and fragile and glittering with raw menace. Even the moon, the tiniest slice of light I'd ever seen, looked like an icicle in the shape of a sickle above my head.

Quinn's consciousness stood by her gate, so focused on her conversation with Dazmine that she was completely unaware of my presence as I tiptoed around her and nudged open the door.

It wasn't hard to find her memories. Her maze was made of short, angular pathways, and the things she was trying to keep secret were already at the forefront of her mind.

"It's insane here, huh?"

A misty version of first-year Quinn was walking next to Jenia on Bascite Boulevard during what looked like the first hour of our arrival. I crept toward the memory in order to analyze every detail of it.

"Oh—" Jenia flipped a partial curtain of hair over her shoulder. "—I'm from Belliview, so I'm used to all this."

Quinn stared at her.

"So you're like, right next to Bascite Mountain!"

"Well, yeah." Jenia passed an amused smile to Quinn, but there was something keen and hungry beneath the curve of her mouth. "You must be from one of the smaller villages?"

"Yeah, Alderwick." Quinn said the name of our home as if it were a centipede or something else she might squash easily underfoot. "It's kind of stupid there. Everyone knows everyone, and we're all assigned the lamest jobs after our Final Tests. No one ever dances or sings or... does anything else unless it's a special occasion."

Jenia snickered. "God, that *does* sound stupid. My older sister and I—back before she left for the Institute, at least—we would go to these performances on the weekends, where Wild Whisperers would get the flowers to dance and Element Wielders would juggle balls of live fire and Object Summoners would fly you around the room."

Quinn gasped. "Just for *fun*?"

"Well, *yeah*."

Their conversation continued as they pressed further down Bascite Boulevard, but I studied Jenia's eyes, how they swept over Quinn with that same keen hunger as before, and I finally understood: in Belliview, she'd never been seen as anything special surrounded by all that fantastic magic, but here, Quinn slathered her in attention and admiration and awe.

And when I'd showed up a little later that day and Quinn had called me her best friend from home, Jenia had fought tooth and nail to keep that feeling all to herself. Even when she and Quinn ended up in different sectors, Jenia must have viewed me as the wrong person to have been given the same power as her. I'd never looked at Jenia with attention, admiration, or awe. I'd only looked at her with confusion and wariness and—later, when they were attacking Gileon for fun— disgust.

I moved to another memory.

This time, Jenia had cornered Quinn between two Element Wielder classrooms that glimmered with uncut rubies embedded into the alabaster.

"Do you remember what I told you about Kimber? How she's on track to join the Good Council after her Final Test?"

Quinn glanced around nervously. "Yeah? What about it?"

"Well, she found out that one of our classmates isn't what they pretend to be," Jenia said, a cold glitter in her eye. "And if we get her to confess, Dyonisia Reeve might let us join the Good Council, too." She grabbed Quinn's hands. "Daz was too scared, but she doesn't know what we'd get *rewarded* with. She's never been interested in moving up in life like you have."

A flicker of desire stuffed out the nerves written in every line of Quinn's face. She closed her fingers around Jenia's hands.

" *Who* isn't who they pretend to be?"

Jenia uttered my name, and Quinn and I jolted with horror at the same time.

I ran away before I could hear her response, following the echoes of another memory.

This one was even more jarring than the others. It started off as a giant gap, as if the beginning had been ripped away. But then Lander was there, in his panther form, snarling at her with such vicious, spitting rage that I knew this must have been the tail-end of her memory of that incident in the jungle last year. The part of her memory that Steeler had left intact.

A sob burst from Quinn's throat at the look of such hatred on Lander's shifted face.

She turned and fled.

Branches and brambles snagged at her clothes as she tried to tear through them. She could have used her wind to push them apart and create a path home for herself, but something peculiar was happening to her body: it was growing frost. A hue of blue was washing over her skin, as if her magic was trying to calm down her racing heart. To freeze her panic in its tracks.

Quinn didn't fight it for long. When the jungle became too thick for her to wade through, she fell to her knees with a squelch in the mud that was slowly frosting over.

Ice burst from her chest, forming a wall of glittering, spiked barricades around her. A crystal-clear spire shot through the canopy above, and a mote of frigid water wove around it all.

In the middle of those barricades, Quinn wrapped her arms around her legs and rocked back and forth, trying to catch her breath as it fogged out in front of her. Long after she'd finally rocked herself into stillness, a familiar voice wormed its way toward her.

"Well, isn't this an interesting display of magic?"

Quinn looked up to find Lexington's face leering through her opaque walls of ice.

I continued on, chasing after other memories in search of a hint of Mr. Gleekle.

Parties, classes, one-night stands, drinking games, friends—the chaotic routine of Quinn's life in the last year went by in a blur as I ran past those short, angular paths, merely glancing at their dead ends before rushing on—until I did a double take and turned back.

There, at the end of one, a castle-like structure of... of *shells* cloaked what should have been the space for a memory.

I raced toward it, heart skittering, knowing that another Mind Manipulator had buried whatever this was—albeit clumsily, with their own magic rather than using Quinn's mind to hide parts of itself.

I plunged my hand through the sharp fragments, tossing aside scallops, whelks, and disjointed ladybug wings, until it all came scattering down and the mist burst into life around me.

"Quinn Balkersaff?"

Kimber Leake had cornered Quinn in almost the exact same spot between Element Wielder classrooms... but now, Quinn turned to face Jenia's older sister with fear and wariness knotting between her eyebrows, her fingertips frosting over with blue on instinct.

"Yes?"

I saw her eyes shoot to the little red dot in Kimber's shoulder brand that marked her as an elite. This must have been sometime after Jenia's exile, when Kimber had shown up for the Branding as a Good Council representative. Perhaps even when her parakeet had been spitting names at me on my house's balcony.

"I'm sorry for your loss," Quinn added in a mutter.

Every ounce of Kimber's polite demeanor seemed to snap away.

"My sister's not *dead!*" Chest heaving, she tucked a strand of brown hair behind her ear and said more calmly, "Look, I don't have anyone else to go to. Jenia had a falling out with Dazmine Temperton, our family in Belliview would never even entertain the idea of helping a *disgrace.*" Kimber's voice snagged on a choke with that last word. "And her boyfriend really *is* dead, by the looks of it." She lowered her tone and leaned in close to Quinn. "I can break her out of the prison where they're keeping her, but I need someone to hide her for me if I do—your home village is small, right? Alderwick, right? You could keep her safe there?"

Nothing about my house's old Wild Whisperer princess looked sane right now. She was curling her fingernails into her fists repeatedly—open, close, open, close—and when a very familiar parakeet swooped into the alleyway to land on her shoulder, her body gave a violent tremor.

Quinn backed away, her fear hardening into crude distaste at the mention of how small our home village was.

"I don't know what you mean by *prison* unless that's what you're calling the pirate ships out there. But I can't hide Jenia in Alderwick even *if* I wanted to risk my ass to mess with the dome or run away from the Institute. Those are the rules, Kimber. And you, out of everyone, should know that."

She eyed the brand, the dot in the middle, with such vehemence that it was a wonder Kimber didn't tell her parakeet to rip into her face.

"You're right," she said instead, her own face hardening into smooth, lethal contemplation. "My mistake."

And when she dove into Quinn's mind to smother this memory, I knew my assumption had been correct. Kimber had been branded with a second power sometime during her years at the Esholian Institute: Mind Manipulating, just like me. And if Jenia's earlier claim was true, she had been spying on my mind all of last year. She'd discovered what I was—a half-faerie—and apparently thought she could give her younger sister a shot at joining the Good Council if Jenia claimed that discovery for herself.

Little had either of them known that Dyonisia had known about me and the innate power in my blood all along.

I wanted to dig deeper, but a distant, outward part of me recognized the sounds of a conversation ending in the real world.

Without Dazmine to keep her distracted... I couldn't risk Quinn sensing my presence. I ripped myself out of her mind just as she was opening her door again.

"...so I don't need *you* to tell me how to live my life," she was practically shrieking, and that pale, cropped hair of hers crackled with living flames.

Dazmine opened her mouth to call her back, but I shot a single, shaking thought into her mind: *let her go.*

Sneering, Quinn slipped back into her room, managing to slam the door behind her even though she'd only opened it a crack. From behind it, I could hear a deep, muffled voice, and Quinn answering, "Nothing. Just a girl I used to hang out with every so often..." before her voice faded, too.

I yanked Dazmine down the hall until we'd rounded a corner.

"What...?" she started to ask.

I shook my head at her and tapped my head.

I got a lot of information, I sent into her mind, *but I don't want to say any of it out loud.*

Even though the hallway was empty for now, I could still hear music drifting up from the bottom floor. Distant laughs and groans and screams still melted through the walls of this place. It was better to assume anyone could be listening.

Dazmine cranked up an eyebrow. *And?*

And I think Mr. Gleekle's secret Branding is a part of the Good Council system, I said, still filled with shock at all those pieces I'd picked up in Quinn's mind. *They're picking out students who demonstrate superiority in some way and giving them a second brand—then testing them throughout their remainder at the*

407

Institute. *If they learn to control two powers, they get recruited to the Good Council. If they can't control the two powers—if they descend into madness like Jenia did—they're brought up to that prison just like all the others who fail their Final Test.*

Dazmine dropped her arms with a gape.

So Jenia...

Knew about this because her sister was picked out sometime during her five years here at the Esholian Institute and given a second brand. That whole confrontation in the jungle... it was all just a way for Jenia to prove that she belonged on the Good Council, too. But it seems like she didn't think she could do it by herself, so she asked for help.

Despite the fact that she, Fergus, Jacques, and Quinn had failed their mission, whatever they'd done that day must have caught the Good Council's attention anyway, because two of them had been branded twice now. But while Jenia had dissolved into a screaming fit on her hands and knees, Quinn had apparently been able to manage her Shape Shifting power just fine.

Or... was the new hair a sign that she *couldn't* control it?

A quiet look of horror clouded Dazmine's features.

Dazmine? I prompted.

She rubbed her eyes with a shaking hand.

Jenia once told me she was going to punish you and your friends once she was on the Good Council and had the authority to. I laughed at her. I didn't think there was any way Dyonisia Reeve would recruit her, so I laughed in her face. I didn't realize she was serious.

Yeah, that sounded like Jenia Leake. I wasn't surprised she'd turned to a more willing friend after Dazmine had scoffed at her ideations.

What I *was* surprised about was the second Branding itself. To think that every elite on the Good Council had an extra power...

What did Kitterfol Lexington have besides Mind Manipulating? I'd never seen a single hint of another magic from him.

And was *that* what Lexington had meant would happen to me if I delivered him his batch of pills? I'd join Mr. Gleekle's secret club? I'd get yet another brand—another power?

At that moment, a trio of Element Wielders lumbered past us, absorbed in their own giggling conversation. Dazmine and I fell back against the wall, pretending to fix the fallen strands of each other's hair.

When the trio had faded around the corner, Dazmine asked, *Does Quinn know where Jenia truly is right now?*

No, but... I relayed all the other memories I'd witnessed up to the moment Kimber had cornered Quinn. *Her sister does. And apparently, she's willing to break her out of prison, but doesn't know where to put her.*

As soon as I said it, Dazmine's eyes flashed open.

That's it! She began to pace, her eyes glued to the floor. *That's what Terrin and I have been missing!*

"Dazmine," I started to whisper, but it was like she didn't hear me.

The pirates can't break into the prison, so we need someone to let us in—someone from the inside.

"Dazmine..."

If we could just make contact with an elite, turn them into a double agent—

"Dazmine! Shut your thoughts down right now."

I felt something in the air around us, like another mind was searching. Reaching. Probing. Maybe Steeler was just listening in on

409

our mental conversation, but I hadn't felt his dark, fathomless energy since I'd told him to go earlier. This... this felt foreign.

Yet shockingly familiar.

Horrified, I dove into Dazmine's mind, landing on a surface that rolled with dry, unforgiving waves of sand—just as another figure evaporated, like a shimmer of heat, right near her consciousness.

A wormy figure I'd recognize even in my deepest nightmares.

Lexington.

CHAPTER

42

"Steeler," I gasped out loud.

Within two of my crashing heartbeats, the solid wall of his body materialized between Dazmine and me.

"What happened?"

It only took him half a second to absorb all the information swimming behind my eyes. Half a second for him to understand exactly what I'd learned in Quinn's mind and what I'd just seen in Dazmine's.

Did Lexington see you? he asked urgently. *Did he get into your mind or see that you were in Dazmine's?*

No. I was confident about that. My blockade had been sliced open to listen in on Quinn's thoughts, but I'd never felt or seen anyone so much as brush up against it.

Steeler's shoulders relaxed an infinitesimal amount, but he still stood like a statue carved of impenetrable marble. *Did he go through Dazmine's gate?*

No. I don't think so. He stopped right near her consciousness, as if he was just listening to what she was thinking at that exact moment. Which was that she wanted to get someone from the inside of the prison to let the pirates in. Shit, I tacked on as the enormity of that crashed through me.

I had no idea why Lexington had been in Dazmine's mind, of all people's, but there was no doubt in mine that even if he wasn't on campus, he'd be closing in on us soon after hearing all that.

How far out do you think he is? I asked desperately.

Steeler shook his head.

If he was able to get into her head, it means he's somewhere within Mind Manipulating range. Knowing him and how far he can reach with his power, I'm willing to bet that's a good five- to ten-mile radius, but...

He didn't have to finish that thought for me to connect each painstaking dot. Dazmine wasn't safe here at the Esholian Institute anymore. She probably wasn't even safe at the lighthouse without Walking powers of her own or an ability to flee if Lexington ever found out about that secret haven.

Steeler's jaw tightened, confirming my fear without a word.

"If neither of you tell me what's going on in the next five seconds," Dazmine started, "I'm going to call all the rats out of the walls and have them nibble your—"

"The Good Council knows you know too much," I said urgently, hardly able to bear the way her scowl flashed into alarm. "And they're coming for you now. Steeler is going to have to take you away... maybe for good. I'm sorry, Dazmine. I'm so, so sorry, I—"

I'd been so focused on maintaining my own blockade that I hadn't even thought about trying to protect Dazmine's mind. This was *exactly* what Steeler had tried to prevent from happening to me by keeping sensitive information out of my head until I could learn to defend myself.

"No," Dazmine interrupted before I could say more.

"What?"

"You don't need to do any apologizing, Rayna. You didn't do anything wrong."

"But," I started, "I knew involving you in... in all of this might put you in danger and—"

"—and I accepted that danger," Dazmine said, her chin tilted high. "I bullied you, threatened you, and used you just like you used me, so don't get all self-pitying on me now. Okay?"

I nodded, but it didn't stop the guilt from digging deeper into my gut. I purposely hadn't told Emelle or Lander or Rodhi about anything going on in—

I froze, horrified.

Rodhi.

If Dazmine disappeared out of thin air, Lexington was bound to interrogate the shit out of everyone in the house... and Rodhi would be in just as much danger as any of us. Not because of my secrets, but because of his own.

"Rayna, no."

Steeler's eyes had widened as he caught on to what I was thinking. Mentally, he snarled my way, *even if Lexington didn't know Dazmine was with you, he's going to be pissed when he gets here and he can't find her. Don't throw yourself into that fray.*

I already failed to protect one friend, I said, already backing up. *I'm not abandoning another one.*

Steeler leaned forward as if poised to snatch me away.

Garvis hasn't taught you how to protect somebody else's mind from an actual invasion, Rayna. That's fifth-year magic...

413

...so I'll try my best to protect Rodhi in whatever way I can until you can take Dazmine to the ship and then come back, I snapped.

In theory, that would only take a handful of seconds. Realistically, though, we both knew he couldn't just Walk Dazmine to a pirate ship and immediately abandon her to come back for Rodhi and me. That would almost be worse than dropping her into the middle of the ocean.

Steeler opened his mouth to argue, his eyes flashing with something carnal and possessive, but I just said, "You told me you were learning to trust me! Show me that you can do that now."

His pupils widened at that word. *Trust.*

Had he ever truly trusted me before—that I could handle myself in the face of danger? *Could* he? Enough to let go, even for a second? Not in the way he'd done last year, where he'd left me like a butterfly in a tank for him to protect from the outside, but in a way that would unleash me like the hurricane he'd always said I was?

As if it caused him indescribable pain, Steeler dipped his head. Dazmine glanced at him, then back at me, and nodded, too.

Nodding back, I turned and sprinted downstairs.

I didn't have to look over my shoulder to know he'd done it: Walked away with Dazmine just like I'd asked. The absence of his dark, fathomless presence left an ache against my heart, but the knowledge that both of them were out of the danger zone was a palpably sweet relief on my tongue.

I nearly stumbled over the lower lace of my dress as I barged into the Element Wielder foyer and pushed into the throng, desperate for any signs of a boy with a goofy grin all over his carefree face.

"Rayna! What are you—"

"Have you seen Rodhi?" I panted, fighting my way to Emelle as soon as I heard her voice. She looked beautiful tonight—clad in a silver dress with hooped earrings winking like starlight in her hair—and Lander looked just as handsome in a silver tie beside her.

"Um." Emelle squinted over my head. "I think he went somewhere over th—"

BOOM.

The entire room shook as the front doors blasted open and a group of Good Council elites stormed inside.

Kitterfol led the front, his cloak flowing behind him in a flash of scarlet that matched the livid blood vessels popping in his eyes.

The conversation in the room crashed into deathly pale silence. The musical instruments overhead stopped playing. Every drunken, confused gaze turned to Lexington and the three other elites behind him.

" *Where*," Kitterfol said in a tone that oozed venom in every syllable, "is Ms. Dazmine Temperton?"

By the way his mouth trembled with the urge to scream... oh, he *knew*. He knew Dazmine was gone, but didn't know *how*.

I pushed my pride, my deep appreciation for Steeler's innate power, back, back, back into the distant horizon of my mind. No way was I letting the Good Council anywhere near my true feelings for him.

Lexington turned to his other elites and gave a significant nod.

They streamed past everyone, rushing deeper into the Element Wielder mansion and up the stairs as if Dazmine might still be hiding somewhere inside. Lexington himself stayed stock-still, breathing heavily as he surveyed the halted party.

"Where is she?" he whispered.

Nobody answered.

"WHERE IS SHE?" he snapped, and lunged for the nearest student.

It was a girl in a neon two-piece. She screamed, but nobody dared step forward to help her as Lexington grabbed her by the arms and shook her back and forth, evaluating her mind and whether she had any relation to Dazmine in one smooth sweep.

The fact that he hadn't immediately landed his sights on me meant he didn't know I'd been with her tonight. If he'd gone past Dazmine's gate and rifled through her most recent memories back in that hallway, he would have seen our alliance and the lighthouse... but he must have felt confident he'd be able to pick her brain apart piece by piece in person, so he'd withdrawn with a false sense of victory.

Good.

As Lexington moved to the next person with unnerving swiftness, I used the precious time I had to scour the room for signs of Rodhi—and found him near the drinking fountain on the other end of the room, surrounded by a variety of friends from other sectors.

Lexington was moving closer to his group with a rising frenzy. This was nothing like the cool, smooth contemplation he had used to investigate Mr. Fenway's death last year, but something wild bordering on mad. It reminded me of how I'd felt when I'd first been Branded with Mind Manipulating and heard the outpour of everyone's thoughts at once. His eyes nearly popped out of their sockets as he turned from person to person and found no connection to Dazmine, no connection to Dazmine, no connection to Dazmine.

Because Dazmine had had no friends besides Jenia.

Dazmine had been a loner after Jenia.

Dazmine was just Jenia's ex-sidekick who'd fallen into everyone's periphery after her exile.

I pushed all of those thoughts out into the open as hard as I could.

As if he'd heard it, Lexington's eyes snapped toward me.

416

Exactly what I'd wanted. Because as much as I'd forced bravado into my voice when I'd told Steeler I could protect Rodhi, he was right. I *couldn't* protect him from the most advanced Mind Manipulator on the Good Council. Not mentally.

Lexington changed course, pivoting toward me instead. The crowd parted, cutting him a straight path to where I tried not to tremble.

I didn't even realize Emelle was clinging to my arm until I felt her nails pierce my skin like little anchors. Anchors I appreciated as Lexington's snarl sent drops of spit flying into my face.

"What a happy little coincidence! Just the girl I've been meaning to have a nice, long chat with, *and* you're Ms. Temperton's roommate."

He grabbed me by the sleeve and dragged me away from Emelle.

"Rayna!" she cried, reaching after me.

Lexington must have shot a command into her mind, because the next second she fell back into Lander again with a blank expression slapped over her face.

I trotted alongside Lexington until he'd pushed me up against the empty stairwell around the corner, where nobody could hear us.

Take out your knife and press it against your heart.

His command was more sudden than I anticipated. For the first time, I could actually *feel* the strings of it try to latch onto my consciousness.

Shaking, I yanked my mother's knife from its sheath and flipped it until the curved point rested just over my left breast, dimpling my skin.

"Good, good," Lexington mused.

I expected him to worm into my mind like he always used to, but he paused to observe me with his lip curled in disgust.

"It's been *months*, girl. Dyonisia is getting impatient for a status update that *I* haven't been able to give her, because you're here playing dress up at a frilly little ball instead of working on acquiring what you promised me."

At those last few words, my grip tightened on the knife, pressing it a fraction of an inch deeper into my skin.

A pinprick of pain flared against me where a warm bead of blood swelled at the point of contact and rolled down between my breasts.

"I'm getting closer," I rasped.

"*How* close? *When* can you get me those pills?"

My hand pushed the point of the blade in even deeper.

"This weekend!" I burst out, forcing out the fraction of the truth I could give him—the pills *would* be ready this weekend. But I knew I needed to provide a few more maybe-not-quite-as-true details to make it believable. "Steeler said he's taking me to the ship this weekend," I made up. "That's where the pills are made and stored. And I'll have direct access to them because he trusts me *completely* now."

Lexington exhaled heavily through his parted mouth. I'd barely had time to smell his breath on my face when he fell with a thud into my mind, the giant worm of his consciousness sliding right up to mine.

"Are you lying to me?" that worm asked.

I willed my consciousness to stare straight ahead. To pretend like I wasn't a Mind Manipulator, that I didn't see him invading my icescape with his fleshy presence.

"No," I said out loud.

To my surprise, Lexington withdrew without tunneling through my gate for any further information. A frown yanked on his mouth, deep and assessing.

"The pills don't make you *truly* love him, right?"

"No," I said again.

"So you wouldn't care about all the other traitors he grew up with in Hallow's Perch?"

I kept my face a careful portrait of appropriate fear even as my heart plummeted to my feet at the thought of that lighthouse and the faeries who met us there every weekend. Steeler's friends. *My* friends now, too. This was clearly a way to test my reaction to a deeper threat, and I was determined to pass it. To pretend like those words *didn't* sink into my gut like stones.

"No. I wouldn't care."

Lexington surveyed me as if he'd never quite seen me before now. The trails of his eyes seemed to leave sticky residues all over my face.

"Good," he said finally, grabbing the edges of his cloak and turning to leave. "I'll give you until the end of this weekend to secure the pills, girl. If you don't follow through by then, I'll let Dyonisia know that you have failed your mission and must face retribution for your crimes. Oh, and..." He paused with his back to me. "If you see your roommate around, go ahead and disable her with that." He jerked his head back at my knife still pressed against my own chest. "She's been spying on confidential government affairs."

I waited several minutes after he'd rounded the corner before I finally allowed myself to remove the blade against my skin and slide it back into its sheath.

You knew? I sent out toward the dark, fathomless presence I could feel hovering on the periphery of my mind.

That you managed to shake off his command in time but decided to play along anyway? Steeler replied, slipping through the crack in my blockade. I closed it back up as soon as his consciousness was safe inside, shielding our thoughts from outsiders. *Yes. Your wrist wasn't quivering with enough resistance.* A growl caressed the edge of his voice. *I would have torn out his throat if you'd been in any real danger.*

Every coherent thought in my brain got stuck in an endless swirl. Steeler had trusted me. Not only that, but he'd known me well enough to see through my deception. Had paused long enough to notice my tells before jumping in to save me...

Which made something vital inside me feel like it was melting away at the edges.

How's Dazmine? I asked instead of trying to respond to that.

I still felt the ring of Lexington's last words in my ears: *she's been spying on confidential government affairs.* So Mr. Gleekle *had* spotted her in the jungle that day and passed the information along to the Good Council. Lexington must have been on his way to wipe her memory of what she'd witnessed. He'd probably never expected to discover that she knew so, so much more than that.

Safe on the ship, Steeler said. *I stayed until she passed the Old Veracious test, or I would've returned sooner.*

A breath of relief whooshed out of me, even while that guilt still clawed at my stomach. Dazmine was off the island, out of Lexington's reach—but still surrounded by a ship-full of lethal faeries who'd held a magic sword to her neck in greeting.

I doubt Terrin will let any of them get within two feet of her, actually.

Under normal circumstances, I might have pressed Steeler for details about the reasoning behind that mischievous tone. But at the mention of Terrin...

Did you hear what Lexington said about your friends?

Steeler's growl returned, nearly vibrating in my own chest. *Yes. But there's no way he could get to them while they're on the ship. Even twenty faeries would be enough to best the entire Good Council. He was just gauging your reaction, Rayna. And you did so, so brilliantly.*

The warmth of his pride crashed straight through me, sending my blood thrumming through my veins.

I tried to hide it by poking my head around the corner to survey the state of the foyer.

Lexington had vanished, but everyone still stood in frozen little groups, shifting from foot to foot uncomfortably and murmuring in low voices, the musical instruments suspended by a shelf of stagnant air overhead. Emelle was the only one moving through the crowd, her eyes scurrying around the room as Lander hurried after her.

"Hey." I popped out and met her halfway.

"Rayna?" Her gaze drifted down to the pinprick on my chest, and the worry on her face deepened. "What was that about? Why did Kitterfol Lexington haul you off?"

I made myself give a confused shake of my head. "I guess he just thought I knew where Dazmine went since I was the last person to have seen her." When Emelle's eyes sharpened, I added, "We showed up at the ball around the same time, but I don't know where she went."

It was my first official lie to Emelle, and even though I'd just witnessed firsthand what would await her if I gave away the truth, the guilt in my stomach... it only dug its claws deeper into me.

Lander scratched his head. "What do you think Dazmine could have *done* to get this kind of search party?"

"Any number of things," I muttered.

My attention skidded over their heads to connect with Rodhi, still mingling with that same group of friends across the room. He raised his glass to me in a silent toast and drained it in two thick chugs.

I smiled back. *You're welcome.*

I'd almost let my shoulders relax when a high-pitched voice pushed into the foyer and all the tension radiated back into the room.

It wasn't an elite this time. It was Cilia, closely followed by Mitzi, Norman, and Pierson. Her frantic gaze snagged on Emelle and me and she came running, hiking up her bright pink dress.

"They've trashed our damn room!" she wailed. "Our beds, our drawers, everything!" She sank to her knees and buried her face into her hands. "My favorite pillow is ripped to *shreds.*"

Emelle and I found each other's looks of horror.

I didn't give a damn about my pillows. But if a bunch of elites had torn through everything that lived in our room...

I was already running at the thought of a little gray mouse.

CHAPTER

43

I tore down Bascite Boulevard, Emelle and the others right behind me.

A deep fog was gathering between the mansions, slathering me in a sticky second skin that seemed to hold me back. My legs and lungs burned by the time I'd raced upstairs and barged into our room to face the chaotic mess the Good Council had left behind.

Dazmine's corner of the room was the worst. Her bed was in absolute splinters, as if the elites had thought she might be hiding clues about her whereabouts in the frame itself. Her dresser was knocked over and cracked down the middle, her bags were torn apart at the seams, and every pot or bowl or mirror around her space had been shattered and now laid in fragments on the floor.

The rest of our spaces weren't much better. My pillow was ripped wide open like Cilia's, leaving an array of feathers spread everywhere like the softest snow. My mattress had been upturned. Even my drawers were emptied, my dresses, toiletries, and spare pens and bottles scattered unceremoniously across the floor.

I couldn't even feel relieved that I'd already removed the handful of little black pearls weeks ago. Not when dread sunk into me at the ringing silence their search had left in its wake.

"Willa?" I called, racing forward to check under the bed, in the corners of the wall, under each overturned piece of furniture.

Footsteps thumped into the room behind me. I heard Emelle's soft gasp of alarm and Lander's curse under his breath, but my eyes had gone blurry as my fingers scrabbled to lift everything I could find.

"*Willa*," I called again. "Are you okay?"

More footsteps joined Emelle and Lander behind me... just as a perturbed, high-pitched voice squeaked from a crack in the wall.

"If absolutely disgusted by this rat's nest counts as okay, then yes."

"Oh, thank God."

I crouched to let Willa scurry up my arm and into my palms. She sniffled at me, her beady eyes peering at me in concerned assessment.

"I have walls to hide behind, Rayna, but you don't—no matter how much you like to pretend you do. I should be asking if you're okay."

"I'm..." I tried to finish that sentence on a positive note, but the word *fine* got sniffed back up. I nuzzled Willa to my cheek.

From the doorway, Cilia whimpered, "I just don't understand— why would they touch *our* stuff if they're looking for Dazmine? And why are they looking for her anyway? She might be a bit..." Cilia wiped away a tear. "...*standoffish* sometimes, but..."

"Well, she obviously ran away," Norman Pollard said beside her. "And running away's against the rules."

"But why would she run away?" Mitzi asked on his other side.

I held in a sigh. I had a feeling I would hear this conversation a lot over the next day, and I'd have to maintain a perfectly neutral face every time. I tried to practice that now as Cilia began to moan about her pillow again, and Mitzi offered to let her sleep with her tonight.

Emelle rested a hand on my shoulder.

"Do you want to stay with Lander and me, Rayna?"

I saw her eyes glance at her own ruined bed. Her birdfeeder laid on its side on the floor beside it, its seeds strewn everywhere. Not that she ever slept here anymore anyway, but tonight was out of the question.

"Yeah, I can Shift my bed into something bigger that would hold all three of us until we can get this room cleaned up," Lander chimed in. "Or I could sleep on the floor while you two..."

"Oh, no thank you." I straightened. Emelle removed her hand from my shoulder. "Don't worry about it." It was a kind gesture—one that I appreciated with a pang of something like homesickness—but I didn't want to disrupt the routine Emelle and Lander had created together. And I certainly didn't want to sleep in a bed that they'd made... memories in. "I'll go ask Wren if I can sleep with her."

Emelle nodded slowly, but both she and Lander were looking at me with something a little too shrewd, a little too sad.

"Rayna," Lander said, surprising me with the insistence in his voice as he lowered it. "I've known you since I was a baby, but one memory really sticks out to me during our whole childhood."

I looked up at him. "What?"

He adjusted his tie thoughtfully before speaking.

"When we were about five years old, my grandma was supposed to be watching you, me, and Quinn, but she fell asleep in her rocking chair a couple hours in. The three of us snuck out of my house to go play some street pentaball. Remember that?"

I nodded, though the memory was a vague one for me. I could have probably dug into my own mind—or Lander's—to assess it properly, but I was too transfixed by the intensity of his gaze to do anything besides stare at him.

"You fell and skinned your knee," Lander continued. "There was blood everywhere, but you refused to wake up my grandma and ask her for help bandaging it. Do you know why?"

"Why?" I whispered.

"You didn't want her to feel bad for falling asleep on babysitting watch," Lander said. "You chose to bleed until your wound scabbed over rather than cause someone else the slightest bit of discomfort by asking for help. And you've been that way ever since."

Emelle nodded beside him.

"It's okay to inconvenience people when you need help," she said. "The people who love you will help you anyway, knowing that you'd do the same for them." She gave that same sad smile.

I wanted so badly to tell them everything right here and now. The words were climbing up my throat, but... I wouldn't just be inconveniencing them if I gave in to the urge. I'd be putting them in the exact same situation I'd put Dazmine.

"Okay." I nodded. "Thank you. I'll let you know if I need help with anything. Promise."

Emelle nodded back, disappointment flickering in her eyes. "Well... see you tomorrow at the Testing Center?"

"See you tomorrow," I told them both with a soft smile.

It was only after they'd left that Willa's whiskers twitched in my direction. "*What a missed opportunity. A Shifted bed sounds nice. You could have asked him to turn the sheets into cheese.*"

"Oh, not you too," I sighed quietly. Cilia and the others were still helping her pack up her own stuff, and I didn't want them to hear and feel sorry for me. "I'm sure Wren's bed will be perfectly fine."

I wasn't sure, actually. Wren was probably the least cuddly person I'd ever met, and I wouldn't be surprised if she made me sleep on the floor.

"*I think I'd rather share a wall space with Barty tonight.*" Willa wrinkled her nose. "*And he sings opera in his sleep.*"

I sighed and brought her up to my shoulder so I could begin packing an overnight bag on my hands and knees—a nightgown from here, a bar of soap from there. Anything I could find in the rubble that looked somewhat useful, I threw in one of the ransacked bags.

Was there anything else I needed? Anything I didn't want the Good Council getting their hands on if they returned to investigate further? The pearls were safe, but...

"*... and he doesn't wash his tail and keeps shitting on your book.*"

"What?" I asked Willa.

I didn't need her to explain further, though. As soon as she'd said that last word, I could feel another memory dislodge itself in my mind and come to life in an explosion of mist that involved a request from Jagaros, a conversation with Ms. Pincette, and a map I'd stowed away in the wall behind the cuckoo clock in our foyer downstairs.

A map I was determined to never hide again.

Ten minutes later, with Willa safely deposited back into the walls and Ms. Pincette's tome tucked away in my overnight bag, I poked my head into Wren's room to find that I wouldn't, in fact, be sleeping on her floor after all.

She and Gileon were slumped against the headboard of her bed side by side, their heads lolling against each other as they snored with a pawn-scattered board game between them. Their clothes were on, and nothing about their positions screamed romantic to me, but I still felt that same strange pang of homesickness at the sight of them together. Even Nuisance was buzzing in his sleep in Gileon's lap, his shelled wings fluttering with every breath.

Well, now I knew why they hadn't come running at all the Good Council commotion.

I eased Wren's door shut again, hoisting my bag over my shoulder and gnawing on my lower lip.

The echo of my first night here at the Esholian Institute seemed to be closing in on me. Even though I still had holes in my memories, I could remember peeking into tent after tent and feeling more and more unwelcome and out-of-place as I went. The same deep-rooted loneliness I'd felt then was creeping over my bones now, twining around them and pulling tight.

Bascite Boulevard was shrouded in mist by the time I crept outside to trudge to that same tree I'd slept in once upon a time.

Everybody else must have gone home after the Good Council incident, because nobody passed me as I walked. No lights flickered through the fog, no music permeated the air. Even the usual background noise of nighttime animals—the chirping of crickets, the far-off hoots of owls, the clicking and screeching of bats—had dissolved in the haze.

Just one night, I told myself as I made it to the Wild Whisperer sector. I would take my second quarterly test tomorrow, get those pills from Nara, give them to Lexington, and then.... well, then there would probably be a lot bigger things to deal with than sleeping in a tree.

I almost ran into a thick wall of warm muscle before I saw him through the thickness of the mist.

Steeler was standing before that tree, his arms crossed.

"You can't be serious, Rayna."

My bones heated and shook off their restraints.

"I'm a Wild Whisperer," I shot back, glad for the mist that hid the color warming my cheeks. The fact that he hadn't gone back to the lighthouse, that he'd stayed here to make sure I found a bed safely... I cleared my throat to keep my voice steady and carefree. "Sleeping in a tree is, like, the one thing I'm good at."

"I'd say you're good at a lot of things, actually."

His gaze didn't flick down the length of my body, but I felt the weighted heat of it as if it had. As if he'd already memorized every part of me and devoured them whole.

"Just one night, little hurricane."

Steeler's voice was so soft, so achingly fragile, that I wanted to cradle it in my palms. When he offered his hand to me, something irrevocable shattered in the smoky quartz of his eyes.

"I know I don't have any right to keep you," he said on an exhale. "I know I don't deserve to love you. But please, Rayna—give me one more night to be with you."

My breath eddied away at the expression on his face.

He wasn't asking to sleep with me—not in that way. He may have made certain suggestive *claims* in the past, but I knew by now that he wouldn't ever pressure me into anything physical.

But could I even *sleep*, knowing he was in the same room as me? Could I stand it, with no Garvis there to stand as a buffer between us? What if I wanted to taste him again without the excuse of a Mind Manipulating lesson? What if I couldn't smother the hunger within me that was reaching for him?

I had to say no.

It was for the best to say no.

It hovered on the tip of my tongue to say no.

"Yes," I said, stepping toward him.

And that pang of homesickness inside me melted away.

CHAPTER

44

"*Raynie!*"

A bright voice greeted me as soon as the darkness dumped us into the middle of the lighthouse cottage.

No sooner had I stood up than Felicity bounded into my arms and wrapped herself around my neck. "*I didn't think you'd be here until Sunday. Come look at what I've been learning to make.*"

She bounced out of my arms again and tugged on my dress until I stumbled, laughing, toward the kitchen table.

There on the gnarled wooden surface sat a variety of glass jars and containers filled with swirls of different-colored wax and topped with wicks made of twine. I leaned in to smell them, inhaling a mixture of caramel and lavender and vanilla.

"*Candles!*" Felicity announced proudly. "*I made the wax from palm leaves, melted it over the fire, and mixed in all the oils. My favorite is the lotus blossom one, by the way. Did you smell it yet?*"

I lifted the jar with the cream-colored wax to my nose.

"I could just eat it up. This is amazing, Felicity."

And I meant it. The proud smile on the monkey's face, the fire crackling in the hearth, the soft breeze that floated in from the ocean outside the window—it was all like a pocket of deep calm before an oncoming storm. I wanted to sink into this warmth and never let go.

But there was one last thing lingering on my mind.

I waited until Felicity had busied herself with her candles again to say it.

"Did you know?" I whispered, my back still to Steeler.

"What?"

"Did you know that the Good Council is recruiting people when they're only students? That Mr. Gleekle is giving them a second brand?"

I couldn't fathom how else he would have known to give me one, and by the intake of silence behind me...

"Yes," Steeler said finally, and I rotated to face him. "When I was a first-year at the Institute, I came to realize that my Mind Manipulating power was... stronger than my peers'—all my peers except for Garvis. We figured our faerie blood gave us a heightened ability to wield it, but I didn't realize until I was messing around in an upper-classman's mind just for the hell of it and saw that he'd been double Branded how dangerous that heightened ability could be." Steeler looked down at his hands. "I knew if Mr. Gleekle got ahold of any of us, he'd discover our true identities, so the others and I... we held ourselves back. That day that you first arrived in the courtyard..." He looked back up at me. "... it was the first time I ever flexed my power, just to see what it was like. And I regretted it instantly."

My gaze snapped up to his.

"Why?"

He gave a sad smile.

"Because I got a taste of what I was missing out on and knew it would consume me, if I let it." He held my gaze. "I never expanded my power again until the end of last year, when I erased everyone's memory of me at the Institute and found that it was scraping my limit."

When his face twisted with self-revulsion, I knew he didn't just think I'd never forgive him; he didn't think of himself as *forgivable.*

He didn't think he was worthy of it.

The words I should have said lumped in my throat as I set my overnight bag down on the floor and watched Felicity absentmindedly set her homemade candles on various surfaces around the room. The coffee table. A side table. The mantle. A windowsill.

Outside that window, the breeze had picked up into a whistle.

I couldn't exactly blame Steeler for keeping the secret about the second Branding from me—not after witnessing the Good Council's ruthless hunt for Dazmine. Just like Jagaros, he'd been waiting until I could shield my own mind to give me those pieces, and I...

I could respect that. I had a right to my own mind and information about *me*, but I didn't necessarily have a right to information about others. I could force my shoulders to deflate and breathe out the anger coiling in my chest and come to terms with the fact that my anger wasn't justified. It was just hiding a deep-rooted pain.

Trying to force cheer into my voice, I got to my knees to dig through my bag for a toothbrush and nightgown.

"Any other stories you want to tell me before we go to bed?"

A blush was already settling, not in my cheeks, but deep into my core at the thought that I'd have to change in the same room as him. Would we sleep in the same bed? Or would he insist on taking the sofa? But that warmth faded instantly when Steeler whispered, "Yes."

I looked up at him in question.

"Mine." He cleared his throat. "I'd like to tell you my story. If you want to hear it," he added.

I dropped my bag again and sat on the edge of the coffee table.

"Of course."

I'd thought I'd re-discovered everything important about Steeler's life since he'd stopped erasing my memory—he'd grown up on a pirate ship until the faerie fleet decided to use him and his friends as pawns in a much bigger game. Then he'd spent his remaining years in Hallow's Perch until he'd gone to the Esholian Institute for half a decade.

The look on his face couldn't have been clearer, though: there was more to it. So, so much more.

"Do you want anything to drink?" he asked suddenly.

"Oh... um... sure."

"What would you like?"

He was stalling, I knew, but I humored him anyway. "Do you have any wine?"

"*Ha!*" Felicity called from a corner of the room where she'd just lit the lotus blossom-scented candle. "*Do we have wine? What kind of question is that, Raynie?*"

"Wine, then," I repeated to Steeler, who removed two dusty glasses from a cabinet before wiping them with a cloth and digging out a bottle that definitely looked like it had been stolen from one of the neighboring villages.

He handed me a glass just as Felicity inhaled deeply and pressed her padded palms together with a smile.

"*Ah, that's perfect, isn't it?*"

She'd lit two other candles—the vanilla and what smelled like a sandalwood one. The result was a mix of intoxicating scents that flowed throughout the room in defiance of the increasing wind outside.

"You're very talented, Felicity," I said after taking a sip of my wine. "You're the best cook, hairdresser, and candlemaker I've ever met."

"*Oh, and I plan on being good at so much more.*" A determined glint lit up Felicity's eyes as she bounded forward to give me another hug. "*I'm going to hit the rafters now. Tell Coco sweet dreams for me.*"

"I will."

"*And don't worry about making too much noise, by the way,*" she added over her shoulder, shooting me a wink that I definitely felt was way too inappropriate for such a young monkey. "*I'm a heavy sleeper.*"

We both watched her jump her way to that bedroom in the hallway and close the door behind her, leaving Steeler and me very much alone with only two glasses of wine between us.

Steeler sat next to me on the sofa, his body angled forward.

My heart galloping in my throat, I dared to rest my free hand on his knee for the smallest space of time before I removed it again.

"You don't have to tell me if you don't want to. As long as it doesn't involve me or my life..."

He shook his head, inhaled through his nose, and sighed out, "It does, in a way. As much as I know you hate to hear it, our lives are very much intertwined. And with your mother being the lost princess..."

He fingered his glass as a look of memory clouded over his face. I kept my blockade firmly locked up—to let him tell it at his own pace.

"I told you about my own mother," he said finally. "That she died before I could remember her."

"Yes," I said somberly.

"Well..." His jaw twitched, his whole face hardening. "She died because the queen of Sorronia murdered her. I'm almost sure of it."

"What?"

435

My hand clenched in my lap. I'd always sensed some deeper animal rear its head inside me whenever he mentioned this so-called faerie queen. My biological aunt, apparently. But if I was going to be honest with myself, I'd always feared it was jealousy at the way he said her name. How he served her. How I had to share him with this faceless ruler across the sea.

Now, the animal in me understood what it really was. The way Steeler's whole body had just tensed up, hatred pouring from him in waves...

I wanted to *protect* him from the queen. I wanted to shield him away from whatever she had done to him in a fierce, desperate kind of way I'd never even felt regarding Dyonisia or Lexington.

"How do you know she killed your mother?" I put my hand on his knee again. Whether we were friends or enemies or something in between, he obviously needed the pressure of a touch to keep him grounded.

Steeler's body softened ever so slightly. He turned toward me.

"For the most part, Sorronia is a glamorous realm. The queen's palace is a glittering spread of spires surrounded by gardens, and the inner cities are just as breathtaking. But the outer cities... they're crammed with faeries who get by in squalor. Faeries with lower powers or who never matured and don't have any powers at all."

He rested his spare hand over mine, and his heat sunk through my skin. Or maybe that was just the heat of the flames in the fireplace that licked the air, the logs crackling and the sparks popping.

"I was just a bastard born of a homeless whore, they told me," Steeler breathed out. "And the queen so generously swept me off the streets and took me in when some disease claimed her. The only thing I got to keep of my real mother was that pendant."

His eyes shifted briefly to the back of my neck.

"Oh my God. I'm so sorry."

My heart was sinking for him, even as new thoughts and revelations rocked this way and that in my mind. I wanted to tell him to never think of himself as a bastard or his mother as a whore, but I knew my voice wouldn't stand a chance against the many voices who had told him this in his past.

So instead, I opted to ask him a question that would propel him forward.

"Did she raise you, then? The queen?"

Steeler gave a half-laugh. "Not for long. I'd been living at the palace for a couple years when I caught on to the whispers that always seemed to follow me around and learned the truth."

"The truth?"

"The truth." He nodded, then took his deepest breath yet. "Which was that twenty years ago, Her Majesty's esteemed General of War retired at the ripe old age of 875. Rumor had it that she couldn't decide whether to replace him with Lieutenant General Magees or Admiral Fennelly, so she went to pay a visit to Fate in one of Sorronia's most notorious temples." When my brows pinched together, he added, "Not to request a mating bond, but to ask Fate which of the two candidates was destined to acquire more soldiers, kill more enemies, win more wars."

"And did Fate give her an answer?"

I couldn't for the life of me see where this story was headed. I couldn't even imagine what a visit like this might *look* like. Was Fate a solid, flesh-and-blood woman? A spirit? A voice or a vision?

Steeler had lowered his head.

"Fate did indeed give the queen an answer. But that answer was neither Magees or Fennelly: it was a two-year-old bastard born of a homeless whore on the streets of one of the outer cities."

I blinked at him in a sudden flare of shock.

"*You?*"

Steeler let out a dry laugh and took a swallow of wine. "Me."

"But you were a *baby*. You couldn't be a general of *war*."

"Exactly why my mother probably wouldn't have agreed to it. And why I think the queen murdered her so that she could have access to me without a pesky little faerie whining in her ear about it. Besides..." He shrugged, but his voice sunk into a deep bitterness. "Her Majesty has lived so long that a couple decades to let me grow up.... it was nothing to her. Not in the face of the armies I have been fated to conquer."

I stared at the planes of Steeler's face lit up by the fire and candlelight as if seeing him for the first time. To think that Fate had already whispered his name to the most powerful faerie in the world...

"So you didn't actually grow up on the ship?" I asked. "You grew up in the palace?"

He snorted. "Oh, no. As soon as I found out about my so-called *fate*, I started acting out. Knocking over suits of armor in the Grand Hall, refusing to wear the clothes they laid out for me, making friends with the servants' children instead of the pompous little nobles they tried to force me to play with." He grimaced. "And so when I was five, the queen sent me and those same friends to the ships that she had posted outside the island of Eshol to await the day her treacherous sister's dome of magic finally collapsed from overexertion—to help me learn the ways of my new position, she claimed." He shook his head. "Really, it was just a punishment. Both for me, and for the servants who had let their children run around with me."

"Terrin, Garvis, Sasha, and Sylvie were the children of the servants," I whispered.

"Yes. And Mattheus." Pain cracked in his voice at that last name. "They were all forced to join me later, too, when the queen thought planting me *inside* the dome would help... speed up my maturing process. She had no fear that the experience would actually kill me, you see. Being named by Fate means I will not die anytime soon. But as for the others..."

A knot in his throat tightened as he swallowed a lungful of air.

As for the others, one of them was already dead.

Outside the window, rain was pelting the lighthouse in droves now, and that deep rumble of familiar thunder was rolling in with the tide. Lightning flashed in forks through the gloom.

I sat in silence, my hand still on his knee as if it had been melded there.

"*You're* the Fated General," I said at last.

He looked up, but there was only resignation in the gesture.

"Yes. Once I officially accept my oath, that is—*on the day you explode into power, you will serve the queen of Sorronia as her General of War and conquer her enemies forevermore,*" he whispered. "She spoke that oath into being long ago, and it has been hovering over me since the first moment the darkness claimed me and I landed here at the lighthouse. But..." He turned to me with an expression I'd never seen him wear before—almost *pleading*. "I didn't want to conquer her enemies when that would have taken me away from *you*. So I've been procrastinating. Biding my time for as long as I can, telling the captain that my powers aren't fully formed yet, that I'm still working on perfecting them."

Again, something animalistic inside me bristled at the implication that he was thinking about the queen—and that it was scaring him.

"If you don't want the position, then don't accept it."

"I can't refuse." His voice had fallen flat, dead, and cold. "As soon as Lexington gives Dyonisia those pills and I know you're safe from her, I'm going to have to accept it. I can't delay any longer."

Another roll of thunder crashed into the lighthouse. The lightning outside seemed to flicker in my own veins, filling me with electricity.

"Steeler, you have the power—literally—to go anywhere in the world you want to go."

Just like that, I'd removed my hand from his knee, set my now-empty wineglass on the coffee table, and bent to rummage in my bag again.

"I have a map, look." I brought out the tome and flipped to page nine hundred and ninety-nine. "We can find someplace where you could lie low."

"I can't," he said again without looking at the map.

I stood on legs that quivered just as much as the windowpanes.

"You can. Because you know what I just saw when you talked about this queen and Fate and your title as General of War?" I pointed a finger at him. "I saw that damn light in your eyes—every hint of your smirk and your smugness and your confidence that I wish I could hate so much—I saw that all *disappear*. You cannot accept this role, Steeler. You—"

"I have to."

"You don't have to."

"I HAVE TO," he said, finally standing up to tower over me. "I can feel that oath thickening every day, ready to explode. If it goes unanswered, the queen of Sorronia will kill everyone I've ever loved—and that includes you."

I didn't realize that my hand was a furious fist clutching at his shirt against his chest until I looked down in bewilderment.

Steeler dropped his voice again, but his shoulders heaved up and down as he said, "I am going to stay and help you through everything until Dyonisia Reeve is dead, and then I am going to accept my role as the Fated General of the Sorronian Army, and I am going to leave you alone. I will not stalk you, I will not leave you little black pearls, I will not kidnap you, whisk you away and hold you against your will forever. I will not enter your mind again, I will not look at you again. You will be free of me and all the torment I have caused you."

"Steeler."

Just one more night, he'd told me, and now the desperation that had gripped his tone made sense. *Just one more night* because he wasn't planning on any more nights with me after this one.

No matter my true parentage, I was just a girl who'd grown up in a small village on a relatively small island, raised by two wonderful but very normal fathers. He... *he* was destined to be in charge of whole armies, to win wars around a world I would never travel.

I backed away several steps, my entire body buzzing with the urge to scream and thrash like every drop of my blood was on fire. Steeler's own face shone with that same kind of wild, starving energy—two predators facing off, resisting their most-anticipated meals.

What if I *wanted* him to look at me again? What if I *wanted* him to enter your mind again? What if I *wanted* him to hold me?

But what if I told him all that and he rejected it? What if I kissed him like I'd been wishing I didn't want to and he left again?

"Fine."

The word fell out of my mouth and hovered in the air like a raised weapon.

To the delight of the animal inside me, Steeler didn't back down in defeat.

He stepped forward.

441

"*Fine?* Really? What kind of *fine* was that?"

I raised my chin. "The kind that means I'm fine. You're fine. We're all fine and this situation is fine and it's fine if you leave me again."

"Oh, no." He took another step forward. "We're not playing this game again."

"What game?"

"The game where we both pace and prowl around the thing we really want to tell each other."

I felt the friction of the air vibrating between us as he moved a final step toward me, so close I could smell his skin and every unspoken word on his lips.

"I didn't realize you have more to say to me," I breathed.

"Oh, I have plenty more to say to you, Rayna." Every one of Steeler's features shone on high alert. His nostrils flared, the tips of his fangs glinted, and his eyes ravished mine. "But let's start with you. My new faerie maturity heightens all my senses, you know, and those senses are picking up on some mixed signals."

"Mixed signals?" I scoffed, crossing my arms.

"Yes, mixed signals. For instance, you *sound* like you want me to get out of your sight sooner rather than later, but you *smell* like you want me between your legs. So which is it?"

Heat poured into me in waves as I looked down at myself in mortification. My chest was heaving in the lacy red dress I'd never changed out of, and my legs—dammit, they *were* pressed together in an attempt to stifle the burn growing between them.

I dared to look up and meet his gaze.

"Why can't it be both?" I challenged.

Steeler crossed his arms back at me. "Because even with my Walking power, I can't be in two places at once. So choose."

"I'm not going to—"

442

"*Choose.*"

"Fine!" I shrieked. "I want you. Right here, right now."

For one heart-stuttering moment, we stared at each other.

Then the wineglass on the coffee table shattered as Steeler swept it aside and it hit the floor. Lightning forked across my vision when he cupped one hand around the back of my neck and eased me onto my back with the other until *I* was laying on the coffee table instead.

He lowered himself over me until he was hovering above my face and whispered, "Was that really so hard to tell me?"

"Yes."

"Well, then, let me reward you for being so brave."

He stood to his full height and marveled down at me, grabbing my ankles and slowly sliding his hands up my left leg until he found the knife sheath I always wore.

Without taking his gaze off me, he unclipped it and threw it to the side, where it landed with a thump on the floor that got drowned in the next roar of thunder from outside.

That wretched heat writhed and squirmed in my core as his fingers moved further up and grabbed my underwear, sliding them off with smooth precision and tossing them aside as well.

The lower half of my dress still covered everything that pulsed and ached for him, though, and when he just stood there, towering over me while I lay on my back, I almost screamed.

"Steeler, if you don't touch me right now, so help me God..."

"I'm just curious." He tilted his head, eyes gleaming. "Do you still gasp when I do this?"

He placed a hand on each of my knees and yanked them apart.

A gasp tore through me.

He grinned with all the wickedness and humor I'd come to love.

"Do you still curl your toes when I do this?"

443

Moving his hands up my legs, he shifted the dress upward until I was completely exposed to him before shifting his thumbs to my clit.

I just barely managed to resist crying out, but my toes... they curled. My back arched at the delicious hint of touch, desperate for *more*. More pressure, more movement, more *him*.

"Do you still make the same sounds when I do this?"

I watched through a daze as Coen Steeler sank to his knees on the coffee table before me and spread me wider, wider, wider, until he was eye level with that most yearning, aching, desperate part of me.

"So beautiful," he repeated, and caught my eye for an instant. "Every piece of you, Rayna." Then his attention flicked back down, and he smiled with those fangs on full display.

By the moonbeam and the *mist*.

The thought that he was *that close*. That he was just staring at me with such wonderment and possession and hunger and *ferocity*...

"We can stop whenever you want," Steeler said, his breath hot against me. "No matter what, if you want me to stop, if you change your mind, you say so. Okay?"

I nodded.

He yanked down my legs to repeat, "*Okay*? I need to hear that pretty voice of yours say it out loud, Rayna."

"O-okay," I gasped. "Okay."

Then I flung my head back and closed my eyes.

"This is what I would have done to you if I had won our bet," I heard Steeler say.

Just before the warmth of his mouth sank into me.

CHAPTER

45

A moan fluttered out of my throat.

Steeler's fangs dragged down my clit, his tongue gliding down my entrance and back up again with a brutality that had my hips rolling forward against their will, wanting more, more, more...

He raised his head before it could reach a crescendo. When I opened my eyes briefly, it was to find him staring down at me with lips that already glistened from how wet he'd made me.

"You taste even better than I remember," he said, eyes blazing with the reflection of the fire. "But you're holding back."

Of course I was holding back. Mere months ago, I'd wanted to drive into him with a knife. Now, he was driving into me with his tongue, and I was scared to let myself enjoy it too much.

His hand circled my throat—not too tight, but tight enough to get my attention, to make my eyes flare wide open.

"I want you to grind on my face as much as your body is begging you to," he said with carnal intent. "Suffocate me if you must, strangle

me, smother me. But do not hold back. I want all of you, little hurricane."

I nodded, remembering the same words I'd used in regard to him
all those weeks ago: *I want to see everything.*

"Okay. I—I won't hold back."

He lowered himself again, diving into me with increased ferocity.

At the sweep of his lips, I moaned again and wrapped my ankles
around his neck, yanking him in closer.

At the scrape of his tongue, I rammed myself against him, bucking with pure madness, letting the most intimate part of me feel every
hard ridge and curve of his face: the hardness of his chin and jaw
against my entrance, the slope of his nose against my clit. And those
fangs...

Oh fuck, those fangs...

The world broke and reformed into a million colors at the feel of
those fangs.

Every time I grinded against them, their sharp tips pierced my
most sensitive skin—not enough to draw blood, but enough to sting
in the most delicious way.

"Steeler," I gasped without knowing what I wanted to say next.

Lightning flashed inside me, a chaotic whirlwind of buzzing energy and light and God, God, God, I was going to fall *into* it.

Steeler just rammed his tongue deeper into me, filling me, feasting
on me, drowning in me...

I tipped over the edge.

The pleasure his tongue and teeth created... it exploded inside me,
blinding me with white-hot light that flared against my eyelids, and I
screamed.

Finally, when my body had gone completely limp against the coffee table, Steeler removed his head from between my legs and stood up.

He looked wonderstruck, his face dripping with me and a deeply satisfied smile playing along his mouth. I shuddered in a breath, trying to get air flowing through my lungs again...

Only to catch sight of his own want straining against the seam of his pants.

He noted my wandering eye and shook his head slowly, like the taste of me had gotten him drunk and he couldn't move as fast as usual.

"Don't worry about me. I just need a few minutes to—"

"I want the rest of you inside me, Steeler."

His head snapped back to me as I picked myself up off the coffee table, already feeling the heat return to my core again, as if that lightning had exploded into ashes that were settling back into place.

Slowly, I began to unbutton the side of my dress where the fabric joined and parted. Steeler watched the movement with an increasing sharpness until I'd shrugged out of the dress completely.

The lace fell into a heap of crimson at my feet.

"Fuck," he whispered, looking almost pained. His eyes roved over every inch of my skin, and my nipples ached in the face of such meticulous attention. "Look at you."

"Can't," I whispered, echoing his past words. "I'm too busy looking at you."

He moved around the coffee table, surging forward to hold my face in his hands, but I shook my head at his touch.

"No. Don't..." I squeezed my eyes shut. "Anything—*every-thing*—but that."

I still couldn't bear the thought of his mouth against mine. Maybe it was truly because I was afraid he'd disappear behind my closed eyelids and I'd open them to find nothing but mist. Or maybe I was just too afraid to face whatever emotions were swimming beneath that mist.

Maybe I could face them later.

Tonight, I just wanted to give in to my physical need for the male who had haunted every one of my dreams and blessed every one of my nightmares over the last year.

Steeler removed his hands from my face, his eyes hardening.

"Your lips are too tempting, Rayna. You want to fuck but don't want me to kiss them? Then turn around."

I would have done that in a heartbeat, but he was already flipping me around until I was facing the glowing embers of the fireplace.

He pushed me onto my hands and knees and sunk to his own behind me, threading his fingers through my hair to hold me tight.

I arched my back on instinct to bare myself fully to him, already throbbing with need again. The sound of him unbuckling his pants...

My fingernails dug deep into the rug beneath me.

"I want you to see just how pretty you look taking my cock from behind," Steeler said.

His dark, fathomless presence hooked onto my consciousness and reeled me into his, merging us together in a way I'd never felt before. I wasn't just reading his thoughts now—I was seeing through his *eyes*.

My legs were parted, my ass rounded, my pussy spread wide open and waiting for him. Beneath his fistful of my hair, he felt the scars of the brand on the back of my neck.

The heart does not falter.

No part of Steeler faltered as he finally grabbed his pulsing cock and pressed the tip against my entrance.

I squirmed against him, desperate for the friction as much as he was, and he delighted in the way my body moved when I did so. I was so needy for this that it made him want to hold back just to watch me keep squirming under his iron grip—

"No!" I shouted, my voice a hoarse whimper that only made him harder. "Don't make me wait. Please, Steeler."

"Such good manners," he said. "Saying please like that."

And he sunk himself into me.

We both cried out in unison, but he was already moving out and back in, both of us stunned at the sight of him sliding into me again and again. I was gripping him so tightly, taking the length of him so well, my body rocking forward with every stroke, my ass thrusting back to meet him again every time.

This... this was everything he'd never dared dream he could have again. But better. So much better after all that had expanded between us. My hips moved with an aggression that finally matched his. He was no longer scared of breaking me, of scaring me, of being too much for me—

So he slammed his entire length into me with all the force he'd always wanted to use, pulling a delirious shriek from my mouth as we finally lined up completely, flesh to flesh.

"See?" Steeler grunted, our minds still fused together, me still viewing myself through his eyes from behind. "You see how good you are at taking my cock, Rayna?"

"I see," I moaned.

"Say it, then."

The delicious drunkenness of pleasure was hammering at every one of my senses, so it took me a second to realize what he wanted as his length slid out and drove into me again. "I'm good at it."

"Good at what, Rayna?"

"At taking your cock, Steeler. I'm good at taking your cock."

"Damn right you are." He let my consciousness go, and I catapulted back into my own mind, breathless with the alternate pleasure I had just experienced... just in time for me to feel the small nip of his fangs against my ear. "And you know what, little hurricane? I'm good at taking all of *you*." I jolted forward as he plunged back into me. "Whether you're in the mood to kiss me—" I jolted forward again. "—or kill me—" I jolted again. "—or somewhere in between—I've got you," he said earnestly. "No matter what, I've got all of you."

"You've got me," I repeated.

Now Steeler increased his tempo, pulling my head back with that fistful of hair and using his other hand to circle back under me and massage my clit again.

The thump of his thrusts vibrated in my very bones, taking over the thump of my own heart. Pure bliss hammered into me each time, and I gripped it tight with the possessiveness of someone who never wanted to let go of what was rightfully *theirs*.

A storm twisted around my core. Wind shrieked in my lungs. Sparks exploded in my head.

I unraveled. Sinking my face low into the rug, I screamed out his name as if it was the only one I would ever remember again.

Steeler roared mine through his final thrusts as he came apart inside me.

For a moment, we both quivered to stillness, him still inside me while I faced the dying firelight on my hands and knees.

A boom of thunder made me jerk. Steeler slowly untangled his fingers from my hair and eased himself out of me with a tenderness that I once would have never imagined possible from a male so brutal.

"Are you alright?"

A laugh escaped my mouth. "Alright?" I sat back on my heels as he circled around to face me, his naked body glimmering so beautifully in the low light. "I think I'm more than alright, actually. I just hope Felicity *is* a heavy sleeper."

He didn't chuckle back, but bent to brush a thumb across my face. I didn't realize he was wiping away a tear until I felt the wetness of it streak across my skin.

"What's this?" Concern slid across his features.

"Oh, I..."

I was about to say I didn't know. That beneath all the pleasure and passion we'd just given each other, there was no reason for me to be sad.

Instead, I blew out a breath and asked, "Why don't you like my mind anymore?" If I was going to demand honesty from him, he deserved to get it from me. Even if that meant saying my insecurities out loud.

"What?" His brows pinched together.

Lightning flashed outside, illuminating the room for a split second before it disappeared again.

"You told Garvis you didn't want to train me because you couldn't stand being in my mind, but that was back when I felt nothing but hatred for you. Yet now that there's... more than hatred, you're still avoiding it." I wrapped my arms around my bare breasts. "Whenever you talk to me mind-to-mind, you loiter on the outside and never stay longer than you have to. Just... just then..." My belly fluttered at the mention of what had just happened. "...you pulled me into your mind rather than planted images in mine. And whenever you talk about how... beautiful my mind is, it's always in the past tense. Is it too barren now? Too cold? Too—"

Steeler kept a strong hold on my face.

"I once told you, Rayna, that the first time I laid eyes on you, I saw you had the most beautiful mind I'd ever experienced. No, not just beautiful—striking. Breathless. Wild and captivating and everything I'd never known I needed. It took every bit of control I had to let my eyes slide past you, to remember my job, to not sink into you and lose myself in that stunning labyrinth."

I blew out a breath of disappointment.

"And all that is gone now."

"*No*," he said firmly. "It's still there. But it's my fault that you had to wrap it in ice to protect it. My fault you had to hide it all in that armor. It's not that I don't like your mind anymore, Rayna. I am in love with your mind just like I'm in love with the rest of you. But I do not deserve to be inside it."

I stood up, and he followed suit, our naked bodies separated by nothing but a thin strip of candle-warm air.

He started to turn. "I'll go get us a washcloth..."

I tugged him back.

"I think you *do* deserve it, actually. To be in my mind. I think you *are* forgivable. I think all of your thoughts come from your heart, too. And I think your heart has always been in the right place, no matter how dark it had to become to survive."

I was close. So close to telling him the thing my subconscious knew that I didn't want to admit, even to myself.

"Co—" I started.

BOOM.

The bang of thunder was so much like Lexington's rampage into the Element Wielder house that we both broke apart, our heads whipping toward the front door of the cottage.

"No one's there," Steeler said. "I don't sense any minds."

I lowered my blockade to test that out for myself—

And heard the clicking of hundreds of little minds seconds before the creatures themselves came streaming through the crack under the door.

Spiders. Streams and streams of spiders of various sizes and shapes came scuttling up to my feet, and I backed into Steeler in alarm.

I hadn't seen this many spiders in ages. Had Rodhi sent them? Had something happened to him?

"What...?"

"*We come on behalf of the Good Council,*" the spiders said in unison, the overlap of their words and thoughts like an avalanche of fingernails tapping against glass, and my heart plummeted.

If Dyonisia had made one of her Wild Whisperers send them, then she knew about the lighthouse.

She knew where we were.

I tried to keep fear out of my voice, keeping my blockade down so that Steeler could use the flow of my thoughts as a translation.

"And what message do you bring?"

I could have sworn the spiders smiled, revealing all their little fangs dripping with venom.

"*That Hallow's Perch will be attacked at dawn.*"

CHAPTER

46

Dread swamped me as Steeler and I exchanged panicked glances.

You wouldn't care about all the other traitors he grew up with in Hallow's Perch? Lexington had asked me back at the Element Wielder ball. I'd thought he'd been talking about Terrin, Garvis, and the twins, but now I knew deep in my gut...

The Good Council must be behind the attacks on their own people, and Lexington was about to destroy Steeler's entire home village.

Just to see if I'd come running.

Just to see if I truly cared.

"How did you find us?" I asked the spiders as a trembling rage blossomed beneath the lids of my eyes. "Have you known about the lighthouse the whole time?"

"*No,*" the spiders said in that scraping discordance. "*When Kitterfol Lexington was last in your mind, he caught you thinking about this place and had a Wild Whisperer send us here.*"

Shit. I hadn't kept control over my thoughts at the Element Wielder ball after all. I'd let them slip, and now this meeting place, this safe haven... it was compromised.

"Leave us," I snapped with tears blurring my vision. Steeler had gone completely still behind me, and I half-thought I'd have to stomp on the spiders by myself to get rid of them.

To my surprise, they all scuttled back toward the door immediately, disappearing beneath the cracks—to get inside the walls of the lighthouse or to return to the storm outside, I didn't know.

I lurched toward my bag and threw on one of my spare dresses as quickly as I could, clipping my sheath back around my thigh. When I straightened, Steeler was still stuck in the same position as before, still naked, still staring at where the spiders had disappeared.

"Steeler," I said, "you have to get dressed. We can't stay here anymore—the Good Council knows about this place."

I bit back a sob at the sight of those still-flickering candles Felicity had made, at the mess in the kitchen and the home she had finally felt like she could be herself in. The monkey would be devastated when we woke her up to tell her the news, but it was better that we move her somewhere safe.

"Steeler?"

His head jerked up, and I saw that his eyes... they had gone wholly dark. Darker than their usual smoky quartz.

He cleared his throat. "You're right. Do you think you and Felicity would be safe if I brought you back to the Institute?"

"*Me* and Felicity?" I stepped toward him. "No, Steeler. You're not running to Hallow's Perch all by yourself."

He blinked at me.

"They're going to attack the Esholians who raised me for four years of my life, Rayna. The closest thing to parents I've ever had."

"I know."

In my mind's eye, I could still see that older man who had held young Steeler back as his childhood friend was whipped to death in front of the entire village, and I knew I had to tread carefully. Steeler looked like he was on the brink of flight, but if he went to try to stop that attack alone...

"Think about it—Sasha and Sylvie have loved ones from Hallow's Perch, too, right? And so do Garvis and Terrin?" I asked urgently, grabbing him by the arms. Maybe if we recruited others to help us, we'd have a shot at defeating whatever monsters the Good Council was about to release on his home village. "They'll want to fight with us to protect their own families. So let's go get them, and then we'll fight."

Steeler's muscles tensed beneath my fingers at the mention of *we*.

"And before you try to convince me not to come with you," I added sharply, "I'm calling in my bet. I get to have whatever I want for winning it, and what I want is for you to continue treating me like a true equal. I know that you would help me save Alderwick and my parents, so let me help you save Hallow's Perch and yours."

Lightning flashed in repetitive streaks as Steeler's eyes drank me in. The candlelight stuttered, sending jittery shadows over the floor.

I held my breath.

"Okay," he let out. "I wouldn't want you anywhere except for right by my side anyway." He looked out the window, toward the raging sea, before hooking back onto me. "Let's go get the others and fight."

Ten minutes later, my feet touched down somewhere outside the island of Eshol for the first time in my nineteen years of life.

I landed with a gasp on a platform of rocking wood, my head swooning at this strange new world that tilted to and fro. It was a good thing we'd dropped Felicity off at the Institute before we'd come here—with instructions on what to do and who to seek out, of course—because I was pretty sure the monkey would be tipping over sideways right about now. I had to drop my bag to plant my palms on the deck and breathe through the swoop in my stomach.

"Get up," came a gentle, insistent voice in my ear.

Strong hands lifted me by the elbows, planting me on my feet just as a great commotion of shouting and curse words barreled toward us. Steeler steadied me, his fingers locked firmly around my waist.

"What is *this*?"

I blinked to find that same four-fingered female from Steeler's memories leering at me. It was still nighttime, but only a single dark cloud hung overhead. The storm was a thrashing beast at our backs, the faint bruises of oncoming dawn illuminating the ship around us:

A sun-spotted wooden deck stretching from rail to rail. Towering masts that flapped with too many sails to count. Ropes and nets and ladders and hatches. A glass-faced cabin on the opposite end of the deck. And beyond all that... water.

More and more and more water.

"This," Steeler growled, "is Rayna Drey Reeve, daughter of the lost Princess Chrysanthia, and she is as welcome on this ship as I am."

Gasps burst throughout the crowd that had formed behind the captain. Through my dizziness, my focus finally landed on the monsters every Esholian had always been taught to fear.

They were lithe and tall and beautiful, all with sharpened ears and fangs that somehow made them look superior. But there *was* a certain unkept savagery that roughened each of their appearances.

Wind-chapped skin riddled with scars. Bandanas tied crudely over their heads. Tattered clothes with rolled-up sleeves that exposed the tattoos swirling along most of their arms. One female faerie blinked back at me with solid blue orbs for eyes. A shirtless male had a gaping hole in the middle of his chest—whether because he'd been cursed or because the hole was somehow part of his innate magic, I wasn't quite sure.

These weren't faeries who'd seen the glitter of a glamorous realm recently. No, these people had grown accustomed to the rock of the sea, the great sails above their heads swishing violently against endless wind and sky.

"Get the sword," spat the captain. My eyes settled on her face. The way her entire jaw clenched, her eyes reduced to sharp slits at the sight of me.

"Do you doubt my word, Captain?"

Steeler had tightened his grip on my waist, just as I caught sight of a few familiar faces in the small crowd that had climbed up from a deck below: Terrin and...

Oh thank goodness, Dazmine was alright.

I tried to smile at her. She mouthed a question at me, but I just shook my head. There was no way I could explain about Hallow's Perch right now with the captain digging into me with that daggered stare. It was all I could do to maintain my mental blockade around me.

"I would doubt the word of anyone who suggests the lost princess Chrysanthia is *alive*," the captain spat. Someone guffawed behind her, and another said, "I second that! It's blasphemy!"

I wanted to curl inward and shrink away from all the accusing gazes. Maybe these faeries weren't the same pirates I'd been warned about growing up, maybe they wouldn't chain me up and suck out my magic or sell me to whatever waited on the other side of the sea, but...

They didn't seem to want to have a tea party, either, that was for sure.

The flash of a jade-encrusted sword stifled every thought in my head. Each glorious inch of it glittered and reflected its surroundings like molten starlight as it was passed delicately to the captain.

As soon as the pommel touched her hand, a silver hook shot out from the socket of flesh where her fifth finger would have been, beckoning me.

"Let the girl come forward on her own."

Cold, dark tension leaked from Steeler at those words. Without looking at him, I pried his fingers off my waist, stepped over my bag, and stalked forward.

"Kneel," the captain said.

My heart began to bounce around my chest as I lowered myself to my knees, trying to find my balance against this surface that wouldn't quit *moving*.

The cold swish of glinting steel arced toward my neck—

And hovered just above my collarbone.

I squeezed my eyes, suddenly hoping that Barberro's eyesight was as good as he claimed. Would the sword actually *talk*? Or would it just transfer its knowledge to the captain in silence? What if Barberro had been wrong? What if it claimed differently?

"Well?" someone from the crowd asked after several stomach-clenching moments had passed.

459

The captain sucked in a breath—and let it out again in a voice that sounded shocked beyond belief.

"She is cleared."

Her hook sunk back into her flesh. The steel vanished from my neck. Exclamations and mutters broke out as dozens of pairs of eyes pinned me to the spot, ranging from awed to confused to suspicious. That same voice called out, "What's that supposed to mean? She's really the lost princess's *daughter?*"

The captain didn't answer. After a moment of heavy breathing where she continued to stare at me in shock, she rounded on Steeler with a snarl, "Why did you bring her? We're not a charity house, boy."

"I know that," Steeler said.

"The amount of refugees you've brought on board in the last twenty-four hours alone would indicate otherwise."

"If you count exactly two refugees as a lot, then you're even less generous than I initially believed." Steeler's back muscles were cording beneath his shirt as if to restrain himself from ripping through the captain's throat. "Besides, we won't be here for long. I've just come to fetch my friends, and then we'll be off—" He glanced briefly at Terrin, who gave him an uncustomary frown. "Where are the others?"

"We're here."

The high-pitched, breathy voice belonged to Sylvie, who had just crashed out of one of those glossy wooden hatches. Her eyes swiveled from the captain to Steeler to me, her hands wringing as if she wanted to embrace us all but didn't dare to in the face of present company. Behind her, Sasha and Garvis followed with confusion and wariness plastered over their faces as they took in the scene.

Despite that, the sight of Garvis, his mild presence and the way he walked steadily forward to take his place beside Steeler—it calmed something frantic inside me. Made me feel more in control of my Mind Manipulating power.

Hello, friend, I shot toward him, and he snatched the thought with a small smile.

Hello to you, too. I assume your being here means bad news?
Very bad, I'm afraid.

Out loud, Steeler announced in a voice so deep and commanding that it sucked every last drop of noise from the muttering crowd, "Hallow's Perch is being attacked."

Sylvie gasped, Terrin cursed, and Garvis exchanged a look of horror with Sasha. Dazmine frowned, chewing on her cheek.

Aiming his hostility toward the captain, Steeler continued, "I know *you* don't see a reason to help the human villages in need, but this particular human village is our home, and we're not going to abandon it."

"You're damn right we're not," Terrin called, rolling up his sleeves and marching toward us. The others, too, instantly converged, reaching out for Steeler, Dazmine herself hurrying forward as if to do the same...

"No. I forbid it."

The captain's words cut through the frenzy like a blade.

My blood ran cold at the sight of her face, pinched with a triumphant sneer.

"You may think you run this place, boy," she said, stepping toward Steeler with her hand still clutching the sword, "but you don't, and you never will as long as you continue shirking your responsibility like a spoiled little baby. You will *not* take your friends to that island any longer," she said firmly, despite the dark, fathomless wrath coiling tighter and tighter around Steeler at each word. "That is an order from your current commander. Their work there is done, and so is yours. If you disappear on me one more time, then I will be forced to draw my hand."

She cast her gaze around and landed on Dazmine.

"I may be ill-advised to kill the niece of the queen, but this one will work well as collateral, don't you think?"

In a flash, the captain had Old Veracious at Dazmine's throat, a grin ripping up the sides of her face.

"GET YOUR HANDS OFF HER!"

The roar came from Terrin. Before I'd even blinked, he'd used his Element Wielder magic to conjure a spear of water from the ocean that crashed into the captain and knocked the sword from her hand.

A body slammed into me just as the shouting started.

Magic exploded as faeries turned on Terrin. I could feel the vibrating, humming energy of it even though I could only see cracks from beneath Steeler's shield of a body: chains exploding from the gaping hole in that one faerie's chest and wrapping tight around Terrin while the female with the orbs for eyes held him in a blue laser beam.

"Stop," I breathed, pushing Steeler off me. "Stop."

He let me go in an instant, and I scrambled to a stand as the captain clutched her throat with her four-fingered hand, breathing heavily as if she'd just been assaulted by more than a little seawater.

"Let Terrin go!" I called, sounding much braver than I felt. But there was no time to cower. The sky was lightening more and more every minute, and I felt dawn hovering over the curve of the horizon like a bated breath. We were running out of time.

"You don't get to talk, girl," the captain said. This time, a silver knife shot out from her flesh, pointing at me like an accusing finger. "I don't care *who* your parents are."

Before Steeler could snarl at her, I said, "I don't care who my parents are either. This isn't about my parentage. This is about him and his family—" I pointed at Steeler. "—and this is his choice."

I saw Steeler's pupils widen as I sent him the confirmation and approval I knew he needed.

It's okay. I understand. Do it.

It *had* to be okay. I *had* to understand. He *had* to do it. It didn't matter how much the possessive, feral animal inside me wanted him to be mine and only mine. It didn't matter how much I ached to protect him from the queen across the sea—my aunt by blood. I couldn't— *wouldn't*—be the seed of doubt that held him back from the one thing that could save his family.

Steeler gave me the smallest of grateful nods before he turned back to the crowd, his face hardening again.

"He is not in charge until he accepts his fate!" the captain was shrieking. "Her Majesty appointed me to lead this fleet until—"

"I accept," Steeler interrupted.

Every face turned toward him. The chains around Terrin loosened. The faerie with the blue orbs withdrew her lasers holding him in place.

"I accept my position as the Fated General," Steeler repeated, and he didn't just step forward—he blinked out of existence and reappeared right in front of the captain's face, making her stumble back. "My magic is mature. The process is complete. I am ready. And I am ready *now*."

No sooner had he said the last word than that single cloud overhead began to slowly eddy above him.

Everyone looked up as it began to rain.

Fat globs of dark liquid plopped down—but rather than hit the deck, every drop hurled toward Steeler and bled *through* his shirt, disappearing into his skin beneath.

Inking him. Marking him. *Branding* him.

I gawked at it, at the dark cloud that had been above his head this entire time. Had I ever really seen Steeler in direct sunlight since he'd matured as a faerie? Or had this been following him around wherever he went, the queen's desires literally stalking him until he said yes to her?

By the time the rain stopped, my bones were quivering with the urge to rip the queen's head off from across the sea. I could see the tapered edges of her intricate, spiraling tattoo peeking out from Steeler's collar, climbing up the back of his neck, still swirling ever so slightly as it settled into position.

It was official. Steeler was oath-sworn to the queen of Sorronia.

And he now commanded every single being on this ship.

CHAPTER

47

Steeler didn't take off his shirt to investigate the official oath pressed upon his back. He only picked up Old Veracious at his feet and looked at the crew of faeries before him.

"Anyone who wants to help is welcome to come with us."

He held out his free hand.

I was the first to grab hold of it. Then Garvis wrestled out of the grip of the faerie who still held him, hurrying forward until his warm hand found ours. Sasha and Sylvie followed suit, then Terrin. Dazmine knelt to pick up my bag for me, slung it over her shoulder, and reached out her hand.

Terrin opened his mouth at her, but she rolled her eyes and snapped, "Get over it. I'm coming."

All around us, the rest of the crew was watching with parted mouths. The captain herself was swinging her gaze between Steeler and me with eyes that nearly bugged out of her skull.

I lowered my blockade long enough to understand: they were shocked Steeler wasn't forcing them to fight now that he was their official commander. More than that, though, they were shocked he'd finally *become* their commander after all these years.

Most of them had known him as a boy.

Now, the ink on their skin chained them to his commands above the captain's. And judging by the hatred clenching her jaw, the captain herself was well aware of that sudden change.

"We're coming!" boomed a familiar voice.

I looked up to find Barberro and that same silver-haired faerie in Steeler's memories ploughing through the crowd. They just barely managed to reach between the rest of our bodies to lay a finger on Steeler's, Barberro's figure looming over the rest of ours by three feet.

He smiled down at me. "Hello again, girl with curly hair."

"Hello, little faerie man."

Barberro boomed with laughter, but it was his mate—his *vigate*—I found myself smashed up against, facing her for the first time in the flesh.

When Nara caught my eye, I could tell she knew exactly who I was.

"They have to brew for another twelve hours," she whispered to me in that voice of softest satin, "but they can brew without me."

The pills. We'd been so close to following through with the plan.

Maybe, if we survived this, we still could.

"Thank you," I told her earnestly.

For coming with us right now, yes, but also for helping Steeler all these years behind the scenes. For helping me now. I hope my voice conveyed everything I meant in those two little words.

Nara nodded.

"Anyone else?" Steeler asked.

None of the other faeries on board so much as twitched forward. I tightened my grip on Steeler's hand, and felt him squeeze back as the first tip of the sun broke the watery sheen of the horizon.

It was dawn.

It was time.

Darkness tore into us from every direction, the eight of us clinging to any part of Steeler we could find as he dragged us through space. The sensation would never stop my stomach from roiling when we landed, but this time I didn't have time to gasp or retch.

Because when we landed, it was to find a world of smoke.

Flames ripped into the sky from every thatched rooftop in sight— and there were a *lot* of thatched rooftops here. Hundreds of seaside cottages and huts had been built into the crags of the giant clifftop that made Hallow's Perch: what would have once been a picturesque sight.

Now, it was filled with screams.

Steeler turned to Terrin.

"Can you put out the fire?"

Terrin's forehead squeezed as he concentrated, but after a second, his face fell. He lifted his hands and chucked a ball of water at the nearest rooftop, but it just dissipated as soon as it hit the flames.

"That's..." Terrin's face had gone pale, paler than I'd ever seen it. "That's not real fire. That's... *altered* fire. Like it's been *Shape Shifted.* It won't listen to me or..." He threw another ball of water that dissipated in a hiss of steam again. "...react to my magic."

We all stared in horror at the flames that only crawled higher and higher into the sky. Was *this* what had ravaged Emelle's village, too? *Altered* fire that the Element Wielders of the town couldn't touch?

"Sasha, Sylvie!" Steeler had snapped into commander mode. "Go help any villager you can find—get them to that bunker that was used for tsunamis on the east side."

The twins nodded and streaked off toward the village square. Steeler turned to Barberro and Nara.

"There's a blacksmith and armory shop side by side over there." He pointed down a street marked with a crooked sign called *Mosscrest Avenue*. "I need weapons. Anything you can find."

The two faeries—*vigates*—didn't hesitate before sprinting off, their gaits so in-sync despite the height difference that I didn't doubt Fate had woven their very souls together.

Steeler spared a half-glance at Garvis, Terrin, and Dazmine before shifting his gaze to me and reaching out to thread his fingers through mine with his sword-free hand. The touch was brief. Too brief.

"Don't leave my side, little hurricane," he whispered.

Then a new scream, closer and louder than before, split the billow of smoke before us, and the rest of us rushed after the source of the noise—up Mosscrest Avenue, thick with falling ash, and around a bend.

A woman was on her knees in the middle of a dirt road, holding two small children against her chest with one hand and screaming as she pointed her other hand outward.

"I can't!" she wailed at us when our thundering footsteps surrounded her and she looked up through red-rimmed eyes. "I can't Summon my husband back! That thing t-*took* him!"

"What thing?" Terrin asked.

"I don't know, I don't know!" Shaking, she pointed ahead, past a little stone church between houses. "But it went that way! My husband's a Shifter and couldn't get it to—it's okay, baby, it's okay." She held one of the children tighter against her chest as the little girl began to sob. "H-he couldn't Shift its claws or teeth in time."

Claws and teeth? I exchanged a single glance with Steeler to find my own confusion and terror reflected in his eyes.

Whatever these monsters were, it seemed they were immune to Element Wielding, Object Summoning, and Shape Shifting.

Garvis bent down to touch the woman's back.

"Can you tell us what this monster looked l—"

An ear-ringing roar burst from behind the church, and the children in the woman's arms shrieked with renewed sobs.

Steeler looked at Terrin and Dazmine, gripping his sword tighter. "Get them to the bunker. We'll go after the husband."

To my surprise, even Dazmine didn't hesitate to obey. She rushed forward to scoop one of the children up while Terrin grabbed the other one.

I snatched at her elbow just as they were about to flee.

"Be careful, Dazmine."

Out of all of us, she was the only full-blooded human. Her lifespan was shorter, and she only had one magic.

She tossed me a dry smile over the strap of my bag still slung over her shoulder.

"I will. And you can call me Daz."

Then she, Terrin, and the children fled down a side alleyway with the mother on their heels, the woman's tearstained face flinging back one more time as if desperate for a last sign of her husband among the smoke.

We'll save him for you, I wanted to tell her.

But another roar had already rattled the air so hard that I felt it reverberate through my very bones.

Steeler, Garvis, and I had barely made it to the church's front door when a ghastly shape emerged from behind it.

A giant of a humanoid figure rose higher than the church's steeple, covered in flakes of gray, peeling flesh and holding a man in skeletal hands that were tipped in long, curving talons.

The man lolled in its grip, head swinging, and as the monster made a rapid five steps forward on skittering legs, I saw why.

One of those talons had completely impaled the man's chest like a needle in a pin cushion. The man was already dead.

But that didn't stop the monster from opening a maw of sharp, jagged teeth and chomping down on the man's head.

Leaving just his impaled body from the neck down.

I stuffed a scream deep, deep down as the sound of a crunching skull mingled with the splats of blood that joined the pavement. Steeler had flung his free arm out in front of me as if that would have stopped me from seeing or hearing, but when he looked sideways at me, I knew it had just been a gut reaction. He glanced at Garvis next, and the three of us nodded at each other.

Side by side, we tried to dive into the monster's mind, but...

There were no thoughts to grab onto. Even when I allowed my eyes to close for the briefest moment, I could only sense more of that impervious fire, as if the element *itself* made up the creature's mind.

Which only left Wild Whispering to use against it. But amid the flames and smoke that was stuffing itself down my throat, there were no plants or animals around to call for help. There was nothing except...

The monster's head whipped our way, a shift in the wind alerting it to our presence.

It leapt, but my hand was faster.

My knives were already spiraling toward it, three of them, one after the other, and blood spurted in arcs as the blades hit their marks: one in the forehead, one in the neck, one in the chest.

Not enough to stop it completely, but enough to make it rear back in surprise, another one of its roars cracking my eardrums.

"Good girl," Steeler said, pride lighting up his voice despite the situation.

Then he was gone.

One second, he had been a solid, seething presence beside me—the next he reappeared in midair above the monster's head, swinging Old Veracious down upon its skeletal gray neck.

Blade cut through sinew and flesh and bone.

The head came thumping down moments before Steeler himself landed, catlike, on his own two feet, straightening up in time to move out of the way as the monster's body followed.

For a moment, I gaped at the sight of him covered in splatters of dark blood and clutching his dripping sword with his fangs bared. He looked every bit like the nightmare I'd always imagined him as. The *real* threat. The *real* thing to fear in the dark. The *real* monster.

Then a voice boomed out from behind that sight, and I jolted.

"It looks like we're all going to need these weapons."

Barberro and Nara had reappeared, this time wielding axes and sickles and a variety of other sharp, shiny objects. They tossed Garvis a machete, and he caught it by its handle with surprisingly deft fingers.

I should have been rushing forward to retrieve my knives from the monster's decaying body, but my eyes had returned to Steeler. A pallid sheen was creeping over his face as he shifted his gaze from the tip of his sword to the body and head of the thing he'd split in half.

"Steeler?" I stepped forward. He raised an expression of utter sorrow and hopelessness to my face. "What's wrong?"

More screams shattered the sky from the direction of the village square, and every hair on the back of my neck stood on high alert at the realization that there were *more*—more monsters who could not be destroyed with the power of our brands, who would have to be ended with steel.

But Steeler grabbed my hand as if I'd tossed him a rope at sea.

"Old Veracious told me who it was the moment it touched his neck," he whispered. "It gave me his real identity."

My forehead furrowed. "His? What do you mean by *his*?"

I looked over his shoulder at the decapitated body, the head pitted with yellow eyes that stared unblinkingly at the destruction it had created, its victim's lower body still skewered in its dead talon.

"I mean he's a man." Steeler was still whispering, and I vaguely felt the others drifting closer to listen. "His name is—*was*—Timothy Grandulous. Twenty-seven years old. Raised in Varchmouth. Given Element Wielding at his Branding. Failed his Final Test four years ago."

The realization crashed into my heart, sending the beats of it into a frenzy. Nara and Garvis both inhaled sharply, and Barberro cursed.

The attackers are pale. Damaged. Altered beyond recognition, the Cardina jeweler had said.

And now I knew why.

The attackers were pale because they were being kept in that prison on top of Bascite Mountain. Damaged because they'd been tortured endlessly since their Final Test. Altered beyond recognition because they'd been given more magic—more *brands*—than their original human blood could handle.

The monsters attacking our villages were the exiled ones.

CHAPTER

48

"By the moonbeam and the mist," Garvis muttered.

I couldn't seem to feel the singe of overbearing flames anymore as a wave of cold crashed over me at the sight of that corpse in two pieces behind Steeler, my knives winking where I had impaled it.

An Esholian.

Steeler and I had just killed an Esholian.

And maybe I whispered that out loud, because Steeler was suddenly gripping my jaw between his thumb and forefinger, wrestling my gaze away from the carnage. Back to him.

"We did," he said, not without gentleness. "But that Esholian just murdered a woman's husband—a father to two young kids. And if the rest of them can't control themselves from murdering more, we're going to have to do it again. Do you understand?"

I started to nod, but his past words seemed to ring through my ears. *I need to hear that pretty voice of yours say it out loud, Rayna.*

"I understand," I whispered.

"Good."

Steeler wrenched one of my knives from the corpse with a sickening squelch and twirled it back to me, handle first.

At the same moment, a vibrating *crash* echoed from the direction of the village square, a new layer of screams pealing after it.

I grabbed my knife from him and slid it back into place before wrenching the other two blades out of the corpse and whirling into a run as Steeler took off at a pounding pace.

"The exiled are immune to our powers because they've been Branded with all five," Steeler threw over his shoulder as Garvis, Barberro, Nara, and I ran after him. "And each of those five powers are blending together in ways they can't control. Their minds are fire, the fire is something else that's been Shifted, and their Shifted forms aren't the right kind of material that Object Summoners can grab onto."

My lungs burned with the acrid stench of smoke that only thickened the further we plunged into it, but I didn't let my footsteps slow even as Steeler took a sharp turn up a street bordered by shops that were collapsing in on themselves. A single thought was roaring over the rush of my own blood in my ears.

"The regular people who pass their Final Tests with perfectly average magic—they're the disposable ones," I panted, terror stripping away at my bones at the thought of Fabian and Don and every Branded adult in this village, Steeler's adoptive family included. "It's the people with excess power who can't control themselves—the *exiled*—that she wants to use against her sister to win the throne of Sorronia."

If that was true, then these attacks... they were all just part of a *test*. Dyonisia was testing out her army on her own people. Testing to see how much destruction they could cause on other magical beings.

I'd never wanted to plunge my blade into anyone's heart more.

"Well, then," Barberro said in a voice that wheezed a bit too much for my liking, "let's show traitor her army will never win."

Finally, we charged into an opening in the smoke, and I almost ran into Steeler's back as he stopped dead at the scene before us.

Seven or eight more monstrous figures filled the village square, raging against the handful of villagers who'd stayed behind to try to fight them. Even as we watched, though, one of them whipped out a giant, tapered tail studded with spikes and slammed it into the nearest woman.

The spikes stuck through her face, her chest, her stomach.

And blood spurted onto the cobblestone.

I could feel, in the way Steeler's shoulders hunched and the air seemed to suck in a breath around us, that he was about to Walk. But...

"Wait!"

He jerked back. Trying to block out the image of the monster's tail whipping the woman's body back and forth, I pointed at it.

"Do you see that imprint on both of its shoulders? And another one in the middle of its head?"

Steeler squinted at the vague circles just barely visible on the monster's scaly skin. I was willing to bet there'd be two more beneath each of its lizard-like arms.

"Yes?"

"Those are its brands. Killing them isn't going to put out the fire they created, but if we can mutilate their brands..."

"...we'll destroy their ability to use magic," Steeler finished, his eyes widening, "and put out the fire. Did everyone hear that?"

"Damage the brands," Garvis repeated, dipping his head and clutching his machete close to his heart.

Nara raised her two spades, and Barberro followed suit with an axe in one hand and a sickle in the other.

"COME AND GET A PIECE OF THIS, *FYKA!*"

He charged at the monster with the spiked tail just as it narrowed its sights on another nearby victim, Nara hot on his heels.

Garvis sprinted for the monster beyond it, but Steeler and I pivoted at the same time when a terrified holler rang out on the other side of the raised dais in the middle of the square. A man was on his knees before a creature that looked more dragon than human, except...no, that wasn't right, either. The body resembled an *insect* more than a lizard: tall, spindly legs, horns that almost looked like antennas, and thin, membranous wings that draped alongside it like...

Like a butterfly.

I was already running, throwing a knife at its bristled, tube-like tongue as it unraveled to lash out at the man cowering beneath it.

My blade sliced through flesh before it could. The monster shrieked and turned to me while the man himself scrambled away.

Two milky, unseeing eyes stared right through me, and recognition hit me all at once, turning my kneecaps into lead.

Jenia.

Her unraveled tongue still drooped with the weight of my knife stuck through it, but she seemed to sense me anyhow. Her wings gave a few angry flaps, her monstrous form lifting into the air until she was bearing down upon me, groping at me with hooked feet covered in tiny, prickly hair.

Steeler used the moment of distraction to disappear.

When he reappeared above her, it was to carve a slice of skin from her sloped head with a flash of steel.

And one of Jenia's brands was no more.

She shrieked again, a sound so high-pitched it had my eyes watering... but by the time she landed on those spindly legs and swung toward him, Steeler was gone.

"Here," he said, his presence solidifying by my side as he handed me back my knife he'd ripped from her tongue.

"Thanks."

I claimed the knife but didn't slip it back into place, holding it poised and ready when Jenia's giant wings began to flap toward us once more.

"Do you trust me, Rayna?" Steeler asked grimly.

My focus never wavered from Jenia, but I found the answer sliding from my lips more readily than I ever thought possible.

"Yes."

"Okay. Then I need you to open up for me."

Every particle in my body sang for his commands. It was easy, easier than anything I'd ever done, to funnel an opening in my blockade in his direction. And with his stream of consciousness flowing freely into my mind, merging with mine, we moved in harmony.

Whirling and ducking beneath wings and legs, we flashed in and out of existence around the monster Jenia Leake had become, slicing off the four remaining windows to her powers but never maiming anything vital. Never touching her head or her heart. Her shrieking reached a crescendo that raked nails through my ears, but...

The glints of Steeler's sword and my knives had fused like stardust by the time the giant butterfly collapsed back into a girl.

A sobbing, rocking girl with gaping wounds on five separate parts of her body and a marred scalp with newly-grown tufts of hair.

Disgust whirred through me. Despite the fact that we'd just saved her from herself, I wanted to rip her waste of a head from her neck for what she'd done to Rayna last year. I wanted to smear her back into nonexistence, where she belonged...

"Sorry," Steeler murmured. "That's me."

The next second, I felt him close his blockade, severing the flow of consciousness between us. The absence of him vibrated in my skull for a moment with a high-pitched ringing, but after a few heavy blinks, my thoughts were purely my own again.

And my own were a *bit* less murderous.

I couldn't see Jenia's eyes because she had them pressed into her knees as she rocked, but I found myself squatting beside her anyway. Trying to steady her tremors with a hand to her back.

"Hey. It's over. You're okay now."

Except I didn't even believe my own words. It *wasn't* over. It *wouldn't* be okay—not for Jenia, who surely couldn't go back to Dyonisia now that we'd dismantled her ability to use her powers.

Just as I thought this, a flash of yellow wings snagged the corner of my eye.

I whipped my head toward it to find a familiar parakeet swooping from the smoke-clogged alleyway on the other end of the square—closely followed by its owner.

Steeler had followed my gaze. We both stiffened as Kimber Leake caught sight of her sister sobbing and rocking before me.

She lurched into a sprint toward us, cloak flapping, the Good Council dot in the center of her brand gleaming like a red eye.

I shot to my feet in preparation. I could feel Steeler's grip tighten on the pommel of his sword as vividly as if he'd squeezed my own heart. If Kimber made a single move...

But by the time she skidded to a halt before us, gasping for breath, she had eyes only for the girl on the ground.

"Jenia. Jenia. It's okay. I'm here."

Kimber sank to her knees to wrap her arms around her sister, her back completely exposed to us and our blades. At that touch, Jenia's tremors finally slowed. Her sobs quieted. Her breaths evened out.

The Good Council elite—the woman who had sabotaged me last year to no end, according to the memories I had resurrected—finally looked up.

Not at Steeler. At me.

It was perhaps the first time I could remember last year's princess of our house looking at me with anything other than pure contempt. This was something deeper. Something spiked with pure fear.

"You... you didn't kill her."

Her yellow parakeet fluttered onto her shoulder and cocked its head at me, but kept its beak shut. No derogatory insults this time.

"No," I said bluntly. "I didn't."

Screams and shouts still flung left and right from behind us as Garvis, Barberro, Nara, and stray villagers still fought the other exiled ones with their various weapons. There wasn't time for pleasantries or heartfelt explanations on why I didn't want to murder a classmate— even if she'd been a horrible one who'd wanted to murder me.

"You'd better get her somewhere safe and tend to those wounds if you don't want her to die, though," I added quickly, nodding down at that oozing wound on Jenia's forehead and the blood leaking from the corners of her mouth. "There's a bunker on the east side of the village." I pointed in the same direction the others had gone earlier, and Steeler's gentle nod in my head, the skim of his fingers on my lower back, told me I was right before I could even ask him for confirmation. "Dazmine Temperton's there. She'll help you." When Kimber's eyes flared, I pressed, "No matter *how* she and Jenia left off, she'll help you."

A single nod was all Kimber could seem to manage. But as she looped an arm around Jenia's waist and hoisted her up on quaking legs, I felt a whisper in my head. Just for me.

The rest of the Good Council is here, Kimber told me, her Mind Manipulating voice like a skewer through my brain: unwelcome but straight to the point. *They're sitting in their carriages on the edge of the clifftop, observing the results of their...*She winced. *Of their test. I managed to slip away, but Dyonisia is going to realize he's here soon.*

Her gaze flicked, for the first time, to Steeler, who still had a hand against my lower back and was watching her retreat with palpable impatience simmering beneath his skin. He didn't trust her enough not to attack us as soon as our backs were turned, apparently, but he was already itching to go help the others.

Dyonisia gave me a second power when I became suspicious of his connection to the other four and reported my suspicions to her in my fourth year at the Institute, Kimber continued in my head, urgency smothering her tone, as if she were begging me to understand. *She wanted me to spy on his mind... but he broke up with me soon after, and I wasn't ever strong enough to break past all of his barriers. Then you came along, and did what I could not.*

She opened her eyes, looking pained.

I didn't realize that Dyonisia was playing me, feeding into my hatred, until they Branded Jenia in the sick bay... they gave her Mind Manipulating, not to recruit her, but to see if she could recover any of her missing memories of that day in the jungle. Dyonisia didn't care that it might make her go insane. She only cared about figuring out how he'd *escaped her clutches.*

Another subtle nod at Steeler, one that he noticed with a narrowing of his eyes, distrust and loathing emitting from him like the smoke around us.

Dyonisia will not let him escape again, Kimber finished.

When she finally turned and hobbled off with her arm slung around her sister and her parakeet fluttering after her, I recognized those words for what they were.

Not a threat, but a plea—from one woman who had once loved a male to another who...

I let the rest of that thought bleed into my subconscious so that I could focus on the point of her message.

Protect him.

Save him.

At that moment, Barberro bellowed out a Sorronian curse even louder than the shrieks of monsters, and Steeler and I whirled toward him. One of the exiled monsters with a mouthful of sharp, needle-like teeth had clamped down on his arm, impaling it in three dozen places up to his elbow. Next to him, Nara screamed as her own arm went limp.

Phantom pain, I realized. From their mating bond.

"Go," I hissed at Steeler.

It seemed I was always telling him that when all I wanted was for him to stay. But there was no denying I was holding him back. With his Walking power, he could have all of these monsters disarmed in minutes, and Barberro needed help *now.*

Steeler didn't need to be told twice. He only flashed me a single look that seemed to beg a thousand things at once before he disappeared and reformed on the other end of the square, already a blur of movement.

I flicked my attention to Garvis, who was battling a boar-like monster in a dance that moved closer and closer to where I stood. It looked like he'd already mutilated three of the boar's brands with his machete—only the left shoulder and forehead still to go.

When the boar suddenly erupted with a new set of tusks along either side of its body, one of them narrowly missing Garvis's abdomen, I hurled the knife in my hand.

The blade embedded in the monster's snout. It twisted in a furious circle in a futile attempt to dislodge it, giving Garvis enough time to jump back and make eye contact with me for a second that seemed to waver on the brink of time.

There's something I need to do, I shot into his head. *If Steeler realizes I'm gone, tell him I'll be right back.*

Rayna, I don't think that's a good—

Behind you!

Garvis whirled back to the boar as it charged him again.

I didn't waste another drop of the time I felt ticking in my veins.

I ran.

Down a side street where I batted swirls of white-hot ashes out of my way, coughing as I went. Up an avenue that climbed a ridge of the cliff, bordered by homes with glass that had long shattered. Toward the vague outline of the jungle I could make out beyond the veil of smoke.

Finally, when the blast of heat had faded behind me and the first unburnt weed appeared in the cracks of the cobblestone, I dropped to my knees and began to crawl, searching, searching, searching...

There. A scurrying dot of brightest red.

"You," I panted, "can you help me? I need to send a message."

I didn't realize I was sweating until a single drop rolled off my nose and splatted onto the stone right beside the fire ant.

It paused its scurrying long enough to lift its antennas in my direction. I lowered my ear to hear its rasping answer better.

" *What message do you need to send?*"

Oh, thank God for my Wild Whispering power. I pressed my finger to the ground long enough for the ant to crawl onto my palm, which I lifted to eye-level so that it wouldn't miss a single sound. Then, after I'd described the specific smells of who I wanted to contact, I let out the words I never thought would leave my lips.

"*Now*. I need help *now*."

I could almost *feel* the hive mind start to work, the red ant in my palm immediately sending out electrical signals to its nearest colonist. A tingling kind of energy zipped off my skin, and then it was gone.

"Thank you," I told the ant. " *Thank you*."

I deposited it gently back into the crack of the cobblestone before hurrying back downhill with my heartbeat pumping furiously in my mouth. How long would it take for the message to reach the other end of the island? How long would it take for them to come?

The smoke was actually thinning out by the time I made it back to the village square.

In the shadows of two smoldering buildings, I watched Garvis finally slice off the boar's last brand, watched the boar crumple into the man he'd been. On the opposite end, Nara was covering Barberro's body with her own, hissing at any monster who so much as looked his way.

Steeler himself was a whirlwind of wrath and glinting sword, his body moving in such a beautifully hypnotizing way that I had to remind myself to exhale. He'd already taken down three of the monsters by himself, their collapsed forms cowering against their own blood-stains on the cobblestone... but alive. They were alive.

He was alive. Not a single speck of blood on his skin was his own.

Just as I felt my mouth hook up in its first smile since the lighthouse, something else seemed to hook around my torso.

And tug me backward.

A single breath whooshed out of me at the sudden pressure, snagging Garvis's attention. I'd barely managed to make contact with the confusion in his eyes that mirrored my own when that invisible hook reeled me around a corner, up an even narrower alleyway, out of sight.

It wasn't until it had dragged me up against a dead-end slab of blackened brick that the pressure around my torso loosened. I gasped for air as a figure stepped into my field of view.

Kitterfol Lexington kept his hands casually clasped behind his back, his irises dancing with glee, as he strolled toward me.

I didn't even have time to grab a new knife and hurl it. As soon as my fingers twitched toward my sheath, every single blade—the crescent one included—zipped out of their pockets and rose into the air, spinning inward to face me instead.

"The benefits of a second power," Lexington said. His eyes never unstuck themselves from mine as he lifted his arm and his sleeve fell away to reveal the imprint hidden on that part of his skin.

I didn't dare squirm or move an inch. Not with my own knives hovering in a cage around me, keeping my back firmly against the wall.

Object Summoning. Lexington's second power was Object Summoning, and now past events were reshaping themselves in my mind.

That time he and I had gone soaring up and over the cliffs, back to the Testing Center, after Steeler had left me last year—I'd assumed it was another Summoner in the group doing the heavy lifting, but no, that had been Lexington. Just as it had been Lexington who'd cranked everyone's heads away from us in the Wild Whisperer dining hall, not with Mind Manipulating as I'd suspected, but with the same magic my fathers had always treated with such tenderness and care. I should have known as soon as those Element Wielder doors had blasted open at the ball last night... not with the kick of a violent foot, but with *this*.

This extra hidden power he kept tucked away.

This extra hidden power that might just defeat both of mine.

Lexington didn't need to lift a finger or break a sweat to keep my knives airborne. In fact, he almost looked... *contemplative*. As if he had all the time in the world to stand and observe me like a monkey in a sharp, glinting cage.

"I wonder—how did you manage to lie to me?" he asked, the stringy braids in his hair falling to the side with a slight tilt of his head. "I began to suspect that you were, but still... I couldn't *sense* it in the way I can with everyone else. In fact, I begged Dyonisia to attack Hallow's Perch instead of Cardina today, just because I had a suspicion and wanted to see if you would prove me right. Which, you did." He gestured at me. "Throwing yourself into danger for the traitor you definitely *do* love."

I forced my voice to maintain a gritty level of fear rather than the boiling hatred that seared the inside of it instead.

"I didn't lie to you."

"Oh, none of that, girl." Lexington waved a hand. "You and I both know you did. Were the pills even real? Or did Steeler plant another fabricated memory in your abysmal wasteland of a brain?"

The insult landed like the blunt edge of a sword to my gut. Abysmal wasteland. That's what I was right now, wasn't I? Empty and alone. My eyes were scampering over Lexington's shoulder, desperate for a certain body to materialize behind him at any moment.

But Steeler and I... we weren't *vigates*. He couldn't intuitively sense my distress like Nara had sensed Barberro's. And right now, he was still fighting monsters in the village square, his focus trained on the immediate threats before him.

I redirected my own focus to Lexington's face, flexing my blockade like a bubble around me. The fire had pushed away all the wildlife in the area, so my Wild Whispering power wouldn't be of any use to me right now. I'd have to rely on Mind Manipulating. If I could just slip into Lexington's mind and command him to let me go…

Lexington himself squinted at me, taking a step closer.

"Did you know that Dyonisia has a strict no-killing policy when it comes to you? I can't slice your throat open right now, or she will slice open mine for disobeying. But there is a part of Mind Manipulating that's not taught at the Institute…"

Another step closer. I lowered my blockade a notch, and my knees buckled at the cascade of ugly, slimy thoughts that barreled into me.

"I can destroy your consciousness," Lexington continued, the glee in his irises dancing with mania. "Your body will live, but your mind…well, you will be dead in the ways that matter but alive in the ways that don't. Then *both* Dyonisia and I will get what we want."

The rest of his thoughts were too slippery for me to grab onto. I couldn't dive into a rotten cesspool like that, squirming and writhing with so much hatred and malice. I just couldn't.

"Please don't."

My knives only floated toward me, one of the tips grazing my nose.

"*Please don't,*" Lexington mimicked in a high-pitched warble. "It's too late for manners, girl. No matter how you did it, you lied to me. And the greatest Mind Manipulator in the world does not tolerate liars."

Then he lunged into my mind.

CHAPTER

49

I fell back into my own mind just as Lexington crashed into my foundation with a resounding *thud*.

His invasive consciousness had grown bigger since last night's events. The length of his fleshy body stretched out like one of the bulbous roots of a palm tree. His head was reared up to twice my height, and the gaping hole in his face spread wider than a spoked wheel.

I no longer had my knives—either in the real world or in my own mind—but I remembered all of my lessons with Garvis like he'd imprinted them on my soul.

Eventually you'll be able to Manipulate your own mind with more ease. But that requires getting to know your subconscious better... which most Mind Manipulators don't do until their second or third year.

If I wanted a fighting chance at preventing Lexington from destroying the integral part of me in here, I needed *her.*

My subconscious.

I was already turning to run, but the sight of my own mind nearly stopped me in my tracks.

My walls—they weren't covered in thick slabs of ice anymore. Only the thinnest veil of frost bordered the edges, while steady trickles of water ran down the moss-lined cracks in stacked stone.

And between those cracks—vines and flowers. Climbing hydrangea, jasmine, and a beautiful, drooping plant of purple petals I'd never seen before, all glittering with dew drops beneath the light of my sickle moon. I hadn't even realized until this moment that my foundation was no longer snow, but a stone pathway leading toward my gate, surrounded by bursts of wildflowers among trees.

There was no time to gawk, though.

I shot toward my open gate and the maze of hedges beyond.

Another thud sent tremors through the ground behind me. From the furious hiss that followed, I could tell Lexington *knew*. He knew I was a Mind Manipulator now that I'd run from him, but I didn't stop even as I flew threw my gate and took the main pathway straight into the center of my mind.

In the real world, my body stayed pressed against that dead-end brick wall, suffocated with a band of exhaustion from all the fighting and running in the smoke. In here, though, my muscles and lungs felt alive with the scenery I sprinted past. The hedges were at once soft and domineering, the rosebushes beautiful and thorny, the trees gentle and powerful. The streams of melted ice gathered along the pathway and streamed inward, a gurgling creek leading me straight to my destination.

Leading Lexington, too.

I could hear his monstrous form sliding along after me, a sort of hissing friction that strung mucus along my foundation. It made me cringe, both inward and outward, to have his presence taint such a sacred place.

Because that's what it felt like in here. Sacred. Something I wasn't surprised I'd had to coat in armors of ice for so long to protect what lay beneath—what had *always* been beneath.

This is what Steeler had seen in me on my first day at the Esholian Institute. *This* is what he'd said he could have gotten lost in. Neither a vicious jungle nor a perfectly-trimmed arboretum, but something in between. A wild garden that was made of more than just trees and flowers: stone and water and the faintest flow of wind at my back.

What would Lexington do to it if he caught me? If he destroyed me? Would it still exist, or would all of this wilt and crumble and decay?

Spurred on by the thought that I just needed enough time to say goodbye to Steeler, even if it was for good, I increased my pace and found myself skidding to a halt in front of that marble gazebo moments later.

The center of my mind was the only place that still needed defrosting. The only place still swirling with flakes of ice and snow. The gazebo itself was still frozen white—and so was the woman sitting inside.

Me.

My subconscious turned her head to look at me, and just as I felt the gaping mouth of Lexington at my back, she lifted a hand.

Ice shot up from the ground around us, curling into a dome above our heads, solidifying into something so hard and strong that when Lexington tried to barge through, his distorted shadow on the other side didn't make more than a vague thump.

Breathing hard, I swiveled back toward my subconscious.

"It's nice to see you again, Rayna Drey Reeve," she said.

I stared at her frozen curls, the snowflakes glittering on her lashes. My breath fogged out in front of me when I finally managed to speak.

"What do I need to do?"

She tilted her head, surveying me with regal curiosity.

"Ask me a question. Any question."

Rubbing my hands together, I peeked over my shoulder to find the shadow of the giant worm sliding along the outer circumference of the dome to encircle us completely.

"Eyes on me," my subconscious said, and she passed me a coy lift of her blue-tinted lips. "In other words—*look inward*."

"Right." I turned back to her, and exhaled a shaking breath, pushing out the question I dreaded most. "What are you hiding?"

"That which matters most to you."

"W-which is?"

"*Him*," she replied without hesitation. "Coen. Every missing piece of him is right beneath our feet."

I glanced down at the snow-laden ice, the last frozen piece of *me*. And my own breath rattled like chips of the sharpest ice inside me.

"*You* stole all of my memories of him? You stole them and hid them here?"

"Yes."

I stared at her. "You..." I almost let out a shocked, humorless laugh as it hit me. "You were the cause of all my headaches, then?"

My subconscious dipped her head.

"It hurt you, when I ripped those parts away. But I knew—*you* knew—that they needed extra safeguarding in case another Mind Manipulator was ever able to dredge up your memories. And if you so choose, I can *keep* safeguarding them, here in this ice."

I swept my gaze from my own palms to the deathly white backs of my subconscious's hands that gripped the edges of her throne.

She wasn't bluffing, I knew. If I asked her to, she'd stay frozen like this, cold and forevermore turning into a bruised blue version of her former self, just to protect the one truth I didn't want to face.

I had loved him.

I had loved Coen Steeler so much that I'd stowed him away in the deepest, most untouchable part of my mind, cutting him off from anyone and everyone who might try to take him away from me. Including myself.

But now...

Now, I loved Coen Steeler so much that I was willing to set him and all my memories of him free. I was willing to set him free and see if he came back.

I shook my head at my subconscious.

"No more. No more ice or snow or barriers when it comes to him. Let all of the pieces out."

The icy mirror of me cracked wide open with a smile.

"As you wish."

And the ice itself began to crack beneath our feet.

The snow melted, pooling around my ankles. Fissures in the ground opened up. I backed up a step as mist began to escape those fissures in twirling tendrils, forming tangible memories as they came up.

There was Coen, pushing open the flap of the tent and locking eyes with me as the power in my chest raged. There was Coen, flinging me over his shoulder and hauling me to an alleyway to share his most vital secret with me in the hopes that it would help me survive. There was Coen, fusing his lips to mine when Kimber had walked in on us in his room. There was Coen, touching me in the cave.

And there was Coen, swimming with me in the Element Wielder lake, our laughs rebounding off the surface of the water that glittered with an inky blanket of starlight overhead. Our arms were wrapped around each other as we bobbed in place, neither of us knowing that a certain giant octopus bore witness to the words we next whispered to each other in the dark.

"If you could have any magic in the world," Coen asked me, smiling into my face, "what would it be?"

"Any magic?" I asked.

"Any magic."

I appeared to contemplate, my gaze sliding sideways to the sparkling reflection on the water's surface.

"I think I'd like the ability to touch the stars," I said finally. "It wouldn't be a useful power to anyone, but... I'd like to be able to know what they feel like without burning myself alive." My eyes roved back to him, and my lips spiked up in a smile. "Why? What magic would *you* have?"

Coen ran a thumb along my cheekbone, seemingly mesmerized.

"I would want the ability to weather any storm—to just stand in the middle of all that raging beauty and watch it come undone. Without getting beaten to a pulp, of course."

I giggled. "I think that would take super strength or something."

"Well, yours would take super long arms."

I splashed water into his face, and soon the mist of this memory showed us untangling in fits of laughter, trying to dunk each other underwater.

Then there was Coen and me, joining together in a boat among the same stars I'd claimed to want to touch. There was Coen, digging a dagger into Fergus's neck and cradling me against his chest as he carried me back to campus. There was Coen, kissing me goodbye.

There was Coen, there was Coen, there was Coen.

And as all of those memories swelled and swelled within the dome of protection around us, the ice gave a last, deafening *crack.*

Then shattered.

All of my missing memories exploded outward.

Lexington had managed to wrap his entire fleshy body around the dome, but as soon as the first hint of mist touched his skin, he retracted.

A hiss left his gaping mouth. The memories pushed against him, so blindingly bright that Lexington had no choice but to retreat. Like a worm to sunlight, he began to crawl back—away from the gazebo. Away from my subconscious. Away from me.

I looked over my shoulder once to meet my subconscious's eyes. A jolt trickled through me at the color that had returned to her: the pink in her lips, the green sparkling in her eyes, the freckles splattered across her nose. Still sitting on her throne, she raised a hand in farewell at the exact same time I did.

The next moment, I felt Lexington wrench himself out of my mind, unable to withstand the brilliance of the memories I'd unearthed.

"You *bitch,*" he panted, and I blinked myself back to reality, where all of my knives were floating in midair, their deadly edges winking in my face. "Where did you get the power to do that?"

Before I could respond, another voice landed in my head.

Hold tight, Rayna. I'm on my way.

I tried not to let my face betray any sign of the communication. *Garvis?*

Yeah. Coen's working on the last monster, but I saw something pull you backward and figured you might need a bit of assistance.

I grimaced. *Maybe just a bit.*

Lexington's face pinched together at my silence. When he spoke next, it was through clacking teeth.

"I'm not going to ask you again, girl. How. Did. You. Get. Mind Manipulating. Power?"

Knowing that Garvis was near, I allowed myself to sneer right into his face.

"The same way you did, Kitterfol. By taking it from a faerie." I leaned in closer, pressing my own neck into the point of a knife until a sting of pain flared against my skin. "Only mine was willing to share."

Lexington's chest swelled. By the looks of those veins popping in his forehead, I could tell he was about to disregard Dyonisia's apparent no-killing orders in light of what I'd just done: beaten him at Mind Manipulating.

But just as he was blowing out a reeking breath and all of my knives were twitching forward, a glint of metal caught both of our eyes.

Garvis came leaping into the alley with his machete raised high. Lexington managed to jolt to the side to try to avoid it, but he didn't make it far enough.

The machete crashed down on Lexington's left shoulder, right over his original brand.

Bone cracked. Warm and sticky pinpricks splattered my face. At Lexington's howl of pain, my knives spun around as if of their own accord, controlled by his Object Summoning power...

Garvis didn't have time to tug his machete back out.

He didn't have time to back away.

He didn't even have time to raise his arms.

The knives burrowed into him from every direction—impaling his stomach, his heart, his lungs.

And my world slid sideways as Garvis toppled.

A scream was fracturing in my mouth, ripping my vocal cords apart, shredding all the words I couldn't say to pieces.

And then he was there—Coen, right in front of my face, dripping with gore and grasping me by the back of my neck.

"Rayna. I'm so sorry, I didn't realize you were gone until I cut off the last brand and heard you scream. What—?"

He read everything in my eyes and pivoted, processing Garvis on the ground, surrounded by a spreading pool of liquid I refused to name. Lexington himself had been staggering backward with the machete still lodged in his shoulder, but at the sight of Coen and Old Veracious before him, he straightened with a hiss.

"You—" he began, eyes moving hungrily to the sword.

Just like Garvis hadn't had a chance to defend himself, though, neither did Lexington.

I had already opened myself up to Coen again, and with our consciousnesses merging just like it had before, we moved as one.

My hands shot forward to take the pommel of Old Veracious while Coen materialized behind Lexington, locking his wrists behind his back, and growling in a voice that dripped with predatory command, "Stand still. Do not use your Object Summoning power or any power at all. Watch the reflection of the light as it leaves your eyes."

Through our open connection, I knew Coen's rage and grief and fear had been strong enough for the command to latch onto him.

Lexington went still, his pupils forced to tack onto the glinting blade before him and the reflection that shimmered in the steel.

But his mouth was still able to move, and I knew he was talking to me.

"I've been in your mind, girl. I know your deepest fears."

I adjusted my grip on the sword.

"You don't want this kind of blood on your hands," Lexington continued confidently as Coen kept his arms firmly locked behind his back. "You're too desperate to prove to the world that you're good." He licked a splatter of blood off his lips. "So prove it, Ms. Drey. Prove to me that you're a good person and drop that sword."

I took a deep breath. We didn't have time for this conversation. Garvis was bleeding out *now*. And with my subconscious stirring right behind my eyes, I didn't need to perseverate on his words or wonder if they were true. I already had my answer.

"I don't have to prove anything to someone who knocks other people down just to feel big," I told him.

Old Veracious hummed in my hands, sending vibrations up my arms, into my chest, into my very soul.

When I pressed the edge of it against Lexington's neck, those vibrations whispered all the truths about the man's identity before me. *Kitterfol "Kitty" Lexington, born of Andrea Brink and Fallon Lexington 37 years ago in Belliview on the island of Eshol. Mind Manipulator. Object Summoner. Good Council Elite. Assaulter. Madman. Parasite.*

But one word stood out above all the others.

Coward.

Lexington's eyes widened a fraction as he saw the determination settle on my face. His own face crumpled.

I hefted the pommel to the side and swung.

"No!" he blubbered. "St—"

The sword severed through his neck in one swift stroke, the cut so precise and clean that I barely felt the impact.

And the most famous Mind Manipulating head on the island bounced to the ground at my feet.

CHAPTER

50

I didn't waste a second longer watching where that head landed.

With a gasp, I pitched forward onto my knees next to Garvis, Coen dropping to his own beside me. Maybe there was a healer in the bunker or on the ship that Coen could Walk Garvis to in time. Maybe the puncture wounds weren't as bad as they looked.

But when I trained my gaze on Garvis's chest, it was to find it drenched in his own wounds, already deflated. His eyes had glossed over, and instead of final words, I heard a fleeting thought waft from his mind like a puff of the purest cloud.

I hope...

"No, no, no," Coen breathed, shaking Garvis's shoulders. "What do you hope? Tell me what you hope! Rayna—" He turned to me, desperation clinging to his lashes. "Tell him to come back so he can tell us what he hopes."

I was frozen, staring at the chest that had not risen again.

Garvis... he hadn't found his spark yet. Hadn't traveled or found love or discovered something new. I hadn't even had time to tell him thank you for saving me—not just now, but with all of those Mind Manipulating lessons he'd so selflessly gifted me time and time again.

He couldn't be dead.

But when I tried to dive into his mind, there weren't any more thoughts to cling to. There was nothing but a vague sense of a hundred empty curtains, fluttering away, away, away...and gone.

Death, it seemed, hadn't been as patient with Garvis as Garvis had been with me.

"I'm so sorry," I told Coen, a sob muffling my voice. I laid Old Veracious by his side, reached out, and gently slid Garvis's eyelids closed.

Coen made a sound somewhere between anguish and fury, and I knew that if he could, he would bring Lexington back to life just to behead him again and again and again for what he'd ended.

A voice in my ear tugged my head sideways. I hadn't even felt the fire ant scuttle up my body and onto my shoulder.

" *We're here,*" it said.

Just in time, too. Because the next second, Coen's eyes flashed open as fat plops of milky mist came drifting down from the dome above our heads. The dome itself seemed to be wiggling downward in ropes of antipower, reaching for us with pale hands.

"We've got to go, Rayna," Coen rasped. "She's coming."

"No."

I turned to find myself facing that same boy who'd watched Mattheus die, too. The Fated General who'd just defeated the last monster in the square was, in this moment, just as terrified. Just as small.

Which meant it was up to me to shove down the biting edge of grief and think for the both of us.

"No," I repeated urgently, even as more of Dyonisia's antipower came spiraling down. "Once she sees all of her exiled ones back in their original states—once she sees *him*..." I nodded vaguely at Lexington's dismembered body. "She's going to know you were here. And if that happens, she'll scour Hallow's Perch in search of you. You don't want her to scour Hallow's Perch, do you? You don't want her anywhere near your adoptive family or the others?"

Coen shook his head, his eyes hanging onto mine as if my words were the only thing keeping him from drowning in the tears surely running down his throat.

"This is what we're going to do, then," I whispered.

With our blockades still open for each other, I poured my entire plan—the one I'd been forming since last night—into his mind, barely registering the widening of shock in his eyes in my haste to get it all out in time. The mist was congealing around us, much like a spiderweb, threads of that milky power swimming closer and closer to us.

But there were still enough gaps in it for me to look sideways at the entrance of the nearest alleyway and note the two shadows stirring just behind that corner. Observing. Waiting.

When I was done, Coen gave a frantic shake of his head.

"I can't leave you alone with her, Rayna."

"Hey, hey, hey. Look at me. Look at me, Coen."

His name—his *first* name—on my tongue stopped his pacing pupils in their tracks.

I placed his hands around the back of my neck, digging his fingers into the ridges of my brand. Into those five Sorronian words. "My heart will not falter," I breathed up at him. "Okay?"

It took him a moment, but when the first rope of antipower touched his skin, Coen winced at the hiss it made on contact and nodded.

"Okay."

I didn't think twice. Life was too short to think twice. Lifting myself up to my tiptoes, I fit my lips against the curves of his.

He tasted like copper and salt on the surface, the residues of battle still clinging to his lips. Death. Destruction. Decay. Everything the Fated General was destined to embody.

But as soon as his shock wore away and he yanked me against his chest to kiss me again, that sweet, dark aroma filled my mouth and sent a deep calm down my veins. Now *this* was Coen. Life. The sparkling starlight in the dark. A fierce, ferocious warmth even amid the cold.

I closed my eyes, basking in the brief moment of bliss.

Until the weight of his lips disappeared from mine.

I opened my eyes to find Coen several paces away from me. Garvis's body and Old Veracious were gone, my crescent knife was back in my hand, and a crow-led carriage was veering down from the sky.

When the carriage touched down, the wheels sparked against cobblestone. The crows, about three dozen of them in harnesses strapped to reins, broke into a frenzy of squawking.

"Well, well, well. The Mind Manipulator and the Wild Whisperer, trapped in the same web at last."

Even after all this time, Dyonisia's voice still grated down my spine.

I watched warily as she used the carriage footstool to step down, her Wild Whispering coachman holding her door open.

The milky mist of the dome had wrapped around Coen and me, thin strands of it sweeping *through* us from every direction. The essence of it burned where it touched my skin, as if those parts of me were struggling for air. As if they were being smothered.

But Coen was worse. Dyonisia had wrapped him up even tighter, spiraling ropes of power around his mouth so that he couldn't speak. So that he couldn't even move.

Her curtain of midnight hair swished to the side as she surveyed Lexington's dismembered head in the opening of the alleyway beside us, her nose wrinkling with disgust.

"I assume you've both figured out my power is the dome itself?"

"Y-yes," I got out.

"Good. I would have been disappointed otherwise."

Dyonisia swept her gaze across Coen, lingering on him for a bit with a lip tugging upward in smug victory, then to me.

"What you might *not* have figured out, though," she said, stepping closer, "is how intelligent my power is. It can sense both of your magics in my little web right now. Usually, I give Wild Whispering and Mind Manipulating powers a pass on the smothering effects, but right now... well, let's just say I wouldn't fancy you asking those crows to attack me."

I said nothing, even as a creeping sense of dread slunk over me.

The crows—they were squawking and cawing in their reined harnesses, but I... I couldn't understand them.

And my blockade had dissolved, but none of Dyonisia's thoughts wafted out to me. I couldn't find Coen's mind or fall back into my own. My Mind Manipulating power was gone, too.

Like she'd said, Coen and I were trapped in this web together.

If only Nara's pills had been ready in time. If only I had Object Summoning so that I could ram that poison down her slender throat.

"What do you want?" I dared ask.

Dyonisia gave me a smile masked in tight skin.

"*You.* I want *you,* Rayna."

She took another step closer. I flinched back, but the sting of her antipower held me in place.

"But," she continued, "how could I ever *have* you if you were in love with the enemy—my *dear* sister's greatest weapon?" She nodded at Coen, still locked in that same position a few paces away. "How could I turn you into my own weapon if you chose *him* and the massacre that is to come from him?"

"Massacre?"

"Yes." Dyonisia nodded, her lips puckering with sincerity. "Look what he did to those poor exiled ones today. He *mutilated* them. And he is prophesized to destroy the entire world if my sister asks him to."

My heart broke into a furious rhythm at what she was confessing to me.

"You knew who he was the whole time he was at the Institute."

It wasn't a question, and Dyonisia didn't bother nodding.

"It wasn't hard to put the pieces together. Six kids suddenly exist in Hallow's Perch where they hadn't before? Please." She tutted a laugh. "My mistake was my curiosity. I wanted to see if their Branded powers were more extraordinary than humans due to their faerie blood—I planned to take them in after their Final Tests, but you made sure they got away in the nick of time, didn't you? You and your little spider spy?"

I swallowed all my protests. If I was going to stick to my plan...

"Well, you have him now." I lifted a finger—all I could manage in the web—toward Coen. "I passed your test. Here he is."

"Test?" Now Dyonisia actually lifted her chin in laughter. "Test? Don't you see, child? This wasn't a *test*. I don't want Coen Steeler anymore. I want *you*. Your mission was just a way to turn you against him—to make you hate him as you should. But it looks like that backfired on me, didn't it?"

502

She gestured at Coen, then at Lexington, and I understood: she knew we'd killed him together. She knew we'd fought together back in that village square. She knew I'd fallen back in love with him. Why else would I be in Hallow's Perch, defending his home village? Why else would we have been standing side by side, covered in blood that was not our own?

"It didn't backfire," I tried to lie.

Dyonisia's perfectly white teeth glimmered in a smile.

"Oh, trust me. It did. But I am nothing if not a firm believer in a little discipline. Prove to me that you choose me—that you choose this *island*—over the Fated General. Prove to me that you are willing to sever his bloody destiny before it hurts the people you love." She examined her nails. "Or I will enjoy dropping a bomb of my own power on Alderwick. And this time, I'll make sure it suffocates every last drop of magic, no matter which form that magic takes."

Fabian and Don. She'd threatened them before, and now she was threatening them again, but in a more tangible way. I could almost see the dome condensing over my tiny home village, prepared to fall.

Tears blurred my vision now as I looked at Coen.

His edges were warping through the mist. His warm brown eyes were fixed on me, though, and I found my answer within them.

Dyonisia flicked a finger. Her power released me, and I stumbled forward, gripping my crescent knife tightly in a fist.

Protect him.

Save him.

"Kill him," Dyonisia said.

"I—"

"Kill him. I'm not in a very good mood, you know. My best Mind Manipulator is dead, one of my elites has abandoned me, and all of my monsters appear to have fled." I barely had time to feel relief at the

503

realization that Kimber and the exiled ones, at least, had escaped her clutches. "Prove to me that I shouldn't give up on you, child. Prove to me that I shouldn't just scrap this whole island and start anew."

My blood chilled at those words, and I turned to Coen.

My muscles screamed at me to stop.

I resisted their cries, dragging myself forward, until I was positioned right in front of his blurring form.

I love you, I whispered into the void.

For Hallow's Perch and Alderwick and the rest of the island, I could do this. No matter what Dyonisia claimed, this was a test she didn't realize she was giving me, and I was determined to pass it.

So I plunged my crescent blade into Coen Steeler's heart.

CHAPTER

51

Warmth gushed over my hand.

The sound of his body hitting the cobblestone was like a crack to my senses, jerking me out of a trance and straight into a nightmare.

I'll find the right version of myself when Steeler is dead, I'd told Willa at the beginning of the year

Now, I was staring at the dead, blank-eyed form of him at my feet, and I'd never felt less like myself: hollow and cold. Oh, so very cold.

Never again. I never wanted to see this image again.

I ripped my eyes back to Dyonisia, who had momentarily gaped in surprise, as if she hadn't thought I'd actually do it.

When she saw that Coen's body didn't so much as twitch on the ground, though, she smiled again—this time almost genuinely.

Her mist dissolved around us.

And as soon as my two powers flooded back into me, I used the opportunity to pounce.

Eat the corpse, I commanded the crows.

They obeyed instantly. Eagerly. Hungrily.

"*Food!*"

"*Food!*"

"*Food!*"

The Wild Whispering coachman couldn't hold them back. With a great flurry of sleek black wings, the crows pulled the carriage toward Coen's body and began to peck at every inch of his exposed flesh.

"No!" Dyonisia shrieked, flapping her hands at them. "Stop it!" She turned to the Wild Whispering coachman. "Tell them to stop! I want that body!"

He tried to order the crows back, but they didn't pay him any mind. In the commotion, I bit down on my lip until I tasted blood, clamping down on the smile slowly rising within me.

Because that wasn't Coen's true body, but a Shifted replica of it... and now Dyonisia would never know. She'd never know that even as the crows ate away at that replica, the morphed flesh was already withering back into its original form: rubble and grit and ash.

I chanced a half glance at the two shadows loitering in that alleyway behind the carriage—Emelle and Lander.

Emelle and Lander had come to save me. To save *us*.

I had whispered my plan into Felicity's mind right before we'd dropped her off at the Institute. Until ten minutes ago, Coen hadn't had any idea that I'd asked her to relay my whole story, along with my plan, to Emelle, who could relay it to Lander.

For I'd known that Dyonisia wouldn't trust me completely until she saw me pierce Coen's heart. And Lander was the only Shape Shifter *I* trusted to help me fake his death without turning me in.

I don't know which of their powers they'd used to get here in time—there was a variety of Wild Whispering or Shape Shifting ways to travel across the island—but I did know that Lander had used his power to make a clone of the male he'd seen me with as best as he could.

That clone had been warping slightly around the edges, and those eyes had been Lander's warm brown color rather than the smoky quartz of Coen's real gaze, but other than that...

Well, Dyonisia had been fooled, at least.

Even the blood that had coated my hand had felt real.

Blood that had turned back into ash and dirt on my hands.

Thank you, I shot into that alleyway. *Thank you so much. I didn't want to tangle you up in all of this, but...*

Although I sensed Lander was panting and sweating with the effort it had taken him to Shift something so small into something so significant, neither of their minds so much as flinched with shock at the sound of my voice in their heads.

I'd asked Felicity to tell my best friend *everything,* which meant both Emelle and Lander now knew about more than just Coen. They knew I was half-faerie. That Dyonisia was my aunt by blood. That I had a second brand hidden beneath my matted and tangled hair.

And their minds were filled with nothing but love and pride as Emelle thought back, *We knew you were hiding something this whole time, Rayna. When that monkey of yours found me, it was honestly a relief for us to be able to understand. To be there for you.*

Lander's mind was straining with exertion, and I could practically see the sweat streaming down his forehead as he maintained the bones of his creation. But he still managed to think, *Thank you for letting us in, Rayna. It means a lot to Melle... and to me.*

My throat stung. I couldn't do it in real life, but I threw them both a mental image of me wrapping my arms around their necks and squeezing tight, picking up on more subtle pieces of knowledge when I did so. Felicity was safe in my room with Willa. Rodhi had set his spiders on the Testing Center during the beginning of the second quarterly test—ensuring that nobody had noticed when Lander and Emelle had slipped away.

I'd forgotten about the second quarterly test. Forgotten how dangerous it would have been for them—for all of us—if we hadn't showed up. Mrs. Smetlar, especially, would have relished reporting us to the same female who was currently shrieking at the crows as they continued to tear apart the replica of Coen.

As if Emelle could sense my guilt seeping into her mind, she added warmly, *I noticed, you know.*

Noticed what?

That you filled my birdfeeder for me when I couldn't. You might not have been able to give much of yourself to anyone this year, but you gave me that. She paused. *I knew it was all you could manage. And it was enough.*

My eyes were watering by the time the crows finally picked their way to the ground, leaving nothing behind besides a Shifted skeleton.

Dyonisia sniffed at what she believed to be Coen's bones.

"Who knows where they're going to shit out all of that bascite I could have studied. Good God, I hate birds."

Now I was extra glad I'd had the birds demolish the evidence of how I'd tricked her. When Dyonisia had sensed a Mind Manipulator in addition to a Wild Whisperer in her web, she hadn't realized she'd just been sensing *me:* Coen's power that ran in my blood. My ruse would have been over if she'd realized that the replica had no bascite at all.

As it was, she merely sighed at me.

"Come, child. Let me take you back to the Esholian Institute—maybe you will stay there like you're supposed to now that you know what I can do to misbehavers."

As if to prove just what she could do, she snapped her fingers.

Her antipower lunged back down, devouring Lexington's remains.

Which promptly disintegrated into nothing more than dust.

"There." Dyonisia brushed her hands against her dress. "Now I have *two* extra spaces on my Good Council to fill—Ms. Leake's and Mr. Lexington's. I'll see to it that Mr. Gleekle contacts you about the initiation process at the beginning of next year. I daresay you'd be a good addition... if you can handle a little more power, that is."

She clambered into the carriage and held out her hand.

I didn't dare glance back at the alleyway now that her focus was trained on me. Coen could Walk Emelle and Lander back to the Institute when the coast was clear.

No, I didn't look back.

And as a dark, fathomless presence returned to the periphery of my mind, hovering and guarding from his space between stars, I stepped forward and took my aunt's hand.

The carriage ride back was much too silent and much too loud at the same time.

Dyonisia, the Wild Whispering coachman, and I kept our mouths shut as the crows hefted us up and over Hallow's Perch—what looked like a pile of smoking ruins from above—and across the gentle rise and fall of the jungle canopy. I hadn't realized until now that the sky above all that mist and smoke had melted back into dusk.

The carriage ripped through the wind. I felt Dyonisia's eyes as she studied me unabashedly, her lips pursing in distaste at the filth coating my skin and the jagged rips in the dress she had given me.

She still doesn't trust you, came his voice in my head.

I'd felt his presence follow me, but I still had to bite back the surge of relief that threatened to well in my eyes at the actual sound of his voice as he rode his own wave of darkness alongside the carriage, trailing us in his in-between space while Dyonisia was none the wiser.

I know, I replied, hardly daring to blink. Indeed, my aunt seemed to be shimmering with an aura of mist, antipower coating her like a second skin—a film of protection from any kind of magic I could possibly throw her way. *But at least now she thinks she can control me.*

Maybe she can. Coen's voice was a whisper. *Maybe she controls all of us. When she had you in that dome of her antipower... I couldn't get to your mind. I couldn't hear you.*

So he hadn't heard me say that I loved him. And now he sounded so heartbroken, so angry at himself, that my fingers curled in my lap with the effort it took to hide how much I wanted to gather his face into my hands and smooth out every harsh line I knew rode his skin.

Well, you can hear me now. And I can hear you.

He still didn't sound convinced.

I should have known you were in trouble with Lexington. I should have been there as soon as he dragged you away. I should have—

Stop that. You were literally fighting monsters. There's no way you could have known anything while your mind was so preoccupied.

Well, there *was* a way... but it was a rarity, an impossibility, and I tucked that small kernel of wishful thinking into the shrine of my mind.

I waited until the carriage tipped forward as the coachman instructed the crows to descend to ask, *the exiled ones?*

I'd asked Coen to whisk them all away before Dyonisia could catch sight of them in their original forms, but...

510

I got them to the bunker in time, he sighed. *The village healers are tending to them.*

So Kimber, Jenia, and the others hadn't run away, after all. Dyonisia had no way of knowing that her own citizens had taken in the monsters she'd set on them, but that wouldn't last forever. Eventually, one of those villagers would talk, and the news that Hallow's Perch was harboring exiled ones would make its way to the Good Council. To her.

Did you see your family? I asked.

Yes. Coen's voice hitched. *My adoptive father is a Mind Manipulator, so our secret's safe with him... but I had to erase the encounter from everyone else's mind.*

My neck didn't so much as twitch in Dyonisia's sharp-eyed presence, but my heart broke for him. He'd been trying so hard to leave other people's memories untouched, only to have to erase himself from the very same villagers who had raised him as a boy.

It's better that way, Coen whispered. *I can't share my Mind Manipulating power with everyone.*

I could see the first sparkles of the Esholian Institute now as the carriage skimmed the treetops, aiming for the courtyard. I couldn't believe how different this descent was from the one I'd made a year and a half ago. I was no longer riding the carriage with Quinn and Lander during the daytime, but touching down with the leader of the entire Good Council in the dead of night... and a voice in my head.

What about Dazmine and the others? I asked quickly. *Terrin, the twins, Barberro and Nara?*

I brought them all back to the ship. Barberro's lower arm is absolutely mutilated, but he'll live. And I'll go fetch Emelle and Lander and bring them back to the Institute as soon as you're back on your own two feet and Dyonisia is long gone.

Thank you.

Thank you, Rayna. You were right. If Dyonisia hadn't watched me die, she would have turned Hallow's Perch upside down in search of me. Your plan—and Emelle and Lander—saved my home village.

At that moment, the carriage jostled as the wheels touched down right before the Testing Center. I could feel the weight of that one name neither of us had uttered yet. Coen's grief sunk into my own stomach like stones—or maybe that was my own, tugging me down into a place that was both sorrowful and... angry.

Out of everyone who deserved such a swift and brutal death, it shouldn't have been Garvis.

Dyonisia had no idea what I was thinking, though, as I climbed out of the carriage. Her lips merely puckered with distaste, once again, at all the blood and grime that had hardened on the silk of my tattered dress.

"Try lemon juice, child," she said, finally waving me away. "I've found that gets rid of the worst of stains."

I didn't move from my frozen position until her carriage had dissolved into the misty night high above my head.

When I had made it back to Bascite Boulevard, a feline shape was waiting for me where the moonbeam touched the shadows in the space between the Mind Manipulator and Wild Whisperer mansions.

Lights pulsed from every house on Bascite Boulevard. Music poured from open windows. Everyone was celebrating the postponement of the second quarterly test. I was pretty sure I even heard Rodhi's boisterous laugh echoing from one of the houses—and good for him. I made a mental note to thank him later for setting his spiders on the Testing Center.

"*You're alive*," Jagaros said.

"Well, hello to you, too."

I had to admit, part of me felt... disappointed at the sight of all his muscle and power just sitting on its haunches here at the Institute. Maybe if Jagaros had joined in our fight, Garvis would still be...

The dark, fathomless presence in my mind flinched, and I stopped those thoughts right in their tracks.

Jagaros huffed.

"*I made an oath a long time ago that I would not interfere in the Good Council's... projects. At least not directly. I couldn't go near Hallow's Perch at the time of the attacks any more than I could chew off my own head. And trust me, I wanted to chew off my own head when I heard that you were there and I could not help you.*"

Oaths. I hated oaths. Jagaros had never sounded so bitter, and suddenly, his black stripes looked like the inky bars of a jailcell tattooed right over his fur, just like Coen's was tattooed on his back.

"You can still help," I whispered. "There's a bunch of exiled ones in the bunker of Hallow's Perch. They're safe for now, but..."

When Dyonisia caught wind that her exiled ones were alive and useless, she *would* hunt them down—and punish all of those people in the bunker for keeping them. Just as Kimber had told Quinn so long ago, a hiding place was exactly what they all needed.

Jagaros's tail stilled. His eyes narrowed into slivers.

"*You wish to aid the ones who have harmed you in the past?*"

I didn't hesitate before I nodded.

Despite how much I still disliked Kimber and Jenia, despite how those monsters had murdered villagers and injured Barberro... it was Dyonisia who had instilled the violence in them. Like Kimber had said, she'd fed into their hatred to play them like pawns in a game they didn't even know they were in.

They deserved a space to heal and figure out who they were without that kind of manipulation. Away from brands and chains.

"That is what I wish."

"*Very well, then. I know of a place on the island where the Good Council cannot tread. Now that the official attack is over, I will go to Hallow's Perch to fetch the exiled ones and take them there.*"

I breathed out a sigh of relief.

"Thank you, Jagaros."

In response, he did something he never had before. Rather than demand *I* pet him, he came up to me and nuzzled the side of his head against my neck, a deep rumble growing in his throat.

"*Stay cautious. Stay curious. Stay clever.*"

Just as he was crouching to bound off, I touched his back.

"Wait. I got all my memories back and now I can see them more clearly. You've been in search of a map of the world, haven't you?"

Those slivered pupils studied me, surprise slicing through them.

"*I thought such a thing might aid both of us for different reasons, yes. You so that you could see where your lineage is from, and me...*"

He didn't finish that thought, and I didn't lower my blockade to snatch the answer out of the air. I was too exhausted, too weighed down, for more secrets—or the revelations beneath them.

"There's one in my bag that Dazmine left in the bunker of Hallow's Perch" was all I said. "When you get there, you can have it."

The faerie king of old twisted his maw in a feline version of a smile, canines glinting yellow in the moonlight.

"*Thank you.*"

With a leap, he was off, that silky, striped coat bunching over the ridges of his back, his tail whipping behind him.

When he was gone, I leaned against the Mind Manipulating mansion, listening to the hum of the vines that crawled up the wall.

I wasn't sure I'd ever get the last twenty-four hours out from under my eyelids. Images of monsters and dead bodies cycled in the darkness behind them every time I blinked.

My plan with the pills had failed, but maybe, if I could secure a spot on the Good Council, I could destroy Dyonisia Reeve from the inside-out. I just had to come up with another plan.

For now, though, I needed to recoup.

As I leaned my head against the wall, just breathing in all the muggy scents around me, a soft breeze toyed with the ends of my hair.

I opened my eyes to find an object floating toward me from the sky, dark and circular. The wind eddied around me, jostling the string of black pearls to and fro before sliding it gently over my head.

The wind is my friend, the Cardina jeweler had told me.

And her friend was finally delivering what I'd been waiting for.

No sooner had it rested against my chest than a voice—not in my head, but one carried by the wind—sent electricity shooting through each of my senses.

"What a pretty necklace."

Coen appeared before me for only a brief slice of time.

Then his hand reached out and tugged me into his swirling darkness, where far-off lights flickered all around us.

There, in that space between stars that I'd come to know and love, we hovered against each other, our bodies fitting together like the God of the Cosmos had carved us side by side during our Making.

Coen grazed my new necklace with his fingertips.

"It's my tally," I said in answer to his silent question.

A melancholy smile lifted his lips.

"For?"

515

"How many times you came back for me." A pause lumped in the base of my throat. "How many times you chose me over everything else. Besides, they were just too precious to sit in a drawer, you see."

All of that was only half of it, though. I'd also asked the Cardina jeweler to make me this necklace so that I could wear my love for the male before me right on my chest, where everybody could see it but only I would know what it meant. My missing memories hadn't triggered that realization in me... it had been developing for a long time. Slowly and painfully, but beautifully, too.

My subconscious had known it all along.

Coen leaned back to thumb my jaw with a tenderness that left my skin aching for more.

"They're even more precious against your skin, little hurricane. And I will gladly spend every day trying to earn back just as many reasons for you to be proud of wearing it."

"I already am," I whispered, "and you already have."

Without even meaning to, we'd fallen into a gentle sway, my arms looped around his neck and his hands gripping my hips. Both of us were still covered in layers of all kinds of filth, but I never wanted to miss an opportunity to dance with him again. Not after I'd seen his dead body on the ground. Not after what had happened to our friend.

"Garvis?" I finally whispered after a few beats of pulsing silence.

Coen exhaled roughly.

"I laid him to rest on a lonely isle to the north of here. It was peaceful and quiet and shrouded in mist, and just seemed like the place he would have chosen for himself, i-if he could have."

His voice snagged on those last few words. I leaned my chest against him, pulling him closer and listening to the strong rhythm of his heart.

Alive. Coen Steeler was alive. And even though I'd spent the last six months loathing him and telling myself I wanted him dead, we were even more officially enemies now.

I was set to join the Good Council. He was the Good Council's greatest threat—an oath-bound monster with a jade-encrusted sword who could breach the dome at any time. The queen of Sorronia's deadliest weapon. The Fated General and head of the entire faerie fleet.

Yet I'd never felt so safe against the chest of someone so deadly.

"Garvis said we had a spark." I tried to swallow the tears climbing back up my throat. "Do you... do you still feel that spark, too?"

Coen stopped swaying us to peer down at me.

"I never *stopped* feeling it, Rayna. Every time you looked at me, even when you wanted my head on a spike, I felt it. Sometimes, it was the only thing that kept me going when everything felt so dark."

My tears climbed higher, but so did my courage. I braved the words that had been brimming inside me for the last day.

"Then I'd like to choose you. And to keep choosing you... if that's what you want, too."

After a moment of surprised silence, during which he traced every contour of my face with his eyes, Coen gave me a smile that ignited in their smoky quartz like an ember among ash.

"You are my devastation, Rayna. My catastrophic event. And you are the one who put me back together into who I am today. I can't think of anything or anyone I'd like to choose more than you."

When he lowered his lips to mine once more and I got to taste that promise on his tongue, the world beyond the darkness around us—I could have sworn it *shivered*.

Because official enemies or no, whether she thought Coen was dead or not, Dyonisia Reeve didn't know what was coming for her.

She and the queen of Sorronia were playing a deadly game with each other, each of them using one of *us* as a weapon.

But what neither of my aunts realized was that together, Coen Steeler and I were two sides of the same blade—a double-edged sword that could slice back.

And we didn't have to be their pawns.

We could be players, too.

EPILOGUE

COEN

"Her Majesty would like a word with you... General Steeler."

I was back on the ship with Terrin, Dazmine, and the twins, the ocean air stinging against my eyes.

It had only been six hours since I'd last seen Rayna, and I already missed her: her warmth, her beautiful, wild mind, the softness of her skin, and that glimmering, jade-green light in her eyes.

But she was at the Institute, currently taking her rescheduled second quarterly test. I didn't want to disrupt her focus, and the captain of our ship was mashing her lips at me with an impatient crossing of her arms.

The captain hated me for accepting the oath, I knew, but there was nothing she could do about it—except, perhaps, gloat in my face when the queen of Sorronia wanted to speak with me.

Nobody in their right mind enjoyed the presence of the queen of Sorronia... even when she was hundreds of miles away, speaking to us through glass.

My newfound tie to Her Majesty was punishment enough.

Spitting out a few curses and catching the pity-filled glances of the others, I stomped after the captain. She led me into a room where crimson drapes lined the windows, casting an eerie red glow around the ornate mirror looming over me.

Her Majesty was already a shimmering image in the mirror. A veil fluttered over her face, covering those eyes that could suck out someone's magic with a single glance. Only her mouth and chin were visible beneath the veil, the lips painted bloodred, the chin dainty and unassuming.

As always, loathing tightened my muscles when I bowed my head before her. The mirror had been imbued with a complex charm from one of her ambassadors back in Sorronia, and the result was a two-way communication device that flowed as well as if we were talking through a watery window. I could practically feel the weight of her attention through her veil.

"I have your first official assignment, General Steeler. I think it will be a good way to practice for some upcoming events I have planned."

Like her sister's, Queen Mydusia's voice was a jagged collection of sharp knives and chips of ice, but with a higher-pitched tone. As if she wanted to sound like an innocent, giggly schoolgirl instead of a cold-hearted bitch.

Well, she was failing miserably at that little endeavor, wasn't she?

I didn't hide the disapproval tightening my mouth as I raised myself back up to my full height. Behind me, I felt the captain shift uncomfortably on her feet.

"An assignment?"

I'd known it was coming, but I dreaded it anyhow. Whatever the queen of Sorronia asked me to do, I wouldn't be able to refuse—even if it meant taking me away from the island of Eshol. Away from Rayna.

Not that I'd ever let it slip to the female faerie before me that Rayna even existed, and thankfully, the captain seemed to be withholding that information from the queen, too. For that, I was grateful.

I shuddered to think what Her Majesty would do in the face of that knowledge: the daughter of her long-lost little sister. Another Reeve with all that potential antipower lurking in her veins.

Queen Mydusia's smile made the edges of her veil flutter.

"I'm getting quite tired of waiting around for my sister's dome to crack. I have to admit, she's gotten good at upholding her power—I should have nabbed it from her while I had the chance, but alas. I was much too merciful and generous to do such a thing at the time."

I waited for the punchline. None came.

Queen Mydusia went on with a bit less flair. A bit more irritation.

"I want you to kill my sister within the next year, General Steeler. Her and all the mutants she's experimenting with. They are abominations to our kind."

The queen began to turn away, but my blood had seized up in every vein.

"What... Your Majesty?" I tacked on. I could feel the tattoo writhing along my back, like gears and cogs clicking into place as the power of her command washed over me.

But I couldn't have heard right. Couldn't have understood what that command *was*. Dyonisia had been raising an army for the last five hundred years, yes, but any regular faerie from ten thousand miles away could see that they were harmless. Innocent. Blacksmiths and cooks and farmers and builders. Not soldiers. Even the exiled ones would never pose a real threat against the queen who currently brewed with a hundred or more stolen powers.

Yet through the mirror, Her Majesty's lips stayed upturned beneath the bottom of the veil, as if my disbelief had seeped right through the glass. She leaned forward, until I could see the whites of her fangs glinting in that flickering palace light.

"You will bring me Dyonisia's head within the next year, General Steeler. And within that same time frame, you will also kill every branded citizen under her rule."

The tattoo came to a shuddering halt, the queen's command sinking into my skin and settling there like an elaborate scar that I would never be able to smooth over.

Kill. Every. Branded. Citizen.

The entire Esholian Institute. My family in Hallow's Perch. Rayna's friends and fathers.

Rayna herself.

No. No. No.

Anyone but Rayna.

My knees buckled. My power shivered around me, darkness tugging on every bone in my body to try to help me escape... but there was nowhere to go where this binding magic wouldn't follow. Not even the Cosmos. Not even that sacred place between stars.

As if to prove it, I felt the invisible hand of the oath *push* against my head, forcing me to bow before this wretched excuse for a faerie queen.

Go fuck yourself, I tried to say, but my tongue wouldn't obey me. Instead, a different set of words left my lips, as if Fate herself had pried them out of me one by one.

And the queen of Sorronia smiled when I said them.

"As you wish, Your Majesty."

Acknowledgments

It shouldn't be a surprise that my list of people to thank has grown exponentially since publishing the first book in this series. I have made so many new friends and formed so many new connections with people over the last year, and I am grateful for all the readers who have messaged me with love and support.

That being said, I'll start with the same guy I did last time: my husband. He doesn't just support me with words of encouragement, but with his actions, too. I can't count how many times he's taken the kids out of the house just so I can write my little stories in bed without any distractions. He's my first beta reader, my voice of reason, and the one who brings me coffee whenever I need it. I love you, JD.

Thank you to Grace Pearce, the best author friend in the world. I can't even count the number of hours we've sent voice memos back and forth, talking about the woes of writing and what on earth to do about it. I'm so excited for our book we're writing together, and I'm so thankful for all the times you helped me during the hardest, rockiest moments of my author journey.

Thank you to my other beta readers: Julia, my kind and creative friend; Bri, my primary smut consultant; Klara-Mei Li, my keeper of secrets; Maddy, my favorite annotator ever; Kaitlyn, my bestie, Abbey, a fellow writer, and Penni and Deven, the two sweetest souls in the world.

I also had the greatest pleasure of getting to know my new street team over the year, and I want to thank every single one of them for sticking with me. They've made me laugh more than any group I've ever been a part of before, and they're some of the most compassionate individuals I've ever met. And thank you to Kelsey, for putting the group together and for being my first ever PA!

Thank you to my Instagram followers, the BOOKLounge Group for Readers and Authors, my ARC readers, and anyone who has ever posted about or recommended BTOATO. I wouldn't have had the motivation to write book 2 without you all. You are the reason I write.

Last but not least, I have to thank God, once again, for giving me the two pieces of my heart. Emmarie and Jayce, I love you both so much more than I can ever describe. I could write a hundred books on the joy it gives me to be your mother, but it would never be enough.

Love,

Mariah

About Mariah Montoya

Mariah is a huge fan of anything with romance and magic. Besides writing, she enjoys runs, hikes, and four-wheeler rides. She currently lives in Boise with her husband and two children.

Don't miss her other books!

Welcome to Zurithia, where anything is possible... except escape.

Cinderella is a stepmother. The Little Mermaid is long dead. A fake fairest rules the land...